Book One of The Nousidian Chronicles

THE ENCHANTMENT OF ABIGAIL BROWN

by Mark Waters

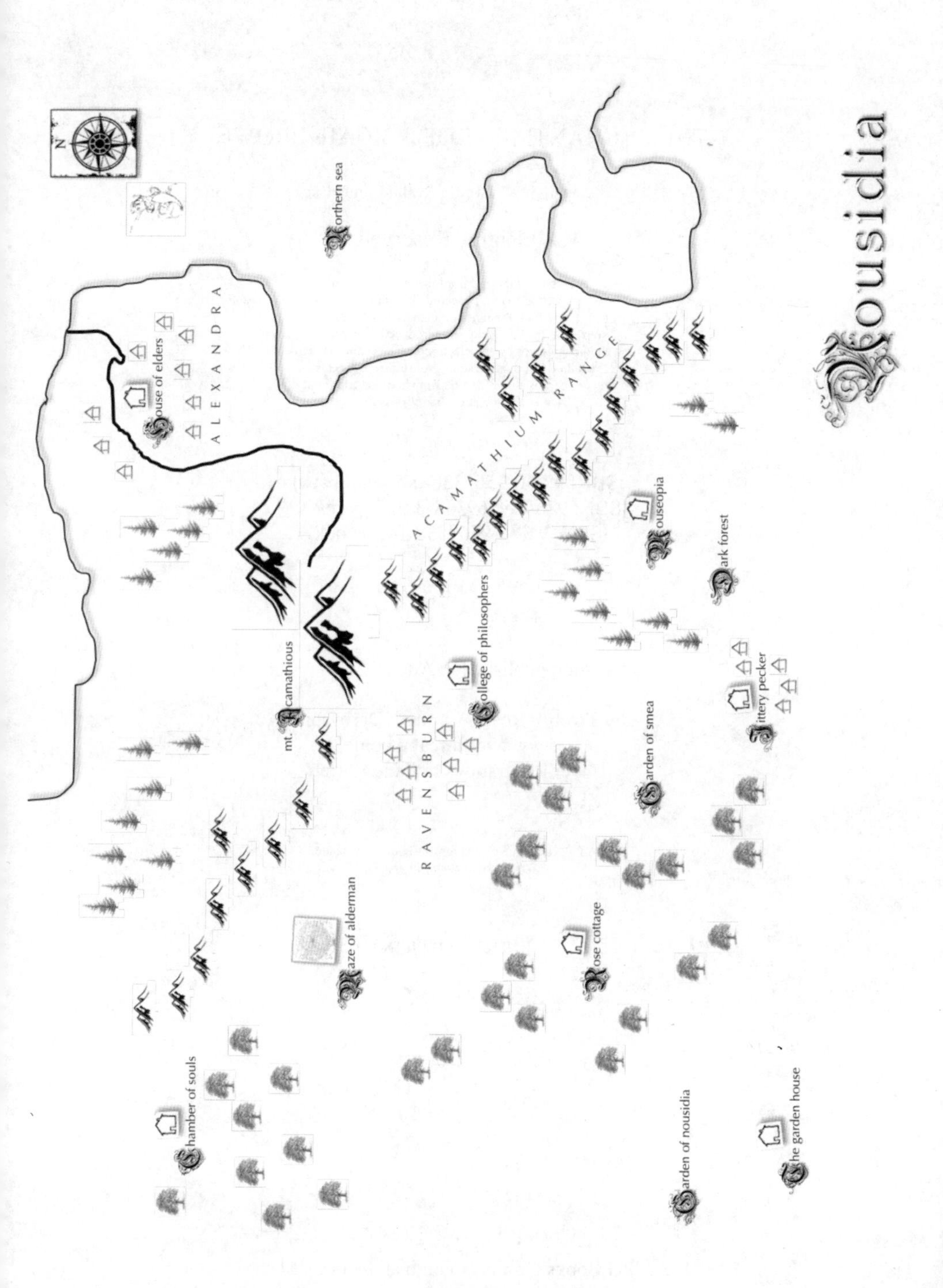
Nousidia
N
Northern sea
House of elders
A L E X A N D R A
A C A M A T H I U M R A N G E
mt. Acamathious
R A V E N S B U R N
College of philosophers
Nouseopia
Dark forest
Jittery pecker
Garden of smea
Maze of alderman
Rose cottage
Chamber of souls
Garden of nousidia
The garden house

THE ENCHANTMENT OF ABIGAIL BROWN

ISBN: 978-0-9569338-0-5 (Hardback)
ISBN: 978-0-9569338-2-9 (Paperback)
ISBN: 978-0-9569338-1-2 (ebook)

First published in August 2011

by Twelfth Realm Limited, Derbyshire
www.twelfthrealm.com
Cover illustrations by Jane Garrett

A CIP catalogue record for this book is available
from the British Library

FIRST EDITION

Printed and bound in the UK by

MPG Books Group, Bodmin and King's Lynn

Book One of The Nousidian Chronicles

THE ENCHANTMENT OF ABIGAIL BROWN

For my father

Thank you

Contents

Prologue

Snow tapped against the ancient window, blown by the icy wind, shaking the thin panes of glass in their decrepit frames. It had been falling for hours, engulfing the surrounding landscape with a blanket of white, covering all that was still.

A baby stirred in its cradle, bitten by a nip of wintry air, as a dark figure slipped into the dimly lit room. A crackle erupted from the open fire, the faltering embers losing their battle for heat over the strengthening winter chill, its struggle the only noise filling the air. The willowy figure glided across the room towards the sleeping babe, its robe fluttering in an invisible wind. No sign of footsteps marked the old rug adorning the floor and no or movement disturbed the frail rocking horse as the figure passed through; for this visitor was not from this world, or the next, but from somewhere in between, existing or not as was its wish.

The infant woke, sleepy but curious as she sensed the presence of her visitor, the faint glimmer of a smile surfacing on her young lips. The hooded figure crouched uncomfortably, its tall frame reducing by half in an effort to meet the low cradle, the hood hanging over its face obscuring all. A quiet murmur broke the silence: its words slow and chanting, a voice devoid of feeling or conscience. The voice grew, as if from nowhere, its volume increasing as others joined, the din becoming deafening as it consumed the dusty room; the sound oozing from the very fabric surrounding the solitary figures, as no others had joined them.

Yet the babe smiled on, a smile without fear or resentment, without the complications of maturity or doubt; this was a sign of unconditional love, a love that had no boundaries or questions: a child's love, and with it came an unfaltering trust.

Without warning a flash of light erupted, bathing the tall figure in a saintly glow, as the dormant fire burst into flame, licking frantically at the stone fireplace with a searing heat.

The visitor abruptly straightened, the hood falling from its head to reveal the outline of a slender face and long hair flowing as though suspended in the room. The stench of burning cloth filling the once still air and a sense of urgency crept into the figure's stiffening form as the heat singed its back. And then, just as abruptly, there was nothing: the figure was gone, the only evidence of its presence a curl of olive-green smoke.

The room was again lit only by the dying embers of the fireplace, the infant alone lying in her cot, a new toy clutched in her chubby fingers: the small stone smooth and warm and somehow familiar.

1
School's out

Twelve and a half years later ...

'Hey, ginger, get a haircut!' The uninspired shout came from a group of boys loitering around the school gate. Their comments were like a bad penny, turning up with annoying regularity.

Abby gave a sigh. *Hang the Nouse, do they ever give up?* she thought to herself. This odd little phrase was one of the eccentricities she shared with her father: it was one of their things.

Her hair was the subject of much ridicule, and also jealousy, she suspected. Her flowing locks ran flame-amber across her shoulders and down her back, the tips touching the waist of her jeans. She did not care for the adolescent taunts of her peers, as she had risen above that, her understanding of the world far outstretching the capability of their paltry minds.

She had refused to wear the uniform usually required as this was the last day of term and she was feeling rebellious. Unfortunately this had made her stand out even more than usual amongst the drab grey and black surrounding her, making her an irresistible target for many of the school bullies.

She mused over the day's events; she had done well, only two fights and no detention. '*Not a bad day altogether!*' she laughed to herself. The first couldn't even be called a fight; she had simply pushed over one of 'the gang', as they were known, as he tortured a first year for his dinner money. The second, however, was.

She had been strolling through the moss stricken structure that had been, at some distant time, a bike shed when they had appeared: three thugs, sporting the telltale short tie and skinned knuckles that epitomised their way of life. The tallest, a bruiser called Jake, flicked a smoldering nub end from his chubby, tar-stained fingers, the projectile falling well short of its target. This was an experience Abby imagined he had become used to, maybe even accepted as inevitable. The three advanced, stomping across the cracked concrete like the onset of old age: predictable but somehow distant. Jake mumbled something incoherent, an insult she guessed as his companions began to smirk, showing hints of yellowed teeth from behind swollen lips. It was Abby who had given them both that particular trait, a move she now considered may have been unwise.

Jake stopped just out of reach, his sidekicks flanking her, the scenario played out like many times before. Their rancid smell was first to reach her, attacking her nostrils in an unyielding sensory assault; the memory of butt-filled ashtrays and stale urine from her one weekend working in a rest home fluttering through her mind. These, however, were not the decrepit, wasted forms in the hospital waiting for their release from this life, but the beholders of suffering for the weak and vulnerable. She hated this scum, and now was her last chance to even the balance: revenge for the years of taunting and hurt.

She quickly stepped forward and punched the leader square on the nose, an eruption of blood and mucus adding to the soiled rag he called a shirt.

He staggered backward two steps, his meaty hand touching the swelling lump at the centre of his face. 'Don't just stand there!' he coughed at his minions, blood pouring down his throat, the strike seemingly improving his sinuses.

A moment later she felt the heavy forms of the bully's henchmen land on her, grasping arms and clothing alike, desperate to restrain this wild creature. Regaining his composure, Jake lumbered forward, swinging a hoof-like fist towards the fine angles of her young face.

Abby closed her eyes, accepting her fate at the hands of this Neanderthal, her chances of escape lying somewhere between impossible and miraculous, neither of which seemed likely.

Seconds passed but there was no pain, a few more and still no pain; something was wrong. She tentatively opened her eyes, squinting into the bright light of day, to be met by the most bizarre scene. Before her stood a donkey, the shredded remains of a tatty shirt hanging from its bloated body. She turned to see the henchmen streak from view, their pathetic screams ringing in her ears as they fled.

'What!' the donkey said, in the unmistakable voice of her nemesis, the boy seemingly unaware of his predicament.

Abby, clearing her throat to regain her voice, simply responded, 'Why, Jake, your Bottom is showing, I always knew you were an ass.' She walked away, looking back only once to see the figure of a boy on all fours with a very confused look on his face.

Abigail Brown was a bright girl to whom strange things just happened. She had grown to expect, and often enjoy, the unexpected; after all you don't look a gift horse, or donkey, in the mouth. She excelled in all her classes, not because she studied exceptionally hard or paid particular attention, but simply because she somehow always knew the answers. She was not like the other girls in her year, being taller by as much as a head in many cases, her long, gangly body sprouting to almost six feet. This had brought problems of its own, as finding a uniform to fit her long frame had proven problematic at best, and had, much to her distaste, resulted in her blazer being unfashionably short, an issue her piers never failed to mention.

Now, perhaps for the last time, the bad penny had returned. She paused for a moment, considering whether or not to respond to the taunts that had become part of her everyday routine and were thus exceedingly tedious.

'What's up, Zackary, can't think of anything new to say?' came a familiar shout from over her shoulder, the voice having the breathless nature of one who had been running. 'Looked in a mirror lately?'

Abby smiled as her only true friend, Tom, stepped into view; she was used to him coming to her defence.

'Drop it, Tom!' she interrupted, her tone a little harsher than she truly meant, tired of fighting the same old battles. 'Let it go, they'll just do it all the more.'

Tom was almost a year younger but very bright for his age and older than his years. She often thought he acted like a grown up most of the time; he just looked like a spotty twelve-year-old. *How would I know?* she giggled to herself; other than her father, and Martha of course, she didn't know any 'mature' people, and they didn't act like Tom.

He was a good deal shorter than her with wiry, dark hair and kind, deep eyes. He wore the school's grey uniform with pride as though it were an expensive suit, his white shirt pristine and freshly starched, his black tie symmetrical in its Windsor knot, the red and blue stripes perfectly aligned, the ensemble completed by the mirror shine of his tailored black shoes. Tom made her laugh, with his gentlemanly behaviour and chivalrous manner. He would defend her honour with the heartiness of a royal knight, even though it was Abby who usually had to step in and dispatch their attackers; Tom's skills as a fighter did not match his bravado. She loved that he tried, as that was what mattered; he was a breath of fresh air in an otherwise polluted, sour world. He seemed to have always been around, the point at which they had first met lost in the haze of early memories.

She defiantly turned her back to the bullies and, taking Tom's arm, walked away. A pronounced confidence in her step signalled that the discussion was over, at least for the time being. Come September she was moving to a new school and these irritations would be behind her, but that was six weeks away: now it was time to forget lessons and enjoy the summer holidays.

'Would you like to join us for tea, Tom?' Abby questioned in her best posh voice as she turned to face him. 'Martha's been baking again.'

Martha was their housekeeper and was always baking. She hoped it was apple pie: that was her favourite.

Tom pondered on the proposition for a moment, a thoughtful look on his young face. 'Well, I am kind of busy, and my diary is rather full at the moment,' he teased, 'but I'm sure I could squeeze you in.'

Abby gave him a shove into the gutter, enjoying the banter she shared with him. 'Well, don't force yourself!' she answered with a smile. 'See you at six.'

Tom shrugged and meandered off towards the gate. 'That's a date then, my dear.' he mumbled, already slipping deep into thought.

She watched him exit the school for the last time and disappear around a shabby hedge. She wouldn't miss the awful seventies architecture, or the ever younger teachers desperate to hold on to what little control over their charges remained, but most of all she wouldn't miss the constant bullying she received from the older girls in her class. If it wasn't her red hair, it was her long gangly legs: being so tall at almost thirteen wasn't fun.

'It isn't easy being told you're so clever!' she announced loudly to no one in particular. 'I didn't want to be in the senior class with the older kids!'

Having said her piece, she strolled out past the rusty old gates never to return. She could feel it in her bones: come September things were going to be different.

A brief glance at the assembly of cars confirmed that her father had again forgotten to pick her up; she was used to it as he got very wrapped up in his work. Sometimes he wouldn't come out of his study for days, and Martha hadn't driven since the accident; she just stayed at home baking and doing whatever else housekeepers do all day.

The two-mile walk didn't bother Abby; it was a balmy day in mid-July and the sun was shining in a pool of deep blue sky. She happily trudged home across Old Man Alsop's farm, dodging the occasional steamy cowpat, jumping over outcrops of rock and tufts of meadow grass. The scenery up here always filled her mind with dreams of faraway places; the rolling hills of grassland dotted with the odd solitary tree, the neat stone walls tidily dividing each field into a patchwork of man-made cells, the rundown barn, neglected and unused, consumed by the strangling onslaught of ivy, its previous life lost in time. A heard of cows lazily observed her from their huddle in a far corner, chewing relentlessly as they stripped the land of its vegetation. A bird of prey hovered in the sky above, waiting, watching for its next victim.

A cool breeze snapped her from such thoughts, the chill unnaturally cold in the heat of the day. She glanced up to the sky where, to her astonishment, the rich blue was being rapidly replaced by angry-looking rain clouds. Thunderheads of deep purple and coal-black bellowed across the sky, flashes of white erupting throughout the thronging mass as it spread from the horizon at a startling pace. She instinctively looked around for cover, spotting a small group of trees a short distance away. Changing direction, she headed for them, sensing the storm would soon break. A flash of brilliant white light sparked in the distance, followed by a deafening crack as a roll of thunder burst across the thickening clouds. Abby's spine tingled, a sudden charge of adrenaline rushing through her tense body, spurring her into a run.

Another crash from above attracted her eyes back to the sky. Over the trees ahead she could see the shape of a large bird, its wings fighting a losing battle against the torrent swirling about it. But it was the bird's foe that caught Abby's attention. Coming to a stop, she stared at the sight playing out in the air above her. A large shape appeared from within the rolling clouds, falling to earth with the speed of a leaden balloon; from this distance she could not be sure, but it looked like a huge cat. She watched in amazement as the shape floundered through the air, grasping at the smaller bird as it spun in circles around its attacker's falling body.

She was shocked into movement by a globule of water landing on her cheek: the beginning of the deluge of rain that accompanied the storm. Doubling her effort, she ran towards the trees, hoping to reach cover before it was too late.

She entered the small copse of woodland as the rain began to pour, glad for the protection the foliage offered. The trees swayed lazily about her, as if being buffeted by a light breeze, but to her surprise the air around her was motionless. She turned to look back, seeing lashing rain in the open fields behind her, the grass cowering like a blanket of seaweed in the swell of the ocean. *That's odd?* she thought, returning to the surrounding calm in which she stood.

Her thoughts were again interrupted by the struggle in the air as the two forms came crashing through the canopy above, showering her with broken branches. She covered her head, layers of fallen leaves rustling under her feet as she stepped back, crouching into a protective ball. A twig snapped under her weight, the noise a thunderous crack that broke the oppressive silence.

After a moment she peeked out from under the cover of her arms, spotting movement ahead: a blur of amber against the neighbouring shades of green. Intrigued, she squinted for a better look, but the shape had moved behind a sizeable bush of vivid hues and vibrant flowers, its majesty paling the surrounding foliage into insignificance. Her curiosity overwhelming, she strode over, past an overgrown holly bush and into a small clearing, tall trees and shrubs surrounding her on all sides.

Am I imagining it, she thought as a tingle meandered down her spine, *or did the foliage close in behind me?*

'Good afternoon, Abigail,' a deep voice stated grandly from the shadows, breaking through her thoughts with a clarity that surprised her. 'And what a lovely one it is too.'

She took a step back, fear flooding through her veins like iced water, the sharpness of a branch pressing through her blazer.

'Who, who's there?' she stammered, pushing back against the holly bush, the chill of fear spreading to every inch of her body.

'Don't you be frightened, young miss; I won't hurt you.' said the voice calmly, its tone full of friendly humour, and with a rustle of leaves its owner stepped into the clearing.

Abby's jaw dropped open. 'This can't be right.' she mumbled as her brain raced to comprehend what she saw, desperately searching for a rational explanation for the wonder that had presented itself; for sat in front of her was a fat cat who appeared to be talking, seemingly oblivious to anything being wrong.

'Let me introduce myself,' the cat continued, his broad accent something similar to Border Scottish but not quite. 'My name is Arnold Buttersquick, and it is an honour to finally meet you.'

He was at least twice the size of an average tabby and rather plump. This, combined with oversized paws and unusually large fangs, gave him the appearance of a miniature lion rather than a household pet. His huge round eyes were as green as freshly cut grass and shone with a luminescence like disks of glittering jade in the dappled shade of the forest. Long white whiskers protruded like curved blades from either side of his Romanesque pink nose, twitching constantly as though absorbing the vibrations of his surroundings. He was a handsome beast and sat with the confidence of one who is in complete control.

Abby opened and closed her mouth, trying to speak, but the words got stuck in her throat.

'What's up, lass: cat got your tongue?' continued the feline with a chuckle, a grey feather falling from his fanged jaw: remnants of his unfortunate prey. 'It's been a long time since, waiting for you to come of age.'

Abby was totally bemused by the whole event. She desperately tried to think of something intelligent to say, or at least something imaginative, but instead she blurted out the only thing that came to mind; the default of anyone brought up in England.

'Strange weather we're having,' she stated nervously, fidgeting against the sharp prickle in her back, and then adding almost apologetically, 'I've never met a talking cat before.'

The cat strolled over to her, lazily rubbing against her leg. 'Sure you have,' he said with a soft purr in his voice. 'You've just not been listening.'

'W-what happened?' she asked in an attempt to understand recent events. 'Was it you I saw fall from the sky, and if so … well, if so … where did you come from? And why aren't you hurt?'

A moment or two passed in silence: Abby contemplating what to do next while the animal before her busied himself with a little preening.

'Okay!' she blurted out finally, her impatience boiling over, 'if you can talk, why can't everyone hear you? Or is it that the whole world doesn't listen?' She folded her arms in a show of defiance.

The cat sighed, breaking from his grooming regime, and looked her straight in the eye. 'You have a lot to learn about the universe my dear princess. Let's just say you're a very special girl, Abigail. It's time you learnt just what you can do, and my being here is a very long story.'

With that he turned, tail in the air, and sauntered out of the clearing, a path opening through the undergrowth as he went.

How does he know my name? Did he call me princess? Only Daddy calls me princess! Abby thought as she lunged forward to follow him, not wanting to be in such a curious place alone. She was very confused about the whole situation, but also in a strange way felt comfortable with the idea; after all, she listened to the house all the time. The soft voices that came to her in the dark of the night, once petrifying, had become soothing, their slow chatter helping her sleep in the lonely small hours of the morning, so why not a talking feline?

'I wonder what else this day will bring?' she mumbled to herself as they stepped out into the glorious afternoon sun, any sign of the ferocious storm evaporated by the burning heat, and turned towards home: cat and girl side by side.

2
Secrets in the study

'Got a new friend?' Tom called out as he ran across the narrow country lane to catch up.

Abby hadn't realised how late it had become. 'This is Arnold,' she replied nervously. They had never had secrets from each other, but she wasn't sure how he might react to a talking cat. 'We met in the forest over at Alsop's farm.'

'Looks like he's adopting you!' teased Tom, winking at the cat as he picked a leaf out of Abby's hair. 'Another mouth to feed, eh.'

He bent to stroke her new friend, the feline arching his back in response. Neither seemed to be very surprised by the other; they seemed to be already acquainted. The notion prickled a thought in the back of Abby's mind; something from her past, tantalisingly close, but just out of reach. She pondered on it for a moment and then brushed it away; there were more important things to think about right now, like what was for dinner.

They passed through a large pair of open iron gates, suspended from weather-worn sandstone pillars, their hinges rusted by time and lack of use. Abby couldn't ever remember seeing them closed; she guessed there was no need as no one ever visited, and besides, the entrance was now so overgrown with greenery it was barely visible. She liked it that way; it was like entering a secret garden, and it was all hers.

The once opulent grounds were now overgrown and unkempt due to the lack of human influence. This neglect had attracted all manner of wildlife, from the rabbits and foragers that burrowed in the undergrowth to a beautifully speckled brown owl that sat in the tree outside the front door like a feathered sentry watching the house in the twilight hours. Abby had spent many a summer's evening wondering aimlessly through this garden, watching the birds darting between the bushes and squirrels racing up and down the colossal specimens of oak and ash.

The trio trudged up the long curve of the driveway, majestic trees standing to attention, although rather shabbily, to each side in an avenue of green and brown; their leaves forming a mottled ceiling high above their heads like the vaults of nature's cathedral.

As they turned the last bend the old house Abby had always known as home came into view. It was a grand old place, with tall windows and a gothic tower at one corner. An ancient creeper covered most of the aged stonework, its skeletal frame bare and leafless. For the most part, other than a few slipped slates, the old place had worn well, its period grandeur still appealing. The tower itself had lost its roof the other year in a particularly violent storm, but Abby figured it gave the house the historic credibility of a partial ruin. 'She just needs a bit of TLC,' Martha would regularly observe in her usual nonchalant manner.

She idly picked at the flaking paintwork on a nearby window as they passed the front of the house; something her father scorned her for as he saw it as disrespectful to the old place, but it was habit. She felt comfortable here, like she belonged; she guessed it was because it was all she had ever known.

A pair of rain-stained gargoyles watched blindly from the corners of the portico, like grotesque winged sentinels frozen in time, as they approached the large oak door. Abby grasped the polished brass handle, its shine contrasting with the blistered surface of the surrounding timber, and gave it a firm shove. The door swung effortlessly on its hinges, revealing the cool house beyond. The heavenly smell of fresh bread instantly filled their nostrils.

They entered, and were met by the thundering of paws on the old staircase. It was no surprise to Abby as her best friend and companion came hurtling towards them, full of excitement at the return of his mistress.

'You're all wet!' Abby protested playfully as the soggy pooch bounded into her arms. 'What have you been up to?'

The collie gave her a loving lick across the cheek and sat proudly in front of her. She slipped a half-eaten corned beef sandwich from her school bag and tossed it towards him: the dog plucking it out of the air and guzzling it down in two bites. She always saved a little something for him - it was tradition.

'Good evening, Apollo,' greeted Tom, giving him a pat on the head. 'How are we today?'

His reply was a soft murmur and a roll over to have his belly scratched. He had the shape and temperament of a border collie but the golden coat and deep brown eyes of a retriever, and a reputation for mischief. Abby had no idea how old he was, or why he was called Apollo: she had once asked her father, who had explained that he was found asleep in her room when she was just a baby, and he'd been around ever since. Like many things in their home, she had grown to accept that it was just the way it was.

They followed their noses down the long hallway, trying not to leave any marks on the highly polished floor, grand portraits of proud ancestors unnoticed in their eagerness to sample the delights ahead. They entered the kitchen; the sweet smell of freshly baked goodies dancing on their taste buds, the air thick with the pungent aroma. A loud growl erupted in Tom's belly, sending the friends into a fit of giggles.

'Shoes and jacket in the cupboard, then sit y'self down an' I'll pour you a nice cuppa tea,' said a plump woman at the kitchen sink without looking round, her hands immersed in a bowl of something gooey. 'You too, Tom,' she continued. 'I guess you'll be staying for dinner? It's your favorite – lamb stew.'

Tom levered off his wellingtons and Abby her shoes, depositing them in a little cupboard as instructed.

'How does she do that?' Tom whispered behind his hand. 'She always seems to know I'm coming before I do!'

They both giggled at the idea and took a seat at the table.

Martha was a large, stumpy woman with a heart of gold and eyes as sharp as an eagle; her dark skin contrasting with her immaculately pressed yellow dress and white slippers. Abby scarcely saw her without her blue apron (with matching oven cloth) or her warm smile. She had arrived a month or so after her mother had died, *to look after us for a bit*, as her father had put it, and never left. She was part of the family now, and Abby couldn't imagine life without her.

'Good evening Arnold,' Martha stated very matter-of-factly as she placed two huge mugs of tea and a plate of freshly baked cookies in front of them. 'It's nice to see you've finally decided to use the front door.'

She strolled back to her goo.

'You know this cat?' Abby asked, totally bewildered. 'It followed me back from Alsop's farm.'

Martha continued to knead the goo. 'Yes, my dear, Mr Arnold has been visiting since I started 'ere all those years past. He's usually waiting for me at the back window 'ere.' She gestured towards a small window with an elbow. 'Got a taste for me cooking, I think.'

Abby looked down at the fat tabby as he sat smugly on the floor next to Martha watching for crumbs, and wondered how she could have missed the sight of such a large feline hanging around her home.

Her thoughts were suddenly interrupted by a loud crash, followed by a thud.

'That'll be your father then,' Martha stated, wiping her hands on a towel. 'Better wash up for dinner, don't want y' stew going cold now, do you.'

With that she ambled out into the hallway.

Dinner was served in the dining room, as was tradition when Tom came to visit. Abby sat on one of the eight tall, and very uncomfortable, carved chairs placed around a large oval table, with Tom climbing onto the chair opposite. *Manners, you know*, he would always say in his best posh voice, *a gentleman always sits opposite his lady at dinner*. The dog strolled in and curled up in his favorite corner, followed by Arnold, who sat next to him as if on guard.

This was a very formal room, with heavy patterned drapes and large ancestral paintings of people Abby had never met. A huge golden chandelier hung in the centre of the room, cascading light and shadow in equal proportion that danced in the cool breeze from the open windows. She always felt a little uneasy in this room and swore the strangers in the paintings were watching her. Even the white horse pictured standing alone in the field behind their house seemed to turn as she passed.

'How was your day, my dear?' boomed a deep voice from the doorway.

'Daddy!' squealed Abby as she jumped from her chair and ran into her fathers waiting arms.

'I've missed you pumpkin,' he said as he wrapped his thick arms around her. 'Have you missed your old dad?' he quizzed warmly.

'But I saw you only this morning, Daddy,' replied Abby into his chest, keeping up the game. 'Am I allowed to miss you so soon?'

Gilbert smiled and released his daughter, his hands on her shoulders. 'Of course you can. As long as you remember to tell your father you love him.'

Abby hugged him again, muttering 'I love you' into his soft jacket, breathing in the faint musty smell of aftershave and cigar smoke she loved so much. He was tall and sort of handsome, in a rugged way, with a small paunch of a belly befitting his senior years. Not bad for a man in his forties, Abby thought, and those glasses make him look kind of brainy. He spent most of his day locked in his office, writing a new book she guessed, but always tried to make time for her when she got home from school.

'Good evening Tom,' Gilbert welcomed as he took his place at the head of the table. 'Nice to see you again; doesn't your mother feed you?'

Tom laughed. 'Not as well as Martha!' he replied, tucking into an exceptionally large bowl of lamb stew. 'Mother's out at one of her do's, so she won't be back till late.'

Tom's mother was always out at some sort of function. She was a socialite with a list of 'must do' events all year round, and thus was never home. He had never known his father, as he had left before Tom was born; he had asked about him once and had discovered, with a clip around the ear, that the subject was taboo. He was under the charge of a nanny: a tall Irish woman who, although well intentioned, liked a tipple or ten of whiskey and spent most evenings snoring very loudly.

Gilbert shot his daughter a quick smile, saying, 'Well, I had better ask Martha to make up the bed in spare room then.' He knew Abby had few friends at school, and certainly none as loyal as Tom.

Martha entered with a large bowl of dumplings, placing them in the centre of the table and sat down to Gilbert's right.

'Hang the newt, Martha, what a magnificent feast!' Tom gasped.

Abby shared a knowing smile with her father. Tom could never get their special phase right, but she had given up correcting him, for it was something he could never truly understand; the kind of bond that a daughter shares with her father.

'Abby. Time to say grace,' Martha prompted, seemingly oblivious to Tom's comment.

Tom immediately put his fork down and looked apologetically toward the housekeeper as Abby put her hands together as if to pray and boldly said, 'GRACE.'

They all burst into laughter, and dug heartily into their meal.

Tom groaned and held his bulging belly as he slumped into one of the old armchairs in Abby's room, dust escaping from the tired material, spiralling into the evening air.

'I've eaten too much!' he complained. 'I shouldn't have had that third helping of apple pie, or so many dumplings.'

Abby sat down beside him feeling equally full. 'Martha's cooking is just too scrummy!' she stated and let out a loud burp.

'*Touché!*' exclaimed Tom, laughing. 'A sign of good food I think.'

They laughed until they thought their sides would burst, not noticing, in the dim evening light, something small and furry slip into the room through a crack in the wall. Tom was busy relating how Miranda Smith, one of the school bullies, had got her long blonde hair trapped in the gymnasium door, and how she had pulled out a large tuft of it trying to get free, when they heard a muffled squeal from behind the bed.

'What was that?' asked Abby as she lazily got up to investigate. 'It sounded like a tiny voice.'

She rounded the bed to see Arnold poised, one of his big paws pinning something small against the wall. As she got closer she could make out the shape of a grey mouse, its whiskers twitching madly.

'Let it go, you bad cat!' she screamed, swiping at the fat moggy with her free hand.

Arnold ducked away from her grasp and lost his hold on the rodent, which quickly stepped out of reach.

Then, to Abby's surprise, it spoke.

'Thanks a lot m'lady, that mog's got whiffy paws!' it said, shaking its head in disgust. 'Reginald Cockle's the name, and I owes you me life.'

Abby was dumbfounded: two talking animals in one day, and this one in the presence of Tom.

She glanced at her old friend, the look on her face asking for his acknowledgement of what was happening, or even the offer of a way forward in this rather unusual situation. Tom's unspoken reply was an echoing look of confusion and a shrug of his shoulders, offering no real help.

'You're welcome,' Abby spluttered eventually, unsure how to greet a mouse. 'Nice to meet you.'

'Pleasure m'lady,' squeaked the mouse, collecting the discarded lump of cheese he had stolen and scurrying out of sight.

Abby stood slowly, feeling very confused, and turned to Tom, who was now standing behind her, saying, 'Did you hear that? A mouse that talks.'

'Yes,' replied Tom, his voice full of skepticism, 'yes, indeed.'

They talked for hours, trying to make sense of the day's events. Abby reiterated her initial encounter with Arnold earlier that day, confirming that she was not completely mad, or at least not mad alone. The longer they talked, the more confused they became, until weariness took its toll and they both fell into a restless, dream filled sleep. The only conclusions reached were that this was very exciting, very peculiar, and very much a secret.

The following morning Abby woke to bright sunlight flooding in through the tall windows of her bedroom. She carefully opened her eyes, squinting in the glare of the room, unsure what had happened the previous evening. She sat up to see Apollo fast asleep at the foot of her bed, lying on his back with all four paws in the air, a look of bliss on his face. Her room was one of the biggest in the house, filled with old, musty smelling furniture, a large rug covering most of the floor. She loved it – it was home.

She lay back against her plump pillows, her hand instinctively wrapping around the small green gem that hung around her neck. She rolled the stone in her fingers enjoying the warmth and smoothness of its surface, admiring the way the sunlight appeared to be captured within its semi-opaque body and the elaborate gold setting her father had made for her first birthday. As she lay warm and comfortable in bed, her mind wandered to distant lands of magical beasts and exotic people. 'Someday I'll come visit,' she mumbled.

'Where's that then, London? Always fancied a trip to the big city,' said a loud voice protruding into her daydream, snapping her out of her peace.

Abby opened her eyes to see Tom beaming down at her. He was standing next to the bed holding a tray full of tea and warm toast.

'Made it myself,' he stated proudly, 'Come on, shift over, before it gets cold.'

She shuffled over to make space and they tucked in. The toast was a little burnt and the tea rather weak, but welcome anyway. Tom was always nice to have around, like the little brother she'd never had – except less annoying.

After breakfast and Gilbert's departure for the day the two sat on the rug in the middle of Abby's room playing cards. She was winning as usual, although she suspected Tom was letting her. The TV was playing away to itself in the corner, a news show talking about 'global issues' being completely ignored. Her dog, Apollo, lay next to her; his head lay softly on her lap, eyes tightly closed. The weather had turned: rain pouring down the windows as a storm bellowed outside, the sky as dark as night with angry-looking grey clouds.

'I guess we won't be taking that walk just yet!' Tom suggested merrily. 'We'll just have to stay here in the warm.'

Abby laid down her winning hand, a look of mockery on her face. 'Read 'em and weep!' she jibed.

Tom, faking disappointment, threw his cards onto the dishevelled pile.

'Another game?' she asked, collecting the cards. 'And do try to concentrate this time!'

At that moment they heard a loud thud from downstairs, followed by the tinkling of broken glass. Abby jumped up and ran over to the window, searching for the source of the commotion.

Peering out into the storm she could see Martha fighting with a clothesline in a comical attempt to retrieve her sodden washing. Her senses tingled: something wasn't quite right; that sound came from below them, from inside the house!

'Tom,' she said, still looking out of the window, 'if Martha is outside, and my father has gone into town, then who's downstairs?'

Tom shrugged. 'Dunno,' he said, looking back at her winning hand.

'We'd better investigate,' stated Abby in her best authoritative voice. 'I'm going downstairs.'

With that she grabbed her dressing gown and strode onto the landing. She stopped when she realised Tom was not following, sticking her head back around the door.

'Come on lazy bones!' she shouted, rousing him to follow.

They reached the hallway at the bottom of the grand staircase. Tom looked for a moment at the study door.

'I'd better be off,' he stated suddenly, an anxious look on his young face. 'Mother will be wondering where I am; you know how much she frets.'

He quickly retrieved his jacket and wellingtons from the kitchen and, fumbling with his zip, said, 'See you later.' Then he stepped into the pouring rain and the door slammed shut behind him.

Abby stood for a moment staring at the blistered paintwork of her front door, wondering what had got into him. Then, with a shake of her head, she made to return upstairs.

As she mounted the first step, Abby froze. A further sound had come from behind the door opposite: the door to her father's study. This second sound confirmed her suspicions of an intruder and reinforced her anxiety at challenging them.

Summoning her resolve, she pushed the heavy oak door with all her strength. It resisted at first but slowly gave way, opening with the low creak of tired hinges. She took a deep breath and squeezed through the opening into the one room in which she had never been welcome.

She scanned the study, her eyes quickly becoming accustomed to the dim light, but found no sign of a trespasser. The room was large; a bulky stone fireplace dominating one wall, with heavy drapes drawn across another. The remaining walls were covered in shelves containing books of all shapes and sizes, and at the centre of the room was a beautifully crafted writing desk. This was also piled high with books and partnered by an equally impressive chair, the stylised motif of a bird as the main feature of its generous back.

She stepped around the desk towards the drapes, carefully avoiding the array of dusty paraphernalia filling the room. Something moved into her path: it was warm and soft as it bushed against her bare leg.

Abby's heart jumped into her throat, an involuntary squeak emanating from somewhere inside her. She stepped backwards, away from the source of her discomfort, stumbling into the desk and dislodging a large book on the corner. It fell to the floor with a thud, dust billowing from its cover into the still air.

'Look where you're going, young lady,' said a voice from behind the desk with a hint of a growl. 'I'm not as agile as I was in my youth!'

Abby's hands began to shake; she was beginning to regret insisting on investigating the noises from inside her father's study. After all he had been very clear when he had told her she was not allowed in this particular room. Her father's voice echoed in her head: 'Now, Abigail,' he had said, 'under no circumstances must you enter my study. There are things contained inside that are not for your eyes, not until you are older.' She remembered asking when she would be old enough, to which she got the reply 'Not yet' and a stern look that meant the conversation had ended.

A shape was emerging from behind the desk. It was low, as if crouching, and she could make out the soft glow of a pair eyes in the duskiness of the room. The low rhythm of husky breathing met her ears, and she realised it was moving towards her. She could feel the muscles in her legs stiffen, the fear spreading through her body. The figure stepped forward, towards the low light spilling into the room from the open doorway behind her. Abby's mind was screaming, telling her to leave while she still had the chance, but her legs had become like stone; paralysed by fear. Her eyes darted around the room, settling on a lamp lying on the floor in the far corner. Its glass shade had shattered into a thousand tiny fragments splayed around the carpet like some crazed form of abstract art.

At least I know what the noise was, she thought, her mind clearing for a moment of rationality.

Movement from the figure in front forced her attention back to the moment and what she was about to confront as it stepped into the light.

Then, in an instant, all fear melted away as she recognised the face that greeted her: it was Apollo, her faithful dog; he must have slipped in after her and snaked around the desk. The feeling of relief was overwhelming. She slumped into the chair in a hot flush, closing her eyes to the stars that danced in front of them. Her dog landed lightly on her lap, pushing his snout affectionately under her chin.

'Sorry if I frightened you,' the voice spoke once again, its tone soft and comforting.

Abby took a sharp breath, her eyes snapping open. She could see the outline of her dog sitting in her lap, but who was talking?

'Don't be afraid,' he said, shuffling position to look Abby in the eye. 'You are opening up to your true potential, and yes, you can understand us. You've just never listened before.'

At that moment another now familiar voice spoke. 'I've already told her all this, you canine twerp.' Arnold Buttersquick strolled out of the shadows, sitting on the corner of the desk where the book had been, his feline form majestic in the dusky light from the open door. 'She just needs a little time to adjust to the idea.'

Can you believe it, the cat and dog are arguing? she thought as the realisation finally dawned on her: she really could understand animals; or was it that they could understand her?

'Will you two stop it!' she ordered, and both animals fell silent. 'So what's the deal? How come I can suddenly understand you, and why couldn't I before?' she questioned, her need for understanding overwhelming her fear.

Both animals sat quietly for a moment and then Apollo, the dog she had known all her life, turned to the cat she had just met and said, 'Its time she knew the truth.' He strolled over to the large bay opposite. 'Would you be so kind as to open the curtain for me, my dear? I think you'll find the view quite illuminating.'

Abby looked at the cat for reassurance, although she knew not why, but he was busy removing a large knotted clump of fur from behind his leg, so, she somewhat reluctantly, she walked over to the drawn curtains.

'Well go on then!' prompted Apollo from somewhere in the gloomy darkness. 'There's nothing to fear.'

She grasped the curtain with both hands and pulled it open, the heavy drape sliding back with ease, flowing on its rail.

At first it revealed a window, through which she could see the storm outside, blowing harder than ever. A figure framed in this scene appeared to be dancing with a white shirt. She realised Martha was still struggling with the washing, the wind taunting her with bellowing gusts. She was about to suggest she should go out and help when the most extraordinary sight appeared in front of her.

The curtain had continued across its rail, revealing a glazed doorway though which she was bathed in glorious sunlight. The view through this doorway, however, was quite different. This vista was not her unkempt garden, full of weeds and neglected grass, but a neat lawn with beautiful borders containing flowers of every colour. A high wall enclosed this, with a statue standing proudly in the centre of the lawn, surrounded by ornate railings and manicured hedging. The subject was a man, tall and handsome, surveying the delights of his environment. He was wearing a grand uniform and a hat with a feather in it. His features look somehow familiar, Abby thought, as if from a distant memory blurred by time.

She turned her head in disbelief, looking out of the adjacent window to see dark skies and pouring rain. It was then she noticed that the curtain had revealed another window on the far side of the door. To her surprise this also showed the storm and the tatty garden she had played in only yesterday.

She took a step back, in awe at what had been revealed to her and the seemingly impossible view through the three portals; a door showing a gloriously bright and mysterious garden in the embrace of summer sun flanked by the dreary vision of the world she knew.

Arnold brushed past her leg, awakening her from her wonder, his bristly fur tickling her ankle.

'Are you coming?' he questioned, motioning towards the door. 'It's a beautiful day.'

3
The garden of Nousidia

Abby couldn't believe her eyes. As she took a hesitant step forward a faint glow appeared in the lock and the large door swung open, creaking on its ancient hinges. A gust of humid air filled her lungs as she stepped over the threshold, the warmth of the sun instantly soothing her pale skin. The smell of flowers was strong and sweet as a large bee floated lazily past her nose, busily searching for its next fix of nectar. She felt strange; but not in a bad way, just different.

Then the voice she now knew as Apollo's spoke from behind her. 'Welcome to Nousidia; welcome home.'

Abby turned to face him. 'Where?' she questioned.

She was confronted by a lofty young man of no more than twenty years with flowing golden hair, pale skin and dark eyes. He was wearing an immaculately presented dark uniform and boots that Abby could see her shocked face in. Across his chest he wore a crimson sash that was lined in gold, the motif of a bird at the collar.

'Who are you?' she questioned, taking a step back.

'I am Apollo, commander of the guard and keeper of all that is sacred,' he replied with a smile and discreet bow.

Abby was dumfounded. 'B-but you're a dog!' she exclaimed in astonishment, recoiling and tripping over her own feet, landing rather clumsily on her back.

The young man laughed. 'In the human world, yes, but here in our world I am what you see now.' With a triumphant flurry, he offered his hand in assistance. 'Up you get,' he said, helping her to her feet. 'We have much to discuss.'

Abby had so many questions: Where were they, how did they get here, how was it possible for her dog to turn into a man? She was contemplating where to start when another familiar voice broke the silence. 'Wait for me,' called the cat from the doorway.

Abby turned to see Arnold step out into the sunlight, but as he did so he began to transform. Through the shimmering haze of the already hot day she saw him grow many times in size, a mane sprouting from his collar, long incisors and claws protruding. He was an impressive sight, with the majestic, proud head of a lion held high, his green eyes shining like emeralds, reflecting in the dazzling sun. As he continued his transition into this world, his body became more akin to that of a bear; large clawed paws padding on the soft grass, long shaggy fur darkening and swaying with the movement of his sturdy torso.

He ambled towards them, the bulk of his muscular frame moving with the ease of youth, razor-sharp teeth glistening in the morning light.

'Hello, brother,' said Apollo, moving to greet him. 'Good to see you again.'

Arnold rose to his hind legs, swinging a paw in an arc to pat Apollo on the shoulder. 'Good to be back home!' he bellowed, his accent more pronounced with the booming of his voice. 'And how's our princess?'

Stepping forward, he sank to one knee and bowed deeply in front of her, Apollo swiftly joining him.

Abby could not understand what all the fuss was about, and quickly ushered them up. It was then that she noticed the house. It was the same shape and size as her home, she could even see her bedroom window, but it shone like new. The stonework was smooth and straight, the paintwork fresh and the tower still had its roof. She distinctly remembered the day that same roof had given way: it made such a racket and shook the whole house. She had used the now open top floor for sunbathing last summer; it made a great suntrap. But most curious of all was the creeper. It twisted and spread over the high, stone walls and appeared to be moving, like a gigantic snake writhing all over the house. Except this snake had the most beautiful flowers; bunches hanging in abundance along its length, giving it a shimmering effect in white and yellow.

'I don't understand,' she uttered, her voice faint, barely audible even in the quiet of the garden.

She walked over to the boundary wall; it was three times her height, the stone smooth like the house but older and worn. It obscured any view of what was outside the garden, with the exception of an iron gate in the far wall.

Curious about the extent of this new world, she wondered over to the opening, feeling the warm sun on her face and the soft grass under her bare feet. As she came closer she was amazed by the elaborate craftsmanship of the gate's construction. It was at least twice her height and as wide as her dad's old car. The ironwork was in the style of a vine, carved in the shapes of branches and grapes. The most ornate mock flowers covered the frame, with a lion's head embossed in the centre.

Through the gate she could see a lawned avenue flanked either side by tall trees, their branches arching over, forming a natural cover. Like the garden, it was kept meticulously tidy.

Abby stood on her tiptoes to get a better look at the lions face. It had a serene appearance with its eyes closed, like it was asleep, the finest details carved into the slumbering mask. She reached forward to touch it, to feel the texture of its surface.

The mask's eyes sprang open as it came to life, snapping at her fingers with sharp teeth, a forked tongue lashing at her, venom secreting from its tip.

'You don' want to be upsetting a gatekeeper, my young princess,' Arnold stated from behind her. 'That vemon'll put yer to sleep for a week as soon as touch yer. Lucky you caught it resting.'

'Y-yeah. Metal doesn't tend to bite where I come from!' She laughed nervously, backing away, her natural confidence returning as the acceptance of such things began to dawn on her. Her thoughts returned to the view through the gate.

'What's out there?' she asked.

'The kingdom, naturally,' was Arnold's response as he turned and walked back towards the house. 'All will become clear in time.'

Abby paused, her attention pulled from the gate to Arnold, to Apollo, to the garden, to the statue at its centre, then back to the gate. Her need was to explore, not to retreat, but she knew it was safer to stay with her companions so reluctantly she followed.

It's a shame Tom isn't here, Abby thought as they relaxed in the afternoon sun, *he would love this place.* Her head was so full of wonder; she couldn't wait to show him and share this magical, yet seemingly impossible, new world.

'Your father loves this garden also,' stated Apollo out of the blue. 'He spends much of his time out here with your mother.'

Abby sat up, startled by his statement.

'Don't you mean "did" spend time out here? My mother has been dead since just after I was born. Anyway how did you know what I was thinking?'

Apollo allowed himself a smile before he replied. 'I am Gordorian. Our first language is thought.' He hadn't realised how little she knew of their culture. 'So naturally I can hear the thoughts of others.'

Abby was fascinated. 'Really? That's cool. Can all your people do this?' she asked excitedly.

Apollo's face darkened. 'Among our people it is as natural as breathing, but to focus on an alien mind takes many years of training, and only a handful achieve it …' He paused, a sadness seeping into his eyes, the memories disturbing him. 'The rest go insane or die trying.'

Abby pondered the gravity of this statement, and after a prolonged moment she said, 'I'm sorry if this is an insensitive question, but if in trying you risk death then why take the risk?'

'The ability to communicate with other races is considered fundamental to our existence. To my people a life without communication is worse than death.'

With that he turned and walked to a nearby tree, his back to them.

'The fate of his people weighs heavily on his shoulders, young lass,' Arnold said in explanation, joining her. 'Been like it for many thousands of years, it has, and don't look like changing.' He took a seat on the grass, looking her directly in the eye, and asked, 'Now what do you know about magic?'

They sat and talked for hours, until the shadows grew long and a nip had crept into the air. Abby yawned as she watched the sun setting into a glorious bed of crimson clouds. She had spent the afternoon questioning her two companions but with no success, and had finally given up. All they would let on was that there was a lot more to the universe than she knew, it was something to do with magic, and her father would explain all upon his return. She had reluctantly accepted this and had spent the remainder of the afternoon exploring the garden.

'It's getting late,' Arnold stated as he rose, a hulking silhouette in the glow of the setting sun. 'Best get back inside before your father gets home.'

Abby really had no idea what time it was, or even if her father had already returned, but she did know that she didn't want to leave such a beautiful place; it felt so right, like she had finally come home, back to where she belonged. She hesitated, gazing longingly around the garden, taking in the vibrant colours of the flowerbeds, the finely preened surfaces of the box hedging, the climbing jasmine as it writhed over the house.

'Princess,' Arnold pressed, a hint of impatience creeping into his voice, his eyes flicking from her to the setting sun. 'We must retire to the house.'

Abby gave him her best pout. 'Can't we stay a little longer?'

'No!' came the stern response from behind Arnold's shadowy form as Apollo came into view. 'We have already outstayed our welcome. Come now, Princess, we must go indoors.'

Realising the futility of further resistance, she rose and stomped off back towards the open door, muttering objections under her breath.

Back in the study she busied herself with erasing any signs of her intrusion. As she stooped to retrieve the fallen book the cover caught her eye. 'Nousidian Royalty – The Past Ten Thousand Years,' she read out loud in her best posh voice. 'Sounds a real hoot,' she commented and lifted the thickly bound cover. It was filled with pictures, each with a summary of name, rank and position. It was all very stuffy. She flicked through the pages, losing interest rapidly, when a name caught her eye:

Gilbert Alexander Xavier Brown – The Grand Nouse and King of Nousidia.

She gasped, looking at the picture.

'But that's Daddy!' she squealed to her two companions then, correcting herself, said, 'He looks very much like my father.'

Arnold jumped up onto the desk (he was, of course, a fat tabby once again), sitting in front of her. 'That is your father, Abigail, and he is the true ruler of all Nousidia.'

Apollo joined them, a look of sincerity on his canine face. 'And you are his daughter and only heir – Princess Abigail Catherine Nubia Brown the Second.'

Abby could do no more than stand and stare at the two animals.

'Named after yer grandma you were. She ruled Nousidia for over a thousand years she did,' Arnold stated proudly. 'I was but a wee kitten of one hundred an' twelve when she finally passed over. A grand age of two thousand eight hundred and twenty-four she was.' Tears were forming in his eyes. Then he rolled over to remove a sticky bud from his chest.

'My grandmother lived to over two thousand years old?' Abby murmured, her head suddenly prickling with heat, the strength melting from her limbs. And then the light of the room faded from her mind as she collapsed in a heap on the floor.

'This will not do!' complained Apollo, a hint of annoyance in his voice as he shuffled between her and the desk. 'We'd better get some help,' he said to Arnold. 'We don't want to get caught in here when the king finds out.'

Abby woke with a start. She was tucked up in bed, warm and cozy, unsure whether the previous day's revelations were a dream or she had really visited another world with a talking dog. She gingerly opened her eyes and a feeling of relief flowed over her: she was lying in her bed, in her room, surrounded by her faded wallpaper and her ancient furniture. It was all welcomingly familiar.

She could hear hushed voices in the doorway but could not make out what was being discussed. She tried to sit up but was halted by a shooting pain in her temple. 'Ouch!' she murmured and sank back onto her pillow.

The voices halted and a moment later Tom's face appeared above her.

'Morning sleepy head,' he greeted far too brightly for so early in the morning. 'How's your noggin today?'

Abby touched a small swelling on her forehead. 'What happened?' she questioned, trying to remember how the previous evening had ended.

'You fainted and bumped your head on your dad's old writing desk,' Tom informed her in his usual stiff manner. 'You've got Apollo to thank for me finding you; he wouldn't stop barking at the study door when I got back until I investigated and found you lying there.' A look of concern covered his face. 'You had us worried for a moment. What were you doing in there anyway? You know it's out of bounds.'

Abby opened her mouth, eager to tell him all about her adventure, when a heavy lump landed on her chest. Apollo licked her face and snuggled his head under her chin, his fur causing her to sneeze – twice.

'Bless you, me dear,' came a familiar voice from behind Tom. Martha had brought a tray full of tea and treats. There were cakes and biscuits piled high, and enough sweets to make them both sick.

'Thought me little patient might like somethin' to cheer her up,' soothed Martha, placing the tray on the bed. 'Well, come on,' she ventured, a smile forming on her lips, 'b'fore the mutt gets 'em!'

Abby wrapped her arms around her faithful dog, all interest in story-telling gone, and tucked into a huge cherry muffin.

The weather was awful again; the rain had continued to pour and the wind howled around the house. Abby and Tom had spent most of the morning playing games in her room, Abby filling him in on the events of the previous afternoon while Tom sat quietly, listening.

'You have an amazing imagination,' he commented once she had finished, assuring her that she must have dreamt it, while her dog, Apollo, stayed very quiet.

Tom had kept a constant watch since she had bumped her head, claiming it was his duty to look after his best friend in her time of need, and she had to admit she did enjoy his company.

Contented silence had long since replaced their game playing, the two slipping into their own thoughts.

'I'm worried about my father,' Abby suddenly stated as she sat in the window seat watching the pouring rain. 'It's not like him to stay away overnight without calling.'

She turned to Tom to ask what he thought, but he was curled up in a large armchair, a low whinny escaping from his slumbering form.

'So much for conversation!' she muttered to no one in particular.

She returned her attention to the storm outside, idly watching her reflection in the thin pane of glass that separated her from the swirling torrent. It was then she noticed a bird on the windowsill next to her likeness, the rain running off its sleek feathers, its breast a vivid shade of red. She watched it hopping about, pecking at bits of foliage on the sill, enjoying its business, until it stopped and looked directly at her. Its stare seemed somehow intense, as though the bird was examining her, and then it hopped up to the window and tapped lightly on the glass with its beak.

Abby sat staring for a moment at the scene in front of her: the bird seemed to want her to open the window. Hesitantly she reached for the latch and eased the sash upwards.

The bird quickly hopped inside, shaking its small body and spraying her with rainwater.

'Thank you, it's raining cats and dogs out there!' the bird said in a high-pitched voice. 'Shut the window before we both catch our death of cold.'

Abby obediently pushed the window closed in bewilderment.

'So I wasn't dreaming,' she mumbled. 'I can talk to animals.'

'Technically, I'm a bird,' corrected the robin. 'But naturally you can understand all of your subjects.' She was very well spoken, even with such a squeaky voice. 'My name is Eleanora Stub, royal advisor, and I have some disturbing news.'

Abby leaned back against the deep window frame and gestured for the little bird to continue.

'It's your father,' the bird squeaked, the statement rushed as though unburdening the speaker of a hefty weight.

Abby gasped. 'My father!' she repeated, sitting bolt upright, fear swelling in her throat. 'He's not hurt is he?'

'Calm yourself, my dear, your father is in good health. He is, however, the prisoner of a dark witch and queen of our lands, your aunt Belladora.'

'Imprisoned?'

The robin stooped her head, her tiny form visibly shrinking.

'I have a confession to make, dearest Abigail,' the bird offered, its voice no more than a whisper. 'I am in the service of the queen, although my allegiance will always be to the true king, your father.'

Abby did not understand. 'If you claim loyalty to my father then why do you serve the woman that imprisons him?' She was becoming suspicious of this feathered visitor.

'It is my purpose to serve those that rule these lands without question or hesitation. I can no more disobey my mistress's word than cut off my own tail feathers,' she stated in a glum voice. 'It is the way of our world.'

Abby pondered this information for a moment, then finally asked, 'What does this dark queen want?'

The bird looked up, a sparkle of moisture glistening from the crimson of her feathered chest.

'She wishes you to attend her five hundred and twenty-seventh birthday celebrations.'

'That doesn't sound so bad.' Abby giggled in relief, bemused by all the fuss. 'I didn't even know I had an aunt, let alone one called Belladora who is over five hundred years old; that will be a sight to see!'

The robin gave her a stern look.

'The situation must not be taken lightly,' she scolded, 'for only on the anniversary of one's birth can the right to rule Nousidia be claimed in the absence of the true heir.' She took a deep breath before continuing. 'You are that heir, Abigail, and to claim the throne as her own Belladora must sacrifice all that have blood right. She has your father, and now she is trying to get to you. It is important that you remain out of harm's way.'

'If this is true why doesn't my father just get rid of her?' Abby asked, not sure what to believe any more.

'Your father was stripped of his powers two centuries ago and banished to this house,' the bird replied. 'Your aunt has become a powerful witch, turned to darkness by greed and envy. She claims the throne for herself and will stop at nothing to get it.'

Abby contemplated this for a moment then quietly let the robin back out of the window, promising to stay put and keep out of trouble.

'I'm going to ask Martha,' she said defiantly as she watched the little bird launch into the torrential rain. Abby trusted their housekeeper; she would know what to do.

She gave Tom a kick as she strode past; she needed an ally, and one that was awake. Slipping into the corridor she shouted 'Are you coming?' to Tom through the open door.

Martha was in the kitchen whipping cream with a very attentive tabby cat by her side. 'Good morning, young lady,' she offered as Abby entered the kitchen, followed closely by a sleepy Tom. 'And how's yer head?'

Abby had forgotten about the lump on her head.

'It's fine, thanks. Where's Daddy?' she enquired, sitting herself down at the table.

Martha dutifully placed two mugs of tea and a plate of biscuits on the table, saying, 'Yer father's had to take a trip to the city.' Her manner relaxed like this was normal. 'He'll be back for lunch.'

Tom joined her at the table, picking up a mug and two biscuits.

Abby shot him a confused look. 'Daddy never goes to the city!' she whispered, trying not to let Martha hear. 'I don't understand.'

She had a strange feeling in her stomach, like she was going to be sick, and a nagging thought in her head that something wasn't quite right. She punched Tom in the arm.

'Are you listening to me?' she demanded, her voice a little too loud.

Tom shrugged, a thoughtful, if tired, look on his face.

'Daddy never goes to the city!' she repeated.

'Sorry,' he replied eventually. 'I was daydreaming about a double helping of apple pie and Martha's homemade custard. People go to the city all the time, it's no big deal.'

Abby punched him again, but this time in jest. She could feel her worries melting away, her concerns for her father seeming somehow less pressing, fading away to the back of her mind.

'Do you ever think of anything other than food?' she quizzed, feeling a smile force its way onto her face, the bird's news seeming increasingly less plausible.

Martha suddenly interrupted, appearing over Tom's left shoulder. 'Now then, lass, what's troubling yer?'

'Urmm. Oh, it's nothing really,' Abby mumbled distractedly, taking a slip of tea. 'I just wondered where my father was.'

Martha smiled, a warm smile that never failed to melt her heart, the last cobwebs of doubt drifting away on wings of happiness.

Abby turned to Tom, all concerns for her father gone. 'Come on let's watch some TV.'

Abby was back on the window seat sometime later, idly gazing out over the rain-drenched garden, and she was bored. Tom had curled up into a ball on the bed and was sleeping again, a position that was not uncommon. A thought passed through her mind, suggesting that maybe he was purposefully ignoring the strange events of the last few days, but why? She quickly returned to her peculiar conversation with the little bird. She had given up trying to comprehend why she could suddenly understand the animals around her, but was disturbed by what the bird had said.

'Right!' she stated suddenly, her manner determined. Tom woke from his slumber with a grunt. 'We're going to investigate.'

With that she pulled on her favourite old jeans, Iron Maiden T-shirt and trusty All Stars.

'What are we going to investigate?' mumbled a very sleepy Tom.

Abby shot him an angry look.

'You haven't been paying attention, have you; where have you been the last two days? I have to go back into my father's study, and you're coming with me.'

4
The return home

Abby squeezed through the gap in the oak door, not daring to open it too far for fear of the old hinges creaking. The study was in darkness, the heavy drapes at the window once again drawn closed.

'Come on, Tom,' she whispered.

He repeated his objection to them entering the study, reminding her that it was strictly forbidden.

'It'll be fine,' she reassured him, dragging him through the gap by his shirt collar.

She felt soft fur pass her leg and saw Apollo join Arnold, who was waiting by the desk she realised as her eyes adapted to the darkness.

'I guess you pair are coming as well,' she laughed as she made her way to the window, a mixture of excitement and dread filling her mind.

She pulled back the drapes and the scene was revealed once again. The last of her doubts that this world truly existed evaporated like the morning dew in the brilliant sunshine that flooded through the central glazing; a sunshine that was framed by the drab environment in which she had grown up.

Again as she strode to the door it opened, and she stood on the threshold, enjoying the warm breeze in her hair, the sun on her face, before stepping into the other world. It felt good to be back: the air was sweet and the sun rejuvenating.

A thud from behind caused her to turn. Tom was lying face down on the grass, having apparently tripped on the doorstep.

'What are you like?' she laughed, her smile broadening as she bent to help him up.

'Sorry,' offered Tom, brushing himself down. 'Guess I was too busy taking in the garden.'

Abby looked at him, confused by his lack of surprise upon seeing this other world, but more so by his appearance. His eyes still had the sparkle of youth, but his face had wrinkled with the fissures of age and was the texture of old leather. He seemed to have matured tenfold in the second it took to pass from one world to the next, his appearance in the human world apparently a mask of his true age.

'Hang the Nouse, Tom!' she gasped, concern in her voice. 'What happened to your face?'

Tom shot her an apologetic smile. 'I'm not sure what's happening to me. The last few days have been a blur of half-realised memories. Like this place, for instance, it feels familiar; like déjà vu. I didn't want to say anything because…'

A voice from behind her interrupted. 'He has visited this place many times, Abigail. He is, after all, from this world; as are you.'

It was Apollo who had spoken. She turned to face him; his handsome features were caught in a smile of admiration.

'Your wonder at this world is to be expected, as you have both been under a powerful forget-me spell, cast to protect you from the evil that holds our homeland in its grasp. It is time you discovered our past, and began your journey into destiny.'

Abby opened her mouth, a hundred questions stampeding through her mind, jostling to be voiced in her need for understanding. Then she closed it again, her mind clearing, her questions fading into obscurity, as one thought dispelled them. This one idea, this one conclusion, was as clear as the sun sitting in the sky and held a truth she could not dispute: her father had the answers; she had to find him.

'O-kay,' Abby sputtered, a little unsure what she was letting herself in for. 'Guess we'd better get going then, eh! Lead the way.'

Apollo strode across the lawn towards the gate, joined by his brother in arms, Arnold.

Abby couldn't help thinking they looked an awesome pair: the tall, slim figure of Apollo, full of grace and poise, and the lumbering form of Arnold, rippling with muscle with a confidence that defied the very world around him.

'Thank you my lady,' Apollo stated out of the blue.

She remembered their previous visit and the gift of his people. 'Cut it out!' she shouted, faking annoyance. 'They're called private thoughts for a reason.'

She gave him a kick in the buttocks to drive home the point.

'Yes my dear!' taunted Apollo with a chuckle.

Arnold burst into a loud belly laugh, his whole body shaking with a force like that of an earthquake. 'There's a long road ahead of us and good humour will make a great ally. I think we're going to get along just fine.'

Tom nudged Abby, a look of confusion on his lined face.

'What's all the mewing and grunting about?' he asked, seemingly oblivious to the previous conversation.

It was at that point she realised. 'You can't understand them, can you?' she said, looking Tom in the eyes. 'I seem to have the ability to talk to animals, I thought you did too.'

Arnold interrupted. 'Nousidian royalty can understand the language of each of their subjects; it is part of their gift. Tom is human, and therefore primitive in this world; the gift of understanding seldom exhibits within their creed.' He turned to look at her. 'Your power of understanding is what makes you special, my princess; it allows all in your presence to share their thoughts with you.'

'What did he say?' blurted Tom, figuring that the grunts and whines coming from the beast ahead were words to her.

'I think he likes you,' Abby suggested, trying to look sincere.

They reached the gate, stopping a safe distance before it: Abby remembered their last encounter and stayed well out of range.

The lion's head opened its eyes, staring at each of them, one at a time, before defiantly asking, 'What is your business?'

'We wish to enter the kingdom,' stated Apollo, making a subtle bow towards the gatekeeper. 'The princess wishes it.'

The lion's eyes snapped over to Abby, its penetrating stare making her feel very uncomfortable. 'Let our princess utter your request in the ancient tongue so you may pass,' it stated and fell silent.

Apollo rummaged inside his robe and pulled out an ornate wand. It was about a foot long and carved with dragon-like beasts entwined around its shank of polished rosewood. At the tip it had an opaque stone, not too dissimilar to the one Abby wore around her neck, also housed in a golden setting.

'I was entrusted with this just after you were born, with instructions to return it to you when you were of age. I believe that time is now,' he announced to Abby. 'It was your mothers, and now it is yours.'

He bent on one knee and presented it to her with a flourish.

Abby stared at his offering, the whole idea of a magical wand seeming a little childish for someone who was almost thirteen, and a mature thirteen at that.

Sensing her hesitation Apollo flicked the wand into the air. It rose like a feather caught on a sudden breeze, somersaulting as it floated into the sunlight. Higher it rose until it hovered over Abby's head. It quivered once and then dropped like a stone, falling back to earth. More by reaction than thought, Abby raised a hand above her head to protect herself; but there was no impact, only silence.

After a moment she opened her eyes, squinting at the return of the bright midday sun, to see the mysterious baton hovering only inches from her hand. Somewhat reluctantly she leant forward and wrapped her fingers around the wand, feeling its warmth in her hand, an energy swimming through her body. The hairs on the back of her neck stood to attention, every extremity touched by the tingling force, before culminating in the pit of her stomach. She felt oddly warm and fuzzy, a new confidence filling her conscience, and with it a strange clarity forming in her mind.

She stepped forward, unsure why, and tapped a shaky circle on the stone adjacent to the gate, being careful to stay out of the keeper's deadly range.

'Enthra,' she said, the word coming from somewhere deep inside, its volume surprising even her.

She took a step back as a crack appeared in the stone. It spread, forming a rough shape in the wall. A soft glow radiated from the fissure, brightening as it spread. Once it had completed its course the panel inside swung slowly open to form an arched doorway of grand proportions.

'Wow!' gasped Abby, looking between the two. 'So the gate isn't the entrance after all!'

'Smoke and mirrors, my dear,' replied Apollo, 'one can never be too careful.'

'W-wow!' stammered Tom, echoing her astonishment. 'I didn't know you could do that!'

Abby looked over to him. 'Neither did I,' she said and walked through the newly formed archway into the kingdom beyond.

5
The real world

The forest was thick with trees either side of them and the group stood at the head of a long, straight thoroughfare of grass that stretched into the distance as far as the eye could see. The grassland beneath their feet was manicured as in the garden, small white flowers sprouting around their footfalls, inspired by the presence of magic. The trees either side arched over high above, giving mottled shelter from the warmth of the midday sun.

'Better get a move on then,' stated Arnold impatiently, striding off, his huge paws padding on the soft lawn. 'We've got a long way to go b'fore nightfall.'

The group followed, Tom running to walk by Abby's side. She linked her arm through his, giving him a comforting smile.

'Don't you worry Tom, I have a feeling we're embarking on a great adventure,' she said soothingly. 'Who knows where it will take us; it's quite exciting!'

With that Tom relaxed a little. He seemed rather nervous about their trip, which was unusual, as he was normally the adventurous type. Something didn't feel quite right; a nagging thought in her head that was just out of reach for her young mind. She guessed it must be normal to be a little scared when faced with the possibilities a new world. Patting his hand, she gave him a knowing nod and set the pace for what looked to be a long walk.

They had been walking for what seemed like hours when Apollo suddenly stopped. Abby walked into him with a thud.

'Sorry!' she apologised. 'I was daydreaming.' She could feel a flush of red in her cheeks, her embarrassment poorly concealed.

'There is someone in the bushes over there,' Apollo stated, apparently not noticing that his young charge had walked into him.

Arnold joined him as he strode over to a large bush of brightly coloured flowers at the side of the road, moving silently as if floating through the air, gesturing for the others to stay put.

Just as they reached the oversized bush, two giant men strolled out in deep conversation. They were easily two feet taller than Abby's already tall frame, with small, beady eyes and short, dark hair all over their bodies. Both were identically dressed in tatty, off-white shirts, with baggy trousers and large flat shoes. Abby noticed that one had string tied around his waist, to hold his trousers up she assumed, and they were both covered in stains and soil. One of the men looked straight at Abby and walked over to her, seemingly oblivious to the two warriors in his path, striding straight past them. He sank to one knee at her feet and took her shaking hand in one of his mucky mitts.

'Welcome back, Princess!' He said, his voice surprisingly soft; the sound comforting, like being wrapped in the finest velvet. 'We've missed you these past years.'

Abby's mind raced; she didn't recognise this giant of a man, why would she? A moment passed, like the slow tick of an under-wound clock, the grimy figure beaming under his dirt-stained fur.

Finding her voice she uttered a polite greeting, shifting uncomfortably in the giant's grasp, a pang of fear spiking in her heart.

'Bet you don't remember us, eh, lass; it's been so long.' He continued in his soft purr, 'Let me introduce myself: I'm Bit, and this is my twin brother Bot.'

He gestured to his companion who offered a subtle nod.

'He doesn't talk much,' the kneeling giant confessed with the hint of an apology. 'We are your royal gardeners and it's our job, nay pleasure, to look after all the gardens in Nousidia, though I must admit, since your aunt took over we've been a little bored! She has taken so much of the land to build her new city, there aren't that many gardens left to tend.'

Abby was warming to this gentle giant; responding with a renewed confidence. 'You've made a lovely job of the gardens around the house: they're beautiful.'

The giant kneeling before her flushed under his covering of fur and mud, releasing her hand. 'We love to work at the house; your mother's spirit is strongest there,' he said as he stood, rejoining his twin.

After a short, hushed conversation Apollo returned with news that the gardeners lived nearby and had offered them shelter for the night.

'I suggest we join them as nightfall brings a chill from which no number of cloaks can protect,' he said, and without waiting for a response he turned his back to them to follow the twins onto a small pathway hidden in the undergrowth.

Abby shared a silent moment of indecision with Tom and then they both ran to catch up with the others.

The group reached their destination as the sun was setting: the low, orange-red glow penetrating though the gaps between the columns of the surrounding forest. The dusk air had taken on a haze, like the foggy curtain that hung over the fields at home on a winter's morning, its tint that of putrid green. The temperature too had dropped considerably, tugging at their skin with its icy fingers. Pulling her jacket closer, Abby focused on the train of walkers she was following, her vain attempts to ignore the blistering cold weakening by the minute. She brushed past a low bush, the movement causing its leaves to glisten in the dim light, the unmistakable sparkle of frost forming on their surface. The group continued to follow the pathway around a huge oak and into a small clearing amongst the dense foliage.

'Welcome to Rose Cottage,' Bit stated proudly. 'It's not much, but it's home.' A giggle passed between the twins as they strolled up the garden path.

The cottage was built from red brick, the roof, clad in an ancient thatch, containing a pair of dormer windows nestled within the old reeds. Windows glowed either side of a bright red door with the flicker of candlelight only partially hidden behind a thin veil of muslin. As they approached Abby wondered how these two giant men could live in such a small house: it didn't look much taller than them; the only consideration for their height was the size of the front door, which was so tall it protruded into the thatch.

The twins strode forward, opening a tiny wooden gate in the white picket fence that surrounded the front garden. As they entered Abby noticed a creeper similar to that she had seen around her own house. It too appeared to be moving, but this had the most beautiful crimson roses adorning its length. The sight of this caused further confusion in her already befuddled mind, as the creeper's foliage was fresh and green, with no sign of ice or damage from the now very wintery air. She turned to look over the garden; the manicured lawn was as white as snow, the surrounding plants withered with the touch of frost.

'Come along, my dear,' whispered Arnold, urging her forward, 'we don't want to get caught out in the chill now, do we.'

The large door opened as the group reached the house, the now familiar glow appearing around the frame. A gust of warm breeze billowed into the cold night air as if to welcome them home. They entered one by one, Abby's view obscured by the bulk of the giant in front of her, until after entering he stepped to one side.

A gasp escaped her throat at the sight that met her eyes. They were standing in a tall entrance hall, its size only outdone by the grandeur of its design. The walls were smooth sandstone with a dozen mottled marble columns along its length. The floor too was a pale rock, a large, elaborately woven rug adorning its centre. Abby looked up to see a beautifully painted ceiling high above her, with reliefs of gold leaf and what looked like precious stones. The scene depicted a garden with fountains and follies, the focus being a grand gothic palace.

'How can this be?' Abby ventured. 'The cottage is so small and this room is so big!'

'This is just the entrance hall, my dear,' Bit explained proudly, grinning like a Cheshire cat. 'We have four reception rooms, eighteen bedrooms and a swimming pool!' He was starting to gloat now. 'All built by Bot and me it was, back in the good old days when yer dad was in charge. I dread to think what the old witch would say if she knew the free magic used to create this place.'

'The old witch?' Abby enquired, unsure as to whom he was referring.

'Sorry m'lady, I forgot who I was talking to. I was referring to your aunt Belladora. I'm afraid she's not too popular around these parts. She banned the free use of magic, you see, some one hundred and ninety years ago, after the last uprising. That's when you and your father was banished to the garden house.' He was blushing under his stubbly fur. 'I'm afraid we've been a little naughty these past years. It's hard for us magic folk not to use our powers – it's in our nature.'

'If I was in charge you could use your powers whenever you wanted,' Abby stated, her manner defiant as her gaze returned to the ceiling. 'So where is that?'

Bit followed her gaze; even his towering frame seemed small in the sheer size of this room. 'That'll be the House of Elders, my dear. That's where you were born,' he answered, looking down at her. 'You'll be coming of age soon, young lady, you must be nearly two hundred by now.'

'I'm sorry. You must be mistaken. I'm thirteen next week!' Abby exclaimed, shocked; she knew she was mature for her age, but she hoped she had kept her youthful looks.

Apollo stepped over to her side, a look of amusement on his face. 'Time moves differently in Nousidia,' he explained. 'You were born in our year ten thousand seven hundred and eighty-three, and are a few days short of your two hundredth birthday, this coming Wednesday.'

He paused for a moment, searching her eyes for signs of understanding. Not seeing any, he continued, 'This is your time, Abigail, a time for you to come of age and return what was taken from us when your mother passed from this world.'

Abby could feel the blood rushing to her head; how could she be two hundred years old, she hadn't even finished school yet! She opened her mouth to argue, her hand instinctively reaching for the smooth pendant hanging around her neck. The touch of the stone instantly comforted her, its warmth soothing the confusion in her head, a clarity forming through the mists of her mind. It was at this moment she began to understand the meaning of the wonders around her. The world in which she had grown became a distant memory, allowing her recollection of this world to return. Although they remained hazy she could recall a grand palace surrounded by beautiful gardens, her parents holding her as a baby, and ... Tears formed in her eyes, the pain of the memories reminding her of what she had lost. She missed her mother more than she had ever allowed herself to believe and now she was worried for her father. Then, as quickly as it had begun, the memory faded as all turned to black: the mists returning to her mind, the reminiscence gone.

Apollo interrupted as he sensed her confusion returning. 'Don't worry Abigail, your memory will return in time. You have been under a powerful forget-me spell, cast by your father to protect you all those years ago.' He gestured to a door at the opposite end of the room. 'Let's get some dinner, and then I think we could all do with a good night's sleep.'

He walked off, followed by Arnold and the twins, leaving Abby and Tom staring at the ceiling. Abby turned to Tom with a quizzical look on her face, hoping for some explanation.

He simply shrugged and said, 'I wish I could shed some light on this, Abbs, but I'm just as confused as you are. Anyway I do believe I smell food. Let's go.'

With that he strode off to catch up with the others.

Abby remained in the hall alone for a moment, letting these recent revelations flow over her like the wash of a snaking river. She was beginning to feel comfortable with the idea of this world; she had a feeling of belonging she had never experienced in England and her new friends were loyal and true.

'Maybe this isn't such a bad place after all,' she murmured to no one in particular then ran though the door to the waiting feast.

6
The Minatox

Abby woke to the sound of bird song. She opened her eyes. Sunlight was creeping through the gaps in the heavy drapes at the window, casting deep shadows on the walls around the large room. She was lying in an opulent four-poster bed; the sheets engulfing her were of the finest silk and gloriously soft to the touch, the pillows under her head firm but comfortable. The smell of fried bacon and eggs was wafting through the open door. She lay still for a moment, enjoying the comfort of her surroundings, her thoughts returning to the previous evening.

They had feasted on huge plates of meats and vegetables, some of which she had never seen before. She had never been a fan of vegetables, but these had the texture of butter and the sweetness of chocolate, with gravy to die for. Naturally this had been followed by enormous helpings of the best apple pie and custard she had ever tasted, with the finale being a dollop of peanut butter ice cream. They all ate like it was their last meal, and afterwards agreed never to eat again.

Abby had been tired after such an exciting day and thus had retired to her room. She had continued to enjoy the stories and laughter from the library below through her open door until she had fallen to sleep while listening to a fanciful tale about a three-headed tiger.

After a hearty breakfast, Apollo informed her that Bit and Bot had agreed to accompany them on the next stage of their journey, and one quick shower later, the six friends set off back into the woods. It was still early morning and Abby could see the remains of frost in the more sheltered pockets of forest, the cold not yet dispersed by the heat of the morning sun.

They were meandering through the trees, taking in the freshness of a new day, when Abby caught sight of a shape hiding in the dense undergrowth. Intrigued, she left the path, heading towards the figure, its form shifting slightly but rooted to the spot as if scared. As she got closer the outline became clearer; it looked like a roe, but was jet black. The shadows were hiding its muscular form; the only giveaway in the surrounding shade was the faint amber glow of its eyes.

'Not too close Princess!' came a shout from behind as Arnold urgently padded through the undergrowth towards her. 'That's a Minatox. They look cute but will rip yer arm off as soon as look at yer.'

Abby continued toward the beast; her senses told her she was safe and she had always felt she could trust them. She leant forward and touched the animal on the forehead. It stood rigid for a moment, unsure how to react, then pushed its snout into the palm of her hand.

'Hello there,' Abby offered in a soothing voice, pleased to meet this majestic creature. 'You see, it's fine,' she called to the others, who had all joined her by that point. 'She's very friendly.'

'It's not her I'm worried about,' shouted Apollo, drawing his sword. 'It's the mother who you need to watch!'

Abby looked up to see a fierce beast crashing through the undergrowth towards them. It was three times the size of its offspring, with glowing orange eyes and very long fangs. Abby instinctively stepped backwards, tripping over a tree root as she went, falling on her back. She closed her eyes, feeling the thundering of her attacker's hooves on the ground beneath her, scrabbling in the soft earth to escape her doom, and then suddenly it stopped.

After a moment of silence she gingerly opened an eye to see the beast held firm in the air above her head, the branch of a nearby tree tightly holding the muscular body mid-pounce, its hooves restrained by smaller entwined branches that were spreading over her torso.

Abby took a shaky breath.

'Do you realise who this is?' a deep voice questioned from somewhere within in the forest. 'This is Abigail, daughter of Gilbert, rightful ruler of Nousidia.'

The beast's muscles relaxed, its eyes dimming to an amber glow.

'I am sorry your highness, I did not recognise you after all these years,' the beast uttered in a surprisingly soft voice. 'I was just protecting my young, you understand.'

Abby squirmed out from under the suspended form standing in front of her, 'I- it's Okay. Who are you?'

The tree released the beast, allowing it to stand at the edge of the forest. 'I am Kyi of the Minatox.' She took a step toward Abby, the remaining tree branch tightening. 'I mean you no harm, Abigail; the Minatox are loyal to your father and therefore to you also.'

'Release her!' Abby ordered in the general direction of the forest.

The tree branch obediently loosened and retracted into a nearby tree.

'Thank you,' she called loudly to whoever was listening, hoping she had made the right decision.

'Your kindness reminds me of your father, young princess,' said the Minatox, stepping forward to look Abby directly in the eyes. 'Yes – I can see it now. You have goodness in your heart and a good brain in your noggin. I think we can be friends.'

Abby's hands were shaking. The beast was standing over her, razor-sharp fangs only inches from her face, its rancid breath blowing in her face, but she stood strong. She was used to facing bullies in the schoolyard and could look after herself, although she had to admit this was a little more extreme.

Seconds passed in silence then the Minatox reared onto its hind legs, jumped clearly over Abby's head and thundered into the forest behind her. Her foal turned to Abby, gave her a wink, and launched after her mother.

'That was close!' exclaimed Abby with a sigh of relief once the beasts were out of sight. Her heart was pounding so loudly in her chest she wasn't sure whether the others could hear it. Her head spinning, the reality of the last few minutes hitting home, she flopped down hard on the nearest tree root. As she fell the roots started to shift; intertwining to form a rough chair into which she landed. Too overwhelmed by recent events to move, she relaxed into the makeshift seat as it molded to fit her body, supporting her weight easily.

'I see the forest recognises you,' Apollo laughed, stepping up to check her over. 'There is a strong bond between your family and the wood of the forest. It has been this way for all time.'

He turned her head from side to side checking for cuts; thankfully she was unharmed.

Abby threw him a mocking look, saying, 'How can a tree remember me? Trees are inanimate objects.' Her head was still a little fuzzy but she was sure she was right.

'You are thinking within the restrictions of the human world, dear princess,' Apollo replied simply, a smile appearing on his handsome face. 'In Nousidia all living things are capable of thought, even gardeners!'

He shot a look at Bit and Bot who were busying themselves taking cuttings from a brightly coloured bush.

'I heard that, dog breath!' shouted Bit, laughing.

Apollo returned his attention to Abby. 'The bond between your family and the forest is much stronger than just mere understanding, however,' he continued. 'It comes from an ancient ritual in which the oldest trees would sacrifice themselves to be incorporated into our grand buildings, forming part of the structure. The fact that the timber used is a willing participant means the tree's essence, or soul, is transferred into the building, living in harmony with its occupants. The House of Elders, where you were born, contains a full copse of woodland. They will be pleased to see you!'

Abby's head was beginning to hurt again.

'Better get a move on, we're burning precious time sitting here talking to trees,' moaned Arnold, his irritation poorly concealed. 'We have much distance to travel before nightfall.'

With that he padded off.

Apollo sighed and added in explanation, 'He doesn't understand trees.' The he trotted ahead to catch his brother.

Abby was scratching her head, wondering whether this day could get any stranger, when the root she was sitting on pushed her up and nudged her to follow the others. Tom, who had been hiding in a nearby bush, fell into step by her side, his wizened face as white as a sheet.

'Did you see the size of that deer, Abbs? It was huge!' he commented.

Abby patted him on the back, agreeing, 'Yes, Tom, she was pretty big for a girl,' and pulled him into a run to catch the others.

7
The garden of Smea

It was late afternoon and a low sun was burning in the sky. The forest was providing some shade, but the trees were beginning to thin, giving way to open fields. After spending so much of their time surrounded by trees Abby was quite relieved to be out in the open again and was taking in the scenery. They had come out on top of a hill and could see for miles. The land was green and lush with undulating hills and valleys. White specks dotted the grassland in the distance and on the horizon Abby could make out rocky mountains topped with snow, like a dusting of icing sugar.

'It's good to be back in the valley,' stated Arnold.

His companions nodded with enthusiasm, broad smiles covering their faces like excited children at a visit to a fun park.

He turned to Abby and asked, 'Do you remember this place, Princess? Your mother used to bring you here all the time; it's her favourite spot.' He could see the look of confusion on her face and, realising she could not remember it, he announced, 'Welcome to the Garden of Smea.'

Abby looked over the panorama, taking in the beauty of the land her companions called home. 'Do you have any memory of these parts, Tom?' she enquired, but there was no answer.

Her heart jumped as she spun around, but Tom was nowhere to be seen. She was turning to Arnold to ask where her friend had gone when Tom stepped out from behind a tree. His arms were laden with bright red berries that glistened in the sunlight.

'Juju berries!' exclaimed Bit, breaking into an even broader smile. 'Good man, Tom.'

He strode over with the others following, each taking a handful and sitting on the soft grass. Seeing Abby's hesitation Bit ushered her over to sit next to him.

'Don't you worry that pretty face, me dear. Juju berries are used in almost every recipe here in Nousidia. Why, the apple pie you ate last night was full of juju juice.' He shifted position to face her as he continued. 'The juju bush is as native to these lands as we are. Their juice supplies all the nutrients we magic folk need for our – well, shall we say, gifts.'

Abby was sure she saw signs of a blush under the stubbly fur covering his face, but before she could say anything he continued.

'It's nice to be able to talk freely 'bout our abilities again,' he said. A look of concern suddenly covered his face. 'It is okay to talk about our magic, is it, Princess?' he asked, going a deeper shade of red.

'Of course,' she replied. 'I'm fascinated by these "gifts" you possess. Why should you hesitate to talk about such a wonderful thing?' Then, she added, 'I wish I had such powers.'

Apollo's face appeared over Bit's shoulder. 'But you do, my dear. Would you like to try something?'

He offered her his hand, gesturing that she should stand. They took a few steps away from the group to a rocky outcrop overlooking a field of yellow flowers.

'We'll start with an easy one,' he said, a note of mockery in his voice. 'All you have to do is turn the flowers red.' He stepped back and gestured towards the field. 'When you're ready,' he prompted, feeling her hesitation.

Abby sat on a small rock sobbing into her hands. 'I can't do magic. I'm just a little girl!'

'Get off with yer!' boomed Arnold's voice from behind her: he had joined them, his muscular features beaming with humour. 'You're a member of the Nousidian royal family, and as such you have the abilities of all your subjects. Now get on yer feet and change them flowers.'

Abby reluctantly got to her feet, wiping the tears from her cheeks. 'But I don't know how,' she mumbled. She honestly had no idea how to change flowers from yellow to red.

'Well, you'll be needing yer wand, me dear, and a few of these wouldn't go a miss.' Arnold offered her a handful of berries. 'Then just relax and think of what you want to happen.'

Abby had forgotten about the wand Apollo had given her the day before. After a minute of rummaging in the makeshift rucksack she had made that morning from an old sack and some string she found her wand and pointed it at the field. A moment of sheer concentration later she turned to Arnold in frustration.

'It's no good, I can't do it …' she began, deflated.

The sight that met her was completely unexpected. There stood Arnold, all muscle and might in a nice shade of pink! The group erupted with laughter. Tom was laughed so hard he fell over into a nearby bush. The only one not laughing was Arnold, who had a very stern look on his face.

'I'm sorry,' Abby squeaked between giggles. 'I told you I was no good at this magic thing!' She erupted into another fit of laughter. 'I'm afraid pink just isn't your colour.'

With that Arnold's face cracked into a broad guffaw, his whole body shaking with laughter as it faded back to normal.

'I think we need to work on your focus,' suggested Apollo, his face red from laughter. 'But first we must find cover as the rains are coming.'

He turned and strode towards a nearby copse of trees. 'Better hurry, you don't want to get wet!' he shouted to his dithering companions.

They stood looking into the clear blue sky, the sun beating down on their faces.

'But there isn't a cloud in the sky?' stated Tom to no one in particular.

As if on command a raindrop landed on his forehead.

'Where did that come from?' he began to ask, but was cut off by a deluge of water falling from the heavens.

The friends ran towards the trees as one. Abby was sure the outer branches were spreading to form a canopy, for which they were all glad, and no one else seemed to question this. She guessed it was another thing that just happened.

I think I'm going to like it here, she thought as she huddled close to Apollo for warmth.

'I'm glad,' he whispered into her ear. 'This is all yours – your true home.' He wrapped his strong arms around her.

Abby snuggled into his jacket and promptly fell asleep.

She was woken by a large drip of water splashing on her cheek. It sent a cold shiver through her body, surging through her like a blast of cold wind. She shivered in an involuntary spasm with the shock of it.

Apollo, his arms still wrapped around her, softly wiped the water from her face.

'Have a nice nap?' he asked, his face only inches from hers, his soft brown eyes like deep pools of molten chocolate.

'Yes, thank you,' Abby answered abruptly, suddenly feeling a little uneasy with the situation.

She got to her feet, not knowing why and stood uneasily in front of her travelling companions. They remained seated, looking up at her in expectation.

'I had a dream about my mother,' she blurted out, and then to justify such a comment she added, 'I need to talk with her; she will have the answers I need.' Realising how absurd that must have sounded she added, 'If it were only possible.'

The two warriors looked at each other, as if in a silent conference, and after a short moment Arnold spoke.

'It is possible that you may be able to speak with your mother's spirit at the Chamber of Souls. It is many days travel on foot and a treacherous journey through the lands of the dark people. Our allegiance to the king will not aid us there, as those who live in those lands are rumoured to be tribal; they either exist or not as is their wish. Matters of the Nousidian world matter not to them, only the power to control their own destinies, and that is something we cannot predict.'

Abby interrupted out of the blue. 'Free spirits, eh? We call them "dudes" where I grew up!'

The group looked at each other, an air of puzzlement shared amongst them until Bit broke the silence.

'You have met these creatures?' he asked, a look of fascination on his face.

'Yes,' Abby replied, unsure what all the fuss was about. 'We have a couple at school. They're usually talking about "radical moves", riding skateboards all over the place and jumping off things. I always thought they were from another world!'

Bit was fascinated with the whole idea, asking, 'What's a skateboard?'

Abby was contemplating how to describe a skateboard when Arnold announced they had better move on before the remaining sunlight was gone. The group busied themselves in preparation for the journey ahead. Bit shuffled off to pack his trowel.

The group set off as the sun was beginning to set. Arnold suggested they head for a nearby village. 'There's an inn around those parts where we can get food and shelter for the night,' he said, remembering a particularly drunken night from somewhere in his distant past; the details were, however, now a little fuzzy.

Abby walked alongside Bit explaining what she knew of skateboarding, although she had to admit she had only tried it once and had ended up bruising her bum.

They reached the inn at nightfall. A sign above the door swayed lazily in an imaginary breeze as the evening air had become as still as death itself; the very atmosphere around them seemed to be freezing solid. Abby squinted in the failing light to read the name on the grimy board.

Arnold informed her by announcing, 'Welcome to the Jittery Pecker.'

The narrow streets surrounding them were empty apart from the occasional hooded figure rushing to a nearby house. Arnold banged on the door with one of his huge paws, the wood shaking in its frame. Minutes passed with no answer. Abby could feel the oppressive cold chilling her to the core. She pulled her jacket tighter around her face, feeling the moisture in her breath solidify on the material. Arnold was raising his paw to knock again when the door opened a crack and deep voice asked, 'Who is it at this late hour?'

'Just some weary travellers in need of food and warmth,' replied Arnold, pushing the door open with ease. 'Do you have room?'

As the door opened the owner of the voice appeared. He was a stout, round gentleman dressed in fine clothes of red and blue with a fine waxed moustache and bushy sideburns.

'Come in, my dears,' he requested apologetically, gesturing for them to enter with an outstretched hand and subtle bow. 'We don't get many travellers these days, what with the rumours that the witch's demons have been spotted in these parts.'

As they entered Abby heard Apollo's voice in her mind. 'Keep your hood low and stick close by me.'

She obediently stepped closer to him, pulling the hood of her jacket over her face.

The heat from the open fire greeted them as they entered the hostelry, the low beams giving the room a cozy feel. Abby could see several small groups of people sitting around marble-topped tables through the slit on her hood. They were drinking with much cheer from goblets brimming with what she assumed was some sort of fizzy beer. One very happy-looking man in a tall hat fell backwards from his stool and landed motionless on the floor with a dull thud. His companions continued laughing, ignoring their companion as though he had never existed.

'We'll take a room,' Arnold was saying to the innkeeper. 'Your best if you please. We have means of gratification.'

'Arnold Buttersquick, you old bugger!' boomed a voice from the bar. 'What are yer doin' in these parts?'

Abby shifted to get a better look at who had recognised him; everybody's attention was on Arnold hugging a figure in a vice-like grip, his muscular arms struggling to reach around the torso of the beast. For this was no human form: he shared the features and stood no higher than his friend but his bulk made Arnold look almost petite.

'What have you been up to, old man?' Arnold was saying, releasing his companion and nodding to the barman for a brew.

'Do yer want a widdit in that?' asked a scrawny youth who had emerged from behind the large slab of slate that served as a bar.

Arnold broke from his hearty reminiscences to ask what in Nousidia a 'widdit' was.

'It's all the rage, my friend,' replied his freind. 'They put a wee fella in yer pint, he gets very drunk, from swimming in the nectar yer see, which gives him the wind …'

Abby burst into laughter. A sudden thought pounced into her mind, reminding her of their need for secrecy; she stifled her amusement as best she could, but couldn't help the odd giggle escaping.

'We'll take that room now,' Apollo said to the innkeeper, his voice smooth but with an air of authority, breaking the wonder of the moment.

The portly man turned without a word and led the group to a small staircase in the corner of the room. After a short climb they were on the floor above the hostelry.

The room was shabby with a row of cots along one wall and a tatty bathroom at the far end. A large, threadbare rug which had seen better days covered the floor and a dirty pair of curtains covered the one window. A fire roared in its stone surround in the outer wall, flames licking around the edges of the mantel.

'This will do,' confirmed Apollo, only slightly masking his disgust at the dirty accommodation being offered. 'Leave us now, we wish to retire.'

The innkeeper gave him a polite smile, turned and left without another word.

Apollo sat on one of the beds, indicating for Abby to take the one adjacent, the others finding cots elsewhere. 'Would you like to try a little more magic my dear?' he asked, a hopeful look in his eyes.

'Can we?' Abby whispered feeling like a naughty schoolgirl talking in class. 'Can we do something with this room?'

'I thought you would never ask!' Apollo replied, handing her a handful of berries. 'These will help.'

She took the berries and threw them in her mouth; they were sweet and juicy and she could feel their energy coursing through her body in waves.

'Now close your eyes and imagine the most comfortable room you have ever seen,' instructed Apollo, handing her the wand.

Abby sat back and focused her mind, closing her eyes to the murk surrounding them. She remembered the opulent palaces she had seen in her dreams, the gold fittings and silk swaths adorning every item, the ornate designs of the furniture and elaborate stained-glass in the windows. Her breathing became shallow, blood washed through her head like a warm blanket engulfing her, and then she opened her eyes.

What met her was a vision in itself: the room had transformed into a suite fit for royalty. The cots had been replaced with four-poster beds surrounded by lavish weaves of silk and gold, the ceiling was adorned with twinkling glass chandeliers, their light filling the space with dancing shadows, the floor was covered in the finest carpet and the air was filled with the scent of flowers.

'Did I do all this?' Abby asked in astonishment.

Apollo gave her a knowing smile, winking at the gardeners as he replied. 'With a little help, now go brush your teeth – its time for bed.'

Abby woke with a start. The room was dark and gloomy, the dull silvery glow of the moon the only light through the lonely window. A soft purr was emanating from the large form of Arnold curled in a corner, a huge paw draped over his nose.

A sharp tapping disturbed the quiet.

Abby glanced around the room, looking for its source, her eyes finally focusing on a small shape at the window.

The tapping came again, this time with more urgency.

Intrigued, she climbed out of bed, pulling on her jacket in the chill of the night air, and padded barefoot across the soft carpet to the small window. A smile formed on her lips as she recognised the figure – it was the robin from her windowsill at home. She quickly released the catch and opened the window just enough to allow the little bird to hop in, fearful of the cold night air.

'Step back, my dear,' chirped the bird. 'I'll need a little room for this.'

Abby backed away as the bird hopped off the sill. The petite bird fell, growing in shape and size, shedding its feathers in favour of soft, pale skin and sprouting a head of jet-black hair, its form continuing to change until before Abby stood a beautiful young woman, her dress flowing with wondrous opaque shades of red.

'Thank you, dear,' she said when the transformation was complete. ''Tis a little chilly out there.'

Eleanora Stub stood only slightly taller than Abby, but it was her commanding demeanour and utter confidence that made Abby feel small. Her stature had served her well these last few centuries, keeping her safe in the role of royal advisor. Although she had spent many years now in the service of Queen Belladora, her allegiance had always been to the true king. It was this commitment to Abby's father that brought her here this night.

'Sit, my dear,' she said, gesturing to a pair of chairs that were obediently sliding silently towards the empty fireplace. Abby hadn't noticed the wand in her hand, its stone now glowing faintly. She stepped over to the chairs now resting either side of the grate of the large fire, which burst into the most enchanting crimson flame. Sitting in the closest, she was joined in the opposite chair by her companion.

Remembering the advice she had been given on their first meeting Abby began to cough out her reasons for not listening, stopping short at the look of amusement on Eleanora's face.

'You have no reason to explain yourself, Abigail,' soothed Eleanora, her voice as smooth as the finest silk. 'You are the heir to the throne, and thus answer to no one. Save for your father of course.' A hint of a smile crossed her lips. 'And I'm sure you always obey him – right?'

Abby joined the humour, saying, 'But naturally!', a grin spreading across her face.

The two sat for over an hour discussing Nousidian politics, accepted etiquette for royalty, even the latest fashion 'must haves' at court, but Abby's real interest was her apparent magical abilities. She learned how, just that day, a battalion of warriors had spontaneously turned a shocking shade of pink, much to the amusement of the crowd who were gathered to witness the changing of the guard. Apollo had told her she was capable of achieving great things, but it had not prepared her for the realisation that she could influence anything in the kingdom.

'That was me!' Abby exclaimed, her cheeks turning a bright shade of red in embarrassment. 'I mean Apollo was showing me how to change the colour of flowers, and I turned Arnold pink.' She smiled at the memory. 'I guess I need some more practice!'

Eleanora smiled, saying, 'Relax and focus, that is the key.' Then, after a moment of silence, she asked, 'Do you remember your mother?'

Abby was shocked by the sudden, personal question. She considered telling her new friend about the dreams in which her mother visited her, but decided against it. 'No. I was only a little baby when my mother died. I can't remember her at all.'

'Shame. She was a great woman. Showed a lot of promise before…' Her voice faltered, the hint of a tear appearing in the corner of her eye.

'Were you close?' enquired Abby, not wishing to intrude but eager to understand.

Eleanora looked the youngster straight in the eyes. For the first time Abby sensed an air of vulnerability behind the woman's crystalline exterior, and something else that she could not quite grasp. Something deeper.

'I must get back,' she suddenly stated, the cold, solid exterior snapping back. 'I will be missed at court.' She stood, towering over Abby. 'You are in the best of company; the warriors that travel with you are loyal and true. Trust their judgement in the days that follow.'

Her form began to shrink, becoming the bird once more. Abby dutifully opened the window a little, backing away from the harsh chill that rushed in.

'I will be watching, my dear. If you need me I am but a thought way,' Eleanora offered with a wink of her beady eye. Then she hopped out of the open window and flew off into the cold night.

8
The dark people

The robin landed on a stone balcony belonging to one of many staterooms in the castle, exhausted after her long flight she limped inside. Like all the rooms in this grand structure, this was decorated in the finest black silks with antique furniture collected from the furthest corners of the kingdom, an abundance of gold leaf adorning even the most functional of items. Sitting at a table against one wall was the figure of a woman crouched over a glass ball. A servant girl fussed over her, untangling robes and combing hair. Mirrors surrounded the seated figure, giving views of all parts of the room. It was in one of these she noticed the bird crouched in a corner near the door.

'Come here, slave,' the woman screamed, her face contorted with anger, knocking the chair over as she swivelled to face her visitor, 'and show your true form.'

The bird obediently transfigured back to human form, but this was not the statue of beauty she had shown Abigail, but a smaller, timid presence with lank, dark hair and a pronounced stoop in her left shoulder. Being a royal advisor for all these centuries had taught her to show what was expected; keeping up this facade was a matter of survival, even though it caused her considerable pain.

'What news of our little princess?' quizzed Belladora, her contorted features relaxing a little. 'Is she near?'

'She rests at the Jittery Pecker on the edge of the dark forest,' Eleanora answered begrudgingly. Every part of her being hated serving this mistress; but it was her purpose, and as such she was compelled to answer truthfully, serving without question.

Her mistress hobbled closer, her features wizened with age; the cost of black spells cast over the years. 'Soon the true heir will be in my grasp and her death will grant my rule absolute,' she spat, stumbling into a nearby chair and sitting roughly.

'Bring the Meditition, I am in need of potion,' she croaked, waving her hand towards the door.

Eleanora made a swift exit, glad to be released from her mistress's hateful glare.

After an early breakfast the group bade farewell to the innkeeper. His face was glowing with a broad toothy smile as he wished them a good journey. His payment for taking them in had far exceeded any he could have imagined, as Apollo had agreed not to return their room to its previous condition. The sun was shining brightly this morning and the group was in good spirits, their packs jammed with delicacies of all descriptions. Bit and Bot had said goodbye at the edge of the dark forest; their grounds needed tending and the dark forest was no place for a gardener. The remaining travellers stood in the morning sun contemplating the journey ahead.

Abby turned to Tom. 'How come you're so quiet this morning, Thomas?' She only used his full name when he was in a mood.

There was no answer, Tom just stood mesmerised.

She stepped forward, shouting, 'Wake up, sleepy head!' in his ear.

Tom jumped as though coming out of a deep sleep. 'Sorry, my dear, I was miles away,' he offered, knowing it was a feeble excuse. The truth was he had a really bad feeling about this place and wasn't at all pleased with the idea of entering the forest.

'Gives yer the willies, eh, boy,' boomed Arnold as he strode past and into the tree line. 'So it should. There be nasty beasties in these parts!'

With that he disappeared into the unnaturally dense shadow.

'I heard that, you big lump of meat!' shouted Tom after him, at which point the realisation hit him: 'Wait a minute; I did understood him. What's happened to me?'

Apollo turned to him, a warm smile on his face. 'You're getting your old powers back, Tom, that's all,' he laughed and with that stepped into the forest.

Tom turned to Abby with a quizzical look on his face.

Shrugging her shoulders, she took his hand and pulled him forward into the gloom.

They had been in the forest for several hours and it was getting cold. The trees surrounding them were gnarled and misshapen, forming an unnaturally thick umbrella of foliage over their heads, cutting out the warmth of the morning sun. The light breaking through this barrier had a dusk-like property that reflected from particles suspended in the air, as though frozen in time; but worst of all for Abby was the absence of comfort she had become used to when travelling amongst the trees. This was different: this felt wrong.

A shape moved to her left, a darker shadow in the surrounding gloom; then another to the right, this one closer, its form almost visible.

Apollo's voice was in her head, quietly calling, 'They have been following us for some time. We need to find some open space.'

Their pace quickened, a sense of fear spreading through them all like the chill of a cold breeze on a hot summer's day. The shadows surrounding them multiplied with every heartbeat, every breath laboured with the need to escape. Arnold tapped on her shoulder, pointing to a clearing amongst the trees.

'Over there, my princess. Quickly, if yer please,' he whispered.

Apollo was already striding over with Tom in hot pursuit. Abby broke into a run, the adrenalin coursing through her veins, fuelling her fear of what surrounded them. Just as they reached the opening a figure appeared in their path; its features were blurred as if not quite in focus, with limbs protruding from a central body. It was hazy, but solid enough to stop them in their tracks.

'Who are you that dare enter the realm of the dark people?' boomed a voice in Abby's head; its volume was deafening, leaving a ringing aftermath. 'Leave while you still can,' it continued and it was absolute.

'Move into the light,' shouted Arnold over the din as he pushed forward, his bulging arms outstretched.

The rest of the group joined him and pushed in unison against the apparition, forcing it to step back into the clearing. The morning sun touched its ghostly head, causing a surprising transformation.

Arnold burst into a roaring belly laugh as he too stepped into the light, closely followed by the others, and the giggle was soon shared by each. For before them stood a young boy. He was no more than four feet tall and wore a brightly coloured raincoat with peacock feathers protruding from it in all directions.

'Don't hurt me, mister' pleaded the boy in a voice that had the pitch of youth. 'I didn't mean no harm. Just a joke y'know.'

Tears were forming in his eyes; he was plainly scared by the beast standing over him, a roar coming from between its curved fangs.

Abby stepped forward, ushering Arnold back with a wave of her hand. 'Don't be afraid, little boy,' she soothed, hoping she sounded more confident then she felt. 'No one is going to hurt you.'

The boy stepped back, unsure about the tall girl moving towards him, her wild red hair blowing in the breeze.

It was then that Abby noticed the gathering shapes surrounding them in the shadow of the forest: hundreds of figures, all blurred and shimmering. A solitary figure stepped into the light. He was a lightly built man of average height with brown hair and bucked teeth. It was his eyes, however, that portrayed his true nature: cold, steel-gray with the unblinking stare of a killer. He walked directly towards Abigail, his gaze unfaltering.

Arnold stepped into his path, Apollo joining his side, their weapons raised.

The figure stopped just out of the reach of the warrior's glistening swords. A moment of tense silence passed before he asked a simple question.

'Is that you, m'lady?'

Abby stepped forward, although cautiously remaining behind her protective wall of warriors. 'Who are you?' she ventured.

'Tis me, Reginald Cockle,' replied the figure, a smile spreading across his face. 'You saved me life from this lumbering moggy and his whiffy paws a couple o' days ago – remember?' He took a further step forward. 'You have no fear in these parts: I owes you me life.'

The little boy ran to his side, grasping a handful of his father's tunic.

'Don't worry 'bout this little one; they love to play puttin' the frighteners on people. Keeps unwanted visitors out, yer know.'

All around them figures appeared from the forest, filling the little clearing with chatter and twitching noses. They all had mouse-like features with long whiskers and brown wispy hair, but each was unique; except for those cold, grey eyes.

'Come along,' Reginald continued, his voice becoming excited, 'you must join us for lunch; we're having cheese!'

He turned to walk out of the clearing, a path opening through the crowd as he went. They followed him as he strode through the dense undergrowth, understanding the pointlessness of argument, as a sizeable mob filed along behind them. After a few minutes they entered another clearing in the forest. This, however, was completely enclosed by the canopy of the surrounding trees, forming a natural enclosure, not unlike a cave. Dotted within this enclosure sat numerous straw huts of various shapes and sizes built around a central structure that dwarfed them all. This was their destination, the group stopping at a pair of intricately carved doors.

Reginald turned to the others, his head held high, announcing, 'Welcome to Mouseopia, kingdom of the Roden and sanctuary to the true heir!'

This statement surprised Abby; although he had recognised her from her bedroom, she had not realised he knew who she really was. She felt vulnerable in a world where everybody seemed to know her (or this perception of her) but she knew nothing. This was an alien concept to someone who always somehow knew the answer and excelled at everything. The only saving thought in her head was the knowledge that she had powers beyond anything she had experienced before, and the strange feeling of familiarity this world held.

The carved doors opened slowly ahead of them, releasing an odour that could only be described as a mixture of overripe fruit and sweaty feet: a pungent smell that made Abby's eyes water. Light erupted from huge lanterns hung high above in the rafters of the hall, a dim glow leaking out into the dusk of the cave-like clearing through the now open doors but hardly affecting the consuming gloom. Reginald ushered them forward into the light, and as they moved a mountain of provisions came into view. He had to laugh at his guests, their faces frozen in awe at the spectacle. Their food store was an awesome sight: the culmination of a whole month of collecting and scavenging.

Mouse-like people flooded in all around them, filling every corner of the hall, an air of anticipation building. Then all went silent as Reginald raised his paw-like hand.

'Welcome to the feast of thanks,' he called, his voice bouncing from the chamber walls. 'Today we welcome the homecoming of our true heir and daughter of the rightful ruler of Nousidia, Princess Abigail Catherine Nubia Brown the Second.'

A cheer echoed throughout the chamber upon hearing her name. He waited for them to calm before he continued. 'May she return to rule our lands fairly, reuniting the scattered tribes and bringing to an end the hags evil reign.'

A chuckle came from somewhere in the crowd and was quickly silenced by a loud slap.

Abby felt her skin go bright scarlet; her head began to swim, like it was filled with hot lava. She felt Apollo's hand rest on her shoulder, its calming influence welcome.

I can't do all this! she panicked in her mind, *I'm just a little girl who wants her father back.*

Apollo's voice soothed her thoughts, caressing them like the hands of a lover. 'One step at a time my dear, one step at a time.'

Then Reginald's hand was up again as he roared, 'Well, tuck in then!' He stepped aside to let two very enthusiastic youngsters pass and dive into a nearby column of Stilton.

Abby had never seen so much cheese, or for that matter known there were so many varieties. She started with a chunk of what looked like mild cheddar, unsure of what to expect, and found it to be similar to that at home. Gradually gaining confidence, and seeing Tom gorging himself (for a change), she picked up a small block nearby: its bluish-green colour and like sandpaper like texture were a little offputting at first, but it was silky to the touch and smelt so good. She took a tentative bite from one corner, her mouth instantly filling with the most exquisite flavor that melted down her throat like a river of warm honey.

'Wow!' she gasped, the remaining cheese flowing away to leave a glow in her stomach. 'That was something else!'

'It's my own creation,' said a proud, high-pitched voice from her left.

Abby spun around to see the young boy they had confronted earlier.

'Norman Cockle's the name. Reggie's me dad and ruler of these parts,' the boy continued. He shared the wispy hair of his companions but had no whiskers and his bucked teeth were less prominent. Norman was extremely proud of his inventions and took every opportunity to talk about them, especially to such an important guest.

'I call it Supergoatilicious; it's a blend of goat's cheese, honey and juju juice,' he said proudly, a look of excitement on his mousy face. 'Would you like to try some of my other inventions?'

Abby was about to agree when Reginald stepped in and changed the subject. 'Where are yer off to then, with yer merry little band?' he asked.

His question was aimed at Abby but answered by Apollo, a pile of cheese samples in his hand. 'We travel to the Chamber of Souls to consult the ancients.'

Reginald turned his attention to Apollo; he had recognised the uniform immediately. 'Captain of the guard, eh?' he confirmed, 'and judging by the golden locks and passive manner, a Gordorian at that.' He stepped closer examining the soldier, his nose twitching. 'I smell goodness in your aura, despite the company you keep.' He shot an icy glare at Arnold before continuing, 'I think we can help you on yer journey. But first we must eat.'

9
Capture

The group followed Reginald through the forest several hours later, along a pathway cleverly concealed in the undergrowth. Behind them strode a troupe of forty soldiers, shimmering in their enchanted armour; they were carrying supplies of food and cases containing all manner of contraptions which, they had been informed, would help them on their journey.

They had gorged themselves for hours on cheese, exotic fruits and juju juice until they felt they would burst. Abby had experimented with a little magic; much to the amusement of the children who had flocked around her in droves, telling her stories of ancient times. Some of these may have even been true, but she didn't care: it made her happy, happier than she had felt for many long years.

She had also discovered that although, like all beings in Nousidia, the Roden changed into their animal form when they entered the human world, this was the limit of their magic. Most of them were simple farmers who had turned to scavenging when they were exiled from the kingdom.

The effect of so much food was to slow them down with splitting headaches and erupting stomachs: an unfortunate side effect of excessive gorging. Reginald stooped down and, without breaking pace, picked a handful of leaves from a nearby bush.

'Rub these on your forehead,' he suggested. 'It'll take the toxins out of yer system, counter the effects of the cheese. I guess some of the riper ones were a little too pungent for yer folk.' He smiled to himself, remembering the tricks he used to play on his friends back in the castle. 'Looking forward to returning home,' he continued very matter-of-factly.

Abby, very confused, asked, 'Was that not your home in the forest?'

Reginald turned to her, matching her stride perfectly on the narrow footpath. He had not realised just how little she remembered of this world. He guessed he would need to fill in a few gaps.

'Many of the Roden are simple farmers, but a select number had the honour of being yer father's personal guard, b'fore the dark years,' he explained, his cold, grey eyes staring into her. 'After yer mother, the queen o' these lands, passed through the veil of light to the spirit world an' yer father got sent to the garden house in exile…' He paused for a moment, the grief of the memories taking its toll. 'Us Roden are loyal, yer see, and we refused to denounce yer fathers rule. That upset the old hag, I can tell yer! Sent her 'enchmen into our camp an' massacred many of our kin. We are but a few survivors hidin' in the forest.'

Abby looked into those steely eyes; hatred glistened there, the desire for revenge immeasurable, tugging at the very fibre of his being. A shudder passed down Abby's spine; she was glad he counted her as a friend.

'Why can I not hear the forest here?' she asked. The question had been bothering her since their arrival. 'I mean, well, I could sense the forest before, even hear it, but now there is nothing.'

Reginald sighed, his thoughts weighing heavily on his simple mind. 'This was your mother's place once,' he began, 'a place where she would spend her days listening to the thoughts of the trees, be amused by the squabbles of the foragers, even occasionally bring a friend to share the harmony of this place. Then one day she just didn't come. The forest fell into decline; its love for your mother was so strong, so addictive, that it could not survive without her, and gradually, one by one, the trees simply stopped growing. The same can be said for the abundance of wildlife that once filled these parts; those that were lucky escaped, the remainder following their great love into the next world.'

'Wow!' Abby gasped, this revelation bringing her own longing for her mother into sharp focus. 'I wish I'd known her.'

'You will!' laughed Reginald. 'You will.'

Then he was off, sprinting through the foliage to clip one of the younger members of the congregation around the ear.

Abby pondered this comment for a moment, remembering Apollo's suggestion in the garden at home. *Could it be that her parents had found a way of bridging the barrier between the living and the dead?*

A particularly bright purple flower said 'Good morning' as she passed, tearing her back to the wonders of the present.

Several hours passed before the forest ahead became brighter and the trees began to thin. Before long they were on the far edge of the forest and back into the afternoon sun. They sat for a while, soaking up the sunshine and filling their flasks with water from a small stream.

Some of the Roden were busying themselves: opening cases and assembling what appeared to be some sort of huge mechanical cage. Abby had not seen anything like it: it was taller than her house and wide enough to fit three, with countless cogs, levers and other paraphernalia jutting out. The remaining soldiers were erecting tents at the forest edge and preparing a makeshift kitchen.

Abby sat on a low rock, feeling a little redundant. She cast her gaze across the green fields to a river in the valley and beyond to the mountains of the horizon. Squinting, she tried to focus on a column of smoke rising below the highest peak.

'What's that?' she asked anyone that was listening, pointing towards the column of black.

It was Reginald who answered. 'That, me dear, used to be our home: the city of Ravensburn, the city of our elders. The smoke you see is the burning of the forest around our once great settlement.' A look of sorrow covered his face: He missed his old life. Forcing a smile, he continued. 'Since yer fathers departure the queen 'as built many new buildings an' monuments, destroying park an' forest alike in the pursuit of her vision.'

He stopped, shaking his head.

'What vision?' Abby prompted, not sure what he meant.

Reginald, his head lifting somewhat, said, 'She is creating a city of steel an' glass an' somethin' unnatural that looks like stone but is man-made in giant moulds.' He shuddered at the thought, his eyes wide and staring. 'A group of us sneaked in just last month. There's no grass! Just smooth grey stone not even the sharpest claw can cut. It's hideous!' His head shot up, his grey eyes meeting hers. 'But worst of all, these new buildings, they didn't answer our calls: I think they're dead!'

'What do you mean "dead"?' Abby quizzed, her mind not comprehending his meaning.

'In this world, my dear, things are very different to what you have accepted as normal.' It was Apollo who answered as he joined them, sitting on the soft grass next to Abby. 'All buildings in Nousidia are formed by the willing co-operation of nature's materials, the occupants who choose to share it, and naturally a little magic; just like the trees in the forest of Smea gave themselves for the construction of your home. These new structures, however, are different, as they are built from man-made materials: a process that kills the living aura of the material it consumes, leaving it cold and dead.'

As he paused Abby looked around the small group that had assembled to hear news of this new city. Each had a look of horror and disgust etched on their face; the thought of it was beyond belief: how could such a monstrosity exist in their world? There had always been rumours of such things from the human world from those who had ventured across, but most accepted them as idle ramblings, blamed on the sickness in those who returned. But now such horrors were being built in their city: a city they had once called home.

'Enough o' this tittle tattle!' stated Reginald, sensing an air of apprehension within the group. 'We have work to do. Back to your posts.'

With a shake of his paw-like hand the soldiers scurried off, returning to their duties.

Reginald turned to Abby, his mousey features calm again, and said, 'Best not dwell on such matters, eh.' His eye caught a shape in the sky. ''Tis time to arrange your transport.'

Abby followed his pointing finger, squinting in the low sunlight. She pinched herself to ensure she was awake as swooping out of the sun towards them was the biggest flying beast she had ever seen, not in her waking hours anyway, for she recognised it immediately from her dreams – it was a dragon! The beast landed close to the opening in the cage structure the Roden had built, its beady eyes focused intently on the contents, its crimson scales glittering with the reflection of the low sun.

Abby stood and took a few steps towards the scene for a better look. She felt Apollo's hand rest on her shoulder and, sensing his hesitation, ventured no further.

Fire erupted from the beast's snout, filling the cage with smoke and flame. A solitary character was standing in the contraption covered by a now smouldering cloak, steam pouring from every aperture. It was Arnold.

'He'll be fine, my dear,' Apollo confirmed, the grip on her shoulder strengthening, his voice so close she could feel his breath on the nape of her neck. 'He's a tough old cat.'

The dragon lunged forward into the cage, reaching towards the warrior inside. Arnold calmly stepped to his left, a sharp claw passing only inches from his nose. Then he was in the air, landing with the poise of a gymnast on the beast's shoulder, his claws embedded into the back of its neck.

A blood-curdling roar came from the beast's throat as it thrashed around in an attempt to rid itself of the unwelcome rider, slamming against the walls of the cage as a group of Roden inched the doors closed. Abby could see smoke as black as soot bellowing from the beasts jowls, the green glow from a frantic eye shining through the smog. Then the beast slumped to the floor, its strength exhausted. The ground under their feet shook as it landed.

The assembled crowd cheered as Arnold jumped to the ground beside his beaten opponent, joining in with his own roar of satisfaction at the beasts defeat.

'Surely he hasn't killed it!' screamed Abby to her companions, not wanting such a fabulous animal slaughtered.

Apollo smiled, shaking his head. 'Don't worry, Princess, Arnold is a master at his art; he has not damaged the beast. It will wake in the morning with a clear head and little memory of this evening's events.'

Abby returned his smile, although shakily, content with his explanation but remaining concerned for such a majestic beast.

After a hearty meal Apollo announced it was time to retire. The sun had reached the horizon, casting a mirage of reds and purples across the twilight sky, and the air had cooled, droplets of ice forming on the surrounding grass. The four were guided to a tent in the centre of a group; it was taller than the others but, Abby guessed, only big enough for two to lie comfortably.

She was about to ask where the others were going to sleep, as she did not want to be alone in this unfamiliar place, when they stepped through the canvas door.

'Why am I surprised?' she mumbled to herself. Before her was a room so stately in size and decor that it could have been equally at home in a grand country house. High above her head the canvas billowed in a gust of evening breeze then settled back to its smooth slope, the movement the only evidence of the structures temporary nature. 'Magic, I guess!' she said to no one in particular then, looking around, continued, 'Bags I get the big four-poster over there!'

She squealed and ran over to an extremely large bed covered in soft pillows and opulent fabrics. She lay on the mattress, enjoying its softness. Warmth enveloped her like a blanket of the finest lamb's wool, lulling her immediately into a deep sleep.

Apollo strode over and covered her with a sheet embossed in green silk and gold leaf, wishing her a good night's sleep as he did so.

'Let her sleep well,' he said to his companions as he turned from the bed. 'She will need all her energy for the days ahead.'

'As will we all,' agreed Arnold. 'You too, laddie.'

He helped Tom onto the bed next to Abby. Tom began to ask why, but his eyes immediately grew heavy. A yawn escaped from his throat then he too fell into a deep sleep.

10
A mysterious visitor

Abby woke with a start. The room was dark and gloomy; the only illumination was the faint glow of moonlight through the canvas of the ceiling. Something had disturbed her, an irrational feeling that urged her to go outside. She lay still for a second, listening to the rhythmic sound of sleep around her, wishing herself back to the safety of slumber. But her mind was focused; she had to know.

Carefully climbing from the bed, she slipped on her jacket in the cold night air. Pulling on her All Stars, she glanced back to the bed, and as she did she noticed something very odd. There on the bed was her sleeping form, wrapped in a blanket, a look of calm on her face. Her heart jumped and she released a squeal from somewhere in her throat.

'I must be dreaming,' she whispered, an involuntary statement.

She looked around the room, but nobody stirred. She walked over to the sleeping form of Apollo, leaning forward to wake him; he would know what was happening. She touched his shoulder, but got no response. She pushed a little harder, rocking his slumbering body, but there was still no response.

A knot of fear was building in the pit of her stomach. *What was happening to her?*

She punched his arm as hard as she could, hoping to break into his dreams. He murmured something incoherent and rolled onto his side, oblivious.

A sudden noise distracted her; a cracking, like the breaking of a twig on the far side of the tent wall. She moved swiftly to the door, opening a slit in the canvas to see who was there. The surrounding landscape was draped in a sparkling blanket of ice, as if frozen in time. Nothing was moving; there was no breeze or nocturnal activity, just still. Abby could see the vapour of her breath crystallising as it met the frozen night air, the intense cold painful against her skin.

It was then that she noticed a figure standing in the shadow of an adjacent tent. It wore a long cloak with a hood that hung low, obscuring its face, and stood with the stoop of old age. She felt a wave of sickness envelop her; although she could not see its eyes, she knew the figure was staring at her, and it was the cold, hard stare of a murderer.

A movement to her left diverted her from the horror of these thoughts; it was one of the Roden guards, wrapped in thick layers of fur and weave, his sword unsheathed.

'Who goes there?' demanded the guard, his manner bursting with the confidence of a warrior, as he strode towards the hooded figure.

Abby tried to call out, to warn the guard against the evil she sensed in this visitor, but her words were trapped in the congestion of fear at her throat; the words formed on her lips, but she uttered no sound.

'What is your business here?' Another question, but still no answer.

The figure raised one gnarled hand and uttered three words of such unimaginable depth and clarity that Abby felt them penetrate her inner being.

'Det faiteus Obsilute.'

She could not understand them as they were of a tongue she did not know, but she understood their intention as clearly as the winter's cold. Without thinking, she jumped out into the night. The bitter air was thick in her lungs, burning her skin with an instantly unbearable pain, but still she pushed forward.

The guard was on his knees clawing at his furs in an attempt to loosen the invisible demons attacking him, his face a grotesque portrait of horror and pain.

Abby lurched forward, her hands instinctively reaching for her wand. She held it out towards the figure, a single enchanted word flowing from her mouth, the emerald stone at its tip glowing brightly, bathing the camp with light.

'Prohibitous!'

The hooded figure broke its hold over the soldier, staggering back against a nearby tent, grappling with its own demons.

Voices were coming from all around as guards emerged from every direction. Abby looked down at the figure now slumped on the frozen ground as the first of his brethren arrived. His form was still, a film of sparkling frost already forming. She looked around, searching for the cloaked figure, but it was nowhere to be seen; only a wisp of crimson smoke remained where once it stood.

She felt a heavy fur dropping around her shoulders and strong hands holding her, shaking her. She opened her eyes, looking around to find she was back in the warmth of her tent: back in her bed. The sounds of a commotion outside filled her ears; men were shouting, and through the canvas wall she could make out the shadowy forms of bodies running from tent. Amongst it all she could she a solitary hooded figure standing motionless over a heap of rags, the soldiers apparently oblivious to its presence.

'What's happening?' she tried to ask. Her head was swimming; the words slurring into incoherence as they escaped, and then consciousness left her, leaving her in a deep, dreamless sleep.

11
The flight of Draconan

Abby opened her eyes then quickly shut them again. The sun was high in the sky and too bright for her sensitive, tired eyes, even through the canvas ceiling above her. She tried again, this time shielding herself with her hand. Apollo was sitting on the bed watching her with a profound intensity, those deep brown eyes pools of affectionate concern.

'Good morning,' he said, a smile spreading across his handsome face. 'You had us a little worried there for a moment.'

Abby sat up; her muscles were aching. 'What, what's wrong?' she enquired.

Apollo explained the events leading to her passing out and the fact she had been asleep now for three whole days.

'Three days!' exclaimed Abby, shaking her head to clear the fuzziness that befuddled her thoughts. 'Well, I have had a lot of excitement recently!' she reasoned.

Apollo's smile turned into a laugh, but more from the relief that she had woken than her joking. Once his guffaws had ceased, Abby set about telling him what she remembered of her out-of-body encounter with the hooded man and what she had seen when she returned to her body and bed.

When she had finished Apollo simply nodded and strolled across the room. At the tent's flap he turned and said, 'Interesting.' A pensive look had formed lines on the smooth brow of his young face. 'Better get yourself up, young lady. We have a busy day ahead of us.'

He left the tent, leaving her alone with her thoughts.

Abby slipped into the early morning sunlight, the air smelling refreshingly cool against the already warm heat of the day, a perfume of wild flowers dancing in its wake. She found her way through the maze of tents to the clear ground where the cage stood.

'I'm sure there weren't this many tents last night, or whenever it was I fell asleep,' she mumbled to herself as she went.

'There weren't, my dear,' replied Apollo, who was suddenly next to her. 'News has spread over these lands of your return. More of your subjects have been arriving by the day; coming out of hiding in the hills and forests to join us – to join the rebellion.'

'What rebellion?' Abby asked, realising she must have missed some important events over the last few days.

'The council of war has met, and we have decided to take back what is truly ours,' boomed Arnold as he joined them. 'Yer return has provided the catalyst that will reunite our people. Come, Princess, let me show yer.'

Without waiting for permission he wrapped his muscular arms around her waist and hoisted her to his shoulders. Abby felt a little giddy, but from her platform of muscle and fur she could see tents far across the valley, white and shimmering in the heat. It was a hive of activity with people striding around purposefully, working towards a common goal: freedom. But these were not just Roden, as she had expected, but beings of all shapes and sizes, some in human form but others so diverse she wasn't sure they were real.

She could see a small group about the same height as her in the distance. They appeared to be naked apart from brightly coloured feathers protruding from their heads and more private areas. Their skin was the colour of coffee beans and shimmered in the sunlight, giving it the appearance of being almost liquid in form. They were performing a strange dance that involved an impressive series of jumps and rolls.

She continued to survey the sights open to her until those huge arms were around her waist again, lowering her back to the earth.

'It is time,' Arnold stated, guiding her towards the cage.

The beast roared as they entered the cage, defiantly flapping its huge, web-like wings against the bamboo walls. Abby stayed behind Arnold as she had been instructed, a precaution made necessary by the unpredictability of dragon kind. As they skirted around the beasts huge body Abby caught sight of a carriage strapped to the creature's back, its timber construction creaking with the movement of the beast below. It swung its head around, focusing its emerald-green eyes on them. Arnold stopped in his tracks, the two staring, unblinkingly, daring each other to strike.

The beast's tail swung from the right, hitting Arnold square in the chest and launching him across the cage.

'Sneaky bugger!' he shouted, his voice husky from the impact to his chest, shaking the dust from his coat. 'Feeling a wee but feisty this morning, are yer?'

Abby was feeling very exposed. Arnold had landed on the far side of the cage and the beast had manoeuvered itself between them. It lowered its head, so low its snout was level with her face. The sparkling emerald of an eye focused directly on hers, the burning stench of the beast's breath filling her lungs with the putrid stench of decaying meat. They stood like this for a moment, fire burbling from the dragon's nostrils like molten lava erupting from a pair of miniature volcanoes. Abby was standing bolt upright; her limbs felt like they had been turned to stone; her heart was beating so heavily she wondered whether it would escape from her chest.

Then the most peculiar thing happened: the dragon gave a low bow and clearly spoke. 'Good morning, Princess. It is good to see you again.' His voice boomed with the depth of maturity.

Abby was dumbfounded, and so, it would appear, was everyone else; they were all standing around the pair, weapons drawn and their mouths wide open, for they had all quite clearly heard the dragon speak.

'Have we met?' enquired Abby, unsure what to think but not entirely surprised the beast could talk.

A look of mock hurt covered the dragons face. 'Why, don't you remember me, Princess? We used to fly together when you were a babe and I was slightly younger. We would fly for days: scare your mother silly we would!' He was grinning by this point; the memory always made him smile. 'My name is Draconan, king of dragonkind and friend to your parents. How is your mother these days?'

Tears formed in Abby's eyes, the shock of this sudden question hitting home. 'Did you know my mother?' She asked, trying to stifle the tears.

'Of course, since she was a wee nipper herself,' replied Draconan. Then, realising this had brought her pain, he asked, 'What is the matter child?'

Abby broke down and wept. The release of her grief finally overwhelmed the stony resolve she had maintained all these years. She fell to her knees, the tears flowing unchecked across her pale skin, the flow expanding to form a puddle in the soft earth. As the final spasms of grief jerked from her she noticed a reflection in the puddle that had formed around her knees. Through the blur of tears she could make out a sprig of green, a shoot growing from the watery mirror, and it was growing quickly, rising into the sunlight. She rubbed the remaining moisture from her eyes with the sleeve of her jacket and looked again. It was even larger.

A familiar tang drifted into her consciousness; the smell of jasmine filling the air and with it came a distant memory of her mother. As it continued to grow the creeper enveloped her, wrapping its tendrils around her limbs like a swath of silk; for this was not an aggressive movement, but the comforting hold of a parent. She pictured the figure of a woman she knew was her mother, a voice sounding in her head, comforting her, urging her on.

'Mummy!' she called, the desperation of grief echoing in her voice.

But the apparition faded, and once again she was looking into the face of the dragon, the only evidence of her vision a wisp of opal smoke drifting away in the breeze.

Preparations continued for hours, eased by the now co-operative dragon, but still painfully slow. Eventually Reginald announced that the carriage was secure and Draconan was ready for flight.

'We're going to fly on a dragon's back?' Abby asked upon hearing the news. 'Cool!' She looked over to her companions who weren't showing quite as much enthusiasm. 'Come on, guys, it'll be fun,' she prompted.

Not waiting for them, she clambered up the dragon's scaly back and into the carriage. Reginald was busy making final adjustments to pillows and blankets to ensure the group were comfortable.

'It can be a tad drafty up there, me lady,' he explained as he fussed. 'I will not be joining yer, Princess; there are lots of preparations to be made and my people need me here.'

The two brothers, Arnold and Apollo, joined her in the carriage, but there was no sign of Tom anywhere. Looking over the side she could make out the figure of an old man leaning heavily on a stick of twisted yew; he was making his way over to the dragon.

'Who's that?' Abby asked anyone who was listening.

Reginald gave her a knowing look. 'That's Tom, me dear,' he replied. 'He has returned to his true form. Can't hold on to the energy of youth forever, yer know. It is time for me to depart. Good travels.'

With a wave of his paw-like hand he scurried off.

Abby returned her attention to Tom; he looked very old and shriveled with time, and wore a deep emerald robe, its long hood pointing down his back.

He looked up, as if sensing her stare, and gave her a wink. Out of nowhere a gust of wind billowed his robes and his frail body lifted towards her. Abby could only stare in amazement as he drifted through the air on his lofty chariot until he landed in the carriage, taking a seat next to her.

'Good morning, my dear,' he said, his manner relaxed, as though nothing had changed. 'Did you sleep well?'

Abby shut her mouth. She guessed she ought to get used to this sort of thing as the rules of the human world did not seem to apply here. *This world is far more interesting!* she thought as the carriage jerked forward and they all quickly took their seats.

Draconan bounded out of the cage and across the open lands towards a rocky cliff edge some distance away, the carriage swaying from side to side on his back, its passengers held in by invisible restraints. The ground below them stopped abruptly, falling away into the canyon below, and they were in the air, the movement smooth and natural, the wind blowing in their faces, tangling Abby's long auburn locks as they danced about her.

'This is the best rollercoaster ever!' she screamed into the rushing air.

She looked over at Arnold; his huge muscular frame was rigid with fear, his face a distinct shade of green.

'I don't think Arnold flies well!' she stated to Tom, shouting into his ear over the wind.

'There's no need to shout my dear,' he replied, his voice booming over the noise of flight, not with volume, but with clarity. 'Your overdeveloped friend over there is a Chunkett: a beast of immense power and loyalty in battle, as long as he is on the ground.' He turned to her, looking directly into her eyes. 'His race have an understanding with earth and rock that enables them to achieve great feats of balance, manipulating them to their advantage,' he explained.

Abby looked into the old man's eyes; his pupils were large and elliptical in shape. She could see a depth in them, like pitch-black caverns cut from the rock of weather-eroded mountains. They were engulfed by a brilliant iridescence whose colour changed with the angle of the light. Red, purple, green, yellow, they appeared to be constantly changing. Even the white surrounding them sparkled with a gem-like quality.

'Hence his problem with flying, you see,' Tom was continuing. 'Too far from his beloved earth.'

He broke eye contact and the noise surrounding them returning to Abby's ears: the creaking of the invisible harnesses and howling of the wind again suddenly filling her senses.

They had been flying for hours. The smooth movement of the dragon's wings cutting through the thin air had become rhythmic, even soothing, and Abby had taken to watching the scenery race below them. They had passed over the river into the valley beyond; fields of grass stretched out as far as the eye could see to the south and west whilst an expanse of forest reached out to the east and north to their destination. She could see the mountains in the distance, the smoke rising in the foreground, a sooty column of black amongst the cleanliness of the surrounding vegetation.

Occasionally she caught sight of a clearing in the trees. Some contained settlements with little houses and livestock, faces turned upwards to catch a glimpse of the beast high above, but nothing to showed signs of a great kingdom.

Sensing her interest, Apollo murmured a secret word to release his bindings and rose to join her on the far side of the carriage. He knelt beside her, pointing out the occasional oddly shaped tree.

'These are the markers of our people,' he told Abby as he pointed out a peculiarly shaped branch. 'Nature is protecting our camps and villages from those who look to destroy them. Evil spies swoop through the skies searching for survivors of the old ways, twisted to obsession in their goal to destroy every last one of us.'

He stopped, looking over the side to somewhere into the distance.

'LOOK OUT!' he shouted suddenly. 'A Monthaton Sear, and she's coming in fast!'

The group was on their feet at once, searching the sky for a sign of the visitor. Abby felt the pressure holding her into her seat slacken, enabling her to rise and join the others. In the distance she could see what appeared to be a woman flying directly towards them. In one hand she held a large metal pole, its tip containing a brightly glowing purple crystal, and in the other a lumpy woven sack that appeared to be moving. The woman stopped short of the carriage, hovering in the turbulent air. Her eyes were as dark as night, her ebony skin covered in a chalky dust that dulled her natural glow, her clothes, once the fine outfit of a lady, now in tatters.

'Who is she?' Abby asked, tugging on Apollo's sleeve.

He turned to her, putting his hands on her shoulders. 'She is the spirit of a once noble woman turned to evil by Queen Belladora,' he replied. 'The name Monthaton Sear is given to those who have lost their way, devoting an eternity in death to evil.' He looked around, searching the skies around them. 'It's her twin you have to watch, though, my dear, and there she is!'

Abby twisted to follow his gaze, focusing on another womanly figure flying directly towards them on a gust of icy wind. Her skin was as pale as snow, a mane of long white hair billowing about her. Even from such a distance Abby could see her sapphire-blue eyes, glowing from the swollen apertures of her face, stark against their pale background but lifeless in a state of death. In her wake a swarm of black clouds was building, flashes of white erupting from their depths; she was a Storm Bringer, and she was angry.

The wind picked up, lashing around the dragon and its passengers with increasing ferocity. Draconan fought against the swirling eddies buffeting his vast wings. Loosing his battle for flight, he suddenly dropped like a lead brick towards the earth below. Abby let out an involuntary squeal as the platform they stood on suddenly dropped from beneath their feet.

They plunged towards the forest below, the world becoming a swirling blur as it spun out of control around her, the sharp foliage getting closer by the second.

Suddenly her back crashed against the timber floor as the carriage lurched upwards; Draconan regaining flight, snapping branches from the tallest trees with his hooked talons as he brushed the canopy below. Her fellow passengers pulled themselves to their feet as Draconan flapped his vast wings, regaining altitude. Apollo strode over to Abby, helping her stand on the sloping platform, and checking her for injury.

'LOOK OUT!' he shouted, a warning from her side. 'A storm comes from the north.'

Obediently the Roden crew set about tying down boxes of supplies dislodged by their impromptu dive. Two of the soldiers were heaving a tarpaulin free, uncovering a machine that loosely resembled a large catapult. It had a rotating sling action and a sight along one side. Next to it was a mound of slimy balls, the stench of which filled Abby's nostrils, making her retch.

'What are they?' she coughed in revulsion. 'They stink!'

Apollo staggered over to the machine, checking it was in working order.

'I haven't seen one of these in years,' he said, a hint of humour in his voice. 'This is a Roden mud slinger, and those are Muffenhair balls; get hit by one of those and you'll stink for a week!'

Abby didn't understand. 'How will that help us against them!' she shouted above the growing din; the storm was getting very close.

'I'll show you,' replied Apollo. 'Just give me a minute.'

Donning a thick pair of gloves, he loaded a ball into the sling, being very careful not to get any on his clothes, and cranked a handle that made the arm ratchet back until it clunked into place. He looked down the sight, carefully taking aim, and released a lever.

The slimy ball shot into the air, gaining speed as it careered towards the Storm Bringer, but narrowly missing her.

'Close!' Apollo shouted over the howling wind, busying himself with loading another ball.

Abby looked back at the woman; her features had hardened into a mask of hate, the vapours around her swelling into a black torrent of swirling clouds. The wind suddenly dropped, bringing with it a foreboding calm in which everything seemed to gain a vivid clarity, the colours surrounding them brightening to a comic-like shine.

Then came the rain, lashing down onto the deck of the carriage, instantly drenching all, and with it returned howling winds and thunder so loud Abby felt her ears pop. The clouds enveloped the surrounding sky, pounding the little carriage with hail and lightning. Draconan's flight was becoming more erratic with each shocking strike, the charge weakening him.

A lightning bolt struck the sling as Apollo released the second ball, shattering it into kindling and throwing him to the deck. Fortunately his aim was good and found its target, hitting the Storm Bringer square in the chest. A howl emanated from the creature as she writhed in agony, spinning out of control into the sky above, the sound vibrating in Abby's head like the pounding of a migraine. Then suddenly all went quiet, a moment of breathless apprehension, before the Sear exploded in a shower of fizzing purple sparks.

A terrifying scream came from across the deck as her sister swooped towards Apollo, her face a carbon copy of the hateful mask they had seen only moments before, her arms outstretched, reaching for him.

He turned to face his attacker, drawing his sword in one fluid motion. But he was too late: the creature slammed into him, forcing him to step backwards. She lashed out with clawed fingers and rabid teeth. Apollo tried to raise his sword to dispatch the creature but his arm was trapped between their bodies. Then he lost his footing and tumbled backwards towards the open edge.

'LOOK OUT!' Abby screamed, seeing the peril he was in, but he was gone, into the torrid sky.

She rushed over, seeing him falling towards the forest below, the Sear in pursuit. Without further thought she closed her eyes and jumped. A moment passed before her mind cleared and she realised she was flying, not falling, although very clumsily. She focused on the two bodies descending rapidly towards a carpet of green below, speeding forward through wisps of cloud and rain to reach the struggling enemies as they fought, seemingly oblivious to their deadly fall.

Upon reaching them, Abby landed a kick into the face of the creature, connecting directly with her nose. With a squeal she let go of Apollo, falling away from her prey: blood pouring from the flat mess now in the centre of her face.

Abby instinctively took Apollo into her arms, slowing the rate of fall with all her might and increasing the distance between them and their attacker.

There was a shriek from below as the creature regained its poise and came back towards them, blood and venom pouring from its flattened nose.

Abby was bracing herself for the impact, knowing she could not outrun this foe, when from above came the swoop of dragon's wings and a plume of blue flame, instantly incinerating the Monthaton Sear in a swirling ball of purple smoke.

They landed rather clumsily moments later on the deck of the carriage as the dark clouds dispersed; making way for the low sun of dusk.

'Nice to see you remember your flying lessons young lady!' teased Draconan, looking back towards them.

'Hear, hear!' agreed Apollo as he sat on the wooden deck, his normally immaculate uniform dishevelled and torn, 'Hear, hear.'

He looked at the tears in his clothing, muttering a few chosen words no louder than a whisper. To Abby's surprise the torn material slowly bound itself back together, the dirt and stains falling off its surface like dust from polished marble.

'That's better,' he stated, brushing the last of the dust from his arm. 'It wouldn't be fitting to attend royalty in such a raged state, now, would it!'

Abby smiled, comforted by the calmness of his demeanour. 'What's that?' she asked, pointing at the hessian sack clutched in his hand.

Apollo looked down at the lumpy sack. 'I caught it when the Sear met her demise,' he said, lowering the sack to the damp deck. 'Lets have a look what poor soul she was carrying.'

He carefully untied the rope, holding the sack closed, and stepped back as the contents moved of their own accord. Gradually a figure emerged from its hessian prison, mewing like a newborn kitten, until before them sat a small, furry animal. It sat back on its haunches, staring at its new capturers with huge saucer-like eyes, the coarse black fur of its coat ruffling in the passing breeze. It was no higher than Abby's knee and looked very young.

Arnold padded forward, a friendly smile carefully positioned on his face, for he recognised what this was and he wasn't fooled for a moment by its soft, cuddly appearance. He held out a paw, touching the new arrival on the nose, and retracted it quickly when sharp teeth appeared, snapping so viciously it surprised even him.

'What we have here,' he said, watching their little visitor carefully, 'is a Nibblet.'

Abby let out an involuntary giggle and then stopped herself when she saw the serious look on her companions' faces. Instead she decided to inquire what a 'Nibblet' was.

'A Nibblet, my dear,' stated Tom in his schoolmaster's voice, 'is native to these lands. They are generally considered to be extinct, although looking at this odd little fellow, obviously not.'

Arnold took a step back. 'They are also known for their aggressive manner and unique abilities.'

Abby stepped forward, her arm outstretched towards their new guest. 'He's scared, that's all,' she said as she approached. 'Look, he's shaking.'

With that she put her hand on the animal's furry head, stroking down its back until she reached the long fluffy tail. The Nibblet stood, arching its back, and releasing a low growl. Abby quickly retracted her arm, stepping back out of reach, and was about to concede that Arnold was right when it jumped into her arms.

The warriors around her drew their swords immediately, surrounding the pair in preparation to dispatch the beast.

Abby began to giggle; the long fur of the Nibblet's ear was tickling her nose as it nuzzled its head under her chin, the soft mewing returning with increasing volume.

'Well, I'll be Snotwart's uncle!' bellowed Arnold. 'I think it likes yer!'

Shortly afterwards they swooped into a large clearing, landing with the delicacy of a moth. The group climbed down from the remains of the carriage; carefully climbing over the wreckage to the ground below. Arnold, who had been very quiet throughout the flight, bounded onto the ground, rolling over in the dusty earth, a purr of satisfaction releasing from his throat.

'I think someone is glad to be back on the ground,' Tom laughed as he stepped from the wreckage. He was again leaning heavily on his stick, looking around at their surroundings. 'Our destination is just through those trees,' he confirmed.

Abby turned to Draconan, looking into his emerald-green eyes. 'Thank you, my friend. Will I see you again soon?' she asked.

The dragon lowered his head, pushing against her with his warm snout. 'I have lived many thousands of years and look forward to many more in the service of the rightful heir of these lands. All you need to do is call my name and I will be at your side.' He gave her a wink and with a whoosh of his mighty wings launched into the air. 'Goodbye for now, my sweet princess,' he called as he rose high into the dusky air, discarding the remains of the carriage with a shake of his huge body.

Abby watched as the dragon flew towards the horizon, towards the mountains he called home.

'Let's have yer then!' called Arnold impatiently as he padded towards the tree line. 'It's getting late. Won't be long till a chill fills the air.'

The group set off, strolling into a nearby copse of trees. Abby was pleased to feel the warmness of the forest around her again; she could sense the closest branches reaching out to welcome her home. The Nibblet, which she had named 'Pook' due to the noise it made, had attached himself around Abby's shoulders and stared with intense scrutiny at the surrounding foliage, chattering in a short succession of 'pooks' as though in conversation with some invisible companion. After a short walk the trees thinned to reveal a beautiful garden filled with all manner of colourful flowers. An avenue of rose bushes lined a grassy pathway that led to a small stone structure at the far end.

'This way,' Tom called as he hobbled towards the structure, 'and don't dawdle.'

The brothers looked at each other, sharing a knowing smile, as they followed the old man, ushering Abby to keep up. The group finally reached the only opening in the structure: a cracked timber door with a tarnished iron handle and rusting hinges.

Pook began to wriggle frantically in Abby's arms as they got closer to the door, finally dropping to the floor with a soft thud. He sat staring at her with those huge dish eyes, and emitted one long 'poooooook'.

'What's up with the wee beast now?' demanded Arnold, barely hiding his annoyance with the little monster.

Abby bent to pick him up. ‘He’s just scared, that’s all,’ she said, offering words of comfort to the shivering animal. She leant forward, but as she touched him he disappeared with a soft pop.

‘Where’d he go?’ she asked, bewildered by the sudden disappearance.

Arnold gave her a disapproving look. ‘He’ll be back, my princess. Of that I am sure.’

Tom stopped at the door and turned to his companions, a look of apprehension growing on his face as he said, ‘Welcome to the Chamber of Souls.’

12
The Chamber of Souls

The group stepped over the threshold and into the darkened void beyond. The air inside was chilled and dank, pulling on their lungs as though clotting the tissue. The ground underfoot changed from the soft bounce of manicured grass to the solid echo of stone, the comfort they had enjoyed for the past hour gone in an instant, taken by the bitter, stale air. The door slammed closed behind them, plunging their forms into total darkness. Abby felt isolated by the absoluteness of the surrounding black, the hair on the back of her neck rippling. The only comfort was the soft murmur of her companions' breathing, its rhythm increased by their mutual fear, for it was the ultimate fear: that of the unknown.

A door opened at the far end of the chamber, the low flickering of candlelight casting dancing shadows across the walls. Abby could make out the silhouette of her companions, like dark sentinels poised and ready to strike, but also other shapes, some standing like statues on the floor while others appeared to be floating in the darkness. *It looks like a grotesque gallery of shadows amongst a sea of blackness*, Abby thought, the memory of such a description flitting through her mind.

A grunt came from somewhere in the darkness. She recognised the voice as Apollo's and, remembering his ability to read her mind, focused on the door ahead. A figure appeared in the doorway, only partly obscuring the light as it were only half as high of the opening. The dwarf stepped forward, clapping his hands once. The room was suddenly bathed in light as twelve huge candles burst into flame, filling every corner of the vast chamber with their brilliance.

Large portraits dominated the walls, their frames intricately carved and covered in aged gold leaf. Abby walked over to the nearest frame; its content had caught her eye.

'We have this picture in our dining room at home,' she said to anyone listening, then stepping to the next, said, 'and this one!'

'These are your family, Abigail,' said a voice that came from behind her. It was unnaturally high, almost squeaky. 'This is their mortal resting place.'

'This place is a tomb?' Abby questioned, knowing the answer was affirmative. 'Cool!'

The dwarf, who introduced himself as the caretaker, led them from the entrance hall into an antechamber. He said nothing further other than uttering a high-pitched squeak, which seemed to be understood by Abby's companions to mean 'Follow me'.

This second room was much smaller than the previous, with a low ceiling and a large fireplace in one wall. A fire was roaring on the hearth, giving the space a comfortable, welcoming air, unlike the room they had just left. Again light came from candles, but smaller, more discrete versions of the others. Abby noticed there were no windows in this room and only one other door, partly hidden by a heavy curtain.

It seems odd not having any windows with such beautiful scenery outside, Abby thought. She looked at Apollo and wondered whether if he was listening to her.

'You have travelled far under the earth, my dear,' came the reply, it was deep, like a murmur in her head, but not a voice she recognised.

She stepped back from the caretaker, the motion involuntary, more surprised than frightened by the sound. Her thoughts randomly asked questions of how she could hear him when she could clearly see he had not opened his mouth, or could someone else hear her and was answering?

'Don't be afraid, Abigail,' said the voice again. 'You are in the house of your ancestors. Here you can share your thoughts with those who have passed to the next world.'

'How?' Abby blurted to the group surrounding her. She could feel her cheeks reddening as she looked at the puzzled faces around her.

'I guess you didn't hear that then?' she asked in explanation of her outburst. She was getting uncomfortable with the whole idea of voices in her head. 'Someone has just told me I can talk to my dead relatives!'

With that she slumped into a nearby chair.

It was the caretaker who answered her question, strolling across the room with the grace and poise of royalty. He was a good foot shorter than anyone in the room, even Tom, and his face was lined with the passage of time. His long hair and beard were immaculately groomed and woven with beads of the most enchanting colours. His gown was made from a soft opal weave with hints of gold and glittering stones. What struck Abby, however, were his kind eyes; they were chocolate brown with depths like bottomless pits. She felt comfortable in his gaze, even though they had just met.

After a moment of contemplation he spoke. 'I understand you are troubled by confusion, Abigail,' he said, his eyes never leaving hers. 'You are among friends in this place; the forces of evil that hold this land in their icy grip cannot reach you here.'

The mention of evil and ice sent a chill down Abby's spine, making her shiver even in the warmth of the room. She lifted her legs, curling herself into a ball as she always did when she felt vulnerable. Apollo stepped over with a blanket conjured from the air, wrapping it round her like a mother to a babe.

The caretaker, his gaze never faltering, continued, 'As you are aware, you are a member of the Nousidian royal family. Not just any royalty either, as you are the true heir to the throne and, if I may say so, also my niece.'

He let out a little chuckle; he was so pleased to be finally reunited with her.

'The room in which you are sitting is called the Chamber of Souls,' he continued. 'It is a place of reverence and meditation in which a select few can, as you say, talk to their dead relatives.'

Shuffling noises around the room pulled Abby's gaze away for a second. She could see the others gathering around her and a twinge of fear crept into her mind: *Did she really know these people? Could she trust them? Why was she feeling so tired in the middle of the day?* Her eyelids had become very heavy, her mind was floating, and then an idea hit her: *They must have drugged me!*

Then consciousness left her.

She opened her eyes, shocked into movement by a swirling breeze of cool air. She was standing alone in pitch-blackness: there were no sounds or smells, no movement in the consuming void, no evidence that this place existed, just nothingness.

A hint of essence wafted past her nose, the fragrance igniting a memory of something from her distant past. Her mind raced to place the recollection; images of the garden back at home fluttered in and out.

'Jasmine!' she mumbled into the blackness. 'That's what I smell.'

The fog of her mind was clearing now, a form appearing in the distance, the shapes of a beautiful garden surrounding it. She was a tall woman with long, flowing auburn hair. Her figure was athletic in build, but with the subtle curves of womanhood showing under her simple white dress. Her feet were bare and made no imprint on the grass below them. The still air held no sound, just the pungent perfume of the jasmine flower.

The woman spoke, her smooth lips forming the words in a sweet melody. Abby heard those words, but not with her ears, as the sound was not in the air, but in her head.

'Hello, my dear Abigail,' the voice sang. 'It's so good to see you again.'

Abby's heart jumped into her throat, the sound stirring memories long forgotten.

'I know you, don't I?' Abby questioned. She understood the pointlessness of speaking the words, but she could not remember to whom she was speaking.

The voice chimed again, its melody hypnotic, instantly addictive. 'It has been so long since I have looked upon your young features, dear child, like an eternity of darkness.' The figure moved closer, the perfume intensifying, filling her being. 'Do you remember me, child?' it asked, its voice longing for recognition.

Abby stepped backward unsure of the feelings she was experiencing. Her mind was swimming with questions and doubt, but her heart was full of sweetness and a longing to be reunited with this lost soul. Another voice broke into her thoughts; she recognised it as the now familiar voice of Apollo.

'Trust your heart, my dear,' he said, his voice calm and understanding. 'What beats there are the truth and the path to your real self.'

It was then that Abby felt the fear drain from her body, like snow melting in the morning sun, any doubt washed away with its watery residue.

'Mummy!' she called, a sudden wish enveloping her, a need to be in the arms of the one person she had never known: her mother.

She staggered forward, weakened by the torrent of emotion she felt, and into her mother's waiting arms. The woman held her, tears pouring uncontrollably from her eyes, damping the soft material of her dress. Abby felt delicate hands stroking her hair, the mewing of soft words offering love and belonging in her ear.

Then, suddenly, it was all gone. Abby opened her eyes to see the small room around her, felt the heat of the fire and the smells of her companions, her eyes stinging with the sourness of tears. Through the haze she could see the outline of the caretaker, a broad smile spreading across his face.

'Your mother has waited so long to finally meet you again,' he soothed, aware of Abby's discomfort. 'Her spirit lives within these walls, along with the rest of your distant family.'

The dwarf moved closer, putting emphasis on his next statement.

'Your father is in danger, as was every member of your royal line. Now you are our only hope.'

He stepped out of sight, the weight of this revelation heavy on his shoulders, standing by the fire to warm his hands.

'I want to go back!' Abby cried, her whole body longing to return to the place where she could be in her mother's arms. 'Send me back now!' she snapped.

'Conserve your strength young Abigail,' the caretaker soothed calmly, still facing the fire. 'You will need it before the day is out. There are many other members of your family who wish to meet you. Their lives were also cut short in the culling during your father's exile.'

She felt Apollo's strong arms wrap around her, his soothing presence softening her feelings but not quashing them. His voice was in her head, telling her that in time she could be with her family, but first she must gather her understanding and strength for the battle ahead.

Abby, somewhat comforted, fell back into her slumber.

Over the following days Abby spent many hours in the Chamber of Souls. She was becoming familiar with the process of communicating across the worlds and needed her uncle's help less each time.

Finally one morning she crept into the crypt alone, the need to be with her mother overwhelming. The chamber was in darkness when she arrived. She was careful not to ignite the candles in the hall so as not to wake her uncle, the caretaker. The questions that filled her mind were personal, and although she had grown to love her uncle over the past few days, she felt these would be better asked alone. She entered the crypt, slowly closing the door behind her, the hinges letting out a low creak as the door met its frame. She froze, listening for any signs of movement from the hall. After a few minutes she was satisfied that no one had followed so she thought the candles alight. *Not bad*, she considered, the last few days of practice had paid off; she was glad simple spells did not require the caster to mouth the words into the air.

Taking her usual seat at the edge of the room, Abby prepared herself for the meditation. She had brought some juju berries for luck and gobbled them down now, feeling their energy flow through her body. Closing her eyes, she felt her heartbeat slow and the haze in her mind shift. Now all she had to do was focus on her mother.

A figure appeared through the darkness, and as it came closer she recognised him as her great-grandfather, his uniform freshly pressed, his youthful looks carrying a smile of happiness to see her. Abby had got used to meeting her relatives as young adults as that was the period most chose to retain in spirit. She welcomed him to the chamber.

'What troubles you, my dear?' he asked, the words echoing in her head.

Abby knew she could trust him as the spirits of this world had no reason to lie or agenda with which to corrupt the truth, and anyway he was her favourite.

'I need to see Mummy,' Abby stated, getting right to the point. 'Is she here?'

Her great-grandfather stepped to one side, a hand outstretched to guide her, and simply said, 'Off you go. Cassandra is waiting.'

Abby didn't need any persuading. As she ran past him he give her a wink and she suddenly found herself in the garden of their house. She looked around to see the figure of a lady clad in a beautiful yellow summer dress. She was standing next to the statue, shading herself from the midday sun with a paper-thin parasol.

Abby called out and ran to her, arms outstretched.

The lady turned and held out her arms, the parasol discarded, and Abby jumped into them, tears of joy flowing from her eyes, the perfume of jasmine filling her nostrils. They embraced for several minutes, catching up on a lifetime of happiness, then her mother released her and beckoned her to sit on the soft grass.

'My you've grown,' Cassandra began, stroking a silky hand across her cheek. 'I have missed you so much.'

Abby, fighting her compulsion to cry again, replied that she had missed her too and she was so glad to be with her again.

Cassandra smiled, a smile that filled Abby with a joy beyond measure. The warmth of her mother's love soothed her broken heart.

'Are you hungry, my dear?' she asked.

A picnic of cakes and sweets appeared between them. Abby tucked in; she couldn't be happier. They talked for what seemed to be hours; her mother wanted to know everything. Eventually Abby could not contain the one unanswered question burning in her heart: she had to ask her mother what had happened to make her leave when she was so young.

Cassandra sat back, her yellow dress fanning out about her. 'It is time you knew the truth,' she replied, her tone decisive. 'Your father and I were very much in love, married, and I became pregnant with you. All was well in the kingdom, as it should be; all except for one dark sorcerer, a man called Marrick Bitendor. He was obsessed with power, and above all the throne of these lands. He bewitched my sister, your aunt Belladora, and wed her in a secret ceremony at the top of the Black Tower. When the true king, that's your father, my dear, discovered this treachery he hunted down Marrick and his followers, killing him on the field of battle.'

She straightened her posture; the past still haunted her like it was yesterday. Then she continued. 'When the news of his death reached Belladora she was furious. Consumed by hatred, she took the ceremonial knife from the chapel and slipped past the guards into my bed chamber where she plunged it into my heart.' She shuddered at the thought; it was still very real to her.

After a moment she regained her composure, putting a steadying hand on her daughter's shoulder. 'Your father returned to find me dead and you, although premature and weak, alive. He fell into despair at his loss; the only light in his eye was you, my dear, and he tended you day and night until you were strong. He was unaware of Belladora's treachery and allowed her to get close, even look after that which was most dear to him. One day he discovered a way to retrieve my soul from its resting place here in the chamber and, stricken with grief, he conjured a powerful spell to allow me access back into the world of the living.'

A smile spread across her face, the memory so pleasing to her.

'Well, let me tell you, that really upset the Grand Council! They set about stripping him of his powers and banished him to the garden house to contemplate his actions, returning me here. Thankfully our royal gardeners had planted a very special jasmine in the grounds of our home, allowing me to be with you both, if only in spirit. I have been looking over the old place ever since.'

Abby looked over to the house with its creeper engulfing every corner, the clarity of understanding entering her mind.

'So you have been close all my life,' she said. 'It was you who spoke to me in the dark hours of the morning when I felt so alone.' As Abby gave her mother a hug a thought crystallised in her head. 'How did aunt Belladora come to power?' she asked, curious.

'Your aunt has become a powerful witch, and the minds of the council, although wise, are weak. She took the oath on the anniversary of her birth many years ago, with no one willing to object through fear of repercussion and no true heir available, and assumed the roll of queen.'

Abby stood, her hands on her hips, and stated quite categorically, 'Well that's not fair!'

Her mother looked over her shoulder, an expression of sadness covering her beautiful features. 'I'm afraid it is time for you to return, my dear,' she stood, taking Abby into her arms. 'I will be with you always in your heart; when your need is most, I will be there.'

A mist began to envelop her as the garden faded into darkness and Abby opened her eyes to be greeted by a smile from her uncle.

'So now you know the truth,' he said, his voice cheery. 'Now you are ready to face Belladora.'

13
The Maze of Alderman

The sound was like the song of angels. Gryphus Minior had only come of age some thirty years previous and thus still retained some of his boyish features; his long, dark hair jutted out in unruly outcrops unable to be tamed, his long, gangly limbs not yet achieving the bulk of adulthood. This was only his second night as guard at the Chamber of Souls and his heart was full of joy at being selected for this most important of duties.

It was the deepest part of the night when all living things are still and the world itself seems to be slumbering. The sound had found its way in through the gap under the great oak door, filling his head with sweet melodies so intoxicating he wondered how he had lived so long with their absence. His fingers fumbled with the lock, the old key stiff in its housing. With a solid clunk the door was released and he tugged at it, eager to be closer to the heaven that awaited him. He stepped out into the cold night air, his winter robes forgotten in his intoxication. He staggered, dreamlike, towards a soft glow in the forest, convinced this was the source of the music. From behind him he could make out the muffled sound of voices, sounds he would have obeyed only hours before, but this was the only desire for him now: he had to find the source of this pleasure and become one with it.

He entered a copse of trees, brushing away clinging branches and climbing over jutting roots in his singular focus until he reached his goal. She was the most beautiful thing he had ever seen. Her hair was the colour of pure gold, her skin as pale as snow. Her silken dress floated in an unearthly breeze, a flowing, vivid crimson, like it was made from the blood of the purest virgins. He was in love that very instant, words of devotion spilling out into the night. He did not notice her sister, sitting on a fallen tree in the background, her dark skin camouflaged in the night air, or the ice forming on his tunic with each new breath; he did not care. He reached forward; every part of his being wanted, no needed, to be with her. She leaned forward to meet his outstretched arms, matching his actions.

Their lips touched, the need fulfilled with the slightest touch, lifting the veil of deceit cast upon him. It was only then that the true horror of his fate struck him, for what hovered only a hands width from his still pouting lips was death itself. He felt a blow between his shoulder blades, the cold steel igniting a fire in his chest like the very heat of hell. His vision blurred as he tried to turn for the comfort of home, opening his mouth in a vain attempt to call for help, choking on the hot blood now flowing freely from his throat. He fell to his knees, the world becoming dark, the glow of lust, the singing of angels lost forever to his senses as he passed into another existence.

The group sat in the garden enjoying a hearty breakfast of cakes and pastries. Some had flavours Abby had never experienced, but all were so wonderfully appetising and sweet; they danced on her taste buds like a flock of humming birds on a summer's day. The early morning sun was burning through a low mist that covered the garden in a veil of white, the last remnants of ice melting from the foliage surrounding them.

'Why does it get so cold at night?' Abby asked no one in particular as she devoured a sticky bun.

The group looked from one to the other until the caretaker, whose name, she had discovered was Tyrillious, spoke.

'It is the true way of the world, my dear,' he said, his deep eyes settling on her. 'The kingdom of Nousidia is ruled by nature's old ways, the way this world was created: in harmony and balance.'

He had developed the sort of pose that Abby had seen many times before back in the classroom at her old school, back in the other world. His stature had straightened and he wore the look of knowledge her old science professor used to have in class. Seeing Abby's mystified look, he adjusted his wire-rimmed spectacles and continued.

'Nousidia has three seasons,' he stated. He gave her a look like she should already know this. 'They are, of course, summer, winter and dusk.'

Abby screwed her face up; surely she must have misunderstood him.

'Dusk?' she questioned.

'Yes, dusk,' Tyrillious replied in a very authoritative manner. 'Dusk is the period between summer and winter each day when the eternal battle between good and evil is fought.'

Abby couldn't believe her ears. She tried to imagine how it could be summer and winter in one day. Finally she gave up, asking him how.

'I am no expert, my dear,' he replied, his features softening, 'but I'll have a go. Simply put, summer is the time of good when the sun enhances the magic within all living things. This is our time: when we are awake and the world around us is alive and growing.'

He shuffled closer, his voice lowering into an undertone as if what he was about to say was not to be spoken aloud. 'Winter is the time of evil,' he whispered. 'A severe cold takes hold of the land, killing all in its path.'

He stepped back, assuming his professor's stance again, the volume returning to his voice. 'We have all three seasons each day,' he reiterated matter-of-factly. 'Summer is during the day when we are awake; then dusk is a transitional period in which both good and evil are present and the struggle for dominance is fought. This then passes into winter, where the sky is cold and dark and all living things are frozen in a blanket of impenetrable ice.'

He uttered an involuntary shudder at the thought, pausing as if for effect.

'It is the will of Belladora that all that lives in the warmth of the sun become still with its setting; hence the cold and ice each night,' he said in explanation. 'You will do well to ensure you find cover come the setting of the sun. It has been this way since your mother …' He paused, a sadness creeping into his eyes. 'Well, for quite some time.'

Apollo interrupted, standing. 'It is time to leave this place.'

He had regained his more formal tone. Over the last days he had experienced a calm which he had never truly allowed himself before, and it felt good. But now it was time to rekindle the warrior within him and push forward to what lay ahead.

'We leave after breakfast,' he said, and with that he marched back to the house.

'Can't we stay a little longer?' Abby pleaded with her uncle, giving him her best pout. 'Just one more day? I want to learn more about the seasons.'

Tyrillious stepped forward and gave her a hug, the wispy hair on the top of his head tickling her nose. 'As much as I would love for you to stay, my dear, a great task has been bestowed upon you, a task that will not wait.'

He released her, trapping her in those deep brown eyes.

'Each day the witch's spies get closer to discovering that which we have kept safe for so long. Just last night the shrieking of a Monthaton Sear was heard in the forest and the body of one of our brethren was discovered at first light.'

'I don't understand,' admitted Abby, very confused. 'I thought we were safe from my aunt's evil cronies in the chamber.'

Tyrillious gave her a knowing smile. 'You will discover as you come of age that the minds of men, although full of good intentions, are weak and can be twisted by temptation of the flesh. A trick I'm sure you will learn in good time.'

Abby did not understand. A knot was forming in her stomach, a feeling of uncertainty she had not experienced before, and she didn't like it.

An hour later the friends, Abby, Apollo, Arnold and Tom, were making their way into the forest. Abby was sad to leave her uncle; she had only just got to know him and now it was time to leave. He had promised that they would meet again very soon; she looked forward to it, but something deep inside her mind was telling her that next time they met life would be very different. She shrugged off the feeling, dismissing it as she would a dream, linking arms with Tom as they strode off amongst the trees.

After stopping for lunch in a clearing the group turned west to follow a high ridge into the valley below. They stepped from the tree line to be met by a wall of green. The bush, not unlike the garden hedges at home, Abby thought, was formed so thick that it appeared almost solid. She reached out to touch it, curious as to how it could be so dense, stepping closer as she did. Her fingers brushed the closest leaf; its texture was like that of leather, like the polished shoes her father wore when he went to town, only with the deep veins of plant life.

Her touch spurred movement within the vegetation ahead of her; a window began to form, the branches parting like the leaves of a folding screen. The opening continued to grow until finally it stopped, leaving a slot the width of a door. Abby looked at the others, hoping for some explanation, only to be met by bemused faces.

'This is a new one to me!' admitted Apollo, looking at Arnold. 'How about you?'

Arnold shrugged his huge shoulders, uttering a low grunting sound.

Abby looked at Tom, 'How about you Tom?' she asked, hopeful that he might remember something.

'Sorry, my dear,' he replied, looking at the sheer height of the hedging. 'Can't help, I'm afraid. It looks like you've opened a door of some kind. May I suggest we take a look inside?'

Arnold stepped past them and into the opening, his body filling the width, brushing off loose leaves from either side with his bulk. The friends followed one by one, entering a corridor of tall walls. Abby was the last, stepping carefully over the threshold, looking up to see the faint glimmer of sunlight high above their heads framed by the leafy walls around them. As she stepped through the gap she could sense a consciousness around her as if the bushes were talking to her, whispering in a voice she could not quite hear. She stopped, straining her ears to hear what they were saying, but the only sound she could comprehend was the rustling of leaves in a light breeze that had sprung up around them.

It was then that she realised that the opening was shrinking, the doorway back to the ridge now a blur of vegetation, and then it was gone, as if it had never existed.

'I guess we will have to see where this leads,' Abby said in an attempt to be positive. She certainly didn't feel that way; her senses told her something wasn't right with this place, and she had always relied on them to guide her; it was a haunting feeling of loss she could not shake.

Arnold looked around. 'Could this be real?' he asked.

It was Apollo that answered. 'I feel it too. I assumed this place was just a fairy tale.'

Feeling a little out of the loop, Abby asked what they were talking about.

'This way,' Arnold stated, an air of authority in his voice, ignoring Abby's question. 'We must traverse across the maze to reach the city, but beware, the Maze of Alderman is a treacherous place; we must stay together.' With that he marched off, taking the path to the right.

Abby broke into a brisk walk as they set off in convoy, catching up with Apollo in a few strides of her long legs, questioning him about this maze.

Apollo looked at her, his stride not faltering even slightly. 'The Maze of Alderman is the oldest of natural structures in Nousidia,' he said, his voice low and soft, settling into the tone of on etelling a long story. 'Many centuries ago, when our ancestors first settled in these lands, an understanding was formed between humankind and the varied forms of nature abundant in these parts. This understanding, although never written or confirmed, formed the basis of the co-existence enjoyed by our people and the surrounding nature. This blossomed, as time strolled by, into the utopia we have enjoyed for thousands of years.'

He paused, unsure whether to continue.

Abby was fascinated by the idea of people and nature living together, and how it all worked, so she prompted him to continue.

'All life in this world - from the trees to the juju bush, the birds, fish and the bees - has the ability to understand other's needs and therefore work in harmony to create balance in the universe.'

'Sounds great!' Abby commented, not understanding the problem. 'It all seems to be working fine to me,' she stated simply.

Apollo stopped abruptly. 'The problem started some five thousand years ago when a small group of humans became greedy,' he stated quite categorically, looking her in the eyes. 'They were not content with the limitations of nature and began to experiment with unnatural chemicals and ores from the ground. As they grew in confidence more followed, and the traditional ways of working in harmony with nature were gradually forgotten. After two millennia the lands to the south were consumed by great cities of stone and glass. The only remaining sanctuary for those who believed in the old ways was the realm of Nousidia, once a great capital of these lands, tucked up in the north but not forgotten. The land was divided as the people of the south, led by a young wizard called Marrick Bitendor, denounced the old ways of magic and the bond with nature as heretic and set about destroying what remained of the old world. He had been consumed by the lure of evil and used his powers to control the minds of his subjects till their eventual end.'

Apollo's face showed a shadow of bereavement as he remembered the loss of so many souls.

'What happened?' Abby asked, afraid she knew the answer.

'A war ravaged these lands, a great war, an all-consuming war, a war that took the lives of many of our kin. Until, after almost a century of fighting, a delicate truce was agreed. The land was to be divided, not with borders and rules like the world in which you have been living, but with the conjuring of a powerful spell to create two worlds, both existing at the same moment but completely separate. Thus the new world was created, the world in which you have lived for so long: the world of the humans.' He gestured around him. 'The Maze of Alderman was one of nature's defenses against further attack. It is said that if a being that is not pure of heart enters the maze it will never leave, spending the rest of eternity trapped within its walls.'

He stopped, the memories physically draining him of strength. His legs buckled, his weight, although only slight, toppling him to the ground. Abby jumped forward, cushioning his landing as best she could, calling out to the others who were now quite a distance ahead.

On hearing her distress Arnold and Tom began to run back to them. They had been in such deep conversation they hadn't noticed the others fall behind. Abby skirted around Apollo's dormant body, brushing against the leathery leaves of the high wall. She ignored the rustling of foliage around her, such was her concern for her friend, until she realised a wall was forming across the path, stopping the others from reaching them. A pang of horror chilled Abby's heart: she was trapped, her best friend was unconscious, and the only people she knew who could help were on the other side of a dense wall of foliage. She clambered to her feet, reaching for what remained of the air between them. She thrust her arm though the gap, touching Tom's outstretched hand for a second, before pulling back to safety.

She sank to the ground, all her strength leaving her, tears flowing from her eyes, the fear of being lost overwhelming. She sat hugging her lifelong companion, feeling his shallow breathing against her cheek, wishing she could do something to help him.

She sat there for sometime in sheer exhaustion, her will to continue faltering. Then a voice spoke in her head: it was her great grandfather, as clear as if he were standing next to her.

'Good afternoon, my dear,' he said, his voice full of pleasure at speaking with her again. 'What troubles you?'

Abby looked around, her conscious mind desperate to rationalise what was happening; the only movement was a butterfly drifting in the air, its wings a vivid blue that shone against the dull background.

'Grandpappy?' she uttered so quietly she barely heard herself. 'Are you there?'

The butterfly landed on Apollo's slumbering head, its sapphire wings folding flat along its back. It appeared to be examining her, its antennae twitching in the now still air.

'Free your mind,' came the response in her head. 'Believe in your abilities and you will succeed. Find your way to the centre of the maze, for there you will be reunited with your companions. But hurry; time is short.'

Then the voice was gone, replaced by the rustling of leaves around her and the soft murmuring of Apollo's breathing. The butterfly fluttered up into the air.

'But how?' Abby murmured to nobody, feeling the frustration mount.

It was then she remembered her lesson in the valley. Slipping off her backpack, she rummaged until her hand touched the shaft of her wand; the wood of its length was warm to the touch, like it had a pulse of its own, and as she pulled it out the jewel at its end was glowing brightly.

'Just think of what you want …' she recalled, attempting to clear her mind of her bewildering fear, '… and you can make it happen.'

'I want to be in the centre of the maze,' she said a little shakily, and pointed the wand at the nearest wall, adding, 'Please!' for good measure.

Nothing happened and she slumped down onto the soft grass, resigned to the fact she was lost. Suddenly there was a flurry of movement as branches obediently folded and leaves parted to reveal an opening slightly over to her left. She could hear movement further away too as openings appeared throughout the maze. She turned to Apollo; his resting form remained slumped on the ground and she realised she would have to carry him. With great strain she lifted him onto her shoulder; he wasn't as heavy as he looked but his limp form was cumbersome and would slow her movement considerably.

After several hours and many wrong turns Abby discovered a clearing. It was overgrown with all manner of creepers and bushes, having the unkempt look of her garden back in the other world. In the centre she could see a stone tower, its sides made of open colonnades, with three levels and an ornate green-copper roof. A stone staircase spiralled around the outside, giving access to the first two floors, but had long since collapsed to the remainder.

A strange statue of two figures stood in the middle of the upper floor. It was eerily lifelike in its detail, she thought, even down to the stubbly fur covering the subjects' bodies. A peculiar thought slipped into Abby's mind: they looked just like Bit and Bot, the gardeners who had travelled with them a few days ago. It couldn't be them, she rationalised; they were tending to the Garden of Smea back on the other side of the valley. Nevertheless she could not shake the thought, so she laid Apollo on a clear area of grass and started pushing her way through the undergrowth towards the tower.

After what seemed like an hour's hard labour she finally reached the structure and clambered onto the lower floor, quickly climbing the steps to find her way to the statue. It was covered in a creeper not too dissimilar to ivy which wound itself around the sculpture like a crushing serpent. Abby looked closely through the covering of green. She was right: the statue did look exactly like the two gardeners she had left at the edge of the dark woods. She reached forward, unable to resist touching the surface of such lifelike carving, pulling away some of the creeper enclosing them as she did.

'Don't touch it!' screamed a tiny voice from somewhere behind her.

Abby jumped at the sound and instinctively spun round to face whoever had screamed; but there was no one there, just Apollo's still form lying on the grass and the maze stretching for miles around.

She was about to turn back to the statue when out of the corner of her eye she caught a glimpse of something small and so intensely bright she had to shade her eyes. Her head started swimming, the clarity that had got her so far fading into a whirlpool of despair, each breath becoming more laboured than the last until she lapsed into unconsciousness on the stone floor.

She woke with a sneeze, but not just any ordinary sneeze as this one shook the surrounding stone. Abby's head was buzzing, a blur of bright lights flitting across her vision. She lifted her head to see what they were and a familiar voice spoke, its soft tone a welcome sound.

'What yer doing up here?' enquired Bit. 'In fact, what are we doing up here?' he continued, a distinctly curious tone melting into his normally confident voice. He looked from Abby to Bot.

Bot just shrugged, tearing lumps of ivy from his muddy shirt.

A very small voice answered his question with another. 'What are two royal gardeners and you, Princess Abigail, doing in such a dangerous place?' it said. Its volume was so timid that Abby, Bit and Bot had to strain to hear.

'Who's there?' Abby asked, oblivious to the presence of anyone other than the three of them. 'And turn that light down. You're giving me a headache!'

The light immediately dulled, revealing a group of small insects. They came closer, giggling as they did. They appeared to be floating, suspended the air in front of her, tiny, transparent wings vibrating at a speed faster than her eyes could follow. As they approached Abby realised her mistake: these were not insects but tiny people, no higher than her little finger. The males (she guessed) were dressed in pin-striped suits and bowler hats, their shoes twinkling with a mirrored shine, while the females wore beautiful gowns of red and blue, each with a bow in her hair. They had skin that shone with the luminescence of the moon, their features a mere blur in an overall glow.

A particularly portly one hovered in front of the group, giving Abby a low bow. As he came closer she felt warmth emanating from him like his little body was made of fire.

'I shall not come closer, ma'am, as I have no wish to burn you,' he said with a flourish, his voice distinctly English in character.

'O-kay!' Abby stammered, pulling herself into a sitting position.

'My name is Alexander Puntington-Smyth,' he continued proudly, 'and this is my wife Elizabeth, and our children: William, Fredrick, Victoria, and the little one is Millie,' he said, remaining in his bow.

'Its nice to meet you all,' replied Abby, still in wonder at these tiny people. She felt a little uneasy as they obviously knew her but she was totally unaware of who, or what, they were.

As if sensing her confusion Alexander whispered the answer. 'We are Poggles, or Fire Fairies as your father used to call us. We're on the way up to the castle for the queen's birthday feast.' His face took on a faint red glow. 'But you'll know that already of course, Princess.'

'Y-yes, of course,' Abby responded, hoping she sounded at least a little convincing.

'You were lucky we came along,' continued Alexander, sounding very pleased with himself. 'You and your companions have stumbled upon a very nasty strain of poison ivy. Not harmful in the long term, of course, but it may have made you late for the party; nasty habit of turning people to stone, that one.'

Abby was desperately trying to think of something further to say; the thought of being turned to stone sounded long term to her.

Bit stepped forward and announced that the chill was setting in so they were going to make camp in the tower.

Abby thanked him and returned her attention to Fire Fairy in front of her, asking if he and his family would like to join them.

'It would be a pleasure ma'am,' replied Alexander, a note of gratitude in his voice. He turned to his family, ushering them to the centre of the stone floor, and took out the tiniest wand from inside the folds of his jacket. With a flick of his wrist he swept the remaining foliage away. Comfortable-looking reclining chairs appeared and a shimmering wall enveloped the tower from foundation to roof.

'Wow!' Abby sighed in wonder.

'Not bad for a little 'un!' Bit commented as he sank into the closest chair.

Abby took the chair opposite, relaxing into the soft padding as it formed itself around her. The family of fire fairies broke into a merry dance on the floor between them, heat rising from their tiny forms as they jigged.

Abby lay back in the chair, her muscles finally relaxing. A shadowy figure appeared on the far side of the shimmering wall; she sat up in alarm as it moved closer. It reached the wall and began to step through, the screen flowing around it like a vertical wall of water flowing around a protrusion of rock. First a leg appeared, then an arm feeling its way, and then a head pushed through, the watery screen flowing over it, hiding its features.

Then it was through and to Abby's relief she recognised the face immediately: it was Apollo. 'Look what I found lurking in the undergrowth outside!' he said, a smile spreading across his face.

Two further figures pushed their way through the wall: Arnold, followed by the bent figure of Tom, leaning heavily on his stick as he hobbled along.

Abby jumped up and gave her friends a hug. She was so pleased to see them. She asked how they had found their way to the tower.

They both answered in unison. 'We followed the light.'

Abby understood, remembering how brightly the Poggles had shone when she first saw them.

Three more chairs appeared around the fire fairies and they all settled down to rest. After a hearty meal of juju berries and apple pie, the group settled down to sleep. The fire fairies had already settled some hours before, comfortable warmth rising from their bodies as they huddled together on the stone floor. Abby, her eyes drooping, gave Tom a sharp kick; his snoring abruptly came to a stop. And then she passed into a deep slumber as the chair around her transformed into an elaborately carved bed.

Abby opened her eyes, the chill of the freezing air shocking her back to consciousness. She looked around, her mind fighting to make sense of what she saw. She could see the tower, standing tall amongst the surrounding black of the maze. It was glowing with a shimmering light, casting long, dancing shadows into the night like a huge lantern. The sky was a starless mass of black; the only break was the faint glow of the moon, partially hidden by wispy, swirling clouds.

She looked down to the maze below, realising she was floating above it. She was dressed in a long, flowing white gown that billowed in an invisible wind: the air around her still, as if dead. She could see a figure floating next to the tower, its ebony skin reflecting the brightness of the wall adjacent. It reached forward, towards the shimmering light, a sense of fear in its movement.

Suddenly there was a brilliant flash of pure white light, like the striking of a lightning bolt, and the figure was thrown into the distance, spiralling out of control into the darkness.

A voice shouted, it's pain embodied by the shriek of its cry. Abby looked around, searching for its owner, but saw no one. Another cry; this one longing: a call for its sister to return. Abby's heart began to hammer in her chest, the rhythm increasing, a pounding in her head. It had been her cry; it was her voice she could hear in the night; her loss at the expulsion of her sister.

'This can't be!' her mind shouted, the blood rushing to her head like she was about to explode in a volcano of molten lava. Her world was spinning; she felt she was about to retch.

Then it all stopped.

She wiped the tears from her eyes, her vision clearing with the blurring moisture. She was no longer floating in the cold night air above the Maze of Alderman. Smooth stone walls surrounded her; black silk adorned a door in the far corner, its fineness giving it a transparent nature. Through it she could make out footsteps getting closer with every footfall, excited voices whispering in a tongue she did not recognise accompanying them. She looked around for a means of escape or a place to hide, but the room was empty except for a bed pushed against a dark corner. She quickly stepped over to it, looking for some form of shelter from her impending visitors.

A shape stirred under the covers, fighting as if with the sheets themselves for access to the world outside. Abby stepped back, trapped between the voices in the hallway and the unknown figure in the bed. The sheets finally gave up their battle and released their prisoner into the dull light of the room.

'Daddy!' she called, seeing the face of her father revealed.

'A-Abigail?' he stammered, blinking to gain a better look at his daughter. 'What has happened to you? How did you get here?' he questioned, a look of disbelief on his face.

Abby stared at him, wishing she could explain. She opened her mouth to speak but as she did so her head started spinning. The room was getting darker, only silhouettes remained, and then the blackness returned.

14
A very special day

Abby was woken by the smell of bacon, the clattering of pans and the bustle of people around her. She opened her eyes to see Bot hunched over a stove on which she could see a collection of pans and a rough kettle that was beginning to squeal as steam poured from its snout.

'Tea?' asked a very jolly sounding Tom above her.

'Err, yes, please,' she squeaked. Her head was aching. What had happened last night? She slowly got out of bed and looked around her. The tower had changed beyond all recognition.

'Hope yer didn't mind us sprucing the place up a bit!' called Bit from a fireplace that had appeared in a wall that had not been there last night. 'We thought it was fitting to have a little luxury for our princess, it being yer birthday an' all.'

'It's my birthday?' Abby squealed; she had completely lost track of what day it was.

'Two hundred today, me dear.' cheered Bit proudly, giving her a little bow. 'And a proper lady too I might venture.' He continued to stoke to fire.

Abby settled into an armchair next to him, warming her feet against the chill of the morning air. It was then, as her mind began to clear, that she realised she had not seen Arnold or Apollo this morning. She could hear Tom snoring in the far corner in a large oak bed, the heavy curtains surrounding him drowning out most of the noise.

Clambering out of the chair, she padded barefoot across the room towards a window that had appeared in the wall that now surrounded the tower.

'Where are the others?' she asked as she passed Bit.

'Tom's in bed, as yer can hear!' Bit replied with a chortle. 'The other two are out hunting fer some lunch.'

'Oh,' said Abby thoughtfully, remembering her conversation with Apollo the day before. 'But surely if this world works by the co-operation between nature and humans, it would be wrong for them to kill an animal for food?'

Bit looked over to Bot, who just shrugged.

'She's not quite got a grasp of the way things are here, has she?'

Abby stamped her foot on the hard stone floor, hurting her heel in the process. She could feel anger rising in her, something she had never really experienced before, and it took her quite by surprise. Before she could re-gain control she was shouting, 'TELL ME HOW THINGS WORK THEN, WILL YOU!'

Bit looked round, completely nonchalant about the sudden outburst. 'A little of yer aunt coming out there, I reckon,' he said, his voice as calm as always. 'The witch is getting stronger, me thinks.'

Abby was fuming but she couldn't understand why. 'S-sorry,' she mumbled, her voice faint, like that of a naughty child caught with her hand in the cookie jar.

'Don't yer mention it, m'lady,' replied Bit with a wave of his big hand. 'Not fer us to question yer now, is it?' His tone was formal but underlined with the softness she had come to love.

Abby continued to the window, lifting herself onto a squashy cushion on the sill. Glancing out over the maze she was met by the most unexpected sight: the hedges were covered in a film of white, their shape muted by a thick covering of snow. She looked into the heavens to see the sun shining brightly in a clear turquoise sky, but it did not seem to be having the usual effect on the cold of the night; in fact it seemed to be lightly snowing in the breeze.

She turned back to the gardeners and asked how this could be possible.

Their answer was simple: evil was getting stronger and thus its effect on the weather more profound.

A door opened in the far wall, flaky snow fluttering in with Apollo, closely followed by a lumbering Arnold.

'How's my birthday girl then?' Apollo asked, seeing Abby by the window.

She rushed over into his waiting arms, hugging him tightly as she had done so many times before; well, in his dog form anyway.

'You haven't killed anything, have you?' she spluttered as he released her.

'I'm sorry?' Apollo replied, a confused look on his face.

'You haven't killed anything for lunch I mean!' she said, realising he hadn't been party to the previous conversation.

Apollo searched the features of her face, his soft brown eyes meeting hers. 'We have an understanding with the beasts that graze in the fields of these lands, my dear. We only take what we need to feed ourselves, and no more. It is the way of nature.'

Abby had never really thought of where her meat came from: she assumed it was not from the animals around her. Her thoughts were interrupted by a loud plop from the stove where Bot was fussing over a large pan; she guessed that was lunch.

'Don't you worry, my dear, we didn't kill anything,' Arnold assured her as he padded over. 'We traded some juju berries for a haggi.'

Abby turned to face him; his cat-like face was full of humour, his whiskers and mane speckled with snowflakes.

'Haggi?' she questioned.

'I believe they call it haggis in the human world,' he said. 'But these are bewitched with life, running free in the mountains. Been bred in these parts for as long as I've known. Got to get them free range though, tastes better!' He began to remove his heavy coat. 'Real buggers to catch, mind!'

Abby couldn't help but smile. 'Free range haggis; whatever next!' she laughed, the idea tickling her.

'They're a real delicacy,' Apollo stated somewhat defensively. He did not understand what was so funny.

'I'm sure they are!' Abby squeaked between giggles, all worries about her food forgotten.

Bot nodded to his brother to announce that their food was ready. He had an apron around his waist and a matching oven glove on his left hand. Abby couldn't help thinking he resembled a rather hairy Martha and she collapsed into another fit of laughter.

'Dinner is served,' Bit announced in a very eloquent manner, gesturing to a formal table with six tall chairs that had not been there five minutes earlier.

Tom appeared from behind the heavy curtains of his bed and strolled over to the table, sitting in the nearest chair. His wizened face was looking older than ever and a pronounced stoop was evident in his walk. The others found their seats and waited for Bot to join them. The tiny family of Poggles fluttered in, sitting on miniature chairs at one end of the table; they all looked very smart in what Abby guessed were their finest clothes.

Bot finally joined them, raising a glass that filled with juju juice as he did so, gesturing for them to join him in a toast to the birthday girl. They all stood and raised their glasses (that also obediently filled), wishing Abby a very happy birthday.

'Thanks,' she said, tears forming in her eyes, and then added, 'To my friends!' and drank deeply.

They had all filled their stomachs to bursting point by mid-afternoon, and had retired to the ample chairs around the fireplace. Snow was floating to the ground outside in hand-sized flakes and Abby was watching them hit the windows, marvelling at their structures before they melted in the heat radiating through the glass. The Poggle children were playing in the fireplace, chasing embers as they launched onto the stone hearth, their parents snoozing under Abby's chair.

'I think it's about time we gave you your presents,' Apollo chirped up suddenly.

He rose from his chair and strode over to his cloak, returning a moment later with a small pouch which he handed to Abby. She opened the drawstrings to reveal a small, round, metallic object that looked like an ornate monocle. She had a vague recollection of seeing her great uncle Fredrick wearing one very similar three days before when he had visited her in the Chamber of Souls.

'Thank you,' Abby cooed, giving him a long hug, 'it's beautiful.'

Apollo smiled at her and gestured that she should try it.

Abby had to admit she felt a little uncomfortable trying on a monocle; it didn't really fit with the worn jeans, Iron Maiden T-shirt and All Stars, but she didn't want to appear ungrateful for the gift. Standing, she lifted the piece to her eye, giving a surprised jump as in front of her appeared a scene she had not expected.

She could see a city of steel and concrete, not unlike most big cities all over the world, but this one was deserted. Here too the ground was covered in snow, small mounds dotting the street in front of her like pimples on a pale face. She looked left and then right, taking in the lights glowing in the windows of the tall structures around her, but she could see no sign of life in these buildings; it was like their occupants had suddenly disappeared.

She took a step forward, pushing against the weight of the deep snow surrounding her legs, kicking something buried in her path. Bending down, she reached forward to touch the obstacle. A handprint appeared in the snowy scene below her. Surprised, she reached forward again, clearing imaginary snow in the heat of the room. As she did so the flakes parted to reveal a man's face. His features were frozen in a mask of horror, his eyes wide and his mouth open, showing ghastly brown teeth.

Abby stepped back, tripping over the chair behind her, and landing in a pile of gangly limbs on the floor. The scene was gone as the monocle had slipped from her eye and was lying just out of reach.

'What was that?' she asked as she pulled herself back into the armchair.

'That, me dear, is a looking glass. Allows you to see what's happening in other parts of the realm, it does,' stated Arnold, a look of fascination on his face. He rose and picked up the eyeglass. 'Not seen one of these fer years,' he mumbled as he examined the ornate carving of the frame. 'Must of cost yer a bit of bargaining that one, eh!' he continued as he turned his gaze to Apollo.

'It belonged to your father,' Apollo replied, smiling down at Abby and ignoring his brother's comments. 'He gave me this on the eve of battle, before we rode against Marrick Bitendor and his army of Squakor Raiders. He said it would bring me luck.'

A smile twitched at the corner of his mouth, thoughts of the glory of battle with his old companion bringing back memories of great times lost.

'I have treasured it these last two millennia,' he continued, 'and now it is time it returned to the bloodline from whence it came.'

Abby looked at Apollo's face; his young skin and long golden hair told nothing of age or the hardships of battle.

'How old are you?' she enquired, guessing he must be at least as old as her grandmother.

'Time has no meaning to my people,' he said, sitting on the edge of the chair next to her.

'Eh?' Abby responded; this statement had no meaning to her.

He put his hand to her cheek, his touch soft, almost caressing. 'I am Gordorian and as thus am immortal,' he stated simply, like he was passing on a nugget of trivia. 'I know not how long I have lived, just that I will continue until my purpose is fulfilled.'

Abby's mouth dropped open, then, after a few seconds of tortured silence, she shut it again. 'So you can't die,' she exclaimed, 'how cool is that!'

Apollo gave her a smile, a smile that did not reflect in his eyes, but said nothing, strolling over to the window.

Tom, who was warming his feet by the fire, interrupted. 'What did you see?'

Abby thought about the vision, contemplating the meaning of what she had seen. She told them in as much detail as she could muster: describing the cityscape, with its tall buildings and snowy avenues, and the horrified look on the frozen man's face.

There was a silence when she had finished; her companions were looking at each other, as if making a hushed analysis of what she had said.

It was Arnold that broke the silence. 'Here you go, me dear,' he said, passing her a large, tubular parcel wrapped in cloth. ''Tis for the battle ahead.'

She took the gift, carefully unwrapping the tightly wound cloth, to discover a sword. It was beautiful: the handle was carved in the most ornate fashion in what appeared to be ivory, its surface smooth and comfortable, depicting two intertwined dragons, each breathing plumes of fire. She slid the blade from its sheath; the detail along its shimmering length matched the beauty of its handle, a line of ancient text running from shank to tip.

'That'll be real dragons tooth fer the handle; you've got Draconan to thank fer that one, and Elfish steel for your blade. Only the best fer me princess,' Arnold said proudly. 'Her name is Salankia: it means truth in the old tongue, and she is as old these 'ere hills.'

'Wow!' gasped Abby, admiring the gleaming blade. 'But I've never used a sword before.'

Arnold smiled a toothy grin. 'Then I shall have the pleasure of teaching you, Princess.'

She examined the sword for a moment, taking in the fineness of its edge and the intricate carving of the handle. 'What does the writing on the blade mean?' she asked, holding it up to the light to examine the text closely.

'That'll be an ancient Celtic spell. It was handed down by me father, and his before him. It gives the bearer the power to cut through anything. This sword is very special though, me dear, as it can only be yielded by one that is pure of heart. Should evil ever brandish such a weapon, the holder will suffer an unimaginable loss of power and untold pain so long as the sword is in their grasp. It contains a concentrated goodness that cannot be broken, and now it is yours. Use it well.'

Abby was admiring the weapon when the sight of Tom caught her attention; he was rummaging in the numerous pockets inside his robes as if looking for something.

'Just a minute,' he said, a smile rearranging the lines on his antiquated face. 'Here we go.'

He handed her a small piece of cloth that looked like it had been torn from the lining of his cloak; its edges where ragged and frayed in several places.

'Erm, thanks,' said Abby, unsure what she was supposed to do with a tatty piece of cloth.

Tom picked up his twisted walking stick and lightly tapped the fragment of cloth once. It immediately began to expand, transforming in shape and size, a pattern weaving itself into the fabric. When its task was completed Abby found she was holding a fine tunic of the darkest crimson with the emblem of a phoenix in gold thread adorning the back. She put it on, feeling the soft material mould to her feminine figure like a second skin.

'This tunic is more than a mere item of clothing, my dear,' Tom stated in his well-spoken manner. 'It will keep you warm when it is cold, and cool when it is hot, give you protection in battle and comfort when at peace.'

'Thanks, Tom,' she said, giving him a hug. 'It's so comfortable.'

Apollo suddenly made a noise like a low bark from his position at the window. 'We must continue on our journey if we are going to stop the witch Belladora from taking complete control of these lands,' he said, looking out over the expanse of white ahead. 'We have much distance to travel before nightfall.'

'Back to work!' laughed Arnold. 'An old warrior's toil is never done.'

15
The creation of Alexander

Within the hour the friends stepped out into the freezing afternoon air. Snow was falling all around them like a curtain of white, reducing their vision to no further than they could reach. The group huddled together as they made their way back into the maze, pushing through the now knee-high snow. Abby looked over at her companions: they were all wearing heavy robes and animal skins. All except for the two gardeners that was, who had deemed such garments unnecessary and now she could see why. As they stepped out into the cold afternoon air a rapid transformation occurred: their short, stubbly fur grew, encompassing their huge bodies, like great, shaggy carpets.

Bit caught her eye, giving her a smile. 'Warm as toast now, me dear,' he laughed. 'We are creatures of the land; this is our natural habitat.' He placed a big hand on her shoulder and guided her forward to join the others. 'Come on, Princess, let's keep up.'

They had been walking for over an hour, following the glow of the Fire Fairies as they hovered in the air before them. Abby's feet were freezing - she had lost the feeling in her toes long before - and although the rest of her was warm in her new tunic, her face was numb, the liquid in her nose frozen in spiky crystals.

The group came to the crest of a hill, blinded by the unending white around them, and then Abby hit something hard: she had been looking at the footprints in the snow at her feet and walked straight into a now stationary Arnold.

'Whoops-a-daisy. Are you okay Princess!' he enquired, turning to see whether she was all right. 'Not looking where you're going, eh?' He looked her up and down. 'No harm done now, lass.'

Abby looked into the blanket of white ahead. There were lights in the sky above them, dancing in the air like a hundred Poggles, but these were flickering like the flames of so many candles.

'What are they?' Abby shouted over the cruel wind that swirled around their bodies like a school of frozen fish.

Apollo's voice sounded in her head, clear and calm as if they were back in the garden at home. 'Welcome to Ravensburn; the city of the elders,' he said, his voice proud, a hint of pleasure creeping in.

As they made their way closer to the lights the shadowy forms of buildings began to appear, silhouetted in the surrounding white like giant ghosts guarding the landscape. These were tall, unnatural forms; their edges square, their surfaces smooth and hard.

'I guess this must be Belladora's new city,' Apollo stated, the distaste sounding in his voice as they entered a wide avenue between the structures. 'This was all forest the last time I was here!' He looked at the huge slabs of steel and glass around them and uttered a glum sigh.

Abby was about to comment when she realised how familiar this sight was: it was the scene she had witnessed in the vision of the monocle. Lumps protruded from the snow all around them, their forms smothered by a thick covering of white. She stepped forward, brushing the soft snow from the closest form. As it cleared she was met, for the second time, by the horror-struck face of a man, his features frozen in a glaze of thick ice. She looked up at the faces of her companions; their bodies formed a protective shield around her, only the occasional wispy flake of snow breaking through their wall.

At that moment she felt a warmth against her right ear, a tiny voice speaking to her, the sound so quiet she struggled to make out the words. 'Let me help you, Princess.'

Abby recognised it as belonging to Elizabeth, wife of Alexander the Fire Fairy.

She fluttered down, guiding Abby's hand to the frozen body below, and with the lightest touch placed it on the man's forehead. The ice encapsulating him immediately melted away, the effect spreading to the snow around his body until his form lay in a puddle of warm water, his mouth open, gulping in large quantities of air. Abby knelt beside him, touching his arm as gently as she could, not wanting to shock him further. He slowly turned his head, his thawing eyes blinking rapidly in an attempt to clear blurred vision, his hand raised against the brightness of Elizabeth's glow.

'Is that you Princess?' he asked, a look of wonder spreading to every feature of his young face. 'Can it really be you?'

'Yes,' Arnold responded, his voice gruff in the cold air.

The man shrank back at the sight of the warrior towering over him, the look of horror returning to his face. Abby put a hand on Arnold's shoulder, signalling for him to retreat from sight. The remaining Poggles each took a host and led him to the surrounding humps in turn, until patches of thawing snow surrounded them. Abby returned her attention to the figure at her feet; his muscular frame had relaxed and he was trying to sit up.

'Take your time,' she cooed, attempting to help his movement. 'What's your name?'

He eased himself into a comfortable position before answering her. 'My name is Cornelius Bitendor,' he said; his voice, although a little shaky, had the confidence of experience beyond that of his apparent youth.

The name struck a chord in Abby's mind; the memory of a conversation floated teasingly out of the reach of her conscious thought: annoyingly close.

Cornelius coughed, a long hacking noise that pulled her thoughts back to the present.

'We must get these people inside,' said Apollo from behind her, 'before the night sets in and we all freeze.'

There was movement all around them as twenty or so people shuffled through the remaining snow towards a side street. The friends followed them, hoping they knew of somewhere safe to take refuge, the Poggles flitting back and forth above the crowd, generating warmth in the surrounding air.

They walked through the deserted streets, turning right, then left, and then right again until the architecture began to change: the grey monoliths they had first encountered starting to thin, replaced by smaller, less formal buildings with timber framing and odd, jutting shapes.

'I know where we are!' announced Bit suddenly, looking at the ramshackle assortment of houses around them. 'We grew up in an orphanage not far from here. Had some good times in these streets, I can tell yer!'

They turned a final corner, congregating in a cobbled courtyard surrounded on all sides by buildings of three and four storeys. Cornelius stepped to a large doorway and knocked three times on the blistered wood. After a moment the door opened, allowing the flickering of candlelight to pour into the dusky air, the figure of a woman in its path casting a long shadow across the cobbles.

After a hushed conversation, so quiet that none of them heard a word, she stepped aside, beckoning them all to enter. Abby followed the others, flanked on either side by Arnold and Apollo, their bodies obscuring her from the sight of their hostess. Abby caught a flash of light, like a shooting star in the corner of her eye, and then felt a sudden increase of warmth within her tunic. She pulled at the clasp, urgently trying to free herself from its folds. She finally managed to release the top fastening, a soft glow lighting her face as it opened.

It was then that she realised that the family of Poggles had taken refuge in one of the many inside pockets. Alexander's glowing face appeared; his tiny hand rose to his lips in a gesture of silence. She gave a slight nod, pulling her collar closed, and lowered her head amongst the crowd.

The group staggered through the narrow hallway, their bodies bumping and jostling for room. Abby could not see what was happening around her as she was surrounded on all sides, so she resigned herself to following the crowd.

'So this is what a sheep feels like!' she murmured to herself as her arm grazed the wall.

'What is a sheep?' Apollo asked, his voice sounding in her head.

Abby burst into laughter; the question seemed quite absurd.

'What is so funny?' asked Apollo, a hint of impatience creeping into his voice.

'Don't worry!' she squeaked between giggles. 'I have always known you as a dog: a sheep dog of sorts.' She paused to take a calming breath, looking up at the confused expression on his face. 'A sheep dog,' she stated at last, hoping this would bring a light of understanding to him. 'Turns out you don't even know what a sheep is!'

The group spilled out into a vast chamber, fanning in all directions, glad to be free of the confinement of the corridor. Abby felt a rough hand on her shoulder guiding her towards a corner at the far side of the room. She looked around, glimpsing snippets of wall here, furniture there, until they came to a stop in a wide alcove next to a large chimney breast. She could feel the heat from a blazing fire set in a large fireplace she had glimpsed as they crossed the room, a faint smell of burning filling the air.

She looked up as his was the only direction open to her, marvelling at the height of the ceiling above. Like the one she had witnessed in the gardener's cottage, this was painted with the relief of a great city, mapped out three stories above her but as clear as though she held it in her hands. The scene was only broken by the perforation of small skylights through which the dark night sky was clear, devoid of stars, only the moon shining hazily in the distance.

She felt a warm sensation at her collar, a soft voice whispering in her ear.

'That is your kingdom, Princess,' Alexander whispered in her ear as she gazed over the scene. 'We are in the Royal Square; over there, towards the far chandelier.'

Abby turned her head towards the area he was describing. In it she could see the courtyard, surrounded by buildings, but with no apparent entrance; the buildings just butted against each other like fallen dominoes. One of the buildings, however, struck Abby as being even odder as it appeared to be glowing faintly in the dim light of the surrounding shadows.

'That, my princess, is our current location,' Alexander stated smartly. 'We are in the map room at the College of Philosophers,' he continued, taking on the air of a schoolmaster. 'There are rooms like this all over the old city, though none as grand as this one, I must say. They show not only your current location but also, with a little practice, the location of anyone within the city walls. This has been my life's work, and I am saddened that now it will be destroyed.'

Abby's heart jumped, beating at the base of her left temple.

'Who's destroying them?' she asked, keeping her voice as low as possible in the hum of the room around her. 'And why?'

'It is the work of the Squakor, the protectors of the old witch. They are pulling down parts of the old city in an attempt to flush out any of us that remain loyal to the true king,' he answered, an undertone of hatred in his voice. 'Naturally we are resisting; but they possess a strong, dark magic. We lost three just last month.'

Abby was contemplating this senseless destruction when Apollo's voice interrupted her thoughts.

'Stay close,' he urged.

She felt the pressure of his strong hand on her arm as shouting erupted from the far side of the room: people being questioned in the distance. A scuffle broke out, the sound of angry voices filling the air, echoing from the tall walls surrounding them. Then there was a loud bang and a woman screamed. Abby instinctively ducked to the floor, pulling Apollo off balance as she sank.

She caught sight of a man hitting the floor through the forest of legs filling the room; blood was pouring from an open wound in his chest and a vacant expression consumed his features as life was passed from him.

'This way!' a voice called from somewhere behind her.

It was hushed, but with sufficient urgency to galvanise her into action. She scrambled to her feet, feeling the pressure of Apollo's hand on her arm again, roughly guiding her through a door she had not noticed into the pitch-black abyss beyond.

16
The coming of age

Abby lay on a cold hard floor, her heart pounding like a drum in her head. The angry sounds were muffled now, as if by the utter blackness that engulfed them.

'Luminous!' a voice whispered from somewhere in the surrounding blackness.

The room was immediately bathed in light. A dozen tall candles standing in a circle against the perimeter wall had ignited, spreading their flickering glow throughout the room. Abby squinted, her pupils contracting in the sudden brightness, her vision gradually returning.

'Wow!' she gasped as she took in the wonders of the room around her.

The curved walls were covered in bookcases, filled to overflowing with leather-bound books of all shapes and sizes. The only break was for twelve large portraits hung equally around the perimeter; each had an elaborate iron stand to the side, an ancient candle at its pinnacle. A modest open fireplace had also ignited under the portrait of an elderly man in dark green robes, giving the room a cosy feel. It was heavily furnished with an abundance of mismatched but comfortable-looking chairs and a dotting of small tables. But it was a large writing desk on the opposite side of the chamber that attracted Abby's attention.

She strolled across the room, weaving through the maze of furniture, taking in the intricate carving of her target as she moved closer. She circled the desk to examine an equally impressive chair, the beautiful carving of a bird in flight on its back. It was then that she realised: this was identical to the one in her father's study, except maybe a little less shabby.

'Sit,' ordered a voice from behind her, its tone quietly domineering.

Tom had hobbled to the desk, taking a seat in the chair opposite. He looked ancient, the lines covering his face like the map of some busy city.

'Sit!' he repeated, indicating the carved chair.

Abby obediently sat, giving him a stern look of disapproval. The upholstery was soft, the shape of the chair subtly adjusting to her body as she relaxed, tilting back slightly as the candles dimmed to tiny, dancing specks. Her gaze followed the tall bookcase opposite to the ceiling above, and she let out a quiet gasp as she laid her eyes on it.

Above her, where the ceiling should have been, was a wonderfully star-speckled universe. She felt the chair ease back until she was almost lying down, giving her a perfect view of the night sky above. She could make out each of the twelve constellations, burning brightly amongst the surrounding sparkle, and eight small but brightly coloured planets in slow but constant movement.

'How is this possible?' asked Abby, her eyes following the course of a shooting star as it streaked across the ceiling.

'It is enchanted to show the true night sky, my dear,' Tom replied in explanation. 'Only those with the gift may see it; others will only experience the black void that exists in the sky outside.'

Abby leaned forward to face Tom, the chair obediently reshaping with her movement.

'Why are there no stars in the sky outside?' she asked.

Tom looked from the ceiling to her. 'It is the will of Belladora,' he stated, those piercingly colourful eyes locking onto hers as he continued his explanation. 'The stars guide our people; giving them understanding and knowledge. Without this she retains control though chaos.'

A door hidden within the bookcase to her left opened and with it a rush of voices filled the room, disturbing their thoughts. A woman entered, bowing in the direction of the desk as she did.

'I am sorry to disturb Your Highness,' she said, her voice commanding but respectful.

Abby recognised her as the woman who had invited them in. She had a tall, slim figure and wore a flowing gown of the deepest aquamarine. Her long auburn hair contrasted with the pale, flawless skin of her face, her features soft and feminine. She raised her head to reveal vivid green eyes that penetrated the gloom of the dusky room. Her youth was now apparent: she was no older than Abby herself. A strange thought crossed Abby's mind: she looked familiar somehow, as if from somewhere in her past.

She spoke again. 'The guards have gone, my lords, Princess, and our injured are being cared for. We have prepared a feast for your arrival.'

With that she bowed and left the room, leaving the door open in her wake.

'Grub!' stated Arnold, striding towards the door. 'I was beginning to think I was fated to die of starvation!'

Each in turn followed him back to the great hall. Abby stood and took Tom's arm, taking one last look at the wondrous sky above before following the others.

They entered to see a large table stretching the length of the room; it was laid elaborately with fine china plates and silver cutlery. A row of candles adorned the centre, lighting the otherwise dim room.

Abby noticed a man lying on a bench near the fire. A woman was tending to him, tears flowing freely from her eyes as she dabbed at the constant flow of blood from his chest. Instinctively she walked over to them, subconsciously reaching for the wand she had stowed in a hidden pocket deep inside her tunic. She placed a hand on the woman's shoulder, feeling her stiffen under the touch, and gently eased her to one side. She looked down at the man lying in front of her; his skin was white and clammy, his eyes closed, a tremor shook his body with each troubled breath. She recognised him at once: he was the man she had seen fall; he was Cornelius Bitendor. Apollo had appeared at her side, his hand closing over hers, lightly gripping the wand.

The opaque stone at its tip began to glow brightly as he eased it towards their patient's wound. A haze of pale green smoke poured from the wand's glowing tip, engulfing his bloody chest like the mist of a spring morning. The tear at his chest began to bubble, tendrils of stringy flesh slithering like miniature snakes from either side of the wound, weaving a complicated dance, knitting together to form a fresh film of skin. Within minutes no sign of the deadly injury was present; only the blood stained cloth of his shirt remained. Cornelius gave one final shudder and opened his eyes. The woman, who had fallen silent, was crying again, but this time tears of joy, of relief.

Cornelius raised himself into a sitting position and then back to his feet, the woman manoeuvering to give him support. A moment passed; the warrior standing uneasily, a look of contemplation fixed on his rugged face. Then he took Abby into his arms, hugging her with renewed strength, muttering words of gratitude for his rescuer. Finally he released her and held her at arm's length, a smile spreading across his face, a tear swelling in his eye.

'Thank you, Princess,' he said, the tear escaping along the stubbly angles of his face. Then, regaining some of his composure, he said, 'You must be starving!'

He turned to the room. People were standing, their mouths open, looks of amazement etched on their many faces.

'Join me in welcoming the return of our beloved Princess Abigail,' he bellowed. 'Let it be known that on this day she has saved my life, twice, and I hereby pledge my allegiance to her in this world and the next.'

A cheer rose from the crowd in the room, a mixture of clapping and jubilance filling the air, until Cornelius raised his hands to quieten them.

'Let us feast and celebrate the beginning of this renewed friendship between our people.'

He gestured towards the table, which had miraculously filled with the most sumptuous food and drink. He guided her to the head of the table, indicating she should sit and for the others to join them. Then, without another word, they filled their plates and ate heartily.

Abby retired to a magnificently decorated bedroom with a full stomach and relaxed mind. The sounds of laughter and music continued to resonate throughout the building as the celebration continued late into the night; the bewitched instruments playing gleeful melodies for the dancing horde - for many more had arrived as the evening progressed, the word of her arrival spreading.

Apollo had made himself comfortable on a large couch next to the blazing fire; he was lying on his back with one arm in the air. Abby remembered seeing this look of calm many times in the past but in his canine form, and was comforted by his unfaltering devotion to her.

Donning a silken nightdress, she lay on the bed; the sheets were soft, the mattress firm and supportive. She laid her head on a stack of plump pillows, her mind swimming with contentment as willowy figures danced through the ether of her consciousness, and then she passed blissfully into sleep.

She was back in her father's bed chamber. The only source of light was a single candle flickering in its fight against the oppressive gloom, a drip of molten wax dribbling over the ornate carving of its holder. She strode over to the bed, not wishing to waste any time as she had no idea how long she would linger here.

A lump shifted under the intricately woven blanket covering the bed, a soft murmur escaping into the cold air.

She reached forward, hesitantly touching the form she hoped was her father. Another mumbled phase escaped, the meaning of which she could not comprehend. An overwhelming need consumed her: she needed to see her father; she needed to be in his arms. She leant forward, her face next to his; she could feel his breathing on her cheek, smell the sweetness of his skin.

Placing a shaky hand on the corner of the blanket, she pulled it away from the slumbering figure's face, manoeuvring to allow the dim light to show his features.

His eyes opened. 'Is that you, Abigail?' he murmured in a sleepy voice.

Fighting back her overwhelming tears of joy, she managed to squeak a noise that they both understood as yes.

Gilbert raised himself into a sitting position, the blanket falling away to reveal his old chequered shirt and faded jeans. Abby jumped into his arms, her tears now flowing unchecked. She felt she could stay like this forever: wrapped in her father's embrace, feeling the warmth of his touch and the security of his protection.

He released her slightly, looking into her eyes. 'I see you are coming of age, young lady,' he said, a proud smile on his lips, 'and starting to realise your true potential, it would seem.'

'I don't understand,' Abby replied. 'How come I can suddenly do all these things? How come I'm suddenly here with you?' She stole a look around the room. 'Where are we?'

More questions rolled into her mind, cascading like the relentless onslaught of a landslide; she had always relied on her father for answers, to understand her life.

Gilbert smiled down at her, his demeanour, as always, relaxed as he answered. 'So many questions, my dear! Well, let me think. First of all, you have always been capable of the abilities you find so amazing. As I'm sure you are now aware by now, we have been imprisoned in the garden house this past two centuries, and we - that's your mother and I - felt it prudent to protect you from the true world; to give you a chance to grow strong and healthy …'

'I saw Mummy in the chamber of souls!' Abby blurted out, interrupting his flow.

'Yes, and I imagine she was very pleased to see you,' he continued. 'As I was saying, we felt it was best you were kept away from this world, so we conjured a powerful forget-me spell over you. A spell that has been broken by your arrival at womanhood.'

Abby gave her father a quizzical look. 'But I'm only thirteen, Daddy,' she said, her confusion returning.

'Time moves differently in our world, my dear,' he replied, a smile cracking his dry lips. 'Today is your two hundredth birthday. In the world in which you have grown only thirteen years may have passed, but you have aged in your true form.'

'So it's true,' Abby mumbled to herself, the reality of this extraordinary week hitting home. 'So how come I'm here now?'

'That brings us to your next question,' Gilbert replied, the smile spreading across his tired face. 'As Nousidian royalty - and a pretty talented Majikalt, I would imagine - you have the ability to project your inner being, what we call your spirit, to distant places. This is usually done when the physical body is sleeping as that is when the mind is free to explore. There are some that can induce such a condition whilst their body remains aware, but only the most powerful of our kind have achieved this. It is an art often only pursued by those consumed by evil.'

He paused, seeing a confused look on her face.

'What's a Majikalt?' Abby asked, taking advantage of his pause. 'Is it some sort of magical feline?'

Gilbert laughed. 'I forget how young you were when you last understood our world. Majikalt is the name given to those who posses powerful magical abilities. All citizens of Nousidia have some form of magic within them. Take your friend Apollo, for example: he's a fairly accomplished Majikalt, sorcerer and a talented healer, as I understand it.'

There was a noise from behind the black veil that hung over the room's one door: someone was approaching. Gilbert's hold tightened on Abby's shoulders.

'It is time for you to return, my dear,' he said, an unhappy undertone creeping into his voice. 'My tormentors are coming. Visit me again tomorrow if you can, when the moon is high and all is quiet once more.' He leant forward and placed a kiss on her damp cheek. 'I love you, Abigail; never forget that.'

A group of warriors burst into the room, their black armour having very little reflection in the dim light of the solitary candle, their bulk filling the opening.

'Stop there!' shouted the largest, pulling a wand from a holster at his waist, its tip glowing red.

Abby jumped down from the bed as a flash of pure white light burst across the room. She crouched on all fours, her hands over her head, as another flash soared past, dislodging a large chunk of stone from the wall behind her. She looked up to see him aiming again. Panic surged through her veins, her head buzzed with adrenaline, and then everything went black.

She could hear voices in the surrounding darkness, distant and wispy as though travelling within the very air she breathed. She willed her eyes to open, focusing on returning to the bed where her earthly body lay waiting for her.

Apollo and Arnold's beaming faces met her as she pushed herself back to consciousness, urging her eyes to open once more.

'Have a good trip, lassie?' asked Arnold, an amused tone in his voice. 'I'll take it yer dad's fine,' he continued as if she had just returned from a day out.

'Y-yes.' Abby stammered, unsure how they could know where she had been, or whom she had seen.

'Apollo here has been watching over you, me dear,' said Arnold, sensing the bewilderment in Abby's reaction. 'Good job n'all, what with those Squakor catching yer!'

'Is my father going to be okay?' Abby asked, fearful of the scene she had just left.

Apollo put a hand on her shoulder; the touch was comforting. 'He will be fine,' he assured her, his voice calm. 'They are no match for your father's skill as a sorcerer. He is only allowing himself to remain captive in order to discover Belladora's plan.'

Arnold interrupted as he strode towards the doorway, changing the subject. 'Time fer breakfast! Let the princess get herself out of bed, brother, she must be hungry after such a journey.'

With that he left the room, followed somewhat reluctantly by Apollo.

Abby slid out from under the covers. The room was chilly despite the fire that was blazing in the fireplace. Slipping off her nightdress, she wandered across the room. She poured water from a jug into the bowl waiting for her on the dresser and was pleasantly surprised by its warmth as she leaned over and began to wash. As she did so she caught sight of herself in a tall mirror propped against the adjacent wall, and stopped immediately. Grabbing a towel to dry the dripping water from her face, she stepped over to the mirror. The reflection was of a young woman: her body, although signs of youth remained, had blossomed into womanhood. She looked down at herself in disbelief, not understanding the sudden change, but her body was as the reflection. Her gaze returned to the mirror as she surveyed herself: the swelling of her breasts, her nipples firm in the chill of the room; the curve of her hips as they led to her slender legs; the soft hair that had appeared at the jewel of her womanhood, the same auburn shade as the locks that flowed down her back. She had truly come of age.

She ran her hands across her body, feeling the softness of her skin, the firmness of her breasts as her hands encompassed them, moving lower past her navel and into the soft hair beyond. She felt a mild dampness as she ventured into the unknown flesh, a sense of pleasure she had never known, a tingling inside her inner most core that was instantly addictive.

'Uh-hum,' said a voice from behind her; it was Apollo. 'Are you coming for breakfast? It'll get cold.'

'Y-yes, of course,' she stammered, feeling the heat of embarrassment touch her cheeks. Then, regaining her poise, she shouted, 'Get out with you! Can't you see I'm dressing!'

She entered the great hall enclosed in a wonderfully soft dressing gown, her feet, although wrapped in her trusty All Stars, were a little chilly as the shoes remained damp from the snow of the previous evening. All evidence of the celebration had gone; the only furniture was a modest table positioned by the fire with a chair for each of them. Apollo, Arnold and Tom were already seated, gorging themselves on what looked like waffles. She joined them and a pile of the waffle-like pastries appeared on the plate in front of her, oozing with a syrup the colour of molten gold.

As she tucked in a door flew open at the far end of the hall and the two gardeners bounded in, their fur rapidly regressing, exposing the soil-stained skin beneath. They strolled towards the table, a vase of tired-looking flowers springing into life as they passed, and sat in a pair of chairs that had appeared for them.

'Morning, me dear,' said Bit as he sat.

Bot nodded in her direction, a faint smile showing on his stubbly face.

'Yer have a good night's sleep?' Bit continued as he took a pile of waffles in his shovel-like hand.

'Yes, thank you,' replied Abby, wondering whether any of them were going to comment on her sudden change.

Apollo leaned over and whispered in her ear, 'It is quite normal, in this world, for a woman to flourish on the evening of her coming of age. What I am interested to see is the extent of the powers released by your life step.'

'My what?' asked Abby, unsure what he had said.

Apollo smiled, his watery brown eyes soft like pools of warm mud. 'Our lives progress in stages, my dear. Childhood is the first and lasts for around two centuries. Then comes the reckoning: this can last anywhere from a year to a thousand, depending on the character of the individual. This is a period when the spirit is open to the secrets of nature, a period of great understanding in which an individual's perception of the world is formed.'

Arnold interrupted between mouthfuls. 'And when you get your education, lassie!'

Abby's heart sank a little. 'More school: great!' she said mournfully.

'Do not fear, my lady, as school in this world is not about homework and essays,' Apollo continued. 'It is about focusing your skills as a Majikalt and understanding our bond with nature.'

'And having fun putting spells on people!' laughed Arnold, his whole body shaking with humour. 'Don't listen to old stuffy paws here; education's about finding yerself and what yer capable of.'

'That sounds better,' Abby admitted, slightly relieved. 'But where does this all happen?'

'Why, right here of course,' replied Arnold, a hint of surprise in his voice. 'All royalty attend the College of Philosophers; it's the best.'

At that moment the door opened and an elderly figure appeared looking very windswept. He strode over to where they sat, shedding layers of clothing into a swirl of air around him as he approached, each one vanishing with a puff of faint green smoke. He gave a small bow as he stopped opposite Abby, a crack echoing through the air as his staff slammed against the hard floor. His wizened features wrinkled into what Abby guessed was a smile.

'Good morning, Miss Brown,' he stated abruptly, his voice commanding and clear. 'I am Professor Quirk, headmaster of the College of Philosophers, and I understand you wish to join us this semester.'

'I do? Sorry, yes, I do, Professor,' Abby said, her voice lacking volume or authority. She assumed this was the new school her father had referred to.

'Speak up, young lady,' bellowed Quirk, surprising them all, 'and stand when in the presence of an elder.'

Abby jumped to her feet; she had become used to people in this world treating her gently, like royalty, and was thus a little shocked by this sudden abruptness. Professor Quirk strode around her, looking her up and down whilst muttering to himself.

'Well, I guess you will do, considering your unknown parentage,' he said, sounding mildly disappointed with what he saw. 'Classes start with the beginning of the new moon. I assume you will have the correct attire,' he continued, looking at her dressing gown and sodden footwear.

Abby opened her mouth to correct this obnoxious little man, but catching Apollo's eye, thought better of it.

Without another word Professor Quirk turned on his heel and strode back across the room; items of clothing appearing about him as he went until he was wrapped in several tight layers, ready for the harsh wind outside.

'Bad luck, lass!' laughed Bit, once the professor had left. 'We had Quirky for our reckoning; he can be a real taskmaster.'

'Best tutor in the land,' added Apollo defensively, looking over at Arnold and Tom for back-up.

'You should have let him sense her royal line,' Tom replied sternly, a look of disapproval on his face. 'We don't want our princess treated like a commoner, do we?'

Apollo stood, staring directly at Tom, a look of hatred wavering in his eyes. 'Some of us have not forgotten our common roots!' he stated, and strode out of the room.

'We better get you some new clothes, me dear.' Bit added cheerfully, changing the subject quickly. 'You can't go to classes in yer bathrobe!'

'But I have no money,' replied Abby miserably, remembering she didn't have a bean to her name.

They all burst into laughter, the change of atmosphere welcome.

'We don't have money in Nousidia, me dear!' Bit said between chortles. 'Magic provides for all our needs; we just need ter trade a little, that's all.'

Abby stood and hurried across the hall. 'I'll fetch Apollo,' she shouted as she entered the cool corridor beyond, enjoying the fresher air. A sense of excitement soared through her body.

She found him in her bedroom sitting next to the fire. Walking over to him she wrapped her arms around his neck as she had so many times while she was growing up. He had, of course, been a dog then; but it was comforting all the same.

'It is important your royal lineage is kept secret from the learned professors,' he said in explanation of his behaviour, his eyes remaining on the dancing flames. 'Many show allegiance to Queen Belladora and therefore could be a danger to you.'

'Okay,' said Abby. 'I won't tell if you don't!'

A smile cracked the seriousness of Apollo's face; he could not stay angry for long in the presence of his princess.

'Come on,' she said, pulling at his arm. 'We've got shopping to do!'

17
The city of Ravensburn

Ten minutes later Apollo, the two gardeners and Abby stepped from the door of the map room. Abby pulled the collar of her tunic tighter against the biting wind; the dressing gown underneath flapped around her bare legs. She had tried to lever on her old jeans but her newfound shape was just too rounded, the buttons falling a good distance short of closing. So here she was in a strange new world wearing a dressing gown, tunic and her trusty, although wet, All-Stars.

I'm glad my old school bullies can't see me now, she thought, *they would have a field day!*

The snow had been cleared from the courtyard but the odd flurry floated around them, melting as quickly as it had fallen, leaving the ground damp and the air with a wintery chill. They stepped out into the cold, Abby's shoes squelching with each step.

'Please, let me,' offered Bit, pointing his trowel at her sodden feet.

Before she had time to argue her toes started to tingle, a warmth spreading through her feet like she was standing on hot coals. Steam poured from them, billowing around her ankles before vanishing into the cold air as it reached her knees. After a few moments the heat subsided, giving way to comfortable warmth. She looked down to see her All Stars were not only bone dry, but spotlessly clean.

She gasped at the sight. 'Wow!' You'll have to teach me that one.'

Bit blushed, giving her a little bow. 'A simple drying spell, me dear. Be glad to show yer sometime.'

Abby looked down at the trowel in the gardener's hand. 'Is that your wand then?' she asked, trying not to sound too dim-witted.

'Yeah,' Bit replied his voice guarded. 'Naturally my wand is a tool for the task I'm destined to do. I'd look pretty silly trying to dig up a Hysinthabob with a stick like yours, wouldn't I?'

Abby could feel her face reddening so decided not to pursue that particular line of questioning for the moment, or for that matter to ask what a 'Hysinthabob' was!

'So what am I going to need for my classes then?' she asked, changing the subject.

It was Tom who replied as he arrived behind them. 'Well, young lady,' he said in his best schoolmaster's voice, 'you will be needing a quill – I'd suggest one of those newfangled self-filling ones - a binding of parchment of course, and books, naturally, you'll be needing all the classics; we can get those from Alexander's bookery …'

Bit and Bot let out yawns of boredom in unison. 'We'll meet yer in the Old Squire later then,' Bit cut in, fidgeting on the spot. 'We've got some - err - catching up ter do.'

With that they marched off into the square like a pair of enormous, dirty toy soldiers.

'I guess it's just you two and me then,' Abby remarked to Tom and Apollo as they too set off.

They walked towards a house that was leaning heavily on its neighbour across the square. As they reached the building it started to shift, easing itself straight to form a narrow walkway between it and the neighbouring house. The movement of the building apparently quite normal, Tom and Apollo strolled on towards the gap, with Abby hesitantly following behind. They walked on through the alley and out into a wide, bustling street full of market stalls and elaborate shops selling all manner of goods.

'Welcome to the Avenue of Nu-Nu,' Tom announced proudly, a smile spreading across his face. 'The only place to shop in Nousidia, you know. Named after your great-grandmother, Queen Nu-Nu, the founder of this grand city, with a little help from yours truly of course!'

The threesome strolled down the wide street. The flickering of candlelight shining from the surrounding shop windows displayed the most bizarre assortment of goods imaginable. They reached a particularly vivid shop; a sign over the window was fizzing and popping like a sparkler on bonfire night. A loud boom made the friends jump as a brightly glowing orb launched into the air, showering sparks over the hundreds of faces that looked up as the sphere traced across the cloudy sky. Then, with an ear-splitting roar, it exploded into the shape of a shimmering crimson bird of sparks and fizzing light. It soared over the crowd, so low Abby almost touched it with her outstretched hand; and then, with a single beat of its huge wings, it rose into the white sky before exploding into a mass of whizzing, popping sparkles. People were applauding and cheering all around them; Abby let out a scream of delight as she watched the dying embers fade away.

'That'll be Freaky Freddie's joke shop then!' commented Tom, a hint of amusement in his voice. 'I've heard they're Nousidia's best!'

Abby looked at the brightly painted shop with its fizzing sign and window crammed with all manner of obscure paraphernalia. It was at such odds with the surrounding businesses, with their classical architecture, neat signs and meticulously planned displays.

'It's quite something,' laughed Apollo, sensing her wonder, his face a picture of happiness.

Abby was about to comment further when his face changed: a look of concern consuming the broad smile.

'We need to get under cover,' he stated suddenly, stern and warrior-like. 'The Squakor are coming. It would seem Belladora does not share our amusement.'

He took her arm, guiding her towards a nearby shop, pushing her towards the door.

'Ah, very good,' Tom agreed as they approached, his manner relaxed as though they were on a Sunday afternoon stroll. 'The perfect place for your new robes, my dear.'

Abby looked up at the shop front as they rushed on. It was a small, sombre-looking building with glossy black paintwork and a smart sign over the door. Abby strained to read the gold lettering as they moved closer:

'Satanus Uridius Black – unique clothing for unique people,' she read as they reached the door.

Apollo turned to her, placing his hands lightly on her shoulders. 'I must leave you for a while,' he said, a hint of sorrow in his deep brown eyes. 'A friend to whom I owe a great debt is in need.' Turning to Tom, he continued, 'Look after my princess; I will be back before dark.'

He hurried off without another word, the urgency in his step greater than Abby had ever seen.

Tom opened the door and gestured that she should enter. As she did she glanced over her shoulder to see a group of soldiers approach, their black armour pristine and their swords drawn. They congregated around the little, brightly coloured shop, but Abby sensed confusion in their midst, as if they were unsure what they were seeing. Then her view was obscured by her rushed entrance into the shop, the wonder of which pulled her thoughts from the soldiers immediately.

The interior was cavernous. The walls on either side were filled with rows of clothes in every colour and style imaginable, reaching as far as the eye could see. The shop was lit by a line of glittering chandeliers, each with twenty flickering candles, spaced along the centre of the high ceiling on long golden chains. Under these, in the centre of the shop, was a cluster of deep armchairs and comfortable-looking sofas surrounding an intricately carved table, its glossy black surface reflecting the candlelight above.

'Good morning,' said a deep voice that appeared to be coming from every direction. 'Welcome to our humble establishment.'

A tall figure stepped from the shadows of an alcove Abby had not noticed, giving her a little shock of surprise. He was wearing beautifully woven robes of shimmering black, the surface moving constantly as if made from liquid. As he moved into the light Abby saw his face and hands were blood-red. His hooked nose protruded from an otherwise handsome face and a shock of short, jet-black hair sprouted neatly between two slightly pointed ears. As he stepped closer Abby's eyes were drawn to a small horn at each temple on his forehead; the classical vision of the devil popped into her mind's eye and she tried to suppress a giggle.

'No, I don't have a spiked tail!' said the figure, his voice surprisingly high-pitched and full of humour and joy. 'It's a pleasure to finally meet you, Princess,' he continued with a low bow.

Abby flushed a deep crimson, stuttering a rushed apology.

'Say no more, Princess,' he soothed, his voice taking on a vaguely camp tone. 'My, you have flourished!'

Abby, regaining her composure, asked, 'How do you know who I am? Have we met before?'

The shopkeeper bowed again. 'Let me introduce myself. I am Satanus Uridius Black. Tailor to the famous and royalty alike. And I am at your service which, by the look of this ensemble, you very much need!'

Abby was suddenly very aware of the bathrobe she was wearing under her tunic and was about to start explaining when Satanus interrupted.

'You have come of age, my dear; naturally you will need a whole new wardrobe. I have been waiting for your visit since I sensed your change.'

'You sensed my coming of age?' Abby enquired, confused.

Satanus smiled, a knowing smile of wisdom. 'The commencement of the reckoning is a powerful step in the life of our people, especially in of one with such potential. Those that are sensitive to such things have felt it; I can assure you, I will not be the only one aware of your change. But that's not important right now: we need to dress you.'

Tom settled into an armchair as robes and dresses began to float around the room. Transparent veils and puffy ball gowns amazed Abby as they hovered around her, elaborate shoes and hats that defied gravity appearing to complement her choices. But what pleased her most of all was the softness of the fabrics and the perfect fit of everything she sampled. *This really is shopping to the extreme*, she thought as she tried on a sumptuous gown of the finest silk.

A man appeared at the table. He was no taller than Abby's elbow and wore a black kilt and shirt. His features where gnarled, but not unkind. He gave a low bow and placed a tray of shining goblets in front of them, their refreshing contents welcome as the shopping extravaganza continued.

After a pleasurable hour they were ready to leave: a pile of beautiful garments lay across the various sofas and chairs, and Abby loved them all. She had settled on a long black robe that fitted in all the right places, her tunic sitting perfectly underneath, and a pair of soft blue jeans to finish the outfit. Much to the annoyance of her tailor she had refused to part with her trusty All Stars, which she replaced once they had finished.

'How are we going to pay for all this?' she asked Tom quietly while Satanus was busy collecting her choices.

It was the shopkeeper who answered. 'There will be no need for payment, my princess, the vision of your beauty in the items I have created for you is sufficient. Just remember old Satanus when you return to your rightful place on the throne.'

'I will, thank you,' Abby squeaked as she threw her arms around a very surprised tailor.

Tom raised himself a little stiffly from his chair and stepped to her side. 'We must get a move on, my dear. Lots more shopping to do before the day is out.'

He motioned towards the door.

'Yes, yes,' Abby replied, thanking Satanus again and giving him a final squeeze.

They stepped over the threshold and back into the cold winter air. The street was busy with people scurrying about their business.

'I can't see any guards!' Abby commented as she looked back at the brightly coloured shop she knew as 'Freaky Freddie's'.

'There is a powerful confusion spell on that building,' Tom explained, a thoughtful look on his face. 'It appears like any other shop to those who are not welcome. Very clever.'

He stood looking at the brightly coloured frontage for a moment in silence; then, at a brisk pace, they continued to their next destination.

Alexander's bookery was only a short walk away. They had crossed the street, sampling nibbles from a stall that appeared to sell every conceivable food: both cooked and living. They savoured the delights of the Gumbee Fungus, which, although black and shrivelled, tasted like clotted cream fudge, and the Walker Stick, which resembled a twig and had a taste so sour Abby felt her face contort in horror.

After a few more stops they arrived at the shop. It had a small window containing a pile of dusty books, its woodwork pristinely painted in dark green. A sign hung over the door announcing 'Alexander's' in a flourish of golden swirls.

Their entrance was announced by a little bell that jumped into the air from its resting place on the counter, jangling shrilly in the dusty room. Abby had expected the inside to be much larger, as in the previous shop, but this room appeared to be untouched by magic, its size appearing quite normal. All around them were shelves of books from floor to ceiling, every inch covered in literature. A small counter stood in the centre of the room on which the little bell had settled: quiet again.

A figure appeared from behind the counter, its stature bent with age, a long white beard tangled with equally long hair framing a face cast in the shadow of a wide-brimmed hat. Slowly, and with what appeared to be great difficulty, the figure stood, straightening slightly as it did to reveal features so wizened with age and wrinkles Abby found it difficult not to stare in wonder. Then the figure spoke; but it was not the voice Abby had expected, as it had the spring of youth and a melodic property that led to only one conclusion: its owner was female.

'Good morning, Tom,' she said, her whiskers opening to form a mouth. 'It has been some time since I cast these old eyes on your handsome face.'

Tom blushed, a smile forming in the wrinkles of his own shrivelled features. 'My royal duties have kept me busy these last few years, my dear,' Tom admitted, his voice low and as soft as velvet. 'Let me introduce you to my charge: Princess Abigail Catherine Nubia Brown the Second.' Then, turning to Abby, he continued, 'This is Lidailier Alexander: Nousidia's finest librarian and keeper of knowledge. What Lidailier doesn't know is not worth knowing!'

The bookkeeper stared at Abby, the silence intensified by the depth of her dark eyes, unblinking in the duskiness of the old shop. Then she shuffled around the counter, taking Abby's hand in hers, and, with a deep bow, welcomed her.

The two friends emerged from the shop a few moments later with the promise that all the books Abby would need in the coming year would be delivered to her at the college and, much to Abby's delight, an invitation to visit any time. They had lunch at a quant little stall in the centre of an ancient courtyard just off the main thoroughfare and continued shopping late into the afternoon.

'One more place to visit, my dear,' Tom said as they sat on a bench near a little park.

They were resting their weary legs after many hours of shopping, licking ice cream of such vivid colours that Abby had taken to closing her eyes. Much to her surprise each lick provided a different flavour: first she had tasted orange, then raspberry, then peanut butter and lastly popcorn. Seeing the confusion on her face, Tom had explained that this particular delight was called 'one million and one flavour ice cream', which came with a guarantee that the eater would never taste the same flavour twice!

'Where are we going next?' Abby enquired as she licked the last of the sawdust-flavoured ice cream from her fingers.

'Well, my dear,' said Tom, 'you can't spend the day shopping on the avenue without visiting old Madam Harriet!'

'Madam Harriet?' repeated Abby. 'Who's she?'

Tom smiled, a knowing smile, and answered, 'Madam Harriet is this world's leading authority on, shall we say, special objects.'

'Special!' Abby gasped excitedly. 'What kind of special?'

'You will see,' Tom laughed with a tone of finality that Abby knew was not to be questioned.

18
The house of Madam Harriet

After a few minutes strolling down a twisting, narrow street they were confronted by a grand, old house set in a large parkland garden. It looked so out of place to Abby, standing solitary in its own grounds but surrounded in a large circle on all sides by scruffy looking townhouses jammed side by side with no sign of green between them. Abby imagined giving the first house a push and each one toppling in turn onto the next like a pack of dominoes. To her surprise the first house started to shake, sending a tremor along the nearest row, and then settled again.

'What was that?' she enquired, thinking there must have been a small earthquake or something.

'Be careful what you wish for, young lady,' replied Tom, returning to his schoolmaster's voice. 'With each hour that passes your powers are growing. It will not be long until you will need the training of the philosophers to keep your magic under control. Until then I suggest you keep your imagination at bay.'

With that he opened a little gate in the low fence surrounding the garden and crunched his way up an immaculately gravelled pathway. Abby broke into a trot to catch up and was beside him when they reached the tall oak door.

Tom tapped lightly on the wood and a loud echo resonated from inside.

'*I* caused that house to move?' Abby questioned as they waited.

The door opened, apparently by itself, until Abby noticed a small man in a black kilt and shirt standing before them. She was thinking how familiar he looked when a deep voice broke through her thoughts.

'Madam Harriet is expecting you,' said the man in their path. He then turned smartly on his heel and strode into the cavernous hall.

'Better go in then!' laughed Tom as they stepped over the threshold.

Abby suppressed a giggle as she stepped inside, the wonder of the room enveloping them. The walls were panelled in timber of the softest texture that soared to the ceiling high above. This, like the map room at the College of Philosophers, had an illustration of the realm covering it. Abby searched for their location, catching sight of a grand building softly glowing towards the far corner. She strolled towards it, tracing the route of their day's shopping as she went. Standing directly under the glowing building she could see it had an abundance of land surrounding it, with statues and fountains dotted here and there, and a lake the size of three football pitches. Towards the boundary of the parkland the illustration faded into darkness; leaving an area in the corner of the room blackened; like it had been burnt.

'What happened there?' she asked Tom, sensing him by her side.

He followed her gaze and, after a few moments of contemplation, said, 'That is the darkness spreading over these lands. Those faithful to Belladora are consuming all that is natural in pursuit of their goals.'

'Madam Harriet will see you now,' boomed a voice from behind them.

They turned to see the butler striding across the room towards a large, ornate door in the far wall. He stopped short, indicating for them to enter. As they reached the door it swung open, allowing them to walk through, before slamming shut behind them.

This room couldn't have been any more different to that which they had just left, the ceiling was low and beamed, the walls swathed in a wallpaper of pink swirls and the floor covered by overlapping rugs of various sizes and patterns. Flames blazed and popped in an oversized fireplace against the opposite wall, the only other light coming from candles burning on brackets either side. The room had the dusty, cosy feel of a cottage, with cluttered furniture and chintzy cushions.

'Good afternoon, Thomas.' said a shrill voice as the door behind them opened again.

They both turned to greet their hostess.

Harriet was a tall, thin woman with angular features and pure white hair. She wore a tartan robe of green and blue with heeled boots and held an ebony walking stick in her left hand.

'Good day, Harriet,' said Tom, an air of familiarity in his voice. 'It's good to see you again.'

Harriet shot him a sharp look. 'Is it now,' she said, and gestured for them to sit. 'Tea?' she enquired once they had taken a chair by the fire.

Before they could respond the small, kilted man appeared with a tray full of tea and cookies. He placed them on a nearby table and exited as quickly as he had arrived. They all sat sipping tea and enjoying a cookie, Harriet examining Abby in the finest detail.

'So the true heir has returned,' she stated somewhat abruptly, making Abby jump in her seat, spilling tea in her lap.

'Yes,' Tom answered for her.

Harriet persisted in her examination while Abby dabbed the dark patch on her jeans as discreetly as possible.

'I have something for you, Princess, but it is not for the eyes of such as him,' she gave Tom a sideways glance and continued, 'You must come with me.'

She stood with surprising agility, taking Abby's hand in hers as she rose. Abby reluctantly joined her, looking at Tom for guidance as she did and handing him a sodden napkin.

Tom gave her a warm smile, a look that assured her that she was safe in the company of their hostess, so Abby allowed herself to be guided through a small door that was hidden from sight by a silk screen in a dusty corner.

They stepped through a door and again she was surprised by the difference in the size of the room. This one was long and thin with a tall ceiling and full height windows along one long face overlooking pristine gardens. On the opposite wall were rows of ornate tables covered in bangles and bracelets, necklaces and anklets, broaches, pins and rings: Abby had never seen such a vast assortment of jewellery in one place.

'Pick something shiny,' Harriet requested, watching her like a hawk.

'Really!' Abby squeaked excitedly, looking at the hundreds of pieces.

'Yes, my dear,' replied Harriet. 'But choose carefully, as you can only pick one piece to keep.'

Abby trotted over to the nearest table, picking up bangles and bracelets, trying on tiaras and necklaces. As she rummaged through the mass of gold and silver, Harriet strode over to a cabinet in the centre of the wall. Producing a large black key from within her robes, she unlocked the doors and opened them wide to reveal a small wooden box sitting quite alone on the middle shelf.

'What's that?' Abby asked, stepping to her side to see.

'That, my princess, is my gift to you,' replied Harriet, handing the box to her. 'But you must keep it a secret, and only open it when you are sure you are quite alone. For what is inside this box is for your eyes only; what it chooses to show you may be amusing or disturbing, but it will be the truth. That is for you to discover. You must promise me this.'

'Okay,' Abby agreed, looking at the box in her hand.

Then she gasped as in front of her golden words formed, etched into the smooth surface. She raised the box into the light of the window behind and read the inscription.

'Welcome, Princess, to the casket of the rose,
The truth, in all its pain and glory, is all we propose,
You seek to ask; a question you must now pose,
But be warned, for answers can forebode
Much pain or laughter, offers the rose.'

As the inscription faded Abby looked back at Harriet. 'What does it mean "the truth, in all its pain and glory"? I don't understand.'

'That is for you to discover, Princess,' Harriet repeated, her face cold and expressionless. 'I am merely an intermediary in the passing of objects, of which I have little understanding.'

The old witch turned and walked towards the door. 'Have you picked an item?' she asked as she walked away.

Abby looked back towards the nearest table; a tarnished bangle caught her attention. She stepped over and, picking it up, was surprised by how light it was. It looked like it could be gold and was engraved with the intricate design of a dragon that seemed to fly in a continuous journey around the armlet.

'Come along, young lady,' Harriet called from the doorway, her voice having a distinctly impatient tone.

Abby quickly slipped the bangle onto her arm and trotted over to their hostess, slipping back through the door into the warmth of the parlour.

Tom was standing by the fire waiting for her. 'It is time for us to leave, my dear,' he said the moment she appeared from behind the screen. 'We have an appointment to keep, and we mustn't be late.'

They bade Madam Harriet farewell, although coolly, and left the large house.

'I don't think she likes you,' Abby admitted as they walked along the pathway leading to the street, 'and I don't think she likes me much either!'

'Madam Harriet is old and wise, my dear,' replied Tom as they walked. 'But she has never felt love, and has become cold and bitter over the years. Did she give you anything?'

'Yes,' Abby replied, remembering her vow of secrecy; she had managed to slip the box into her bag without Tom seeing. 'This bangle.'

She lifted the sleeve of her robe to show him the bangle on her arm. It seemed to have shrunk, fitting snugly to her wrist.

'Very nice,' Tom commented as they continued back to the Avenue of Nu-Nu.

The friends continued in silence for a few moments until Tom suddenly stopped in front of a tall building and announced, 'Here we are.'

19
The Old Squire

The Old Squire was a pretty unremarkable building, jammed between Arbuckle's Potion Palace, a cauldron bubbling in its window, its contents a vivid pink with dribbles escaping in all directions, and Alexander's bookery, which Abby recognised from their visit that morning. The stone facade was stained with years of bird defecation; the only opening a grimy black door over which hung a small black sign on a rusty bracket. Abby glanced at it, seeing the emblem of a vivid pink butterfly. She watched it for a moment, amused by the way it fluttered about its dirty frame, alone in its own little world.

'How do we get in?' she asked, looking at the smooth, dark wood in their path.

Tom gave her a wink as a slot opened at waist height in front of them.

'What d'yer want?' asked a gruff voice from the shadow of the opening.

Tom crouched, leaning heavily on his stick, and muttered something quite incoherent into the hole.

'Password?' demanded the voice.

Tom looked around and then said quite seriously, 'Bibble-bobble.'

Abby burst into laughter. Here was the oldest, most wizened wizard she knew uttering a truly ridiculous phrase to gain entry into whatever this place was. There was a scraping sound as several large bolts were withdrawn, then the door creaked open.

The owner of the voice stepped forward, surveying them with his beady eyes as he gestured that they enter. He was no taller than her uncle Tyrillious, but had a look that confirmed he meant business. His black kilt, shirt and top hat were immaculately groomed; his sporran held a crest she was sure she recognised, but couldn't quite place.

They stepped over the threshold into a small shadowy antechamber. Abby looked around the gloomy room but could not make out any other doors leading out, just an empty space. The door closed behind them, plunging the room into pitch-blackness. She felt a breeze brush her face; the hairs on the back of her neck prickled as an unearthly shudder passed through her body. They stood for what seemed like several minutes until the gruff voice spoke again.

'Off yer go then,' he said, and then, almost as an afterthought, 'Have a good evening.'

Abby felt a hand grip her arm and she reluctantly let herself be guided towards the wall on the far side of the room. Even though her eyes had become accustomed to the darkness she could not see a door or any sign of an opening. As they reached the wall she raised her arm, fully expecting to collide with its solid surface, a spur of panic firing into her mind. But then, to her surprise, it melted away to reveal a railed balcony over which there appeared millions of dancing lights. Music met her ears at deafening volume, a thudding bass line causing her eardrums to vibrate in a most pleasurable, although disorientating manner. A flash of pure white light erupted across the ceiling like lightning, a bolt in the heavens.

'Welcome to The Old Squire,' shouted a voice over the din to her left.

She recognised it immediately as belonging to Bit, the gardener with whom they had travelled to the city. As she turned she was met by the sight of him, and his twin brother Bot, dressed in bright green robes, animated flowers pulsating all over them to the beat of the music.

'Like our new threads?' asked Bit proudly. 'Got 'em this afternoon at Freaky Freddie's.'

'Lovely!' Abby shouted over the music. She was feeling a little underdressed in her new black robes and All Stars.

'I'd better get us some drinks, I think,' Tom said, his voice clear in her mind, and gestured to a ramshackle bar in the corner. The four made their way over and Tom acquired four bottles containing a bubbling orange liquid.

'Bottom's up!' shouted Bit, and he took a large gulp from his bottle.

'Don't worry, my dear,' said Tom, his voice again sounding clearly in her head, 'it's Popplejuice; perfectly harmless in small quantities, but might make you a little light-headed!'

She took a swig from her bottle; the bubbles tickled her nose and made her sneeze. As her head cleared she realised that her feet were no longer on the ground. Panic consumed her as she floated over the edge of the balcony into the void beyond.

'Help!' she squeaked: the words seized in her throat with the terror of the situation.

She looked back towards her friends, who appeared to be laughing at her predicament. Then Tom lifted effortlessly from the floor and floated towards her, his face a picture of humour. Bit and Bot soon joined them, swimming past her through the air in a movement a little like backstroke.

After what seemed like hours of floating amongst the glittering lights with very little control, Abby had finally got the hang of dancing in the air and was thoroughly enjoying herself. She was just getting the hang of the forward roll when Tom's voice was in her head again, coaxing her back to the ground. Reluctantly she obeyed and, with a little burp, floated back to earth. They bade the twins farewell and, walking through a nearby wall, found themselves back in the street.

'That was amazing!' Abby shouted as they strolled back to their lodgings; her ears were still ringing, her head full of wonder at what she had just witnessed.

Tom nodded, turning into an alley between a pair of teetering buildings.

'Short cut,' he said in explanation, seeing Abby's questioning look. 'I discovered it yesterday when I – err – when I got lost.'

Abby giggled at the thought of Tom, the wise old wizard, getting lost in the city he had helped build. They strolled on in a comfortable silence. Abby had enjoyed her day of exploring the city with him: discovering the wonders of Popplejuice, which she had found made the drinker lighter than air, and Madam Harriet's magic emporium, where she had been amazed by a room containing all manner of enchanted jewellery. She looked down at the golden bangle on her arm; its shine dulled by the grime of age, the intricate carving glowing softly as she ran her fingers over it.

And then she vanished.

She laughed at the look on Tom's face as she disappeared from sight, tugging on his arm to show she was still there.

'I see you got yourself a vanishing bangle, my dear,' laughed Tom, realising what she was up to, a smile spreading across his wizened face. 'I am impressed. Only a powerful Majikalt can empower such an ancient magic.'

He suddenly stopped, the smile falling from his face. A group of men had stepped out from the shadows and were blocking their path.

'Good evening, gents,' he said in a cheery voice that did not reflect his expression.

A tall man stepped forward. He looked no older than Apollo but his clothes were dirty and torn; his face, although quite boyish, was marred by a scar running across his left eye. Abby caught a glint reflecting in the dim light: there was something in his hand. Her heart was beating hard against her chest, the drumming almost deafening in her ears. Her body frozen with fear as he raised the short blade.

'Give us yer wand, old man,' he ordered, 'or we'll have to give yer a beatin'.'

'Why would you want to hurt a feeble old man?' she heard Tom say, his voice strangely calm and somehow sounding much older.

'Way I sees it, old man, there are three of us and only one of you, so yer better do what I say.'

It was then that Abby realised she was still invisible. She released Tom's arm and carefully circled their tormentors, reaching for her wand as she went. It felt warm in her hand, the gem at its tip faintly glowing; she could feel its energy flowing through her veins, giving her the confidence and strength she needed. She stepped up behind the tall man's two companions, pointing her wand at their backs, and whispered, 'Together.'

Their heads flew together with a sickening crack and they fell to the ground, blood trickling from open wounds onto the damp street, lying as motionless, lifeless lumps in the dull light.

'It would seem things are now a little more even,' she heard Tom say though the haze that had enveloped her mind. She looked up to see the remaining youth lunge towards Tom, the movement slow, almost comical. A wand had appeared in Tom's hand, the jewel at its tip glowing brightly, not with the soft green glow that her wand emitted, but a fiery red whose colour danced as if alive.

The youth stopped in his tracks, the blade falling from his limp fingers, a chilling gasp escaping as the air crystallised in his lungs. He hung lifeless for a moment, like a grotesque puppet in an unnatural play, and then sank to the ground, his eyes wide, staring inertly up at her.

Abby brushed her hand over the bangle, making her form visible again. She knelt beside the still bodies of their attackers, pointing her wand at them, wishing for the life to return, but to no avail: they were dead.

She felt Tom's hand on her arm, roughly pulling her upwards, away from the horror of what they had done, urging her on to safety. They staggered along the street, Tom guiding her. She could not take her eyes from the bodies lying in the shadows, the sight sickening to her core. They reached a corner, the now familiar sight of the College of Philosophers appearing ahead of them. She took one last look down the once deserted street to see a group of hooded figures surrounding their victims, raising the bodies with red, glowing wands.

'They are from the Order,' Tom whispered in her ear as they stopped out of sight. 'Those men were Squakor, agents of the witch Belladora. My fellows will clear up the bodies.' He took her shoulders, looking her in the eyes. 'We must not speak of this to the others,' he said, his voice low but commanding. 'It would not do to worry them with this trivial matter. You are safe, and that is all that matters.' His face brightened, the sparkle in his eyes intensifying as he added, 'You handled yourself well back there, my dear, I am proud of you.'

Abby felt tears welling in her eyes, a lump forming in her throat. 'I killed those men!' she croaked, her voice constricted by the fear in her heart. 'They are dead because I couldn't control my powers.'

Tom pulled her to him, hugging her shaking body, his arms comforting, like those of her father.

'You are not responsible for their deaths, my dear,' he whispered in her ear. 'You are no more capable of killing as I am of becoming a Horn-snouted Bangus! It was I who forced those men's heads together; you merely distracted them, causing their guards to drop.'

'R-really!' Abby stammered, tears now flowing freely down her face. 'I didn't do it?'

Tom released her, smiling. 'You did not kill anyone, my dear. You are an innocent; your aurora is brimming with goodness, the strength of which reminds me of your mother all those years ago.'

Abby, shocked by the mention of her mother, asked, 'You knew my mother?'

Tom gave her a knowing look. 'Well, naturally, you don't get to be my age without getting to know the most influential people. I was at your parent's wedding, you know, a beautiful day…' His voice had become wistful as he reminisced.

Abby could feel her heart lifting; she had not killed those men and Tom had known her parents before she was even born. The feeling of security she had enjoyed since entering this world was returning, the memory of the evening's recent events fading from her mind.

'I'm hungry,' she stated suddenly, cutting Tom off in the middle of a story about a three-legged horse.

'Of course you are, my dear. We had better get back before we are missed.'

20
The call of Salankia

Abby woke late the following morning to the sound of a hushed argument outside her bedroom door. She lazily rolled out of bed and pulling on her dressing gown as she meandered across the room toward the voices. She had stopped behind the door, wiping the sleep from her eyes, trying to stifle a yawn, when something hard hit her in the face and everything went black.

She woke to a vision of two blurred figures standing over her, haloed by bright light: one was crouched low over her, his tall body slim and elegant, while the other was a stocky figure with tufts protruding from his head, his round form flitting around her vision. She tried to raise her head but was stopped immediately by a searing pain in her right temple. She raised a hand to her face, feeling the swelling around her eye.

'What happened?' Abby questioned the two hazy figures somewhat deliriously.

'Drink some of this,' said a familiar voice: it was Apollo.

He raised her head slightly and brought a cup to her lips. She drank slowly, the nectar running down her throat like warm honey until the pain dispersed and her vision began to clear. Apollo helped her into a nearby chair, discretely closing her robe to cover the naked body beneath.

'I say, nasty bump, what!' came a voice from behind him.

Abby looked into Apollo's face, searching for some understanding in his deep brown eyes, and was answered as he stepped back and introduced his companion.

'This, my dear, is Professor Bumblebot. He is your new head of year and human studies teacher here at the College of Philosophers.

'Spiffing to meet you, my dear,' said Professor Bumblebot with a smile full of overly white teeth. 'Sorry about the door an' all, can be a bit clumsy, you know. Not to worry, we'll have you right in a jiffy!'

Apollo stepped forward as the portly man raised a wand of twisted wood, the gem at its end pulsing like a throbbing sprout.

‘I think we will leave the healing to the experts, Professor,’ said Apollo, a look of concern quickly hidden from his face.

‘Okey-dokey,’ conceded the professor without even a blink of argument. ‘Well, lots to do, you know. It was nice to meet you, Abigail. See you in class.’

He waddled out of the room, calling, ‘Toodle pip’ from the corridor beyond.

Abby let out a giggle. ‘What a character, eh!’ she squeaked, and then a question came to her. ‘I thought Professor Quirk was going to teach me?’

‘Yes,’ replied Apollo, deep in thought. ‘Some say Bumblebot is about as kooky as it gets, but I’m not so sure.’

Snapping out of his daze, he looked directly to her.

‘Professor Quirk will oversee your quickening, but you will be taught by the greatest minds of our time. The teachings are not something that one being can master completely: it can take a lifetime to master only one structure in its complexity.’

‘One structure? I don’t understand,’ replied Abby, bewildered.

Apollo took a seat in the chair next to her and began to explain. ‘The teachings are an ancient text that forms the basis of our beliefs. It is divided into three structures: earth, air and water, each having a specific purpose but combining to form the basis of every living being in Nousidia. Bumblebot subscribes to a relatively new theory, for which he has won the right to teach our young this past two millennia, suggesting that the human race, in all its variety, has evolved into a fourth structure, one of flesh and blood. As you can imagine, this has caused a great deal of controversy; some even claim it was the catalyst that started the Great War.’

He stood and stepped towards the door.

‘That’s enough politics for the time being. Better get some clothes on, Princess; we’ve got a busy day ahead of us.’ With that he left the room.

Abby was busying herself with dressing and such when she noticed a humming noise coming from the trunk at the bottom of her bed. It sounded like the flutter of a bee’s wings, but louder and less rhythmic.

She strolled over to the trunk, opened the lid and, after sifting through an abundance of discarded clothing and shoes, put her hand on the source of the commotion. Since opening the trunk the noise had become steadily more urgent, increasing in both volume and movement. She grasped the offending item, the vibration making the nerves in her hand tingle, sending shockwaves up her arm and through her shoulder. She pulled it clear to discover the sword Arnold had given her in the tower of Alderman for her birthday. A blast passed through her fingers, jolting her like an electric shock, and the sword fell from her hand.

Much to her surprise it landed on the tip of its blade, rotated slowly, then fell purposefully, facing the corner of the room. She looked at her hand but there were no marks, no signs of burning or swelling, just her pale, elegant fingers.

But how can his be: I felt a burning and the shock was real, she thought, and then ran out of the room to tell the others what had happened.

After examining the sword neither Apollo nor Arnold nor Tom had any answers. They had resolved to consult the library; but after a morning of fruitless searching, and much coffee, they were still no wiser. They had been through the section on ancient weapons, read countless books on Nousidian history and waded through endless dusty newspaper scrolls, but all to no avail. By late afternoon they had admitted failure and congregated around a large table in the map room, documents spread everywhere around them. Apollo stood with his eyes closed and arms folded, meditating on the question; Tom had curled up in front of the fire with Abby - they were discussing her mother; while Arnold sat idly thumbing through a text on the evolution of the Chunkett.

Suddenly he stumbled on a theory: a memory from his childhood. 'I remember when I was but a wee cub, back in the mountains of Acamathium,' he said, gesturing the others to join him. 'My grandfather once told me a story about this sword and its magic.' He picked up the sword, examining the construction of its sheath, the intricate carving of the hilt, before he continued, 'The sword was made by order of Gratador, husband to Nu-Nu and the first king of Nousidia.'

Tom interrupted. 'Yes, we know all this!' He was becoming agitated.

Arnold ignored the outburst, and continued, 'The craftsman, a dwarf of such skill that others dared not rival him, made not only the sword but also a shield and suit of armour of such beauty that people travelled miles in the hope of seeing them. These gifts were presented to my great-grandfather in honour of his devotion and his help in bringing peace to these lands; for he was among those who conjured the Great Division, thus forming the world in which you have grown.'

He gave Abby a smile, his feline face softening.

'In time my grandfather inherited the fabled suit, and died with honour in that same armour at your father's side during the witch's uprising, some two centuries ago. The armour was burned with his earthly remains, as is our custom, and the sword passed first to my father and then to me. Unfortunately the shield was never recovered.'

He looked back at the sword in his hands. 'Some say it calls for its brother when the righteous have need for their service. I think it is that which you have witnessed this morning.'

A smile formed on Apollo's face. 'I read an article in one of these scrolls. An account from the Battle of Devil's Gorge.' He frantically searched the pile of scrolls on the table before him and settled on a particularly dirty scrap of parchment containing very faded text. 'Here it is,' he said, triumphant, and began to read.

'... *After the bloody battle was over the King surveyed the dead. He had lost many good warriors that day, including his captain of the guard and closest friend, Joseph Buttersquick, a Chunkett of the highest order. His body was returned to the great city of Ravensburn to join the ranks of the honored dead: the greatest tribute to a warrior's life. The funeral pyre burned for three days and three nights under the constant observation of the general's garrison, the warrior elite. His ashes were finally scattered at his home in the mountains of Acamathium. A poetic end to his existence in this world, as the battle that extinguished his living flame was in defence of his own people, outside the village in which he entered this world. We wish him happiness and honour in the next.*

Much controversy has enveloped this story over the week since the funeral, as it has come to light that a piece of General Buttersquick's armour, the famous shield of Salankia, was not retrieved from the battlefield and is currently missing, feared lost.'

Arnold stood, a thrilled look on his face. 'Show me the direction in which the sword lay, Princess,' he said, barely containing his excitement.

Abby indicated the direction with her outstretched arm. Much, it would seem, to the delight of Arnold.

'The shield must be hidden somewhere in Acamuntum: the city of my ancestors, where I was born!' he boomed. He was vibrating with enthusiasm by this point; he had not visited his home since his capture over two centuries ago. 'We must retrieve the shield,' he continued, like a giddy schoolchild with a new project.

Apollo nodded his agreement; the shield would be a useful tool in the battle to come.

'We leave at sunrise,' he said, his tone becoming formal, returning to the air of authority that had been missing these last days. 'I suggest we all get some sleep as tomorrow will bring with it a great journey.'

21
Reunion

It was still dark outside when Abby woke, a hand on her shoulder gently rousing her from slumber. She hadn't been able to connect with her father that night; she was worried for his safety after the Squakor had discovered them at her last visit. She dressed and joined Arnold and Apollo in a rushed breakfast in the map room. Tom joined them minutes later, and the group set off into the chilly morning air.

Arnold had described the journey in great detail the previous evening, telling of the dangers that lay ahead and the difficulty of the route they would be forced to take. The Chunkett were a private people, living high in the mountains above the city, away from society and its trappings, and they did not welcome visitors freely.

The pace was brisk, for they had a full day of climbing ahead of them, and they were soon leaving the tall houses of the city for the ramshackle shacks of the mountainous slopes.

They stopped to rest in a small village at the base of the Acamathium range, acquiring food from a local family who welcomed them into their home in return for a few glass beads cut from Abby's headwear. They ate heartily and engaged the family in polite conversation.

The man of the house had a tall, muscular frame that gave the appearance of youth, along with long blonde hair and a beard the colour of copper. He had introduced himself as Simok and was knowledgeable about these lands, boasting that he had been approached as a guide just the previous day by a group of priests. 'They were dressed in emerald-green robes, the insignia of the Order of Sincerus emblazoned on their bodies,' he boasted.

'Where were these priests heading?' Apollo asked, his tone controlled to that of mere polite interest.

Simok smiled, the chance to share his gossip welcome. 'High into the mountains: a village called Acamuntum, just past Devil's Gorge. They said they were on a pilgrimage to retrieve an ancient talisman.'

Apollo and Arnold exchanged glances across the room and Apollo's voice sounded in Abby's head: a warning not to discuss their intentions or goal. Abby understood and adopted the vacant look she had used so many times back at school, deflecting questions and interest alike.

'You did not take up their offer?' asked Apollo nonchalantly.

'Their generosity did not meet my needs,' he stated, a smile spreading across his face as he gestured towards his children. 'I have a family to support, and the harvest has been poor since the frozen winter came.'

Tom interupted from his chair in the corner of the room. 'We understand your needs. Maybe we can afford you more generosity.'

Apollo shot him a look of bewilderment.

Ignoring him, Tom tapped his stick on the stone floor three times and pointed it towards a tall pitcher in the corner. It immediately began to overflow, its lid sliding off on a river of grain. He then turned his attention to a pot on the stove that began to bubble with the sweetest smelling nectar. Then, to their amazement, a beast of such a size to provide ample meat for the coming year joined them.

'Your generosity is second to none!' oozed Simok, his eyes wide with greed. 'I will guide you in your quest.'

'I thought you might,' laughed Tom. 'We can be very generous to those who serve us well.'

The group set off an hour later, their new guide leading them high into the mountains. The trail was patchy at best; loose rocks and shingle covered a terrain that was more like ice than rock, its surface constantly moving. They forged on throughout the morning, stopping occasionally when one lost his or her footing, but making good ground against the increasing gradient. Abby watched a bird of prey as it hovered overhead, following their progress as if stalking its prey but keeping a safe distance in the warm blue sky.

Upon clearing the brow of the lower hills, the companions paused to take in the panorama laid out before them: ahead the mighty peaks of the Acamathium range towered over the multitude of lower peaks, like nature's skyscrapers; dark and brooding, their peaks white with snow.

'Devil's Gorge is at the base of Mount Acamathious, the tallest peak to the left,' said Simok, his voice full of his own self-importance. 'We should reach it by nightfall.'

Abby winced at the idea; it looked a very long way and her feet were already sore.

They continued at a brisk pace all afternoon, the hot sun beating down relentlessly, only stopping occasionally to fill water bladders and check for position. Abby was glad of her gift from Tom; the tunic felt as light as cotton in the hot sun, her skin feeling cool as if bathed by a sea breeze. She could see the others were not quite as comfortable, although none dared to complain and as they continued their pilgrimage in silence.

The afternoon heat soon cooled into evening, a distinct chill creeping into the air. The faint green haze of dusk enveloped them as they made their way into a hollow worn through the rock by centuries of thawing water and shifting earth. The ground here was devoid of life; no vegetation grew among the rocks, no movement scuttled within its cracks. A silence filled the air, its absoluteness giving an uncomfortable sense of emptiness. Light too appeared to succumb to the effect of this place as an oppressive darkness hung around them.

'The Devil's Gorge,' Apollo stated, his voice cold and emotionless. 'Much suffering and pain lingers in this place, unable to break free from the talons of death.'

'Get on with yer!' shouted Arnold as he climbed a clammy wall opposite. 'There's no such thing; yer just giving 'em all the willies.'

Apollo gave a shrug, looking around as though expecting the worst.

'This'll do!' Arnold shouted from high above their heads.

The group carefully made their way across the smooth rocks, climbing to where Arnold was waiting. He was standing next to an old shack, its mossy walls and silvery shingles looking old but strong. Between a pair of grimy windows a blistered door was standing ajar, inviting them to enter.

They filed into the shelter, the dark walls intensifying the gloom outside. A sharp tap cracked on the stone floor somewhere in the shadowy depths of the room and they were bathed in light. Abby looked up to the ceiling, searching for its source as there was no sign of candles. Above their heads a thousand tiny specks of light danced in the air like a frenzy of miniature stars, filling the void within the pitch of the rafters. Four rickety cots stood against the wall with an old stove in the corner; otherwise the room was empty.

The stove burst into life as Abby looked in its direction; surprising them all, especially Simok, who was leaning over it.

'Better settle in then,' Simok suggested, busying himself with a pan at the now blazing stove. 'Light's going and the winter's bad in these mountains.'

'I'll take first watch,' grunted Arnold, settling in a spot by the door.

They all ate heartily after the day's travelling and settled down for the night. Abby fell into a deep slumber the moment her head touched the pillow, her aching muscles forgotten as she passed into sleep.

She woke suddenly. A cold wind was twisting its way through the room, like a serpent stalking an unfortunate mouse. She jumped out of bed, her clothing dishevelled, and pulled on her tunic, feeling a warmth flow through her. She looked around the small shack for the source of her unease.

A sound met her ears; it came from the depression outside, a soft murmur like that of a child at play. Instinctively she stepped through the blistered door, passing into the cold night air. She sensed a presence around her: not a physical form, but the essence of a person, no people, in the surrounding gloom. She could see the vapour of her breath and the crystalline white of the frost around her, but she felt no cold. She looked down, examining her bare hands, expecting to see the bluish tint of frostbite but was met by the warm pink of her flesh, apparently untouched by the surrounding chill.

The murmur again: its sound emanating from the cave below, its murky mouth open in an eternal yawn. She carefully climbed down into the gorge, finally standing at the mouth of the cave. Straining her ears, she waited for the sound again: wanting to hear it, if only to confirm her own sanity, her senses battling with the fear in her heart.

She caught a glimpse of colour shifting in the gloom, a tantalising peek at her prey, and then she was inside. The darkness was oppressive, the feeling of loss and heartache intense as if focused by the complete absence of light. A shape appeared in the dark, a soft glow in the form of a tall boy, his features blurred, as if being viewed through water. The figure glided towards her, its movement slow and unsure. With each step Abby noticed a sharpness forming in his features, as if coming into focus. He stopped just out of reach: a young man looking at her with such intensity as if he was looking into her, directly at her soul.

Further figures joined him: those of men, women and children, each with a luminescence like the glimmer of the moon.

'We are the Illuminatum: the people of the light,' stated the youth before her.

'Hi,' Abby responded shakily. 'I'm Abigail, daughter of …'

'We know who you are,' the young man interrupted, rather rudely. 'We have been waiting for your return.'

Abby, not sure this was a good thing, opted to say nothing.

'We are enlightened beings,' a tall man of substantial years interjected. 'Cast from our homes by an evil spell, forced to hide here like animals.'

A murmur filled with hatred escaped the thickening crowd, its sound echoing from the surrounding stone. The elder raised a shimmering hand to quieten the unrest.

'Once we lived in peace with your kind,' he continued, 'a mutually beneficial co-existence without fear of our uniqueness. Then came the rein of darkness and evil took a grasp of these lands, bringing death and destruction to all beings: man, beast or vegetation. We hope to see happier days again, young princess.'

'So do we,' boomed a voice from behind her: it was Apollo. 'Greetings and salutations Mizer'ak,' he continued, walking past Abby as though she did not exist. 'It's good to see your radiance has not faded in these troublesome years!'

Apollo stepped to the elder and the men embraced. Releasing him, Apollo turned to the younger man, looking him up and down.

'Is that you, Mizer'an?' he asked. 'You have grown strong and healthy in my absence.'

The youth looked puzzled. 'It cannot be. My brother has returned. Is that really you, Mizer'af? Or should I call you Apollo, commander of the royal guard?'

Apollo smiled. 'Yes it is I.'

'But where is your life glow, dear brother?' questioned Mizer'an, a look of disbelief on his face.

The elder Mizer'ak stepped forward, interrupting their reunion. 'His radiance will return in time now that he has returned to his people,' he said. 'We have much to catch up on and very little time before the dawn arrives. Let us be seated.'

The three took seats on a nearby outcrop of rock and were joined by several others. Before long they were in deep conversation.

'Abigail!' shouted a voice from somewhere within her subconscious. 'Wake up!'

The scene before her faded to black, the sound of hushed voices filling her ears as she woke, back in the shack. Arnold was standing over her, shaking her nervously as if concerned he might damage her.

'Thank the ancients!' he said, a look of worry on his feline features. 'Yer had us concerned there for a moment, lass.'

Abby's head was fuzzy. Had she dreamt the meeting in the cave, or had her spirit travelled without her, like when she visited her father?

'Apollo is missing,' Arnold continued. 'We're preparing to search at first light. Better get yer things packed.' He turned away, busying himself with preparations.

Abby sat up in bed, rubbing her forehead; it ached with the commotion of a thousand thoughts, all demanding to be heard at once.

'BE QUIET, ALL OF YOU!' she shouted in frustration.

The packing stopped around her. Each of her companions turned to her in stunned silence.

'Are you all right, lass?' Arnold asked, an amused look on his face. The outburst had caught them all by surprise.

Abby was about to explain what she had seen when Apollo burst through the door, a concerned look on his face, his clothing covered with a sparkling film of frost.

'I sensed your fear, my princess,' he said, ignoring the open mouths and glaring eyes surrounding him. 'Are you okay?'

Abby's brain began to clear, the thoughts dispersing into the oblivion of her mind, the peace returning once more.

'Where have you been?' demanded Arnold, his voice taking on the tone of a nagging wife. 'We were troubled by your safety.'

Apollo turned to his warrior brother, placing a hand on his muscular shoulder. 'I need to speak with the princess alone. I have discovered much, these last few hours.'

22
Revelations

They climbed in the misty light of dawn, Apollo picking a path through the barren rocks, searching for the right spot. Abby followed close behind, the warnings to be careful still ringing in her ears, their destination now in sight at the peak of the mountain called Acamathious. The climb was difficult and they travelled in silence; Apollo promising to explain everything once they had reached their goal. They scrambled over a ridge and onto a plateau of rock where Apollo gestured that Abby should sit. They made themselves comfortable with rugs and cushions conjured from the air before Apollo spoke.

'It is beautiful here,' He said, looking out over the valley below.

The sun was rising on a distant horizon, casting a shimmering haze of purple and red over the pale sky. Its heat was beginning to penetrate the frozen tundra, patches of green emerging amongst the blanket of white that covered all in its smothering vale. Abby could make out the city of Ravensburn in the far distance to her right; she had not realised they had travelled so far.

Glancing over to her left she caught sight of a much larger city, its extent reaching to the very edges of the forest between it and Ravensburn to the south, and the wide expanse of sea on the horizon. A snaking body of water sliced though the centre of this city, like a jagged border between the two halves, the water of the river flowing rapidly towards the sea. Even from such a distance Abby could make out tall, shimmering monoliths of coloured glass, standing like sentries on the western banks of the river, a stark contrast to the much smaller structures on the opposite side.

'Where's that?' Abby asked, turning to Apollo.

He looked over to the left, taking in the vista towards the ocean. 'That, my dear, is the city of Alexandra. Capital of these lands, and home to your birthplace: the House of Elders.'

Abby looked over the city. She could make out a line of dark columns spiralling into the air before dissipating into the strengthening breeze.

'Is that smoke?' she questioned.

Apollo answered in the affirmative, a note of sorrow in his voice. 'The forest is being consumed by fire to make way for Belladora's vision, her grand design. Our people have resisted such change, only allowing construction of such fallacies on the western bank, but as her strength grows our ability to object diminishes. It is only a matter of time until her evil vision consumes all. That is, unless we can stop her, my princess.'

Abby watched the sprawling city, lost in her thoughts, as the sun spread its heavenly light from pointed spire to thatched roof, indiscriminately sharing its warmth with all, sparing only the deepest of shadows.

'You had a vision last night,' Apollo stated suddenly, breaking through Abby's daydream, 'of my meeting with the Illuminatum in the cave.'

'Yes,' admitted Abby honestly; she knew lying was not an option with someone who could read her mind like a book. 'You know those people?'

'The Illuminatum are my family,' Apollo replied, a smile returning to his handsome face. Seeing the confusion in her eyes, he explained, 'When I was very young, no older than you, my paternal family travelled, with many others of our kind, across the stars. The motivation for our move is unclear, as my memory of such events is dulled with the passage of time; all I remember is that it was for good reason. After many years those who survived discovered this planet and the Illuminatum. They were a greatly advanced race, versed in the arts of science and literature, and they accepted us as equals, allowing my family to settle in their great city.'

He paused, the memory bringing sorrow to his eyes.

'War came in the form of pirates: humans who destroyed the once great city, looting and pillaging, as was their way. The Illuminatum are a peaceful race and as such had no weapons with which to defend themselves. After much loss they had no option but to flee into the caves above the city. My parents died holding off their attackers, thus allowing such an escape.'

A tear broke from the corner of his eye, rolling along his handsome cheek unchecked.

'I was adopted by Mizer'ak, an elder in the tribe, and brought up as his son and brother to Mizer'an. The Illuminatum rebuilt their civilization upon the burnt embers of their once great city and lived in harmony for many millennia. Over time a fragile trust was rekindled with the humans of this world, culminating in the forming of a treaty in which your father, a young king himself, was instrumental. With the death of your mother and the rise to power of the witch Belladora, came another battle: that which resulted in your family's banishment to the garden house, and the further destruction of Acamuntum, the city of the Illuminatum, a city that both Arnold and myself called home.'

Abby interupted. 'Why did they not fight back this time; surely they learnt from the first war?' She felt anger in her heart at this unfair treatment of his people.

Apollo looked directly at her, his dark eyes deep pools of sentiment. 'The Illuminatum have evolved to a state beyond that of the flesh,' he explained. 'They are beings of pure emotion, and therefore do not exist in this world, or the next, but somewhere in between, as is their will. They have no interest in conflict; only the return to harmony between the inhabitants of this world.'

'Is that why their skin glows?' Abby asked, her thirst for knowledge becoming overwhelming.

Apollo grinned. 'What you saw is called the life glow; it is a reflection of a being's feelings.' Seeing her confusion remaining, he continued, 'Their skin appeared to glow because they were happy to see us!'

The two friends sat for a while in silence, taking in the beauty of the world around them as it thawed into a new day.

'So why did you bring me up here?' Abby asked rather abruptly. 'Surely you could have explained all of this down in the valley.'

'You are wiser than your years, young princess,' replied Apollo, 'but I have good reason. The Illuminatum shared further information with me, information I believe it unwise to share with our friends at this time.'

He looked out over the mountains to the south in a moment of deep thought.

'The priests we follow into Acamuntum form an ancient brotherhood, a secret society called the Order of Sincerus. They are an assembly of men versed in the black arts, and are feared in civilization for such practice. Your friend Tom is suspected of once being one of their kin, and as such, in the eyes of the Illuminatum, he is not to be trusted.'

Abby gasped. 'Tom? Into black magic? Don't be so daft!' She laughed at the idea. But as the last of her giggles subsided, the memory of the alleyway in Ravensburn returned to her: those hooded men, their appearance to clear the bodies so quickly, Tom's reassurances that 'his fellows', as he had called them, would arrange everything, and his insistence that she not tell the others.

No, she thought to herself, *Tom's not like that!*

Not wanting to discuss it any further, she informed Apollo that they had better get back before the others became worried. Apollo stood as their seating vanished, and led the way back to the shack and their friends below.

23
Acamuntum

Their first sight of the city of Acamuntum was a disappointment. It consisted of a small group of rough timber huts with mossy thatched roofs, positioned in a circle around a fountain that burbled at its centre. All around them were ruins, piles of stones consumed by creepers and vegetation; very little evidence of the once prosperous society that dominated these mountains remained. Abby had imagined a great city of towering monoliths and grand buildings, fitting for such 'enlightened' people.

'INCOMING!' screamed Arnold as a missile shattered the rock over Abby's head, showering her with shards of splintered stone.

The group instinctively scattered for cover, wildly scanning their surroundings for a sign of their attackers. All, that was, but Simok, who remained in the open, frozen to the spot, his eyes wide and staring, like those of a beast sensing its end in the lights of an oncoming vehicle. Protruding from his chest was the shaft of a crude arrow, its tip fizzing and coughing his blood from an open wound. Then, with a wet thud, Simok was no more.

Further projectiles rained down, ramming into the ground around them, scorching life from the earth.

'Head for the village,' called Apollo in Abby's head, all calmness gone.

Abby instinctively jumped into the open as a flaming arrow scorched the hollow in which she had been hiding. She ran with all her might, willing her aching limbs to push forward into the light of the village. She was reaching out, her shaking hand within touching distance of safety, when a hooded figure stepped into her path. His arms were spread, open in a grotesque gesture of welcome, a staff held in one hand, its tip glowing with a ruby red stone, and a bloodied sword in the other. Abby could not stop herself and stumbled into the arms of her attacker, the momentum of her panic pushing the figure to the ground. They rolled to the earth in a tangle of limbs and weapons. Abby looked up to see her assailant gasping for breath and leaped to her feet, kicking out at the rising figure as she did, her wand already in her hand. She could feel power flowing through her veins, ancient words flowing from her mouth as she levelled her wand at his chest, the gem at its tip pulsing in a vivid green.

A flash of pure white light erupted from the wand, hitting the hooded man squarely in the forehead. His hood fell away to reveal the wrinkled face of an old man. His knees folded under him, his torso teetering like a spinning top, and then with one final rattling gasp he collapsed motionless to the floor.

A thunderous roar erupted in Abby's ears as she watched the life ebb from her assailant, the strength from her legs gone in an instant. Her vision began to fade, engulfing her in a foggy vale. A figure, tall and glowing, was her last memory before oblivion. A memory that seemed somehow familiar.

Hushed voices chattered all around her like the hissing of an angry snake as Abby squeamishly opened her eyes, a sense of foreboding filling her senses. Musky smells wafted tantalisingly close to her nostrils, hinting at exotic spices and sweet flavours, but most of all she could feel the people around her, sense their emotions, touch their thoughts.

She found herself enveloped in the hustle and bustle of a crowded market place. People were milling around her, going about their daily business, seemingly unaware of her presence. She scanned the crowd, hoping to catch sight of a friendly face, maybe some understanding of the sudden change in location, but to no avail. Giving up hope, she made her way over to a stall at the edge of the square where a range of pastries and hot liqueurs were displayed upon a simple trestle table. She was suddenly aware of how hungry she was, her stomach growling in agreement.

'Can I help you, ma'am?' enquired a short, round man in a brightly coloured turban and smock who, Abby could have sworn, had not been there a moment before. 'Maybe an apple flap, or a cup of beeju nectar?' the salesman pressed.

Abby looked at the eclectic range of goodies available but, realising she had no means with which to pay, opened her mouth in an attempt to decline.

'I recommend the Benuvian Clusters,' said a soft voice from over her left shoulder.

Abby spun round to face its owner, the voice instantly recognisable as that of her father. She dived into his arms, instantly engulfing herself in the comfort of his embrace.

'I thought I had lost you,' she mumbled into his jacket. 'When I could not raise you in my dreams, I feared the worst!'

She held him tightly, not willing to let go in case this was all a dream, tears of joy pouring from her eyes. Sensing her fear Gilbert released her, looking directly into her glistening jade eyes.

'You are safely in the custody of the Illuminatum, my dear,' he said soothingly. 'As such you are outside the reach of our enemies. The others will join us shortly in council, as we are on the verge of war.'

'Are you really here?' Abby asked, hoping that her senses were not deceiving her, not really taking in his last statement.

Gilbert smiled, that knowing smile only a father can share with his own flesh and blood, replying with the soothing purr of a parent. 'We are here in spirit as beings of pure emotion, as is the way in Acamuntum: the City of Enlightenment. Our enemies know not of this place, as it does not exist in their world, or ours for that matter, but somewhere in between. As guests here we profit from our hosts protection and the belligerence of their strength.'

'But what of our bodies back in our world; will they not come to harm in our absence?' asked Abby, suddenly fearful for her physical form, her understanding of such things still very limited.

Her father gave her a wink, putting a large hand on her shoulder. 'We are quite safe, my dear. Time has little meaning here; our visit will pass in no more than the blink of an eye and thus it will appear as though we had never left.'

Abby was about to question him further when she noticed the bustle around her was beginning to fade; a darkness was consuming everything around them, until only their forms remained. After a moment lights appeared in the darkness; shimmering orbs in an otherwise pitch-black abyss. Soon tall walls appeared, decorated with fine portraits and intricately carved panelling. A ceiling came into view: a bejewelled landscape of ornate plasterwork with accents of gold leaf and finely painted detail. Then before their eyes furniture appeared: its carving intricate in veneers so thin they were almost transparent, giving them the illusion of being living forms of flesh and blood. As the room gained density a pair of doors opened at the far end and a gaggle of warriors entered, animated in their chatter and reminiscing about their last encounter.

Their conversations came to an abrupt halt at the sight of their sovereign and heir, melting into gestures of welcome and gratitude.

'Sit,' Gilbert ordered so abruptly that even Abby jumped.

The group seated themselves around a large oval table in the centre of the room. Abby took the seat next to her father, proud to be the daughter of such a great man. As she sat, she looked around the table; to her surprise she recognised not only Apollo and Arnold but also Reginald Cockle and Mizer'ak of the Illuminatum. There were many others, of all shapes and sizes, many of whom she did not recognise.

Gilbert stood and the muted conversations stopped. 'Welcome, friends,' he said in the deep, clear voice of authority. 'It is a shame we do not meet under better circumstance, but these are the fortunes in which we find our people and thus we must make do.'

A murmur of agreement rippled through the assembly at these words.

'We find ourselves on the eve of war. A war against those who renounce the old ways and our balance with nature.'

A movement caught Abby's attention. It came from the intricately detailed figure of a woman standing against the wall between equally impressive warrior figures. She was carved from a single piece of rosewood and finished with the most delicate hand.

'Good of you to join us, Emilia,' Gilbert stated, his demeanour that of someone to whom a moving statue was an everyday occurrence. 'Please, take your place.'

She slowly moved across the room, watched by all around the table, and positioned herself adjacent to Arnold, lowering herself into a seated position in an empty gap, settling as if on an invisible chair.

'Forgive me,' continued Gilbert, giving a flourish toward their newest guest. 'For those who have not had the pleasure, this is Queen Emilia of the woodland, regent of the tree people and ruler of all that is green.'

A mumbled welcome resonated throughout the room.

Gilbert cleared his throat and continued his address. The meeting went on for hours, with arguments being thrown from side to side concerning the action that must be taken. Finally an agreement was reached and the meeting adjourned. The outcome was quite simple: the witch had to go.

24
The City of Enlightenment

After a formal meal in a beautiful galleried room adjacent to where they had met, the council bade their farewells and, one by one, faded out of sight. Only Gilbert, Apollo and Arnold remained, relaxing on comfortable cushions and sipping hot beeju nectar. Abby sipped the juice from a small cup that had been presented to her minutes before. Contrary to its pea-green colour and gooey texture, it tasted like a sweet tea and was very refreshing.

Gilbert spoke, his voice softer now that he was safely amongst friends. 'I am pleased to see so many of our subjects have remained loyal. I was concerned that my crimes may have turned our people away.'

Apollo smiled at him, offering a plate of what Abby assumed were biscuits to his regent.

'Your only crime is unfaltering love for your family. If this is a crime then it is shared by many amongst us and understood by all those who are loyal to their true king.'

He offered the plate to Abby, who took it from him gladly.

Apollo, his attention returning to the king, continued, 'The people of Nousidia are behind you, but I am concerned that Belladora has amassed a great army who are well versed in the dark ways, and loyal to her evil vision.'

Gilbert absorbed his comments for a moment of silent contemplation and, once ready, replied, 'The will of a free man protecting his home is stronger even than the blackest of magic. Belladora's army is made from once fine men, women and beasts, twisted by the evils of gluttony and lust to carry out her bidding. They have no passion for their purpose, only greed; and greed does not give a soldier reason.'

He looked at each of his companions in turn, meeting their eyes with his unfaltering stare.

'We are of this land. Our bond with the earth, with all that grows here, the rocks, the water and even the very air we breathe gives us the right to take back what is ours. We will overcome Belladora, and should we pass to the next world in doing so then we will enter in the knowledge that we are free.'

A cheer erupted from Apollo and Arnold upon hearing these words. Even Abby let out a squeal of excitement: this was her father, the true king of Nousidia, expressing such passion. She was so proud to be his daughter.

'Now I wish to spend some time with my daughter,' Gilbert stated once the warriors' shouts had calmed, a smile spreading across his handsome face. 'It has been far too long.'

The two warriors rose, making a low bow in the direction of their king, and faded from view.

'So, my dear,' cooed Gilbert, turning to Abby, a look of pure happiness etched across his face. 'Would you like to take a stroll around the city with your old dad?'

Abby beamed. She was so happy she felt she might burst. 'Could we?' she asked, unsure of what to expect from the city of enlightenment.

Gilbert took her hand, and without another word led her forward and out into the sprawling metropolis that was Acamuntum.

They stepped out onto a wide pavement, father and daughter. The building behind them, like many of their surrounding counterparts, was tall and irregular. The surface was a labyrinth of intertwined layers, like a great oak grown over hundreds of years from a tiny acorn. Abby touched the wall next to her; the smooth coolness of its surface surprised her as the air was humid with the heat of a summer's day. She pulled on the hem of Gilberts jacket, forcing his attention away from the glittering panorama - for every building shone with an iridescence, each a different, subtle shade of white but sufficiently so to enable each building's individuality.

'Why are the buildings so cold?' Abby asked once she had secured his attention.

Gilbert touched the adjacent wall, feeling its texture; the cool, smooth facade had undulating layers with moist condensate globulating over its surface. Unlike the surrounding structures, this was pure white, with no sign of the understated colour the others shared.

'It is stone,' commented a voice from behind them.

They both turned to see Mizer'an, his form solidifying as he approached.

'Good afternoon, Your Highness,' he stated as his face came into focus. 'May I offer you my services as guide during your visit to our city?'

'That would be most pleasant,' replied Gilbert, returning a small bow. 'Have you met my daughter, Abigail?' he added, gesturing towards Abby.

'Very plain, isn't she?' noted Mizer'an, a look of distaste on his face. 'Where is her life glow?'

Abby scowled at him, taking an instant dislike. She would give him something to glow about!

Gilbert placed a hand on her shoulder, his grip firm and adamant that she would not retaliate.

'Abigail has only recently come of age and has therefore yet to develop such intricacies,' he replied for her tactfully. Then before their host had a chance to comment further he enquired, 'How big is this city of yours?'

Mizer'an's face smoothed, placated by his keenness to show the visitors around.

'Acamuntum is only small in comparison to the earthly city that once stood in its place. Its size is limited by the energy required to sustain our protection.'

Gilbert interupted. 'Energy? Is your protection not afforded by magic?'

'It is magic that keeps the city hidden from those who may destroy us, but not the magic that you mortal vessels conjure. We are beings ascended from the material plane and as such cannot derive our energy from nature as we have no physical form. Our energy comes from within each of us, combining through our intertwined consciousness to provide all our needs. Our power is, by simple addition, limited to our numbers.'

'How many of you are there?' Abby asked, taking the chance to participate in the conversation.

Mizer'an looked over to her, his face blank. 'Nine hundred and forty-two souls reside within the city. It has been this way since our ascension.' He returned his attention to Gilbert. 'Shall we commence the tour?' he asked, stepping onto a platform hovering nearby.

Gilbert gave Abby a wink, offering, 'After you my dear' as he gestured towards the hovering podium. She stepped forward, jumping onto the platform, Gilbert following closely behind.

Abby slouched into the nearest chair, its form naturally moulding to her feminine body, exhausted from her day of exploring.

'What an amazing day!' she offered as Gilbert sank into the chair opposite, a fire erupting in the once empty grate. 'The city is beautiful, and the people here are so friendly. Can we not just stay here for the rest of our lives?'

Gilbert gave her a knowing smile. 'If only that were possible, my dear,' he replied, a look of sorrow momentarily crossing his face. 'Unfortunately our time here is limited by that of our flesh and blood. Although time moves slowly in our world during our visit here, it does not stop completely. Our bodies, both yours and mine, are in great peril. Yours from an agent of evil who, even as we speak, holds a blade over your head; and mine that is subject to constant torture at the hands of the woman I used to call sister. This is the world in which we live, and we must both return soon.'

A thoughtful veil covered his face as he contemplated their fate.

'Tomorrow you will begin your training. There is much for you to learn and little time in which to do it. Arnold will oversee this as he is an accomplished warrior and versed in the ways of rock and earth.'

Abby was about to ask what this training would be when a smile spread across her father's face.

'We have a visitor,' he said, suddenly standing, all fatigue dropping from his stature like water flowing from a rock.

The doors opened at the end of the stately room with no sign of whom or what had caused it. Then the figure of a woman came running into sight, her dark hair flowing behind her as if caught in a turbulent wind. Abby sensed her feelings a moment before the sweet smell of jasmine fluttered through her consciousness: this was her mother; she had come to join them.

'Mummy!' she screamed, as she jumped from the chair into her mother's arms. The warmth of her body was welcoming, the sound of her sobbing the sweetest thing she had ever heard. She loosened her grip for a moment, only long enough to allow her father to join them, his strong arms enveloping them both in a ring of paternal protection. They stood for what seemed to Abby like hours; but they were hours of bliss, hours in which they were a loving whole, a family again.

Abby had so many questions, so many thoughts she wished to share with her parents, but none of that mattered now. They sat together, not moving further than within easy reach of each other; not for the fear of parting, as they all understood that was inevitable, but because they had been apart for so long: too long.

The evening passed in quiet conversation, their history taking precedent over the horrors of now. They talked of the old days, when Abby was born and the kingdom was balanced in harmony, of how the Roden guards would play tricks on the human children, teasing them with stories of mythical beasts, and how Abby, even as a babe, had disappeared for hours with the king of the dragons.

This is my real life, Abby thought, basking in the warmth of her newfound memories as they returned full of colour and vitality. The life she had accepted in the human world wilted into the depths of her mind like a bad dream to be forgotten with the waking hours. With this came sleep, not her ordinary, troubled slumber but that of comfort and peace.

25
Training day

Abby woke with a start, her slumber broken by a sudden presence clawing at her mind. She was curled in a ball on a large chair next to a roaring fire, its flame the only light in the dusky room, her parents long gone. Her senses tingled, the hair on the nape of her neck rippling with apprehension. Slowly she opened her eyes, resisting the temptation to move for fear of prematurely alerting her visitor, her body surprisingly aware and alert. She heard, or was it felt, movement from behind the high back of her chair. Fear was rising in her chest with each thud of her heart as it beat against her ribs, but there was also a new sensation: that of confidence and understanding; an understanding that nothing was out of her reach.

Carefully she unwound her gangly limbs from the twist of sleep and reached out to the floor in front. She remembered showing her parents the presents she had received for her birthday the previous evening, including the sword named Salankia that now rested just out of reach. She could see movement across its surface, the scene highlighted by the flickering of the fire. The dragons carved over the handle and sheath of the sword appeared animated, breathing miniature forks of flame into the air.

A footstep sounded, almost invisible on the heavy pile of the carpeted room, pulling her from the wonder that was her sword. She had to act; she had to get her weapon. Her muscles tensed as a rattling breath was exhaled behind her, the fear returning to her young mind. Her heart in her mouth, she sprang forward, pleasantly surprised by the agility of her long limbs. She dropped onto the sword and rolled upright with the precision of an athlete, casting the sheath to one side in a fluid motion.

Her visitor reacted by raising his wand, the bright crimson jewel at its tip glowing with a force not unlike a miniature sun. His eyes, although covered by the long hood of his robes, bore into her very soul: the cold, dead eyes of pure evil. She stepped back, putting distance between them in the vague hope of rescue, shielding her eyes from the intense light. Her foot touched something warm. She instinctively looked down, her eyes focusing on a disk of steel, its decoration a beautiful mass of flying dragons, each breathing tiny flames into the surrounding air.

A bolt of sheer white light sailed over her head as she crouched to collect the shield, slamming into the wall behind her with a shower of fizzing sparks, illuminating the room for a second in an almost comical half-light. She raised the shield, feeling its power flow through her veins like a fresh surge of adrenaline, as a second bolt impacted. The energy dispersed throughout the shield with a roar of anger, licking at the edges with fiery tongues.

Reinforced by her newfound defence, Abby strode forward, slashing out at her attacker with renewed vigour. More by luck than judgement her blade found flesh, cutting her assailant across the chest. He staggered backwards, his hood falling, exposing the wrinkled face of an ancient, the evil in his eyes replaced by fear and longing: the longing for life. As he dropped to his knees Abby's resolve faltered and she lowered her sword; seeing the frail old man cowering at her feet, pleading for his life with those cold, antique eyes, sent a shudder down her spine.

He raised his head, regaining some of his swagger, but remaining kneeling in submission. The fear in those old eyes flickered with the fire of hate as he lunged at her with a blade pulled from within the folds of his robes, putting himself off-balance in his desperation to inflict harm.

Abby swung Salankia in a wide ark, feeling the magic flowing through her arm, the flesh and steel becoming one, and struck true.

The wizened figure stopped mid-strike, his body seizing like a badly maintained engine, the oil finally giving out. His face was a mask of hate frozen in the grimace of death. Then his head simply toppled from his shoulders like a coconut struck by luck in a fairground game, rolling to the carpet in a spreading pool of crimson blood.

Candles burst into life all around the room, spreading into every corner blinding light that dispelled the shadows with its utter brilliance. With it came the sound of worried voices. The doors through which she had laid eyes on her mother only hours before were flung open to be replaced by the heaving bodies of Arnold and Mizer'an.

'Are you okay?' wheezed Arnold, his lungs protesting for air. 'We sensed evil in your presence.'

His eyes slipped from her to the decapitated body lying at her feet and the blood-stained sword in her hand.

'I see you've had a visitor!' he commented, his poise returning. 'And a member of the Order, I see.'

'He attacked me …' Abby began to explain, faltering.

Mizer'an silently strode over to the body, ignoring Abby's protests, and examined the remains with grotesque interest.

'It would seem that even the Order is no longer safe, my furry friend, as this is an elder of Sincerus, one of the highest ranking of their kind.'

He looked closely at the pool of blood surrounding the corpse, sticking a manicured finger in the sticky ooze and placing it gently on his tongue.

'The taste of evil still resides in his blood,' he commented, almost to himself. 'This is Belladora's work. She has achieved that which has concerned us the most: control over those who may decide this war, those who are to be feared above all others.'

Arnold, regaining his composure, stepped to Abby's side. Her body was shaking. The realisation of her deeds toppling through her mind like a ball on the stairs back at home; her old home that was, she reminded herself, as his world was her home now.

An hour later Abby and Arnold strolled through the city towards her first training day. Arnold was explaining that he would not be able to teach her much in the short time they had, but he hoped to get through the basics so she could at least master the simplest of spells. Due to the vast range of abilities available to her, being of royal blood, he had conceded that her training could take years, and beyond even his extensive experience. That would be a task for the scholars at the College of Philosophers.

Abby was only half-listening. Her mind was reeling in shock over that morning's rude awakening and the resultant slaying of the elder: a slaying at her hands. She was struggling with his death; not so much that she had killed him, as it was clear in her mind that she had acted in self-defence, but the fact that she felt no remorse for doing so. This lack of feeling was what really disturbed her.

'… Here we are then, me dear,' Arnold was saying as she returned her attention to him. 'Welcome to the Hall of Justice.'

Abby shot him a quizzical look. 'I thought I was to commence my training, not be put on trial?'

Arnold laughed, his huge, fanged jowls wide in a roar of delight. 'My dear princess,' he said as his laughter subsided, 'in Chunkett society disputes are decided in the arena of battle. Whether it be with sword, paw or magic, opponents release their anger for each other in a battle of wills, the victor being the beast that forces his foe into submission. It is the only place, outside of war that is, where two citizens of Nousidia may legally fight.'

Abby frowned. 'But how can such a fight resolve an argument? Surely the stronger will just overpower his foe and win.'

'Arh yes, that is the secret, my dear. It is our belief that the righteous has the power to triumph over their enemy, if their cause is true. Because of this the rightful winner will always prevail.'

Abby was doubtful that this could work but decided not to press the subject any further. 'So this is where I will do my training; in this arena of justice?'

Arnold smiled. 'It is the only fitting place for such, and will afford us the privacy we must have for your teaching.'

He stepped back and gestured for her to enter.

Abby stepped forward, pushing the carved timber doors inward, to reveal a wide corridor which led to a large open space some distance away. On each side of them were simple timber doors, each closed with a unique symbol inscribed at waist height.

'Where do those doors lead?' Abby quizzed as they made their way along the corridor.

'They, me dear, lead to the stalls; each one to a different level around the arena.' He chuckled to himself. 'You don't want to be getting the wrong door on justice day, no!' His chuckle transformed into a snigger as a memory tickled him from somewhere in the past. 'Each floor is allocated to a different tribe or people. Yer don't want to be finding yourself in with the wrong side, now do yer!'

He laughed out loud now, the roaring guffaw echoing off the chamber's stone walls, amplifying the sound tenfold.

He had calmed by the time they reached the end of the corridor; the sound of his laughter replaced by the clanging of metal on metal as the walkway opened into a vast domed arena. Two beasts were slogging at each other with long broad swords, each looking intent on killing his opponent. Both were bloodied with the wounds of battle but neither was showing any sign of yielding. The battle continued, to and fro, for several minutes, the sounds of the struggle bouncing from the high walls.

Abby looked up to see rows of balconied platforms rising into the heavens above. *It feels like being inside a giant wedding cake*, she thought to herself, allowing a wry smile to form on her face.

Staring out from the many platforms were thousands of shimmering faces, all intent on catching the action. Suddenly a cheer erupted from the glowing mass and Abby's attention was drawn back to the battle below. The larger of the two had faltered, stumbling backwards onto the dusty floor. His opponent immediately took advantage, standing over him with a blood-soaked blade to his throat.

A bell clanged from somewhere high above them and the victor stepped away, offering a hand of friendship to beast he had bettered. The hand taken, they both strode out of the arena without a word.

'Good, eh!' Arnold said, his voice full of cheer. 'Now that's decided we'd better get on; you've got lots to learn in the next few days.'

He stomped off towards the middle of the arena with Abby close behind, trotting to keep up.

'Right then, me dear,' he said, coming to a sudden stop and turning to face her. 'We'll start with some simple stuff and see how yer get on.'

He unsheathed his sword and, without warning, lunged directly at her throat. Abby jumped back in surprise at the sudden movement, her hand instinctively reaching for the blade at her side. She fumbled at her belt, grasping only air where the sword should have been.

'It-it's gone!' she stammered as she looked down to her side, panic rising in her throat. 'Salankia is gone!'

Arnold roared with laughter, the sound echoing through the now empty balconies.

Abby threw him a hateful stare. 'What are you laughing at?' she demanded, feeling anger flowing through her veins. 'And how did you get my sword?'

Arnold shrugged. 'A simple beckoning spell, me dear, that's all.' He stepped to her and handed over the sword with a flourish. 'Very easy if you know a being's true name, as I do in this case.'

Abby looked down at the sword in her hands. 'So if I knew the name of your sword I could take it without you knowing?' she guessed.

'As with any item, or person for that matter, if you know the true name in their heart,' he replied, a look of amusement etched on his face.

'So how do I find out what something's true name is?' she asked, seeing how this could be a great advantage.

'That, me dear, is not so simple,' Arnold replied, giving her a wink, 'as only that with which you have gained trust will give you the name in its heart. Without such, my example is meaningless.' He stepped back and drew his sword once again. 'Now draw your sword and prepare for battle!'

For three days they toiled. Abby learnt the art of swordsmanship and, although she could never beat her tutor, gained a surprising level of skill and confidence. Salankia responded to her every whim, sometimes even before she knew what that was. She also gained an understanding of the magic that coursed through her veins, although only at a rudimentary level, and began to experiment with more confidence, even succeeding in a few simple incantations. But most of all she learnt to fight, and fight dirty. This was an art form in which she excelled, much to the amusement of Arnold, as she constantly surprised him with increasingly more inventive methods of breaking through his defences.

At the end of the third day, as the glow from the sky above began to dim, Arnold and Abby were making their way home through the quiet streets of Acamuntum. Arnold was congratulating his young apprentice on the progress she had made, his expression that of sheer pride.

'I have enjoyed the last few days,' Abby said, a smile of happiness bringing a glow of joy to her face.

As they walked the pair passed a shop window, the glass polished to a mirror shine, a motionless figure standing in the display almost hidden by the reflection. It was this reflection that stopped Abby on the spot: before her was the sight of Arnold in all his grandeur and next to him a young woman she barely recognised as herself. Her muscles had firmed with the punishment of recent days but also appeared to have matured into those of a young woman. Her face had lost its babyish plumpness in favour of a chiselled beauty, her high cheek bones somehow even more prominent. Even her hair had darkened to burnt amber, the long strands arrow straight with the glossy finish of morning dew.

But none of this was what had caught her eye, as the most extraordinary sight was that of a soft glow radiating from her face. It softened her features, giving her an almost angelic appearance. She raised her hands to see that they too were softly glowing as she twisting them to test for tricks of the light.

'What is happening to me?' she asked, turning towards Arnold. 'Why is my face glowing?'

Arnold's smile was becoming that of a Cheshire cat, the pride in his eyes swelling to the point of bursting.

'That, me dear, is your life glow,' he said, his voice full of emotion. 'Your transformation is complete: you have reached womanhood.'

A noise disturbed them from the right, a crack like the snapping of a whip. Abby's senses tingled as a figure appeared from within a doorway some distance along the empty street. His robes fluttered in a breeze conjured from the still air, the dusky light deepening as the very air around them seemed to thicken. Arnold stepped between his charge and their visitor, his bulk obscuring all sight of the mysterious hooded figure.

'I can help you,' whispered Abby as she tried to edge around the bulk of muscle in front of her.

Arnold sidestepped, keeping his body between them.

'No need,' he replied, 'there is only one.'

Abby felt the hilt of her sword move in her hand, the heat of the tiny flames against her skin. She looked down to see the movement of the dragons engraved into the handle, their flames igniting the darkening air as they writhed in their dance of warning. She wished she had brought its brother; the shield would have come in handy right now.

Arnold sprang forward, his massive leg muscles launching him into the air towards their foe. Abby caught sight of the hooded figure as it pounced into the air to meet him, unsheathing a long blade as it rose. They met with a clang of steel and the fizz of sparks as the blades clashed, the bodies returning to the ground with an earth-shuddering thud.

Abby stood and watched, in awe at the sight: the two warriors sparing with such ferocity that each blow looked to be fatal. Although the battle was a vicious trade of blows and parries, Abby could not help but notice the grace in their movements, as if this battle was a ceremonial dance in which only one would survive.

A movement caught her attention, a flash of colour in the corner of her eye, a movement that seemed unnatural even in this wondrous city. She ignored it, giving her full attention to the warriors ahead.

'Ouch!' she screamed, subconsciously putting her hand in her mouth to quell the burning sensation.

Feeling no heat she looked at the offending limb but there were no burns or even a residual heat, just her pale, wet fingers. She looked down at the hilt of her sword and saw the reason for the strange sensation. The dragons swimming about the handle were blowing blue flames with such intensity that they appeared almost as one.

'What?' she questioned as she watched the flame, the battle crashing in front of her forgotten for a moment. 'What are you trying to tell me?'

At that moment she saw - or was it sensed; she couldn't be sure - a movement in a doorway opposite the battling warriors. This time she had no doubt someone was hiding in the shadows. She edged around the ongoing battle, unnoticed in the heat of war, towards the opening, drawing Salankia from her writhing sheath.

It was the eyes she saw first: blood red with the intensity of rubies as they glittered in the reflected light. Then it was upon her, sword slashing down in its deadly arc, its target her exposed forehead. Abby instinctively raised her sword to block, taking the blow head on, the shock vibrating through her arm like an earthquake. She had no time to parry as the next blow rained down on her with frightening speed. She stepped back, trying to make space to think, trying to form logical thoughts. Another blow; she stumbled backwards into a wall. And another. She was trapped. Desperately she glanced towards Arnold, willing him to save her, but he remained locked in battle with his foe. It was up to her: she fought, or she died. As if on command her mind began to clear, one thought pushing its way through the mist of confusion: *PUSH*. She focused on the word, feeling energy cascade through her, and then released it.

To her surprise the barrage of blows stopped. She realised that she had closed her eyes, and gingerly opened them to see her attacker lying on his back some distance away. With renewed confidence she jumped up and strode over to him, raising her sword as she covered the distance between them. She stopped several paces from her assailant as he raised himself to full height, standing equal to her.

Then suddenly he attacked, thrusting a blow aimed at her belly. Abby stepped to the left in a flurry of cloak and hair, landing a blow to her attacker's side. He stumbled but regained his footing at a safe distance, the blood-soaked wound vanishing before her eyes. A manic smile festered on the swordsman's face as he watched her for a heartbeat, analysing her reaction to his ability to heal, and then he was attacking again.

Abby blocked the first blow, parrying with a low cut to the legs. Her opponent was swift and cut the attack dead, replying with an upper thrust at her exposed jaw. Abby jerked back at the last moment, receiving a nick on her chin for her lapse. The swordsman lunged down, driving his blade directly toward her heart. Without thought Abby jumped up and back, performing a perfect loop, landing, slightly wobbly, five paces away.

The swordsman howled and ran forward, lunging with the madness of a lunatic towards her. She faked movement to her left, attracting his attention, and then quickly stepped to the right, bringing Salankia to shoulder height in one fluid movement.

Anger turned to fear in her attacker's eyes as he tried to halt his charge, twisting his body in an unnatural pose to avoid the shining blade. Those terrifying eyes glazed blankly as the steel of Abby's blade sliced into his throat like a hot knife through butter, a spray of crimson blood splashing across her face. His body fell to the ground losing integrity with the movement, its solidness becoming hazy until finally transparent, his form merely an outline. Then, with a barely audible pop, he was gone.

Abby's knees buckled and she sank to the floor. All strength left her aching body with the relief that it was over. Her head sank into her hands, the sword discarded on the ground, tears pouring unchecked from her eyes. She felt movement nearby but was too weak to react, happy to just sit and weep.

'Yer showed him, lass.' said a voice from above her. 'Though he'll be back, of that I can assure you. Come on, let's get you home while there's still light.'

She felt a heavy-set arm hook under her waist and allowed herself to be hoisted to her feet. Only then did she raise her eyes to see Arnold, glittering in the half-light, through her tears, a weary smile etched on his face.

'Come now, deary, let's get you home,' he said, his voice underlined with the soft purr of a feline. 'It's been a long day.'

They turned to continue their journey, Arnold swinging a huge arm around her shoulders in an affectionate hug. Then suddenly Abby's legs gave way. Her vision faded into a black abyss, the brightness of the city extinguished in an instant.

Her final memory was that of the horror on her companion's face.

26
Memories of youth

Abby's eyes snapped open. The confusion of battle filled her ears, the smell of death pungent in her nostrils. Her vision cleared and her focus sharpened on the blade that swept towards her, its blood-clotted steel threatening her very existence. Without thinking she dropped onto her back, the blade passing only inches from its target. From this position she could make out her attacker, his robes hanging loosely from his skeletal frame, wet with glistening blood. She took in the ancient lines on his face, the dull redness in his staring eyes and the surgical slash across his throat through which dribbled the source of his discomfort. He let out a gargled scream, the opening in his throat bubbling with fresh gore, as he staggered toward his prey.

Abby waited, as time slowed with every heartbeat, her mind screaming for understanding: where were the bright lights of the city, where were her companions, where were her protectors?

The figure was standing over her, spraying spittle and blood in her face. She had to think quickly, she had to remember the training Arnold had forced into her. In desperation she raised her leg, driving it into the folds between her attacker's legs, contacting with the soft flesh.

He stopped in an instant, a look of terrible pain overcoming the hate in his features, his blade falling from limp fingers, and then he collapsed onto her.

Abby screamed. The stench of blood and stale sweat poured into her lungs like a river of sorrow, the lifeless body pinning her to the sodden ground. Her mind began to race, desperate thoughts cascading through her mind like a stampede of angry bulls to a red flag. The thoughts turned to memories of the life she knew and the one she had lived but could not recall. The images spun in a frenzied cyclone of colours and sounds, blurring into a thriving mass as they crashed through her consciousness and into oblivion.

She tried to scream again but the air was trapped in her lungs, held by the dead weight crushing her chest. Through the mass of colours she spotted a glowing figure standing calmly amongst the chaos enveloping them.

The weight lessoned slightly on her chest, allowing precious air into her desperate lungs, but remained pinning her limbs. Darkness clouded her vision as her mind retreated into the safety of her inner core, protecting her true self from the evil surrounding her physical form. As she passed into unconsciousness she dreamt, or was it felt, strong arms lifting her, dragging her lifeless body towards a shining light.

Is this it? she questioned in her mind. *Is this the end of life?* Then all thoughts left her.

Warmth soothed her limbs as feeling returned to them, her mind cautiously ebbing back to reality, sense by sense. She could smell the embers burning in a nearby fire; hear the cracking of the flames as they consumed their fuel. She tentatively opened her eyes, unsure what would meet them. She was inside; the room was dark, the only light coming from the fire she had sensed moments before.

A soft murmur reached her ears from somewhere out of sight, the sound rhythmic, an occasional grunt whinnying from the hidden source. She raised her head, searching for the owner, her eyes becoming accustomed to the duskiness of the room. She spotted a figure slumped over the back of a chair, its robes dishevelled in sleep.

Her mind jumped, the memory of the battle returning. The recognition of a robed figure burnt into her mind's eye. Her heart began to flutter.

Had those who wished her harm captured her?

She raised herself into a sitting position. Her tunic was gone, her robes moist with the sweat of fever, her throat parched and in need of liquid.

'Water,' she croaked, the dryness more apparent as she spoke.

The robed figure gave a quiet grunt as it awakened, shifting slightly on its makeshift bed. The figure stood, the stoop of old age evident in its stature, and took a step towards her, the dim light of the room masking any detail of its features. Another step forward. Abby could hear laboured breathing rattling in ancient lungs. Another step and the light of the fire illuminated emerald robes, a crest embossed into the material that Abby recognised from the battle. Then one final step and into the light the figure moved, head bowed, long grey hair hanging loosely about its face. Then slowly, like time itself, the figure raised its head, brushing the loose tendrils of hair from its features with the crooked fingers of a withered hand.

It was Tom.

Relief washed over Abby like a spring waterfall, the tension in her muscles releasing at the sight of her trusted friend, the heart beating hard against her ribs slowing to a less frantic rhythm.

'Tom!' she squeaked, jumping up to hug him, all fatigue forgotten in her delight at seeing him. 'What happened?' she questioned, the memories of recent events clouded in her mind. 'I remember being suddenly back in the battle and that horrible man falling on me …' She squirmed at the thought of this encounter. '… And then nothing, until now.'

The lines on Tom's face rearranged into a smile and the fire in his eyes returned to an iridescent glow. 'Calm yourself, my dear,' he said, his voice soft and relaxed. 'You are safe now.'

He returned to his chair, manoeuvring it so it faced her, and sat with apparent difficulty. 'You have been through a traumatic series of events, my dear,' he said once he was comfortable, 'and I have to admit you had us a little worried.'

Abby chuckled at this. 'You were worried!' she laughed. 'You weren't being attacked by some crazed old man!'

Tom's face straightened, the humour vanishing like smoke in the wind. 'The warrior who attacked you was a member of the Order of Sincerus. A group of which I count myself a part.'

Abby stepped backwards, an involuntary response to this unexpected revelation but one that signalled her discomfort with his statement.

'But he tried to kill me!' she mumbled, suddenly unsure of her safety. 'Before in the city, and then again in battle.'

Her head was spinning as memories poured into her mind: the attack in the city as she walked with Arnold, and then her sudden return to the battle in the hills of Acamuntum.

Tom's smile returned, although it was underlined with fear. 'He was a good man, consumed by the temptations of evil and greed. Many have succumbed to the empty promises of the witch Belladora, and many have fallen because of it.'

His face darkened, his eyes glowing with the ferocity of a bush fire in the heat of the summer sun. 'I will get revenge for my fallen brethren!' he stated, and then, just as quickly, he returned to the mild Tom she had always known.

Abby's head hurt. She lay back down, resting her tired limbs on the soft mattress, feeling the comfort envelop her.

'Has your memory returned?' she asked into the darkness, her eyes closed.

She heard Tom shift as he answered in the affirmative.

'What do you remember? Have you recalled who you are?' she asked, hungry for understanding.

'My name is Thomas de Capolea,' he stated in a very formal tone. 'Grand master of the Order of Sincerus, and …'

He broke off, a silence filling the space between them. They could have been miles, or even centuries, apart at that moment, for their link, their friendship of old, was at the brink of failure. Abby had never felt so alone; emptiness was creeping into her heart, filling the space in which Tom had always resided.

'No!' Abby screamed, jumping into Tom's waiting arms. 'My heart cannot accept what my ears are telling me. You cannot be part of the evil that sours our home.'

Tom smoothed her ruffled hair, his calming influence, although weakened by recent revelations, remained potent and Abby could feel her fear melting like the snow on a spring morning.

Tom released her and, holding her at arm's length, looked into her watery eyes.

'I make no excuses for my past or the acts of my people over these recent centuries, but ask for understanding, given our life together, of the changes I have made and the sacrifices given in the name of love. For I do love you with all my heart, dearest Abigail, and for that I would change the world.'

His eyes lowered to the frail hands with which he held her.

'This is merely a transition, my dear, for your love reciprocated unconditionally will return me to youth and we can be together – forever.'

Abby broke from his grasp, turning away to hide the fresh tears spilling from her eyes.

'I-I don't know,' she stammered. 'This is a lot to take in.'

Tom gingerly took a step toward her and then thought better of it when he saw the look that flashed over Abby's face.

'Do you not feel our connection?' he questioned, his voice low and hopeful. 'Do you not love me?'

Abby raised her head, looking her lifelong friend in the eye. 'Of course I love you, but things are complicated right now and I can't think straight!'

Tom moved forward in a vain attempt to hug her but she shrugged him off with a twist of her body, turning to face a mossy wall.

'I need time,' she whispered, her voice no more than a shallow breath.

Moments passed as silence once more took over the space between them. Abby could not bear it any longer; she spun round to face the love of her life, to face the uncertainty his love would bring, but she was met by an empty space, the only evidence of Tom's presence a wisp of crimson smoke drifting on an invisible breeze. He had gone.

27
The eye of Zeut

The stone room was cold and dank. Wisps of shadow danced about the walls in the jig of wintery death. The sun had sunk below the horizon, giving way to the cold of the night and bringing with it a deep, penetrating frost that even the hardiest of creatures could not survive.

This was Belladora's time; this was winter.

She sat stooped over a ball of clear glass, an image fading away within its depths. She had witnessed the battle at the base of the mountain of Acamathious, revelled in the suffering she had caused by her actions. She, and she alone, had influenced the weak minds of men; she had corrupted their thoughts, driven them to kill. But the battle had not gone as planned. They had not slaughtered the Gordorian or the Chunkett that protected her niece, and now even she had eluded them. She needed her sacrifice, and time was running short.

There was a tentative knock at the door.

'Enter!' Belladora screamed, furious at being disturbed from her thoughts.

The door creaked open to reveal her handmaiden. She sheepishly scuttled forward holding out a bird of prey, its wing broken, the bird crying out in pain.

'What do you want me to do with that?' Belladora spat in disgust. 'Let it die like the others.'

The handmaiden stood her ground, shaking. 'B-but it is your trusted advisor, my queen. It is Eleanora,' she stuttered.

Belladora looked down at the broken bird. Its wing was twisted at an irregular angle.

'So be it,' she spat, her tone uninterested. 'Put the retched thing on the table.'

The maid carefully placed the bird on the table and backed away into a corner.

Belladora ignored the slave and placed a rough hand on the bird's wing. It let out a cry of pain as her touch inflamed the agony. She mumbled a phase of incoherent words and snapped the wing back into shape.

Immediately the bird sprang onto its claws, flapping its newly mended wing to test it.

'Show your true form,' demanded Belladora as she flopped into a nearby chair.

Obediently the bird transformed into the form of her royal advisor, Eleanora, her lank, dark hair hanging over the bulge at her shoulders.

'You have served me well as a spy,' stated Belladora. 'But now I have a new task for you. I wish you to infiltrate the hallowed halls of the College of Philosophers and bring me my niece. This you must do before the rising of the new moon.'

Eleanora raised her eyes, full of sorrow and remorse. 'Yes my queen. I will do as you command as I am bound by my oath.'

Belladora let out a cackle. 'Yes, you will, my young slave. Yes, you will.' Hobbling back to the desk with the clear glass ball, she turned her back on the young girl. 'Leave me now,' she barked.

Once she was alone again she sat and stroked a crooked hand across the surface of the glass, mumbling, 'Show me the girl, oh eye of Zeut.'

28
Sun, moon and stars

Abby stumbled from the ramshackle hut, its door yielding with a sharp kick. The air was thick with smoke, surrounding the village in a spectral veil of grey. She choked on the thick air as it sank into her lungs, the flesh of her organs rejecting the contaminated molecules, causing her to cough. She could make out shadowy forms moving slowly in the hazy cloud surrounding her. One of the forms stopped, pointed in her direction and spirited towards her. Abby took a step back towards the shelter of the hut, feeling the splintering timber of its frame in the small of her back.

The figure emerged from its cloudy cover, the uniform instantly recognisable as that of her companion and friend Apollo. She squealed with happiness and jumped forward into his waiting arms, tears of joy flowing from her reddened eyes. Her heart felt as light as a feather as it floated about her cavernous chest, dispelling the darkness and fear that had befuddled her. She was safe now: held in the arms of her faithful protector.

'Where have you been, my princess? We have been searching for hours,' he questioned, concern rather than scolding sounding in his voice.

Abby released him to see Arnold had joined them. She gave him a hug and then began describing the events since she had last seen them, careful not to miss any detail. Her companions stood in silence, taking in every word as if their very existence depended on it. Once finished she stood quietly, fidgeting with the toggle of her robe, while her companions deliberated on these latest events.

Finally Arnold turned to face her and, with a flash of his pearly white fangs, said, 'It is time for us to return home, my dear, back to Ravensburn.' His face melted into the feline smile she loved so much. 'We can protect you better there, and you have lessons to attend.'

He strolled off towards the hut from which Abby had emerged and returned shortly after with a small, tatty bag; it was her makeshift rucksack.

'I believe these are yours,' Arnold said as he handed her the sack.

Abby took it and looked inside, a smile spreading across her face as she could see the things she had come to hold dear. She pulled out her tunic, glad for the comforting warmth it offered against the stiffening chill in the air, and shrugged it on.

'Best get a move on then, Princess,' Arnold suggested as he padded towards the edge of the circle of huts. 'Well, come on! We've got much ground to cover before dark.'

Apollo shot her a wink and fell in behind his brother, with Abby following closely behind.

After two days of walking Abby was glad to see the bed in her room at the College of Philosophers. They had travelled through the day, staying with Simok's widow that night. Apollo had explained how her husband had died in the service of the one true king and that he had met his end in this world with honour. She had taken the news well, in the circumstances, commenting that she would look forward to seeing him in the next world. They had started their journey early the next morning with full packs and glowing bellies and had continued all day until they reached the familiar structures of Ravensburn and the city they now called home.

A hot bath and good night's sleep had done Abby the world of good. She was busying herself with the long threads of her auburn hair and remembering the reunion with her parents in the City of Enlightenment when there was a loud rap on the door.

Lazily she mumbled 'Come in' and continued with her hair.

The sight that met her when she turned to greet her visitor was not what she had expected. In place of the usual footman, or one of the many townsfolk who had taken to visiting her, she saw what appeared to be a squirrel. It sat in the doorway, its nose twitching rapidly, waiting, she assumed, for her to speak.

'Good morning,' she offered in what she hoped was a confident tone.

Her visitor sat still, watching her with dark eyes, its scarlet coat bristling as if in anticipation of her next move, a long, fluffy tail swaying slightly in an unseen draft. Abby stepped forward, noticing, as she got closer, that her visitor had an envelope in its tiny claws.

'Is that for me?' she asked tentatively.

The squirrel rocked back on its hind legs, presenting the envelope with a flourish.

Abby could see now that it was wearing a miniature waistcoat with the letters 'RSVP' embroidered on the breast. She was about to ask what this stood for when a voice spoke from the doorway.

'Red Squirrel Virtual Post. You'll need a nut!'

Abby spun around to come face to face with an auburn-haired girl. She recognised her as the one who had welcomed them when they had first arrived at the College of Philosophers.

'Oh, hi,' Abby stuttered in an effort to cover her surprise. 'I don't have any nuts, I'm afraid.'

The girl smiled and produced a monkey nut from within the hem of her dress, handing it to the patiently waiting squirrel.

'I'm Emily,' stated the girl, giving a small curtsey.

Abby regained some of her poise and replied, 'Good morning, Emily. How are you?'

Emily smiled, a flush of red flashing through her cheeks. 'I am well, thank you, Princess.' Giving another dip.

'You know who I am?' Abby quizzed, a thought rushing through her head: *I thought my presence was a secret.*

'Yes, Princess, those of us who had the pleasure of being in your presence when you were a babe recognised you immediately. But don't worry: we are few and all loyal to your family.'

Abby gave her a smile, although she doubted it showed much conviction. 'How did we meet? You know - before.'

A quiet cough halted their reunion; it was the messenger, its dark eyes watching their movements with impassive patience. Without further notice it opened the little envelope and removed a folded scrap of paper, reading its content in a clear, if squeaky, voice.

'*Dear Abigail,*' it began. '*You are late for class. Hurry up now!*' The messenger gave a toothy smile. '*Yours, Bumblebot,*' it finished, giving a subtle bow and producing a pencil from the satchel at its waist.

Abby opened her mouth in awe and, once her voice came back, asked, 'What class?'

The squirrel began to scribble.

Emily turned to her, a smile etched on her pretty face.

'Today is the first day of classes. The term was delayed pending your return from your quest. Now you are back we have some catching up to do!'

The squirrel continued to copy their conversation, rapidly scratching at the tiny paper.

Emily giggled, informing the messenger that there was no reply and passing him another nut, while Abby fumbled around her room looking for her books, quill and parchment. Eventually she found them and the two girls ran off to class.

The courtyard was buzzing with excited students: a body of matching youth in their uniform of black robes over white tunics. Abby gazed at the thronging mass of bodies, the scene reminding her of a great school of fish meandering back and forth in the expanse of a river, their chatter like that of a thousand crickets.

With a rumble an aperture formed in the far wall of the courtyard. The bricks rearranged themselves into a smooth archway and a solid wooden door appeared within the opening. The crowd ceased their movement immediately, silence spreading like wildfire throughout. Each of the students stood to attention, facing the newly formed doorway in anticipation of who, or what, was about to emerge. The door slowly opened, its ancient hinges creaking under the toil of their work, a dark void filling the space it left.

A sense of anticipation was building, its gravity so intense Abby could feel the hair on her slender arms prickling, then out of the gloom stepped Professor Quirk. He was dressed in the traditional black robe and white tunic, but with the addition of a red sash tied in the most intricate fashion around his waist. This, Abby was about to learn, was the mark of an educator.

'Welcome to the College of Philosophers,' he called as he stepped into the cool, wintery sun, beckoning them all to enter.

They crossed into the voluminous hall in pairs, forming a line dissecting along its centre. Abby stood with Emily, who was also new to classes. She had discovered that she too had commenced her quickening only days before their arrival in Ravensburn and they shared many of the intricacies of becoming a woman overnight. They had become the best of friends in an instant and talked constantly. Stepping over the threshold in unison, they joined the many gasps of wonder at the sight that met their eyes upon entering the great hall.

The vast room was in the form of a cylinder, like standing at the base of a gigantic tin can. Its walls were covered in intricately carved oak panels and recesses along their length contained life-like statues. Abby squinted in the low light; thousands of candles dotted around the hall battled against the enveloping darkness. She discovered that what she had mistaken for carvings were in fact a mass of names scrawled into the soft timber, each clear in their definition but in such tight configuration as to form a script like the text of a giant book. At either side of the central avenue in which they stood was a circular table, the division forming a pair of symmetrical crescents with benches along their circumference.

'History's great educators,' Emily whispered in Abby's ear, nodding to the statues. 'I hope to join them one day,' she added, a glaze of proud admiration on her pretty face.

At the far end of the room, in a covered alcove, sat a smaller, curved table with five grand chairs; it faced the assembled students, sitting slightly elevated from the rest. At this table stood five black-and-white-clad figures, each with the telltale red sash around their waist. Abby marvelled at the intricacy of each sash, as each was as individual as its owner and thus unique.

Flanking this table were two statues, their slender, cat-like bodies reaching up into the lofty heights of the ceiling. Each held a shimmering orb high above their head: on the left was a shining, golden sun and on the right, a silvery moon.

Abby's thoughts were interrupted by a sharp jab to her ribs. She looked over to see Emily's excited face, a slender finger pointing to the heavens. Looking up, her eyes were met by the most wondrous sight yet. The rafters were filled with twinkling stars, celestial forms of such magnitude and number that Abby found it difficult to take them all in. She recognised the twelve bodies of the zodiac from her studies back in the human world, but they were surrounded by many more of infinite complexity.

This, however, was not what made her gasp. Each of these formations was animated, slowly and deliberately moving about the night sky; but it was more than that, these forms appeared to be interacting, like living beings. She watched as a shape she recognised as the Great Bear padded over to a form that resembled a large bird, which, to her amusement, took a swipe at it with one shining claw.

A ripple of giggles passed over the assembled crowd, confirming that every face was upturned, sharing in this celestial pantomime.

'Welcome to the great hall,' a voice boomed over the assembled crowd, abruptly ending the moment. It was the purposeful voice of Professor Quirk who was standing at the centre of the top table. 'In a moment the testing ceremony will commence, but first I have the pleasure of introducing your educators.' He gestured to his left. 'To my far left is Professor Roughious Miles, a specialist in universal science. Next we have Professor Timothy Bumblebot who educates us all in the intricacies of the human world.'

A quiet giggle passed though the crowd under covered mouths.

Professor Quirk paused a moment, letting the students settle, before continuing.

'To my far right we have Professor Ugier Tintwhistle: history and species. And last, but certainly not least, Professor Eleanora Snakeskin who will show you how to use your natural talents.'

A murmur spread across the room like the low rumble of thunder.

Emily leaned over to Abby's ear and whispered, 'It is said that Snakeskin has a passion for the dark arts, even that she's suspected of being a member of the Order.'

'The Order of Sincerus?' Abby questioned, her senses suddenly alert.

Emily looked at her quizzically. 'Do you know about the Order?'

Abby realised she had said to much and fumbled an excuse, saying she must have heard the name somewhere.

'So what is this testing ceremony then?' she asked, desperate to change the subject.

Emily smiled, taking on an air of knowledge. 'All students are tested as to their particular aptitude. Everyone in our world has a focus toward either light or dark; neither is considered good or bad as a mixture of both is required to bring balance to nature. It is merely a tool with which to guide our education. We will then be sorted into either the school of the sun or of the moon.' She pointed across the room. 'Look, it's starting.'

Up ahead, at the tip of the line, a pair of scarlet squirrels appeared from a recess in the upper level and began hopping from head to head. After the squirrels' visit each student took a seat at one of the benches, some to the left and some to the right. As they came closer Abby could feel a swelling of emotion building in the pit of her stomach; she knew this moment would be pivotal in the path of her life, a moment so brief that would decide her true course. The scarlet rodents hopped closer and closer until finally one landed softly on Abby's head. It rapped lightly on her temple, a touch so light she barely felt it, and then a squeaky voice sounded clearly in her mind.

'Sun.'

A feeling of relief washed though her body like a warm shower after a long day. She did not know why but she knew this was the right choice. She dutifully took her place on the benches to the left, under the gaze of the sun statue. Emily joined her moments later, smiling from ear to ear.

The testing continued until both tables were lined with chattering students.

The thud of a staff on the marble floor brought the room back to silence, every face pointing in the direction of Professor Quirk, who was now standing at the head of the divide.

'Now the testing is completed,' he boomed into the room, 'and you have become part of your respective house. This house will be your family for the duration of your quickening and as such will mould your very existence. But remember this: your future is not set like the history of our lands. We can guide you, but it is your decisions that will ultimately steer the course of your life, in this world and the next.'

He paused for a moment, dramatically underlining the potency of his words.

'For those of you who graduate an illustrious future awaits, but this will require great skill and hard work.'

His eyes flicked momentarily to a boy three seats down, his conversation stopping immediately.

'But less of this seriousness; it is time to celebrate.'

With these words resonating in her ears Abby witnessed the most sumptuous meal appear before them, deposited by a seemingly continuous line of black-clad dwarves. Fine plates of the best tasting meats, sweet vegetables and soft fruits imaginable, followed by enormous helpings of apple pie with lashings of creamy custard.

If this is college life, Abby thought, *I like it!*

29
Macbeth

Abby's first week at the College of Philosophers was full of wonder. She had classes on mythical beasts, some of which she had heard of in fairy tales and some so mind-blowing she could barely comprehend their existence; classes in the wonders of the universe and how the stars guided all life; and hilarious classes in human studies with the very posh Professor Bumblebot in which Abby had to be very careful not to correct some of his more extravagant theories on the evolution of the human race, But most of all she loved her classes with Professor Snakeskin, who, despite her prickly demeanour, was fascinating to watch as she conjured candlesticks from thin air and taught her class the fundamentals of natural magic.

At the request of their parents she had taken to hiding the two oldest Poggle children, William and Victoria, within her robes and taking them to class. They provided welcome warmth in the drafty classrooms and gave the children the benefit of an education not normally available to them. Emily had become her constant companion and Abby had come to value their friendship immensely.

Her evenings were spent in training with Arnold and Apollo, both patiently teaching her skills in swordplay and single combat. But the part she most enjoyed was her training as a Majikalt. Her skills in the art of natural magic had grown so rapidly that sometimes she even felt her tutors might be having trouble keeping up. Her only disappointment was that, since their reunion in the City of Enlightenment, she had not been able to contact either her mother or father; and although her companions assured her that they were fine, her senses told her different. Such a feeling was hard to ignore.

Late on the fifth day Abby was sitting at her bedroom window thinking about her parents - how could she contact them and why hadn't they visited her? – when a commotion outside caught her attention. She looked down to see two men tussling with a beautiful white horse, but this was no ordinary horse as it had a small horn protruding from its forehead: it was a unicorn. Abby jumped down from the windowsill, excitement buzzing through her head like a swarm of bees in the rush of spring. Pulling on her tunic, she ran down into the courtyard, all instructions to stay indoors forgotten.

Upon seeing her, the unicorn broke free of its capturers and trotted over to her side. 'On you get princess,' it said in a surprisingly clear, deep voice as it bent low to allow Abby to climb on its back.

Ignoring her uncertainty over just how friendly a unicorn may be, Abby decided to trust her instincts and go with the beast. She wished they had got to unicorns in their history and species class instead of spending a full afternoon learning how to identify snail droppings; old Tintwhistle didn't half go on!

'Hold on!' snorted the unicorn, jumping into a gallop across the courtyard and through the opening between two leaning buildings, the shouts of the pursuing men fading rapidly as they accelerated away. The gallop continued until they reached the outskirts of the city, but as the buildings petered out the unicorn slowed to a trot, eventually stopping by a small stream, taking in the refreshing water.

Abby took the opportunity to jump down from the beast's back. She walked to its handsome head asked where they were going.

The unicorn raised its head from drinking, splashing her with cool water and looking her directly in the eye. 'Please excuse my manners, dear princess,' it said, its voice raspy after the long gallop out of the city. 'My name is Rufus Macbeth, and yes, I am a unicorn. I believe you have already met my soul partner, Kyi.'

Abby remembered the majestic Minatox. She took in Rufus's muscular features, the long mane and tail and the small, but perfectly formed, twist of horn on his forehead: they made a good match.

'Hello, Rufus,' Abby stated, her tone formal as she had been taught when greeting her subjects. 'Where are you taking me?'

'Your mother wishes to speak with you, Princess,' Rufus confirmed, bowing his head and pawing a rock with his hoof. 'Something at the college is blocking her presence. She asked me, as a loyal subject and good friend, to bring you to her.'

Abby was confused. *The college is supposed to be safe from my aunt's influence*, she thought. 'So where are we going then?' she persisted.

Rufus raised his head, again looking her in the eye. 'To the Chamber of Souls, my dear. But such a journey is full of danger as the witch's Sears are scouring the area for supporters of your father. We had better get moving if we are going to arrive before the chill of winter sets in.'

Abby remounted and held on tightly as the unicorn spurred onwards.

After several hours of galloping though forest and dale alike, they crashed through a wall of foliage into a familiar clearing. Except this was not how Abby remembered it. The flowers that had once been in such abundance about the garden were now no more than petals spread over the lawn like discarded confetti. The avenue leading to the chamber's door, once lined with beautiful roses, was now marked by the remains of burnt trunks, their splendour reduced to that of spent matches.

Abby jumped from her mount. Ignoring the tingling in her legs as the blood returned to her long limbs, she ran to the chamber's entrance. As she reached it she saw that the door hung open on broken hinges, the deep blackness of the chamber obscuring what lay beyond. A pang of fear exploded in Abby's stomach; not only the dread of what lay in wait for her within these walls but a foreboding about the safety of her uncle Tyrillious, caretaker of these chambers.

She stepped over the threshold, the oppressive frostiness of the stone chamber chilling her instantly. She waited for a moment, hoping the familiar candlelight would ignite to show her the way. After several long seconds she remained in total darkness, resolved to the fact no light was coming. She took a tentative step forward, reaching into the folds of her tunic for her wand.

'Luminous,' she murmured, afraid of what she might disturb.

The gem of her wand emitted a soft glow, bathing the room in an eerie half-light. She could see people-shaped mounds scattered about the marble floor, and feared the worst. With her heart in her mouth she visited each of the bodies, confirming that none were her uncle, before heading towards the faint glow at the far door. She carefully stepped into the room, feeling for the presence of evil, her senses tingling with apprehension; but all she could sense was the residual stench of death.

Pushing the door open on its wide arc, she was met by the soft glow of candlelight. Her uncle was sitting on a chair in the middle of the room, his back to her. Abby squealed in delight and ran to his side, but something was wrong: her uncle did not move. As she reached him she noticed the pool of blood forming at the base of the chair, the vacant look on her uncle's face.

'No!' she screamed, the sound bouncing about the stone-clad room as she reached for her uncle's bearded face. 'This cannot be,' she sobbed as the tears burnt her eyes, breaking their seal to run onto her cheek.

Tyrillious roused, a cough spilling from his mouth with his rattling breath.

Abby's heart was pounding in her chest; her uncle was alive. 'Uncle!' she gasped, a mix of emotion swelling up inside her. 'What happened? Are you okay?'

Her uncle let out a pained laugh and wiped the tear from her cheek with a shaking hand. 'Always so many questions, my dear girl,' he said in no more than a whisper. 'My time is short. I feel the pull of the next world on my essence, my hold on this mortal plane lessoning by the minute.'

He let out a troubled rasp as a tremor of pain shook his body. 'Belladora is getting stronger by the day; the winter is gaining a hold on this world, and the world of the humans.' He let out another strained chuckle. 'Global warming, I believe they call it! If only they knew the true nature of the world.'

He grabbed Abby's hand, his grip surprisingly strong considering the frailty of his body. 'The witch is consolidating her grip in preparation for the new moon: an event that coincides with the anniversary of her birth. This is when she will claim absolute rule over these lands, as it is written in our very being. But before she can claim the position of queen absolute, she will need to dispose of all who have blood right before her: that is your father and you, Abby.'

Tyrillious paused, a look of bliss washing over his face. 'It is time, my dear,' he said, a shaky smile spreading across his face. 'Time for me to join our ancestors in the next world.'

Abby lent forward, embracing her uncle in a tight hug. 'Don't leave me, Uncle. I haven't had the chance to get to know you!'

Tyrillious pushed Abby back to look into her eyes. 'Forget your human preconceptions about death, my dear. This body is merely a capsule in which we exist for the short time we have on this mortal plane. One's essence, your soul if you like, moves on to the next world; a world where our departed loved ones are waiting and the next chapter of one's life starts. It is not the end of life, but merely the beginning of the next.'

Abby burst into a fresh flood of tears. 'Take me with you!' she spluttered between sobs.

Tyrillious placed a hand on her cheek; it was cold, like being touched by stone. 'I will take you to your mother, but only because she has summoned you. You will have to return to this world, as you have a great destiny to fulfill, my princess, and many of our subjects to save.'

Tyrillious's body jerked with a spasm and then fell back into the cushioning of his chair: his limbs lifeless, his eyes vacant.

Abby sat back on her heels. Her uncle's face was so calm, his expression one of happiness and peace with the world. She could not help feeling strangely at ease with her uncle's death: his final words resonating in her mind. *Could this really be merely a transition into the next phase of one's life?* She was beginning to dispute the many preconceived ideas that she had taken for granted in the human world; it had been all she had ever really known. She realised that, in the back of her mind, she had always challenged such limiting ideas on subjects such as the finality of death and communication with other species, but had always rationalised such thoughts as the whimsical delusions of an overactive imagination.

Her thoughts were interrupted by voices chatting excitedly. She focused on the room around he. The candles had taken on a greenish shimmer and the whole room, although dimly lit, was possessed by a surprising clarity, each detail somehow sharper and more vibrant. As she looked around the room she noticed a presence: a group of figures appeared to be melting out of the far wall, transparent and wispy in nature but with a solidity reminiscent of fog on a cold winter's morning.

She struggled to her feet, staggering backwards, away from the silent body of her uncle, her back crashing into the solid stone of the wall.

The figures stepped forward, pulling themselves free of the cold stone, wisps clinging to the surface like sparkling cobwebs. They made their way over to her uncle's body, solidifying in size and shape as they moved, until they formed a dense crowd around the corpse.

One of the figures turned to face Abby, a smile forming on his handsome face; it was her great-grandfather. 'Hello, my dear,' he greeted, stepping away from the circle, 'and what are you doing here, young lady?'

Abby's heart softened, the fear dissipating at the sight of her favourite relative. 'I came to see my mother,' she said, her tone more formal than she felt. 'Is she here?'

He stepped over to her, taking her into his arms, his body surprisingly warm and solid. 'I will call her, my dear. We have come to collect your uncle Tyrillious as it is his time to join us in the next world.'

He could see the sorrow in her eyes, the longing for her uncle to stay with her.

'Now don't you worry yourself about such things, my young princess: your uncle remains with you in spirit, as are we all; just look in your heart.' He looked around at the others. 'It is time for us to leave now, my dear. Chin up.'

Abby looked over at the crowd surrounding her uncle; they had been joined by another figure, that of a much younger Tyrillious. He smiled and gave her a wink as they dissolved into the very air around them. All but one.

The lone figure wore a long robe that trailed along the floor as it stepped forward. Pale hands emerged from within the lengthy sleeves, reaching up to the hood hanging over its face. With a sharp tug the hood was flung back to reveal the sweetest sight Abby could imagine: her mother's face.

She jumped into her mother's arms, hugging her with all her might, whispering her love and taking in the sweet aroma of jasmine she knew so well.

'It is good to see you,' Cassandra whispered, the joy ringing in her voice like the chime of wedding bells.

She lowered Abby back to the ground, gesturing for her to take a seat. Sitting on the chair opposite she took Abby's hand, holding it with the gentle caress of a parent to a babe, smiling with the luminescence of the Illuminatum.

'Our time is short, my dear, so please listen carefully,' she began, her demeanour becoming strict, almost teacher-like. 'As you are aware my sister, Belladora, is planning to claim the throne of these lands during the next full moon, at the time of her anniversary. This will require her to remove both your father, my beloved Gilbert, and you, my dear, from the physical plain of existence.'

Abby scoffed at such a flamboyant use of words. 'You mean kill us!' she snapped.

Cassandra smiled; her daughter had become wise to the hardships of life at such an early age. 'Yes, my dear, that means she intends to kill you both by whatever means necessary in order to claim the throne.'

'Well, she's going to have a fight on her hands!' Abby stated confidently, thinking of the followers the Roden had amassed by the dark forest, and her friends Apollo and Arnold.

Cassandra's face darkened, the smile falling from her lips. 'Don't underestimate the witch's power, young lady. She has grown strong over these past centuries. Too powerful for one warrior to defeat alone; even one with such natural skills.' The smile returned to her face. 'I have been watching, my dear, and see a great talent within you.'

Abby blushed, murmuring words of thanks in an embarrassed stupor. She leant forward to give her mother a hug but found nothing but air in the seat opposite.

A thud from the chamber next door shook her back to the present. There was a clang of metal on stone, then shouts of anger. She sprang to her feet, the training of past weeks instantly alerting her, reaching for the trusty sword hanging at her waist. She stepped into the doorway, calling 'Luminous!' as she moved. Light danced off the walls as the whole room was illuminated with the bright glow of sunlight, the scene frozen in shock in the suddenly dazzling brightness.

To her surprise Abby was confronted with the sight of Rufus kicking out at a group of Squakor warriors, the armoured soldiers caught unawares by the presence of a unicorn in the darkness of the room. His hoof came down on the helmet of the closest soldier, splitting the metal in two, exposing the man's soft face. He toppled to the ground as the others rallied, surrounding the beast with drawn swords.

Abby sprang into action, dispatching the first warrior before he had chance to raise a defence. She was quickly onto the next, parrying a high blow with a thrust to the stomach, and then the next, a chilling scream filling the air. One by one the soldiers fell.

Moments later Abby staggered into a wall, her body exhausted by the rage of battle. She looked around to see bodies strewn about the hall, their blood soaking the marbled floor, the smell of death bringing nausea to her throat. She staggered to the door and leaned into the cold night air, releasing the contents of her stomach onto the frozen ground. Once empty she returned to the warmth of the inner chamber, curling into a ball in front of the blazing fire. Rufus joined her, lying at her side, as she fell into an uneasy sleep.

30
Friends reunited

Abby woke to a shaft of sunlight casting shadows across the room. Rufus was lying in a corner, his breathing heavy, the occasional whinny erupting from his floppy jowls and a look of peace on his handsome face. She heard movement from within the adjacent room and memories of the previous evening flooded back in her mind's eye. She sprang to her feet, all sleep washed away by a sudden rush of adrenaline, and collected her sword from its resting place on the stone floor. She carefully stepped into the light, raising her blade in preparation for battle.

'There now, young lady!' said a familiar voice from her right.

She spun round to come face to face with the feline features of Arnold.

'We wouldn't want you poking anyone with that now would we!' he chuckled in a deep purr.

Abby squealed with happiness, wrapping her arms around her feline companion and giving him a good squeeze. 'Am I glad to see you!' she spluttered, nuzzling his nose.

'And are you as pleased to see me?' questioned an equally recogniasable voice from across the room.

Abby released Arnold and sprinted towards the voice's owner, plunging into Apollo's arms and knocking him to the ground.

'Evidently so!' he laughed as he pushed himself back to his feet. 'So this is where you got to last night, is it?' he asked in a tone that hinted at scornful. 'We were very worried when you vanished without a word.'

Abby's face reddened. She had not thought to tell her protectors where or with whom she was going; it had happened so fast.

'Not to worry, my dear,' soothed Arnold as he padded over to them. 'You're safe now, and that's all that matters.'

It was then that she noticed that Rufus had joined them.

'I see you've met this young rascal then,' laughed Arnold, gesturing towards the white steed.

Abby shot him a confused look. 'You know him?' she asked, bewildered.

'Sure,' replied Arnold. 'We go right back; fought together in the Great War, we did. Rufus here was your father's mount, and trusted friend.' He began to rummage in a large sack by his feet, producing a small cast-iron frying pan. 'Breakfast anyone?'

Abby shared the tale of the previous evening while they all tucked into breakfast. She received nods of admiration and congratulations from all for her bravery and scorn for not allowing them to protect her. After eating they burnt the warriors' bodies as tradition dictated. No ambiguity was shown to either side as these were just empty shells, vacated by the essence of the warriors upon death.

As the flames began to die down Abby noticed movement in a nearby bush. Curious, she strolled over to the particularly bright green shrub and peered around its dense foliage. She saw a flash of short white fangs and collapsed backwards into the garden as a small black animal pounced on her chest. Panicking, she screamed out for help, thrashing at the beast with all her might, until, that was, she realised the animal was not attacking her but frantically licking her face. Its tongue was rough and wet; it felt a bit like her cheek was being rubbed with a yard brush. She finally managed to lever the beast off far enough to get a look, and realising whom it was, relaxed until the washing naturally abated. Her face was sodden with sweet smelling mucus that was trickling into her left ear, making her shudder.

Apollo was standing over her when she opened her eyes. 'Are you hurt, my princess?' he asked, the concern sounding in his voice.

She wiped slobber from her eyes with the back of her sleeve, focusing on Apollo's left hand. In it he held a black ball of fur, the blade of his sword resting on its neck.

Abby let out a giggle. 'Don't fear that ferocious beast, my powerful warrior; it won't hurt you.' She clambered to her feet, taking the animal into her arms. 'Don't you recognise him? This is Pook: the Nibblet we encountered on our last visit to the chamber.'

Apollo lowered his sword, content that the animal was no longer a threat, and returned to his work without another word.

Abby was content to recline under a tree, scratching her newly rediscovered friend under the chin, listening to his constant chatter. It seemed a little odd that she could not understand the various levels of 'pook' this animal uttered, as she had the ability, as Nousidian royalty, to understand the languages of all her subjects. However, as the morning wore on she began to notice a pattern emerging in the Nibblet's noises. It transpired that his was a very simple, emotion based language intended to communicate feelings rather than words, and Abby soon discovered he was very happy to see her. He had finally fallen asleep in her lap, purring like a feline after cream, when Arnold padded over to announce they were ready to leave.

'We have received a squirrel from Professor Quirk. The college was attacked last night, less than an hour after your departure,' he said, looking down into Abby's concerned face. 'It would seem there is a traitor amongst us, and as such we have resolved to strengthen our numbers by rejoining the Roden as they return to Ravensburn.'

He looked back towards their companions. 'We will need to move swiftly, young princess. Rufus will carry you. Apollo and myself will travel at your side.' He paused, raising himself onto his hind legs, his muscular body towering over her. 'It is time for you to take command of your army, Princess Abigail, and lead us to victory!' He gave a sort of salute and trotted back to the others.

Abby looked down at the yawning form of the Nibblet lying in her lap. He had woken and was staring at her with those large, bottomless eyes.

'It's time we stood up to these bullies,' she said, a look of determination fixed on her face. 'Show them who's boss!'

The Nibblet cocked his head to one side, his stare unblinking, and uttered a single 'poook'.

Abby understood completely: her life was about to change dramatically.

31
Elvista

After a hard morning's riding the group stopped at the edge a clearing. Apollo gestured for them to rest as he continued forward to check the route ahead. After only a short break he returned with news of a convoy of Roden in the next valley. Eager to rejoin their kin, the group hurried on over the brow of the grassy hill and across the lush meadowlands towards the cloud of dust that marked the advancing troupe.

As they gained ground they noticed that the warriors were stopping and were engaged in a fierce battle, light reflecting from the unmistakable black armour of the Squakor guards as they attacked. Their pace increased, spurred on by the promise of revenge, until they charged into the thronging mass of fighters. Abby, her sword drawn and her shield bound tightly to her arm, thrust at the nearest enemy; his head split like a ripe melon, blood and gore spraying into the air. Killing was easy from her lofty position high on the back of her stallion, and the guards were soon dispatched.

As the red haze of battle faded Abby realised just how many of the witch's warriors had passed into oblivion that day, for it was known that those turned to evil had no place in the next world. Remorse took a stranglehold on her heart. How could she kill so freely? How could she justify taking so many lives in the name of an existence of which she remembered so little? Why did it not feel wrong to commit such atrocities? She slid from the back of her mount and strolled into a nearby copse of trees, her movements unnoticed by the surrounding warriors as they dutifully piled the bodies ready for cremation.

Upon entering the woodland a welcome feeling of calm washed over her body and mind, caressing her thoughts with a cleansing comfort like that of a hot bubble bath, the anxiety of her troubled thoughts washed away by a tide of happiness. Her body fatigued, she collapsed to the ground, the flurry of leaves and branches forming below her unnoticed, the bed of foliage soft and comfortable beneath her weary bones.

A voice spoke within the calm of her mind; it was familiar, and yet she could not place it as belonging to one specific subject, like it was the collective voice of a group speaking in unison.

'Welcome, Abigail, daughter of Gilbert, the true king,' began the voice. 'We are Emilia, queen of the woodland and all that is green in this land. Don't be afraid, young Abigail; we will cause you no harm.'

Abby noticed a branch moving to her left and carefully turned her head to watch its progress. It moved slowly over her body, pausing to shake its foliage and deposit a small pile of juju berries on her lap.

'Eat,' said the voice: not a command but an offer.

Abby welcomed the sweet nectar from the berries as it oozed down her throat and felt the strength returning to her aching muscles as they relaxed.

Once the berries were consumed a face formed in the branches of a nearby shrub.

'Abigail, we have suffered much over these past years, with the burning of our kind and the bloodthirsty culling of many a forest and hedgerow alike. Thus we welcome your homecoming and hope that with you comes a return to the old ways: the true form of nature in cohabitation with all life. We have searched your heart and found a purity that is rare in these troubled times; a purity that is capable of many great achievements and, with the right guidance, a great deal of good.'

The face dispersed from the shrub and reformed in a tree to her right.

'Abigail, a great and bloody battle lies ahead of you. Many good souls will pass into the next world over the coming days.' The voice paused as if in contemplation before continuing, 'Remember this, young princess: the passing of one's essence is not the end; far from it. It is merely a transition between worlds and one from which a pure being can return.'

Abby started to ask how but was stopped by the soft touch of a branch to her lips.

'Such magic will become known to you when the time is right, our princess. Now you must go, for your protectors have noticed your absence and are growing concerned. Farewell, young Abigail, until we meet again.'

With that the branch below her jerked her back to her feet, spinning her to face the beaming smile of Arnold.

Later that evening, as the chill of the air began to nip at their faces, they arrived at the outskirts of Ravensburn. The meadows surrounding the city, now devoid of snow, were covered in a different veil of white: that of bleached canvas. A temporary city had been erected as far as the eye could see, housing the multitude of gathering warriors who had answered the call.

Abby's attention was captured by a crash to her left. She twisted on her mount to see one of the grey monoliths tumbling to the ground, the squeal of twisted steel and shattering glass filling the air, closely followed by the roaring cheer of its tormentors.

'I see the Roden have already started the cleansing process!' remarked Arnold as he stepped to her side. 'By this time tomorrow there'll be very little sign of Belladora's wicked plan in this city. It looks like fun.'

Abby looked down at the feline; his face was a picture of pure happiness. 'You should join them, Arnold. I'm sure they would welcome the assistance.'

He did not wait for further permission, jumping into a gallop towards the nearest tower.

'Well done, my princess,' congratulated Apollo, joining her to view the destruction. 'This work will create a new bond between their species, maybe even friendship. It may be the only hope we have against your aunt.' He looked up at her, a smile spreading across his face. 'I think now is a good time for a long soak in a warm bath.'

Abby joined him in a smile. 'Just what the doctor ordered!' she laughed.

Giving her a subtle bow, Apollo led Rufus towards the city and the College of Philosophers. Neither wished to discuss what was to come tomorrow.

The morning brought the sound of cheering. Abby opened the thick curtains draped across one of the huge windows in her room to see a plume of dust billow into the air. The last of the new buildings had lost its battle against the ferocious Roden demolition team. Hundreds of faces watched with eager expressions from the many surrounding windows, with thousands more on the street, either cheering or helping in any way they could to purge their city of the witch's evil. She could see a mountain of dark metal where the market was usually held; the dented armour of the Squakor guards tangled in a gruesome pile of limbs. She guessed they had attempted to control the upsurge and, judging by the sheer number of dead, failed.

There was a tap at the door. Abby strode across the room, picking her dressing gown from the chest as she passed and, once suitably attired, opened the door.

'Princess!' Emily squealed as she jumped into Abby's arms. 'It's so good to see you. I feared the worst when you … well it doesn't matter now, does it. You're safe, and that's all that matters.'

Emily released her, a tinge of red flushing her cheeks. She took a step back and gave a subtle curtsey, as politeness dictated. She was wearing a long black cloak with a matching black tunic, riding trousers and boots that rose to her knee. Her wand was stowed in the loop of a belt at her waist, the gem at its tip glowing faintly.

'I have something for you,' she said excitedly. 'Satanus dropped it off first thing. I think it's your battle armour!'

Emily handed over a large bundle, which Abby dropped onto the bed. She had started undoing the fastenings when she realised Emily was standing to attention at the door.

'Come on in then!' she prodded teasingly. 'I've got a new outfit to try on.'

After several long minutes, and lots of giggling, Abby was admiring her new outfit in the room's full-length mirror. She had teased on a very tight pair of black riding trousers and substituted the tunic Tom had given her for the black one Satanus had supplied. The knee-high boots fitted her perfectly, moulding to her feet and slim legs like a second skin. The final piece was a long black cloak, not unlike Emily's but with the emblem of a phoenix emblazoned across her shoulders, its tail feathers reaching to the hem at her ankles.

Emily smiled, looking Abby up and down. 'Just one piece left to complete the ensemble,' she said with a giggle in her voice. From behind her back she produced a shimmering band of silver, its surface covered in elaborate scrollwork. 'Your crown, my princess. It was your mother's, and hers before that. It will give you strength in the days to come. Her name is Elvista.' With a bow she placed the shinning ring on Abby's head.

The crown of silver fitted so comfortably, Abby thought it might be made of the finest silk, and it was so light she could barely tell it was there.

'Thank you,' she whispered, a tear welling in the corner of her eye. 'It's beautiful.'

Emily, close to tears herself, motioned that they had better join the others. Today was going to be a big day.

32
A rise to arms

Abby sat astride her faithful steed, Rufus Macbeth. He had been fitted with a saddle and reins the emblem of the phoenix adorning them with a fiery presence befitting the royal seal. Her sword, Salankia, hung at her waist, her wand was tucked into the folds of her tunic and her shield was strapped to her left arm.

How far I have come, she thought, remembering the day she had left her school in the human world, only a few short weeks ago. Yet to her this reality, this alternative life, felt more substantial. The petty problems of the world in which she had grown up somehow lacked substance; even the bullying she had endured for so long seemed inconsequential. How she wished they could see her now.

She looked around at her companions. To her left sat Emily, her long auburn hair tied back into a loose ponytail, her robes flowing over the hindquarters of a beautiful chestnut mare. Her wand was at the ready in her free hand. But it was her eyes that betrayed her true feelings: the fear showed in those deep green pools, and it was a feeling that Abby shared.

To her right stood Apollo, his pristine uniform decorated with ribbons of valour, markings, she guessed, of gallantry in past conflicts. He held his long rapier poised and alert, ready for battle, a look of calm on his handsome features.

Alongside him stood Arnold. He wore a polished, metallic breastplate moulded to his gigantic frame, its surface in constant movement with the rippling of his muscular torso. His head was adorned with a helmet of such intricate design it could have been mistaken for an elaborate tattoo. He had chosen not to carry a blade; his weapon of choice - sharp claws - combined with his agility and brute strength were a match for any foe.

From their vantage point on the brow of the hill they overlooked the city of Ravensburn and the makeshift camp surrounding it. Abby surveyed their army; its ramshackle assortment of shapes, sizes, colours and creeds made for an almost comical sight. That was until one remembered the purpose for which they were gathered. Some had donned armour and broad swords fit for a royal army, while others proudly stood waiting for battle in no more than a swath of material, their bodies painted with bright flashes of war paint.

A company had split from the main group. They were making their way towards them, travelling rapidly, like a herd of gazelle. Abby watched them grow closer, in awe at the speed at which they travelled in relation to their mass. No mistake could be made as to whom they were.

The contingent of around twenty arrived with bowed heads and words of welcome for their princess, a particularly large specimen stepping forward to speak for them. Arnold stepped into his path, blocking him, chest pushed forward in a gesture of dominance. There was a long second of silence as the two warriors faced each other, fangs bared and claws at the ready. Then, completely to Abby's surprise, Arnold lunged forward and took his opponent in the welcoming grip of friendship, a smile forming on both feline faces, as he too was a Chunkett.

After a short, hushed conversation Arnold returned to Abby's side. He gestured that she should lower her head to enable him to whisper a request. She dutifully did so, enabling Arnold to pass on their visitors' words in a low growl. Once he had finished, Abby sat upright in her saddle and pushed her shoulders back, adopting what she hoped would appear a confidant demeanour, and addressed the assembled Chunkett warriors.

'I have heard your words and am aware of your many heroic deeds in battles past.' She paused, swallowing deeply to calm the nerves fluttering in her stomach. 'I am honoured by your gestures of fealty and accept your offer to accompany me in the battle ahead as royal guard…'

Her last words were drowned out by the unified roar of twenty Chunkett warriors, each sharing the elation of the moment, throwing shields and helmets into the air in jubilation that such an honour be bestowed upon them.

Once the roar had calmed, Apollo, his voice clear in Abby's head, informed her that her subjects awaited her word. She focused her attention on the crowd amassed below; each had turned to watch her in a mass of pale faces, a silence enveloping them. in apprehension of what she was about to reveal.

How will they all hear me? Abby panicked in her mind. *And what could I say that would not betray the fear in my own thoughts?*

Apollo's voice was again present. 'Speak only of what is to come, and truthfully from your heart, because it is there that you hold the strength to guide your people to victory.'

Filled with a sense of foreboding, Abby opened her mouth to speak, and then she closed it again. A familiar perfume had wafted tantalisingly under her nose; the aroma so engaging and pure it could not be ignored. It was the sweet fragrance of jasmine, and that could only mean one thing…

'Mummy!' she gasped.

Feeling the heat rise to her cheeks, she looked around at her companions. None seemed to have noticed her little outbreak as they continued in their preparations.

Mummy where are you? she thought, understanding the futility of speaking into the physical world. *I know you are here; I can smell your perfume.*

It was then that a vision of her mother appeared before her. Her form had the transparency of early morning mist and yet held a definition usually reserved for objects of a solid nature; it was as if her mother truly stood almost within reach.

She spoke, the sound a beautiful melody in the hush of the surrounding breeze. 'My dear Abigail, how you have grown since our last meeting.'

She took a step forward, now so tantalisingly close Abby had to fight the urge to jump down and into her mother's arms. She stole a look at her companions; they continued busying themselves, seemingly unaware of the queen in their presence.

'They are not sensitive to my existence in this realm, young Abigail,' she said, sensing her confusion. 'I am only visible to you, my dear. It is the unreserved love we share that makes my presence here possible, and it is that love that will bring you victory in the coming battle. Be strong my daughter; we are with you always.'

Her form began to waver, the misty apparition losing its cohesion in the strengthening wind. The final wisps floated into oblivion as Apollo strode through them.

'Your people await,' he reminded her, tugging at the stirrup of her saddle to wake her from the daydream.

Abby looked down at him, momentarily oblivious to the statement, and then, realising what was expected of her, she addressed the crowd. 'People of Nousidia.' She figured that was a good start. 'Today I sit in front of you on the eve of war…'

BOOM!

The sound resonated through the air like a clap of thunder. Grass, mud and canvas sprayed into the sky like a fountain of litter, the remains of a tent settling to the ground in the far reaches of the camp.

'It is beginning,' Arnold observed, his voice as calm as if he were taking a stroll in the Garden of Smea.

The war had begun.

33
The torment of destiny

The missile had come from above. Abby searched the deep blue of the morning sky in search of its source. She was unable to fathom where it had come from until she spotted a patch of dark on the horizon.

'THERE!' she shouted, remembering the attack of the Sears during their flight with Draconan. 'That's the source: the storm clouds racing in from the horizon.'

There was a flurry of activity around them as her Chunkett guard encircled their little group, forming a protective ring of muscle and fangs. Abby could see soldiers in the camp pulling covers from mounds she had earlier assumed were tents, to reveal numerous contraptions. Some she recognised as Roden slingshots, similar to the one she had seen on Draconan's back but much bigger. Adjacent to them were huge piles of Muffen hairballs, the stench filling her nostrils even from such a distance.

Abby's mind was suddenly filled with the sound of a hundred voices: some shouting orders; some, she guessed, were lookouts, relaying news of the advancing army; and some simply saying prayers and words of love for their families. What was most astonishing about these voices was that she could understand each one as clearly as if its owner were sat on the adjacent horse; but it was not only that - she could also feel them, the anxiety in their minds, the adrenaline coursing through their veins, even the stone trapped in the boot of a Roden infantryman. She sat for a moment, listening to the voices in her head, feeling the emotions of her people, taking in the commotion of preparation for battle. She practised tuning in and out specific voices as she had been taught, even blocking some out completely as fear gripped their hearts, until finally she regained peaceful control over her thoughts and feelings.

Such an avalanche of information, although now under control, had left its mark and she now truly understood her ability. She could move from warrior to cook, from child to grandparent, with the ease of turning a page; she could understand each of the thousands of subjects assembled within the camp and beyond, not just knowing them by name, but so much deeper. She could feel their strengths and weaknesses, experience their confidence and share their doubts, but most of all she understood their motivation. 'So this is how my aunt controls those who have fallen under her spell,' she mumbled to herself.

'FIRE!' The order came from the camp in the valley below.

Abby raised her eyes to see a wall of slime-covered spheres launch into the air. The Muffen hairballs streaked towards a distant figure hovering in the air on the edge of the forest. The figure, a woman of dark beauty, was struck clean in the chest as the balls rained down on her position. A scream erupted in Abby's head, its volume deafening in the peace of her calm mind, the shock physically shaking her.

A cheer bellowed from the assembly below, the many voices of the Nousidian tribes sounding in one triumphant roar as the Sear exploded in a shower of fizzing purple sparks.

Abby shared the jubilation for a moment and then, remembering her legions, released an order to her commanders to search out and destroy the Sear's twin. Immediately the darkening sky was filled with light as a thousand lanterns were lit, their lenses aimed high into the heavens, their beams crisscrossing to form a smoky weave. Abby scanned the angry clouds overhead, searching for any sign of the Sear's pale twin; for she knew that the storm bringer remained, and it was she who brought a chill to Abby's heart.

Minutes passed with no sign. Abby could feel the restlessness of her people, the eagerness to destroy that which had tortured them this past century, as these were the instrument of choice favoured by the witch who sought to control them. These foul creatures, once ladies of the royal court, revered for their smooth skin and fine grace, had taken their children, ruined their crops and killed their partners, all in the name of Belladora.

With a thunderous crack the sea of torrid clouds opened, the movement like the parting of a great ocean, and through it glided the storm bringer. Her long white hair swirled back and forth in the clutches of an unearthly breeze, whipping around her like a tempest of hate, her unnaturally blue eyes scorching those on whom they landed.

The Sear moved closer, the movement relaxed, as if she were taking a walk in a lazy meadow, her long limbs swaying in the surrounding breeze, brushing nearby clouds with her bejewelled fingers.

Then she descended, passing the many warriors in her path with an unholy smile, but this was a smile that was devoid of happiness or warmth, the only emotion a hatred for the nature surrounding her form. She glided into the circle, the Chukett warriors in her path shrinking away as the proximity of such concentrated evil shrivelled their hearts. The woman landed only an arm's length from Abby, the locks and veils surrounding her settling as she took one final step.

Abby stared at the form standing proudly in front of her. Her skin was as pale as freshly fallen snow, her face that of a maiden no older that Abby herself, yet her eyes told of fear and torture, unspeakable acts of vengeance and annihilation.

A voice spoke. This was not the sweet melody of someone so young, but that of an evil tyrant, lost to this world by the atrocities of her malevolent reign. This voice was known to Abby instantly; this was the voice of her aunt Belladora.

'Welcome back to my kingdom, the kingdom of Nousidia,' the voice said, the sound a rasping croak from the girl's arid throat. 'I have been waiting for your return, young one. Now is the time to fulfill my rightful destiny: I will take your life, and that of your father, and through this claim undisputed rule over these lands - forever!'

The girl let out a shrieking cackle that gradually died into a hacking cough.

Abby looked at the warriors around them, willing one to step forward and destroy this vessel of evil, but none moved; a look of horror was etched into each face, pure fear paralysing their limbs. She drew her sword, the blade glowing with the heat of dragon's fire as it slipped from its sheath. Holding the blade over her attacker, she offered a prayer of forgiveness: one last chance to repent her dark ways.

The Sear's face melted into a grin, but this was no return to happiness as with it she lurched forward, hands clawing like a rabid dog, teeth snapping at her very breath.

With a quick flick of her wrist Abby dispatched the beast, severing the head from her shoulders with one fluid motion. The body instantly exploded in a violent upsurge of blood and gore. Only the head remained, and as it toppled to the ground Abby noticed a dramatic change: the maiden's features had taken on an angelic peace, her face somehow free of the evil that had ravaged it so recently. It hit the ground at their feet with a sickening crack and melted slowly into the soft earth from whence it came.

A cheer roused Abby from her thoughts. She looked up to see an abundance of merry faces clustered around her with many more pushing to get a sight of their savior, to see their princess had returned. She looked around, taking in the joy of her people at this victory, but as she surveyed their faces one stood out, a face so familiar she could have recognised it anywhere.

It was Tom.

She jumped down from her steed, pushing her way through the thronging crowd towards her friend, towards Tom. Suddenly she broke into a small opening in the mass of bodies and there he stood, just as she had remembered him.

'Hello?' she wheezed, the breath struggling from her lungs after such effort. 'Where have you been?'

Tom stood silently, a smile spreading across his handsome face, the youth returning with every moment in her presence.

'You have done well, my dear,' he said finally, his eyes glittering in the returning sunlight, 'but now you must give yourself to destiny: return to the House of Elders and finish this war in the name of all the souls of Nousidia.'

Abby was opening her mouth to ask how this may be achieved when the huge bulk of Arnold strode through him, scattering Tom's form like wisps of spring mist. The only reminder of him was a plume of green smoke hanging over the warrior's left shoulder.

'I must return to Ravensburn,' she stated to Arnold. 'I need to consult the great map.'

She turned on her heel and strode back to her steed and, once mounted, galloped towards the city, followed closely by her ever-growing entourage.

34
The plan

Her guardians had left her in the map room of the College of Philosophers. She was protected by the old magic with which these buildings were formed, and she had been assured that no evil could harm her there. Abby had spent the last hour gazing at the wondrous map on the ceiling of this vast room, tracing the various routes through the city she had travelled in recent weeks.

A quiet cough from a dark corner shrouded by heavy drapes disturbed her thoughts. Its owner stepped forward into the light. His stature was not tall but rigid and upright and he had a long mustache covering his top lip curling slightly at the corner of his taut mouth and short hair that was loosing the battle for baldness at his crown. It was Professor Bumblebot, scholar and quintessential Englishman.

'Good morning, young lady,' he welcomed, his statement quite correct even though it was now early afternoon – that was an Englishman's prerogative. 'What, may I ask, is a beautiful young thing like you doing inside on such a lovely day?'

Abby gave him a confused look. Was he not aware of the impending war, the thousands of warriors assembled only a mile away, or Belladora's attempts to rule this world?

'Missed you at class this morning,' he continued, his tone only vaguely interested.

I guess not!

'It would seem the humans are having a few problems of their own, what with last week's tsunami and now arctic conditions. I imagine they're blaming it on this preposterous "global cooling" idea, or is it "warming", one can never remember. If only they knew, eh, Brown!'

Abby decided to go with the flow, answering in a vaguely positive way.

'Well, toodle pip, I'm off to my next class,' he stated suddenly and strode towards the door on the opposite side of the room.

'Professor?' Abby called just as he reached the opening. 'Could I have a word?'

Professor Bumblebot turned to her and retraced his steps, a huge smile spreading across his face as he approached her.

'Certainly, my dear, anything for one of my students, you know.'

Abby decided to cut straight to the question she had been pondering this last hour. 'How do I get to the House of Elders?' she asked, trying to seem only mildly interested.

Now it was Bumblebot's turn to give her a quizzical look, his thick eyebrows rising.

'What would a young lady in the first throes of her quickening be wanting with the House of Elders?' he asked, a hint of suspicion creeping into his voice. 'You're not thinking of joining that rebellious lot intent on banishing the great Queen Belladora, are you? That wouldn't do!'

Abby thought quickly. 'No – no, Professor, nothing like that,' she said quietly. 'It's just that I overheard some of the older students saying how beautiful the architecture was, and I thought it might be nice to visit at the weekend.'

Bumblebot's face lit up. 'Interested in architecture, are we?' he said, his voice rising to a childish squeal. 'Spiffing good show,' he congratulated, patting her on the shoulder.

After a further half an hour and countless stories of his 'misspent youth', Professor Bumblebot finally informed her of the location.

'The House of Elders is the seat of the ruling family of this land,' he said, finally getting to the point. 'It is located in the centre of the great garden on the western fringe of the city of Alexandra, some twenty miles from here.'

He pointed to an outcrop of land on the far edge of the map.

'That's it right there. The garden is protected on three sides by the northern ocean; the only way in on land is through the great forest. But beware, these lands are inhabited by many a magical beast and, rumour has it, even human folk. Anyway, it's not the sort of place for a fragile, young thing like you, my dear; best leave that visit till later, eh?'

'Err. Yes. Thanks for the advice, Professor,' Abby replied, offering a weak smile. *He must be the only being in this world who doesn't know who I really am*, she thought. 'Will do.'

'Good job! Now must be off, lots to do,' Bumblebot repeated as he sauntered back towards the door. 'Toodle pip!'

Once alone again she wandered across the wide expanse of the map room to where he had pointed. The outcrop stood at the edge of a great city and in the middle of the large expanse of green was a building of the most beautiful proportions. Its turreted walls contained tall windows, each with a stone balcony, arranged symmetrically around a central gated keep. As she studied the map she noticed some areas of the surrounding garden were blackened, as though burnt.

'That'll be the witch!' said a voice to her left.

Abby jumped in shock, her heart doubling its beat. She swung around to face her new visitor and came face to face with Emily.

'You made me jump!' she laughed in relief. 'I didn't hear you come in.'

Emily smiled and asked what she was doing.

After explaining Tom's appearance on the ridge and his instructions concerning her return to the House of Elders, she simply said, 'I have to save my father and bring an end to this war.'

She sagged, feeling the weight of her destiny sitting heavily on her shoulders.

'When do we leave?' Emily responded cheerfully, the prospect of such a task seemingly undaunting. 'I will need a little time to prepare travelling provisions. I could be ready within the hour.'

She hurried off without another word, mumbling merrily to herself as she collected items from around the building.

True to her word, they were ready to leave within the hour. Both girls carried woven backpacks stuffed to bursting with food, warm clothing and juju berries, their wands stowed at their waists. Abby wore her trusty tunic, into which she had added several new pockets as the family of Poggles had insisted on joining them. They were just about to leave when a sound echoed throughout the hall.

'Poooook!'

The Nibblet came bounding across the room, jumping into Abby's arms and nuzzling under her chin.

A giggle escaped as his fur tickled. 'You can't come with us, little one,' Abby said, trying to ignore those sorrowful round eyes. 'It's too dangerous.'

The Nibblet gave a short 'pook' and dug its claws into her arm with a surprising grip.

Emily laughed. 'I guess he is coming along; you don't want to argue with a Nibblet once he's got his claws in!'

Abby joined in her amusement. 'Well, I guess that's decided then.'

She allowed the Nibblet to climb onto her shoulder as the two stepped out into the cool air of the courtyard. The sun had reached the horizon, casting a burnt orange glow across the dusky sky intermingled with hues of purple and red of the most vibrant shades.

'It's beautiful,' Abby observed, seeing the sunset.

'Yes,' agreed Emily. 'But it also heralds the beginning of dusk: the time when the battle between good and evil is decided. Many of our people will pass over this day, I fear.'

Once mounted they spurred on their steeds to join the others on the ridge above the camp. Abby rode directly to Apollo and informed him of their plan. After much objection he agreed to drive their army deep into the heart of the city called Alexandra.

'But how do you plan to get into the city?' he asked once the finer details had been agreed.

Abby smiled. 'I'm going to call in a favour from an old friend,' she replied teasingly.

Just at that moment they were disturbed by shouts from the warriors surrounding them. Several were pointing at the sky above as a large shape appeared from amongst the mountains, gliding across the camp and towards the ridge. The Chukett guard readied their weapons in order to stave off this new aggressor, producing spears from a large arsenal of weapons stacked behind them.

Abby stepped forward and, raising her voice, gave the order to stand down. After several confused looks the guards lowered their weapons and the beast commenced its landing. In the diminishing light it was hard to make out the identity of this visitor, but there was no mistaking what it was as a ball of crimson flame erupted from its snout.

Abby stepped forward, welcoming the beast, for this was Draconan, king of the dragons and her friend. Two further beasts joined them within the circle that had had been cleared, each smaller than their king but no less fearsome.

'It's good to see you again, my dear princess,' boomed the dragon. 'Let me introduce my spouses: to my left is Elexia, mother to five and first queen of our kind; and to my right is Cassivna, queen in waiting and mother of three.'

Both dragons bowed in turn and greeted them.

'So, my young princess, I have heeded your call. What is your command?' asked Draconan, a hint of humour in his voice.

Abby smiled, reciting her practised speech: 'Dearest Draconan, I have summoned you here today to ask for your help in ridding our land of my evil aunt and her followers.'

Draconan gave her a look of surprise. 'You know, better than most, that dragonkind have no interest in the quarrels of lesser beings; present company accepted of course. As such we will not involve ourselves in such matters. On what grounds do you ask for such?'

'Friendship, my dear Draconan,' Abby replied. 'All I ask is safe passage into the great garden at Alexandra for myself and my companions.'

35
Alexandra

A short time later Abby stepped into the carriage on Draconan's back with Emily and Apollo, who, after his earlier objections, had insisted on joining them. Arnold, on the other hand, had chosen to stay on the ground and assist in the incursion into the city. Abby suspected this may have more to do with his fear of flying than honourable devotion, but chose not to mention it. After a fond farewell they were ready to leave, the Roden crew busying themselves with final preparations for take-off.

Draconan reared his stately head, releasing a plume of swirling flame to warn all in his path that he, the king of dragonkind, was about to take flight. Abby laughed as the swarm of people ahead of the giant beast fell over each other in their haste to clear a path. Draconan turned to face her, his jowls forming a cheeky smile, fangs glinting in what remained of the setting sun.

'Are you ready?' he asked, his deep voice underlined with humourous intent.

Abby blew him a kiss, and with a smile took her seat. 'Whenever you are, my dear.'

The dragon gave her a wink and with a surge of his immense power launched into a gallop across the ridge and into the air.

Abby settled back into her makeshift chair. Flying felt as natural to her as breathing and she soon settled into the rhythmic flow of the dragon's wing beats. Soon Elexia and Cassivna joined them, flying at the tip of each wing like the wingmen of a battle formation. They soared over the camp, each bellowing a different shade of flame into the darkening air, much to the amusement of the crowd below who spontaneously broke into cheers and applause at the impromptu display.

After several passes Draconan tilted his huge wings towards the west and the city of Alexandra. From this distance the city appeared only as a series of sparkling lights on the horizon, but amongst it all Abby could make out tall columns of smoke reaching into the darkening sky like black pillars supporting a vast ceiling of blue, fed by the many fires consuming the city's vegetation.

She looked back to the camp, seeing lines of warriors meandering westward like enormous snakes leaving their nests for the evening hunt. Each of the three companies took a different route to the city in order to hide their numbers, attacking at different points along the city wall. Arnold had taken command of the Chunkett royal guard who hurried ahead; their aim was to infiltrate the city and provide support for the princess and her team once they arrived, and naturally cause as much trouble as possible for the Squakor guards. Reginald Cockle, with his son Norman at his side, commanded the bulk of the Roden army. Their task was to storm the main city gates, and in doing so draw their enemy's attention away from the remaining forces as they attacked. The plan was simple: confuse the enemy and wear them down.

Abby settled back again, giving Apollo a wink, a motion she hoped would portray a confidence she did not feel. She was concerned for him as he had been distant these past few days; not his usual confidant self at all. She decided now was a good time to confront him, to find out what was troubling him so.

'I am fine,' he said out of the blue. She guessed he must have heard her thoughts. 'Sometimes my people are disturbed by greater issues than those of man. I sense a shift in the fabric of things; things that should not change.'

Abby shrugged her shoulders; she had learnt not to delve into subjects of which she knew nothing.

'Okay,' she conceded. 'But if you need to talk, you know where I am.'

Apollo did not respond; his head was bowed, deep in thought, so she left him alone.

Before long they reached the city of Alexandra. Swooping low over the rooftops, Abby glimpsed her first sight of the ancient dwellings that populated this great capital. Each structure held a distinctiveness that singled it out from its neighbour; be it a crooked chimney or precariously leaning wall, each bore the uniqueness of its occupant, and the nature that coexisted within those walls.

Draconan suddenly dipped to the right, narrowly missing a peculiarly tall building whose upper floors formed a spiralling structure of intertwined rooms, the pinnacle of which was a shining pyramid of light.

'The great observatory,' Apollo commented as they brushed the shingles of an oddly angled roof. 'Many of the great celestial discoveries were made in that tower,' he continued, 'and much of what we now understand about the true nature of the universe.'

Abby looked back at the oddly teetering tower. It was covered in windows of all shapes and sizes. The design was quite staggering as even though they twisted around each other each room had a clear view out across the city and, more importantly, she guessed, the skies above.

She was about to comment on this when the platform under her feet suddenly dipped, tilting at a sharp angle as a fiery object skimmed the timber balustrade, engulfing it in a molten inferno. Abby staggered backwards, falling into strong arms that held her true; soft words were uttered from a mouth somewhere above her, enchanting words, words she could not fathom but instinctively knew contained the strength of ancient magic. Her eyes focused on the flaming balustrade, the wonder of what they told her captivating as the flames faded from the heat of destruction to the cool frostiness of ice, the blaze frozen in the ravage of consumption.

She clambered back to her feet, stepping to the frozen monument that had so recently been ablaze. With one outstretched hand she touched the tip of the sculpture, for that is what it had become: the living embodiment of fire in ice. The moment her fingers touched the frozen form a crazing of miniature cracks spread throughout, like thousands of tiny hairs rapidly growing within a liquid vessel. Then, before she had the notion to remove her finger, it collapsed, spreading across the timber at her feet in a million tiny fragments.

'Wow!' she uttered, watching the pieces melt into oblivion. 'That was neat!'

At that moment the carriage jerked again as several more fiery objects flew dangerously close to their heads.

'I'm guessing the witch is aware of our presence,' Apollo observed as he grasped his seat for support. 'Time to depart for safer air, I think!'

As if on command the three dragons climbed into the evening sky, turning for the safety of a copse of woodland on a cliff high above the city walls. Abby watched the trees swaying lazily under the pressure of the dragon's beating wings and for a moment was lulled by the calmness of the movement. It was as this calmness transcended into her consciousness that she realised that the movement below had taken on a more purposeful agenda; the branches were forming an opening into which they were dipping. The hole extended to allow the three winged beasts to land before closing a dappled canopy over their heads.

Abby jumped to the ground the second Draconan landed, eagerly stepping over to the nearest tree. A welcome was awaiting her as with a rustling of leaves a face appeared in the lower branches.

‘Welcome to Alexandra,’ said the familiar coagulation of voices.

It was the same voice to which she had spoken many times in the forests of these lands: the voice of Emilia, queen of the woodland.

‘I trust your journey was free from peril.’

Abby gave a small bow, a symbol of respect she had learnt over recent weeks.

‘It was, your Majesty. Fight is a joy I savour the freedom it gives.’

The face of branches and leaves formed a smile. ‘A sentiment we cannot share, my dear, as we are bound to the earth, for it is that which gives us life.’ After a short pause the voice continued, ‘Much like your Chunkett friends, I see: their bond with the earth is a strong alliance and should not be broken lightly. They will arrive in the city within the hour. I suggest you get some rest.’

A branch slithered from within the thick foliage, forming a leafy bed for her to settle upon. Another appeared, dripping with juju berries which dropped obediently onto her lap. Abby settled back on the makeshift cradle and gestured for Apollo to join her and relax while they waited.

Before long, with a belly full of berries, she drifted off into slumber.

36
A vision of death

Abby's eyes snapped open, her senses tingling with a change in the air. The vision that met her was far from what she had expected: the dense foliage of the forest had been replaced with the cold, hard surface of stone and the dappled sunlight was no more - the only illumination was the weak flickering of a single candle.

A moan fluttered around her ears, its source hidden by the repeating echo of the confined space, for the room in which she found herself was no bigger than her father's study back home. This room, however, was devoid of such homely features; it had no shelves lined with books, no grand writing desk in its centre and most of all no living essence.

The moan sounded again, this time joined by the sound of movement. Abby scanned her surroundings, her eyes gradually becoming accustomed to the dim light, until they fell upon a pile of rags curled in the far corner. Her heart jumped as within those rags she could see the form of a man, his skin tight over the bones of his head, giving him the look of one close to death.

She hurried over to the figure, willing the knowledge in her heart to be untrue, the fear swelling in her mind to be unfounded. She reached down, carefully placing her smooth palm on the man's cheek, feeling the ravages of time and torture in the very essence of his being. The figure turned his head, nurtured by the warmth of her touch, feeding from the love held within. His eyes slowly opened, pupils contracting even in the dusky light for they had experienced nothing but darkness for what felt like a lifetime. It was in these shimmering opals that Abby truly recognised the owner of this tattered frame, and in that moment she experienced an emotion that had lain dormant in her for so long: an all-encompassing eruption of hatred for those that had done this.

'FATHER!' she screamed as the room disappeared into darkness.

37
War.

She found herself in the warm embrace of a loved one. Apollo knelt next to her shaking body, holding her with the tenderness of a mother with a babe, allowing the energy of his love to smother her in light. She lay for a moment, letting the warmth wash over her like the fountain of a hot spring, until the anger returned, filling her with the blood lust of revenge. She stood, easing herself from his grasp, the uncertainty of her actions befuddling her mind, body very soul.

'It is time for us to strike,' she announced, the clarity of what needed to be done breaking through her bewilderment. 'My father is close to death, and as such requires our decisive action.'

A voice sounded in her head; it was that of Arnold. 'Greetings, my princess. We await your attendance in the great garden. We have slaughtered many, but get bored and fat in our anticipation of the challenge that lies ahead.'

'Saddle up,' Abby ordered, gesturing to the dragon's carriage. 'It is time for us to meet my aunt.'

They witnessed the commencement of hostilities at the city's wall as they glided silently towards their goal, picking off surprised guards in their wake. The trio turned for another pass, gliding over the feuding crowds, raising a triumphant cheer from the Roden horde below. They continued sweeping back and forth, wiping out great swaths of Squakor in their path with flame and claw.

Suddenly the sky was full of sparkling rockets soaring into the darkening abyss before exploding into a fizzing mushroom of colour in the dull surroundings of the deadened garden. This was their signal, a clear marker for them to follow.

The arrival of the dragons was a sight to be seen: gliding into the garden like oversized birds of prey, bursting into view through the gathering darkness, incinerating a group of straggling Squakor as they passed. They landed with the grace of butterflies on an area of shimmering grass, for the frost of winter had already taken its hold on the land and the area around them thawed instantly with the radiant heat of their bodies.

The friends reunited with hugs and words of welcome while the Roden busied themselves dismantling the carriage from Draconan's back. Once this was completed Abby thanked him for his help.

'It was a pleasure as always, young one,' he replied, his voice deep and sorrowful. 'We must leave you now as our traditions dictate that we must not interfere with such matters. The sport of recent moments will be forgiven, as it is our birthright to hunt as we desire, but further involvement may attract the wrath of my people.' He looked deep into her eyes. 'Know this, young princess: your path is just, and although the way may not be clear, you will prevail. Goodbye, my friend, until next we meet.'

With a flurry of powerful wings and a blast of warm air, Draconan and his spouses were gone, lost in the encroaching darkness.

Abby pulled the collar of her tunic tighter, staving off the chill that had consumed the air. She glanced around, taking in her surroundings. The garden was colourless, having a grey, almost monochrome, appearance - *like one of the old black and white films her father loved to watch*, she thought. No flower dared to show its bloom, no tree paraded its blossom, as this garden was dormant and, in being so, dead to this world.

Up ahead stood the towering ramparts of the Palace of Souls, its stone facades protruding into the air like a wall of huge tombstones, covered in lichen and aged with the passing of time. Each face of its cubist structure contained three large balconies jutting out into the dusky sky. Ornate railings, twisting in an unnaturally complicated pattern of steel and timber, rose around them, obscuring sight of the tall doors beyond. Abby knew this building, for this was the place that she had called home all those years ago. She made straight for an outcrop in the nearest wall.

The timber doors towered over her, their height almost double hers with a width she swore even Draconan could squeeze through. Surrounding them was an impressive stone tower, and its windows, although smaller than those around it, were no less impressive, with ornate stone mullions and carefully carved fitments befitting a royal house.

Abby recognised the crest emblazoned across these doors; there was no mistaking her family seal, even with the frenzied scoring caused by unsuccessful attempts at its removal. The image appeared to ooze from the wood as if it were part of the timber's DNA, part of nature itself.

'Looks like the witch has tried to remove your ancestry from the old place,' stated Arnold, a hint of humour in his voice. 'I'm guessing she wasn't too successful!'

He laughed as he traced the path of a particularly deep scratch with a long, curved claw while Abby tried one of the tarnished handles, twisting it to and fro in an attempt to gain access.

'Your aunt won't have left the front door open, my dear!' laughed Arnold, his shaggy mane shaking dusty particles into the still air. 'I can try to break it down, if yer like,' he offered.

Apollo stepped into his path. 'Don't waste your energy, my muscular friend. This door is sealed with powerful dark magic; I doubt even your might will better it.'

He looked around, catching the eye of the nearest Roden soldier. 'You look familiar,' he said, stepping over to him. 'Weren't you once a member of the royal guard?'

The mousey soldier cowered under the gaze of such a renowned warrior. Word of his bravery in battle had rung through their camp on the back of many a soldier's tale, telling of his courage and unfaltering devotion to their true king and, naturally, the young princess who stood next to him.

'Y-yes,' stuttered the young soldier. 'My name is George Buckley, but I was fresh from cadet school, yer see. Only stationed 'ere for a week, I was.'

Apollo smiled, offering a gesture of friendship to the youthful Roden.

'Good lad,' he said, his voice calm and even. 'Now, during your week here did you learn the location of a Roden tunnel into the palace?'

The young soldier looked shocked, his fine whiskers twitching with a vibration like the wings of a frantic wasp, his eyes wide at the mention of something so profound. This subject was a secret within the elite of the Roden royal guard, the knowledge of its existence only given to those of pure blood. He knew of only one who had earned this privilege – their king, Reginald Cockle himself.

'I-I have heard the rumours of course, but such information was not meant for my young ears,' he replied, flushing pink under the soft fur of his mousey face.

Abby shivered, an icicle of chill shooting down her back. Unsure of their next move, she raised her eyes to the darkening sky above, taking in the luminescence of the heavy white cloud that had filled the expanse. She followed a dot as it meandered through the air towards her, falling like on the wake of an invisible stream, skipping through eddies of air rising from the warmth of their bodies. As it grew closer she could make out its intricate crystalline structure, the frosty surface fluffy like that of frozen fur. She gasped in amazement as its size became apparent: it was as big as her hand and yet it danced on the breeze like it weighed less than a feather.

The snowflake drifted past her nose and landed on the frozen earth at her feet, coming to rest against her boot. To her surprise it showed no sign of melting, the chilly form resting against the frosty stone paving as if hovering on an undetectable blanket of ice. Another fell, and then another, the pace increasing rapidly, the flakes quickly becoming a haze through which the world could barely be viewed. The scene was captivating, the icy forms dancing in an enchanting performance of natural beauty, each pirouetting through the air in a celebration of uniqueness yet carefully avoiding its neighbour with an almost choreographed design.

A voice broke through her fascination, a desperate urgency filling the words as if their very lives depended on her, urging her to follow. She turned her head, coming face to face with one of her Roden guards. His eyes were fixed in wonder at the sight around them, apparently unaware of her presence or the look of fear on her face. He was covered in white, the snow forming a smothering veil over his still body, gradually extinguishing all colour from his being as he became one with the smooth, pale shroud that had fallen over the garden.

It was this that galvanised her into action. She pulled her feet into motion, surprised at the stickiness of the settled snow clinging to her every move. She urgently scoured the frozen landscape, searching for her friends, her protectors, in the all-consuming white. She spotted Apollo, desperately brushing fluffy snow from the back of his brother and friend Arnold, pleading with him to show a sign of life. Abby waded over, as the depth had already reached her ankles, instinctively reaching for her wand as she battled forward. Mumbled words of warmth and life spilled from her lips as she touched the tip of her wand to Arnold's forehead, the vibrant olive glow emanating from its tip reflecting in his pale fur.

Arnold's form burst into flame; but this was no ordinary fire, as these flames licked around his huge bulk in an inferno of vivid lime, spreading across the surrounding garden with a thaw so rapid that surrounding flora sprang into life, exhibiting a riot of colour and fragrance.

Gradually, as the roaring blaze subsided, colour returned to the heaving warrior as life flowed back to his limbs. With a shower of watery snow Arnold shook off the last of the binding magic, releasing a mighty roar to announce his return.

Abby set about releasing the other captives, her task made difficult by the relentless onslaught of white falling from the heavens. She managed to release Emily, the young Roden guard, George Buckley and one further of the Chunkett elite, a warrior by the name of Edward Insbrick, before the cold in her hands and the blinding snow became too harsh.

Just as her resolve began to falter, a figure strode out of the surrounding white: the dull black armour and glowing red tip of his wand unmistakable as that of the Squakor. He levelled his wand at Abby's chest, muttering words of pure evil into the snowy air. A flash of light erupted from its tip, like a bolt of lightning, streaking towards her.

38
Snow

The gates to the city crashed open and Roden poured through like a swarm of greedy piranhas, devastating everything in their path in their appetite for revenge. Reginald Cockle, king of the Roden, proudly watched over the advancing horde: his soldiers, although fat and content from over a century in hiding, had served him well, swelling into the city like a cleansing tide.

From his vantage point at the pinnacle of the gatehouse Reginald surveyed their losses. From the ten thousand strong warriors who had marched into battle that morning, seven thousand remained. The cost had been high, as many good Roden had passed over to the next world that day, but the objective had been achieved: their names would be entered into the Book of Heroes.

A flake of white drifted past his nose, dancing in the turbulent air of the battle below, settling on the smooth stone at his feet. Reginald watched as the object slowly rolled towards his leather-clad foot. It touched his boot, instantly burning through the hide, sending a searing pain throughout his body. Instinctively he jerked away, the relief cooling his nerves as the pain evaporated. A realisation dawned on him at that instant: this was the icy embodiment of evil; this was snow.

'TAKE COVER!' he screamed to all within earshot, the revulsion of what was being unleashed becoming a terrifying reality.

Galvanised into action, the Roden hordes scattered in every direction. Reginald watched in horror as his mighty army dispersed into the safety of the surrounding buildings, many falling in the stampede or struck down by the rapidly increasing snowfall.

Taking shelter within the portcullis room above the main gate, Reginald remembered the last time he had experienced such icy wickedness.

It was many years past, in the days before the great upheaval. Reginald, a captain of the guard, was returning home after a day's hunting with his brother, Ronald. It had become late: the hour of dusk was upon them. But they did not fear the dark, as their kind had excellent night vision and fur to counter the freshness in the air. This, however, was no ordinary night, as this night was possessed by an ancient evil, one that had lay dormant for many centuries: an evil that had been resurrected by an unfathomable lust for retribution.

The first flurries had floated past aimlessly, settling on the frosty ground at their feet: flakes of pearly white snow, soft like crystalline moths ambling through the air. Then came the larger structures, their mass growing tenfold in a matter of seconds, and with it the danger they brought. Ronald brushed a lump of cold from his shoulder, but as he did so a blinding pain hit him, firing into his body like the bullet from a gun. The frosty liquid burned through the skin of his exposed paw, melting the very substance of his hand.

Spurred into action by his brother's screams, Reginald pulled his flailing body to cover, using his own gangly frame as a shield against the glacial onslaught, the pain of burning ignored in his desperation to save his kin. From their slumped position in a sheltered doorway Reginald could make out the frenzied screams of his fellow Roden, the snowfall now so intense that even his keen eyesight failed to penetrate the thick curtain of white.

His attention was drawn back by a soft moan from the weight slumped over his legs. Looking down, he retched at the sight that met him. As the nausea cleared he opened his eyes, staring through a blur of tears to watch helplessly as his bother surrendered to the evil that consumed his body, leaving nothing but a dried husk swathed in bloodied rags. It was moments later, through the helplessness of his sorrow, that his own pain was realised; binding him in a blanket of hurt until the blackness consumed him.

He had woken days later, his body covered in bandages, the haze of medication dampening his reactions. It had been weeks before he had finally learned the reason for his brother's demise, and it was that moment he had sworn that he would seek his revenge.

A gust of icy wind roused him from his memories as a young soldier entered the room. Removing his hand from the scaring he had been absently caressing; a perminant reminder of that day, Reginald stood, slipping into the regal pose of leadership.

'Yes, Fred Buckley, how may I help you?' he questioned.

The young soldier, no more than a boy, stuttered his response. 'Excuse me, Uncle, sorry, I mean sir, we, that's me and the lads in me regiment, were wondering how we were gonna get through the snow. It's real thick, and yer know we can't touch it.'

Reginald smiled; Fred, along with his twin George, were his favourites from the dozens of nephews and nieces in their large family, but unfortunately not the brightest.

'Make a fire on the ramparts and spread the dead as far as they will reach. They shall provide one final service to our cause: that of melting this retched snow.'

With that he dismissed the young soldier with a wave of his paw-like hand.

Further along the city wall a small group gathered in the shadows. They were a strange mix: their leaders much taller than the rest, with short, stubbly fur and dirty faces.

Bit looked over to Bot, his expression one of silent contemplation. Then, without a word, the two gardeners pointed their trowels at the soft earth at the base of the high structure. Immediately a shoot appeared, its brightness stark against the night, breaking through the soft earth and rapidly ascending the wall. It grew in height and girth until it reached its goal, forming a natural staircase of branch and leaf to the battlements above.

'Up yer go then,' Bit ordered, snapping his troops from their surprised state.

Minutes later they congregated on the smooth stone of the boundary wall, high above the city of Alexandra. From this vantage point they could see the battle in full flow: the Roden storming the main gate, a bright glow in the sky illuminating the grand palace in the centre of a huge expanse of green, a trio of fire-breathing beasts gliding through the smoky air.

A flake of white landed on the gardener's nose, melting instantly with the heat of the blood flowing through his veins.

'Take cover,' Bit commanded his men, his tone relaxed, as if in polite conversation. 'The snow is coming.'

The warriors scattered for cover, not wanting to be caught in the eternal freeze that came with the night, leaving the two gardeners alone on their rocky perch. The snow intensified, falling like the droplets of a waterfall, closing the world around them in a veil of white.

The gardeners sprang into action and jumped to a nearby rooftop, spraying shingles in their wake as they bounced from one to the next: their target, the plume of light in the palace gardens.

39
The Room of Reception

Abby fumbled inside her tunic, the wand eluding her grasp as the menacing bolt of light careered towards her. Her hand closed on the shaft, its power instantly thawing the numbing cold encasing her heart. She produced it just in time and uttered a counter spell that dispersed the charge into a nearby tree.

'Sorry,' she called, remembering their living nature, a moment of guilt passing through her mind.

More figures stepped into vision, their black armour seemingly unaffected by the mounting snow. Abby and her companions readied themselves for the onslaught, positioning themselves in a circle; wands, weapons and claws at the ready. The Squakor leader raised his wand again in preparation for attack, taking a step toward his prey, his fellows mimicking the movement.

Abby took a deep breath to calm her shaking body; not an effect of the intense cold, but that of an energy welling up inside her. It was the source of this power that caused her to tremble, as it was born from hatred: an overwhelming desire to destroy anything and everything in their path.

A moment of hesitation filled her mind; a moment in which the world became a very different place - a place filled with pain, a place overrun with loathing, a place brimming with evil. She raised her wand, levelling it at the midriff of her nearest foe, the ancient words teetering on the tip of her tongue. Then the most surprising thing happened.

Each of their attackers stopped as if rooted to the spot, their bodies rapidly becoming entwined in the thorny tendrils of a climbing rose. Their bodies were consumed in seconds by a barbed prison that disarmed them without resistance.

Feeling her tension ebbing away, Abby turned to the others, hoping for some explanation for this sudden growth. But her questions were met by equally astonished faces, each looking at her in wonder.

'It wasn't me!' she coughed, her certainty floundering even as she spoke.

It was then that two new figures emerged from the fog of snow, but these wore no armour or carried brightly glowing wands. Their only protection from the blinding cold was a thick covering of matted fur, their weapons dirty trowels.

The gardeners strode over to Abby, bowing low in a display of great respect. 'Hello, Princess,' Bit laughed as he straightened. Abby jumped forward, giving them both a hug of gratitude and thanking them for their timely help.

'Sorry to disturb, Princess,' a voice said from her left: it was George Buckley. 'I'm afraid we have some more visitors!'

Abby looked in the direction of his pointing paw, seeing, to her dismay, more Squakor stepping into their realm of white, wands glowing with malicious intent.

'Leave them to us,' called Bit, assuming command as he turned to them. 'We'll look after these for yer.' He looked over his shoulder, gesturing behind them. 'Take refuge, my princess; we'll be okay.'

He joined his brother, his trowel raised in defiance.

Abby retreated across the frozen tundra, followed closely by her protectors, their movements hindered by the relentless blanket of blinding snow. They reached the high wall that surrounded the royal garden, its stone smooth and straight, designed to resist all who were not welcome. The companions ground to a halt at this barrier, the larger Chunkett, Edward Insbrick, losing his footing and sliding deep into a drift sloping high against the wall.

Arnold stepped forward, a hearty laugh vibrating from his ample jowls, offering a hand of assistance. 'Watch yerself there, laddie, it's slippery stuff this!' he jousted, helping his brother to his feet.

It was then that Abby noticed a small stone hut built into the wall to their left; it was barely visible as the snow had drifted high against it, obscuring all but the top of a blistered timber door. Without a word the two Chunkett warriors made short work of clearing a path, their eagerness to escape the cold, biting weather pushing them on. After forcing the door ajar they stepped inside.

The group huddled together in the blackness of the cramped hut, their laboured breathing eerily loud in such a confined space. Abby flinched as a burning sensation sparked within her clothing. She tore open her robes, grasping at the fastenings of her tunic to release the fire at her skin. Then, much to her relief, the family of Poggles fluttered into the room; their nest within the pockets of her tunic forgotten in the turmoil of recent events.

The Fire Fairies meandered around the room, individually lighting features and walls with the soft glow of their luminous skin, until eventually meeting at the apex of the cabin's rafters. As they joined their luminance increased, casting bright light into every nook and cranny, giving the group a clear view of their surroundings.

A minute squeal echoed around the room, breaking the oppressive silence; it was Elizabeth, the Poggle mother.

'Little Millie is missing!' she screamed, the sound reverberating around the room with surprising volume. 'We must find her!'

Immediately the tiny specks of blinding light separated, spinning around the room like a dizzying array of shooting stars. Abby, who was beginning to get very dizzy by this point, called for them to stop. The five bright specks of light slowed and then assembled in a circle around Abby's pointing finger.

'Right,' she said, an authoritative tone in her voice, 'there's no point getting upset; we just have to look for her. She'll be here somewhere!'

Without a further word the warriors began to search their cramped surroundings, looking in gaps and behind beams, but to no avail: the young Poggle was nowhere to be found.

Elizabeth began sobbing into a tiny handkerchief, while her husband, Alexander, darted to and fro in a vain attempt to find their lost offspring. It was then that Abby realised the tiny figures' glow was diminishing and she stepped over to enquire why, putting on her best soothing voice.

The Poggle mother looked up, her petite eyes bloodshot in a face of glowing pink.

'Our life glow diminishes the longer we are unhappy. We must find little Millie or we are doomed: the heartbreak of such a loss will kill us all.'

She started sobbing again.

As the light diminished, pockets of shadow began to appear in the surrounding walls. It was in one of these that Abby noticed something odd: a dot of dazzlingly bright light was shining at its centre. She moved closer, realising that this wasn't a dot but a keyhole embedded in the wall. Instinctively she retrieved her wand from within the depths of her robes and pointed it at the lock.

'Enthra,' she whispered, not wanting to appear foolish in front of her protectors.

The distant sound of cogs rang out from somewhere behind the wall and suddenly the floor disappeared from below them. The group dropped in unison, plummeting several storeys before landing with the force of taking a small step. Lanterns snapped on, emblazoning the room with a warm glow like that of a summer's day, revealing a long, narrow tunnel in the direction from which they had come.

'It's the tunnel!' squeaked George, a huge grin on his face.

'Millie!' squealed Elizabeth as she caught the whizzing form of her daughter.

'Get off me,' groaned Apollo as he tried to squirm from under the bulk of Arnold's torso.

Once they had dusted themselves down and taken in their surroundings, the group set off down the long, arrow-straight tunnel. Abby gazed at the walls as they walked; their structure was not so much made but grown to form a tall corridor, the intricate weave of branches knitting together in a living sculpture, constantly moving like a pit of slithering snakes.

The Poggles went on ahead, fluttering around the structure like the dancing embers of a bonfire, lighting up the dank tunnel before them. The two Chunkett warriors took the lead, prowling through the half-light like fanged hunters. Abby followed with Emily at her side, merrily chatting about life before the witch's rein, with George bringing up the rear, whiskers twitching at every movement. Apollo was somewhere behind: lost in the darkness.

'So you lived in the palace?' Abby asked, fascinated by what life must have been like. 'What did your family do?'

Emily's face saddened, the playful smile lost in an instant. 'I was only a baby when my parents were slaughtered in the witch's uprising. I don't have any memories of them, or our life here, only the knowledge that the House of Elders was once my home.' A strained smile formed on her beautiful features. 'I was taken in by the college as an orphan and educated at their mercy.'

Abby gave her a look of understanding, for she too had been wrenched from her home as a baby and brought up in a strange world she did not truly understand. At least she had her father; for that she was grateful.

'Don't worry,' she said, the humour returning to her voice. 'You can be my adopted sister. We look so alike, who would question it!'

The two girls giggled as they strolled into the darkening gloom; the soft light ahead guiding them on their journey.

40
House of Elders

Abruptly they reached a dead end, the path blocked by a sheer rock face. The Chunkett warriors began to climb, but the smooth rock gave no purchase, even for their sharp claws, and they were soon returned to the soft earth of the tunnel floor.

'It's a dead end,' stated Arnold, his voice gruff, disappointed. 'We must have missed a turning back there,' he continued, motioning back along the tunnel.

'Don't fret, my brawny friend,' said a voice from the darkness. It was Apollo. He stepped into the soft light, his face beaming with a wide smile. 'We are below the palace,' he continued. 'Directly above us is a chamber known as the Room of Reception, or "the room with no door" as we once called it. The way forward is simple: all we have to do is find the hidden entrance and wish to be received into the palace. But be warned, only the pure of heart can enter here: a fiery death awaits evil should it step over the threshold.'

He looked around at their pale faces.

'Where is this door?' Abby enquired, looking around the dusty walls.

Apollo smiled, a cheeky smile, full of mischief. 'That is a good question, my princess; one to which I do not have the answer, I'm afraid.'

Abby's smile sank, her joy at finding a way into the palace, her chance to save her father, extinguished in a moment.

'Cheer up my dear,' Apollo comforted, seeing her form physically shrink. 'We simply need to find it.'

With a nod the group dispersed around the clammy room, shifting ancient creepers and blowing centuries of dust from all manner of nodules and outcrops. They continued in their work for what seemed to be an eternity for Abby, her anxiety for the safety of her father gnawing at her patience like the rabid feasting of a starving wolf.

'HANG THE NOUSE. JUST FIND IT, WILL YOU!' Her calmness snapped with the frailness of a twig underfoot, the blood in her head boiling over with pure, unadulterated anger.

Apollo stopped his rummaging, his eyebrows raising as he slowly returning a rock to its place in a corner. It was not his princess's outburst that had attracted his attention, however, but a faint glow from the centre of the room. He stepped over as the glimmer faded back to black, disappearing as though never there.

'What did you say, Princess?' he enquired, his eyes not leaving the ground at his feet.

Abby shifted uncomfortably, the heat in her head cooling with the return of control.

'I'm just anxious to save my father,' she apologised defensively, a blush of embarrassment glowing on her cheeks.

'As are we all, my dear,' replied Apollo. 'Repeat what you said a moment ago, word for word, if you please.'

Abby thought for a moment; recalling the words. 'Just find it will you,' she recalled.

The others had joined them, standing in a circle around the leaf covered floor, but nothing happened.

'Before that,' Apollo guided, a twinkle of excitement in his voice.

Abby thought again, the phrase she had used so flippantly coming back to her; surely that could not be the answer?

'Hang the Nouse,' she said simply.

The earth below them uttered a deep growl and a glow, like the burning of a thousand candles, illuminated the foliage at their feet; but not from above, as this eerie light shone from the very ground below. Suddenly the group were swathed in a cyclone of icy wind, whipping leaves around their startled bodies, thrashing them like the slaps of a thousand offended women, each igniting in turn with its own fiery glow before burning out of existence.

Within seconds the soft earth was bare, its only decoration the smouldering ashes of the once lush foliage; but as they fell a outline began to form.

'Shall we?' Apollo invited calmly, gesturing to the ashen shape on the floor. 'X marks the spot.'

Arnold stepped forward. 'I will go first and secure the room,' he stated, his huge bulk stepping onto the mark. 'I wish to enter the Room of Reception,' he said and promptly disappeared.

His fellow Chunkett warrior, Edward Insbrick, followed, and then it was Abby's turn.

She stepped onto the rough cross, her stomach filling instantly with fluttering butterflies, and spoke the words. Her vision blurred and the dim tunnel began to rotate about her, spinning faster and faster, quickly becoming a blur of browns speckled with the odd flicker of colour as her colleagues' faces flashed by. She felt her feet leave the floor, her limbs becoming lighter than air as her body lifted into the darkness above. Then everything went black, her consciousness leaving her, the sense of burning her final memory.

Abby woke with a start, rough hands unceremoniously patting down her tunic, the smell of burnt cloth jerking her back to life.

'What happened?' she asked, her head still spinning as she reluctantly opened her eyes, Apollo's smiling face greeting her.

'Just a little problem with your tunic my dear. It would seem the ancient magic that protects this room has taken exception to the dark forces that formed that particular item. It was lucky I followed you through as you were quite nicely ablaze when I arrived,' he commented, a disturbing lack of concern in his voice.

Abby shrugged and mumbled her thanks as she took in her surroundings. The room was panelled in a rich mahogany, each panel beautifully polished to a mirror shine. The ceiling high above contained a finely painted fresco depicting what she guessed to be a historical reference to the king welcoming a traveller to his realm. What made her gasp in awe at the scene was not the detail or ornate carvings at each corner, but that this king was plainly her father. It was then that the true gravity of the situation dawned on her. She was a princess, her father was the true king, and her aunt Belladora was an evil witch bent on their destruction.

'Wow!' she exhaled as the final shreds of doubt washed away in a tide of belief. 'So this is for real: my father's in trouble, and it's up to us to save him!' She turned to Apollo as the others joined them. 'Do you know where my father is being held?'

Apollo gave her a look of sympathy. 'I'm afraid not,' he replied. 'What do you remember of your vision?'

Abby searched her memories, desperate to remember any small detail that may help their quest. 'All I remember is that it was dark, with no windows, I think, and cold.' She shivered with her efforts to recall. Then she remembered: 'Food. I remember smelling food!'

Apollo and Arnold looked at each other, responding in unison, 'The kitchens: the stores next to the kitchens. Where we used to play as youngsters!'

Without further discussion Arnold gestured to his fellow Chunkett and they exited the room via a concealed door to their right.

'Where are they going?' Abby questioned, confused by the sudden movement.

Apollo took her by the shoulders, looking into the depths of her jade eyes. 'It is time to face your destiny, young Abigail, and with it your future. Arnold will find your father, but we must focus on your aunt. The time draws close, for this day is the anniversary of her birth and as such she can claim the throne in the absence of a true heir.'

Abby returned his stare, her features hardening into that of a true warrior. 'Whatever it takes, we will overthrow the tyrant Belladora, aunt or not!'

Apollo released her and strode over to the others. 'Are you with us?' he asked calmly.

Emily stepped forward without hesitation, offering a curtsey to her princess and a hand of friendship to Apollo. 'I will follow until my death or victory.'

Apollo turned his attention to Fred Buckley. 'And you?'

The young Roden soldier flushed red, opening his mouth in a movement more like a goldfish than a trained killer. 'Y-yes,' he squeaked, his nervousness apparent. 'I-I would b-be honored to serve the princess, and you, o-of course, my lord.'

'That's settled then,' confirmed Apollo, giving Abby a wink. 'This way.'

'What about us?' said a squeaky voice from above their heads.

They looked up to see Alexander hovering over them with his family, his tiny arms crossed and a very put-out look on his face.

'We may be small, but we pack a punch! Just how many of your enemies will be resistant to our blinding luminosity, or being set alight by our touch?'

Abby smiled. 'He's got a point,' she conceded. 'In you get.'

The Poggles dived into the makeshift pockets inside her tunic, settling to rest in the lining.

Moments later they entered a wide corridor via a concealed door in the panelling. This was a grand hallway that ran the full width of the building; to her right Abby could see the grand entrance she had tried less than an hour before, to her left staircases jutted off in various directions along its length, a flamboyant fountain sitting at its centre. Apollo led them towards this fountain, pausing for a moment in apparent contemplation once reaching it.

Abby took this opportunity to examine the structure of this extraordinary water feature: the wide grain of its smooth timber surface, the crystal clear water rushing through thousands of undulations. It was formed from a sprig of three giant leaves, each overlaping the next and slowly swaying as water expelled from its centre.

She leaned forward, careful not to fall into the surrounding stone pool, brushing a leaf-like limb with her outstretched hand. To her surprise the sculpture reacted to her touch, reconfiguring to form the rough shape of a face, water running across it like a head of long, flowing hair.

'Princess! Is that you? Can it really be you? Tell me it's you?' erupted an excitable voice that appeared to be coming from the bulbous lumber of its lips.

Abby looked over to her protector, willing him to explain what was happening, but he was deep in meditation: pondering on the way ahead.

'Hello,' she said eventually, deciding to hedge her bets.

'It is! Just wait till I tell the others, they'll be so pleased,' the voice continued, reaching an almost hysterical level. 'Oh, it's been so long, and you've grown. You were nothing but a wee sapling when I last saw you.'

Abby squirmed on the spot. 'Sorry, do I know you?' she asked, instantly regretting asking such a thing.

'Why, Princess, surely you remember us?' the statue responded, hurt sounding in its voice. 'The woodland in this house has lived with your family for generations. We were present at your conception!'

Abby blushed. She hadn't realised the extent to which the cohabitation of nature and her people reached; she guessed it was further than she understood.

'Sorry!' she offered. 'I have been under a powerful forget-me spell for most of my life. I do apologise,' she added in explanation, hoping to placate the writhing sculpture.

The form visibly shrank, the happiness in its voice lost for an instant. 'It is I who should apologise, your highness. It is just so good to see you after all these years.'

Abby thought for a moment and then asked, 'Do you know where I can find my aunt Belladora?'

A smile appeared on the figurine's mottled face, water redirecting around the aperture with the movement, spittle of spray splashing the visitors.

Abby chose to ignore it.

'Why yes, my dear, she's in your mother's study on the second floor. I do believe she is expecting you; yes, here comes Oswald now.'

Oswald appeared from a hidden door somewhere to their left. He was dressed in the traditional black kilt and shirt of the servant dwarf, looking strikingly similar to the others

Abby had met on her journey. As he came closer she realised there was one fundamental difference: he was much older, his face a mass of lines with openings for his dark, beady eyes. The only feature to break the wrinkled mass was a large, hooked nose from which protruded tufts of jet-black hair. A slit opened below it, showing a rack of decaying yellow teeth and releasing the most rancid of smells.

'Our queen is expecting you,' he said, his voice a low growl. 'If you will follow me.'

He turned and strode to a nearby staircase, mounting each step one at a time, his age evident by the effort required to ascend each one. He continued on his climb without looking back or showing any concern as to whether his guests were indeed following, until he reached the top. Swivelling on his heel, he stopped precariously close to the edge and called for them to keep up before continuing on his way.

Abby looked at Apollo, and then Emily. 'Shall we follow him?' she asked.

Apollo frowned, a look that was an answer in itself. 'It is a trap, my princess,' he stated glumly.

'Are we not here to face the witch!' spat Emily, her usual calm demeanour absent for a flash. 'I mean, it's a chance to finish her off once and for all, is it not?'

Abby looked at her and then back at Apollo, surprised by the reaction.

'Fiery, this one!' he commented absentmindedly as he looked towards the staircase. 'Okay, we will go. But be on your guard.'

The three companions strode forward, reaching the staircase in a few lengthy strides. Apollo opted to lead as the staircase was only wide enough for one grown adult to negotiate. He was about to take the first step when the rickety structure began to move, stretching and distorting until before them stood a grand flight of such proportions that ten could have climbed them at once.

'A staircase fit for royalty,' Apollo observed with a smile. 'After you, my princess.'

They quickly climbed to catch the dwarf who, although ancient, had travelled such a distance they could barely see him. They paced down the elaborate corridor, marvelling at the fineness of the carving on the doors that lined it and the glitter from the many gold fittings and tall lanterns, the light from which glowed with the most enchanting aquamarine flame.

Oswald was waiting for them outside a particularly grand door. As they approached he opened it and silently ushered Abby in, swiftly closing it behind her before the others could enter. Apollo grabbed a handful of the servants collar, lifting his frail body to face him directly. The dwarf lashed out with fist and boot,before finally falling limp, a rasping cackle escaping from his antiquated throat.

'What's so funny?' Apollo demanded, tightening his grip, making the servant's shirt into a makeshift noose.

The lines of Oswald's face smoothed like satin creases in a cloud of steam. 'My mistress has her now,' he whispered and vanished in a wisp of crimson smoke.

Abby spun around at the sound of the slamming door, pulling Salankia from the sheath at her waist, her training kicking in. Stepping back to the door, she pulled at the polished handle, twisting it to and fro in a hopeless attempt to force it open. Giving up, she returned her attention to the room, noticing a figure slumped over a desk in a far corner, the black rags of her robes heaving with each rasping breath. It was then that she realised the true nature of her predicament: she was trapped, alone in this room - alone except for the presence of her aunt Belladora.

41
Honour before death

The veil of white began to thin, the onslaught of snow lessoning by the second. Reginald stood at a great glass window above the city gates, surveying the blanket of white that smothered all below. He could only guess at the number of his kind who had succumbed to this fresh wave of evil incarnate, their ranks dwindling in the face of such terror. A speck of black appeared through the curtain of white some distance away, its size enlarging by the moment, swelling until it filled the narrow colonnade of shops and eateries that crammed the royal mile.

The snow ceased to fall, the occasional flutter blown by a strengthening breeze the only refreshment for the blanket below. Reginald looked at the ground surrounding the gatehouse; the fires that had been set from by those who had passed had melted a corridor, but only of sufficient width for the lightest of defence. As he watched, he could see groups of Roden emerging from hiding, their eyes wide in the horror of such events.

He returned his attention to the increasing mass of black on the horizon, his worst fears confirmed. Individual shapes could now be defined, shapes that struck fear into even his battle-hardened soul: Squakor, and thousands of them.

The air was suddenly filled by a swarm of arrows, launched from within the swelling ranks of the advancing army, streaking towards the exposed Roden below. Reginald screamed for them to take cover, his voice muted by the pane of glass that separated them. Then, an instant later, the glass was gone: shattered into jagged fragments as a dark object smashed into the room.

Blinding pain exploded in Reginald's shoulder, instantly numbing his mind as he toppled to the floor. Seconds later he opened his eyes to see an abundance of familiar faces looking down at him. Scanning them, he finally rested on the young features of Fred Buckley, his faithful nephew.

'Come closer, boy,' he whispered, the pain throttling the strength from his voice.

Fred obediently crouched.

'I have always loved you, my boy, and your rascal of a brother, but now I must ask of you a most difficult task.' He coughed, spittle, fresh with blood, spraying from his lips. 'Lead our people against these beasts, these agents of evil. Fight well and bring honour to our family in the last hours.'

Fred Buckley looked horrified. 'But how, Uncle? I am merely a youngling, fresh from cadet college - how can I lead these men?'

Reginald coughed once more, a smile forming on his haggard lips. 'You have Roden blood in your veins and the heart of a human, one who has tamed this wretched soul. Together they will give you the strength, together they will unite us all.' He leaned back against the hard timber of the gatehouse floor. 'Now go, my young warrior, and show them what we are made of!'

A hand rested on Fred's shoulder, guiding him away from his uncle's body towards the door. 'What are your orders, sire?' a voice questioned, eager to hear his new leader's words.

'We fight,' Fred murmured, as if through a woollen scarf; then, as the courage swelled throughout his gangly body, he shouted, 'WE FIGHT!'

Fred Buckley stood before a garrison of Roden warriors, each committed to giving his or her life, as in Roden culture the female fought alongside her spouse for the just cause they represented: freedom. The Squakor were close now, their dull black armour reflecting in the white of the snow-covered ground. Fred had positioned the remainder of his horde in the surrounding buildings, hidden from the advancing guard behind hastily drawn curtains, awaiting his signal. Theirs would be a heroic fight, a fight to the death, a fight to the very end of their existence, in the name of their king.

The first of the Squakor stepped onto the thawed ground, crossing an unspoken line at the edge of the frozen tundra. Fred Buckley stepped forward to meet his foe, swinging his razor-sharp blade with deadly accuracy, the warrior before him dropping where he stood.

Inspired, each of his fellows followed suit, matching his success with surprising ease. They continued forward, dispatching many more with little resistance, before suddenly the Squakor advance halted.

Fred Buckley struck a further foe for good measure before looking around at his fellows. Much to his astonishment they had also stopped, looking with large grey eyes to the sky above. He followed their gaze and, after a moment of confusion, shared their wonder: above their heads circled the majestic form of a buzzard, its mottled feathers spread along huge wings as it silently hovered. A moment passed in silence before the magnificent bird opened the hook of its beak, emitting a blood-curdling screech.

The Squakor swung into life, hacking at the mystified forms before them, striking several without notice.

This was it: this was their final battle.

The fighting raged on, both sides replacing their fallen with fresh meat for the slaughter, neither side gaining ground or advantage. It was a numbers game, one for which the Roden were ill prepared.

'Look!'

The call came from somewhere to his left as he finished off another victim. Fred Buckley looked to the sky again, searching for the reason of such a call. A shadow was forming on the horizon, a dark mass that soared from the hazy glow of the setting sun. It split, dividing into two and then three like the segments of an orange. Gradually the battle petered out as each of the warriors, both Roden and Squakor alike, watched these newest visitors in awe, the thirst for killing lost in the moment. The three forms came closer, the central silhouette much larger than that of its wingmen, a single flap of huge wings their only movement.

Suddenly their question was answered as a plume of blue flame poured from the jowls of the largest beast, followed in short succession by similar fiery displays from its counterparts.

'DRAGONS!' screamed a voice from the crowd; but this was no Roden tone but that of a man, a member of the black-clad force that encircled them.

'Stand your ground!' Fred Buckley called, beckoning his men to consolidate their ranks. 'We hold, or we die. That is our way.'

All around him Roden solders rallied, filling positions left vacant by those who had fallen, until a solid line of twitching noses and blood-stained blades stood proudly in the Squakor's path.

Another burst of fire from above fed the swelling uneasiness within the ranks of the human horde, the Squakor commanders struggling to retain their control. Then, with a roar of such magnitude the earth beneath their quarry's feet shook, the dragons swooped, bellowing fire into the thronging masses at the rear of the Squakor troop, incinerating hundreds in one flame-driven extinction.

Panic drove the remaining horde forward as this was the only direction remaining for them, directly into the waiting blades of the foe they were so certain to overcome.

'KILL THEM ALL!'

The order came from across the waiting Roden lines, but this was not Fred Buckley's doing: it came from high above, from the gatehouse. Each face turned toward the sound, ears pricking, in anticipation of seeing its owner. Reginald Cockle stood in the open aperture that was once a window, leaning heavily on his companions but very much alive.

A cheer rose from within the Roden masses in elation at their king's survival; none more so than Fred Buckley to whom Reginald was more than just a king: he was family. Each soldier returned their gaze to the mass of black at their front, steely eyes narrowing on their prey - for they were the hunters now, ready to slaughter.

The Squakor commanders lost control, many driving their steeds through the panicking crowd in their desperation to escape, each losing the battle in fiery incineration.

The dragons circled for another run, lifting high into the air on powerful wings, plucking archers from their perches as they rose.

Fuelled by fear and adrenaline the Squakor horde stampeded into the waiting blades of their adversaries, each meeting its end at the tip of a blade. This continued for what seemed to be hours, Roden arms failing as the last of their enemy fell, a weary cheer finally rising from their lips as much for the chance to rest as for their victory.

It was done, the Squakor were defeated.

42
The loss of love

Abby stood rooted to the spot, realising that she was alone and isolated from her protectors. She mutely took in her surroundings: the silk-swathed doors to the balcony open in the cold of the twilight air, the antiquated furniture covered to a point of obsession with aged gold leaf and the sheer quantity of mirrors that had been crammed into the once spacious room. Every wall was covered in a reflective surface: tall mirrors standing at anomalous angles on the plush carpeting, frames of all sizes crammed into every inch, even the high ceiling contained an elaborate mirror of gigantic proportions. Although they were all very different, each mirror contained just one subject: the figure slumped over a desk in the far corner. *Could this really be her aunt Belladora?*

Abby took a step forward, every sinew of her body urging her to stop but her mind forcing her on. Then she halted at the sound of muttering, relief washing through her for this reason to delay. She wanted to speak with her aunt, to find out why she wished to kill her own flesh and blood, to discover the truth about that night: the night her mother died. She wanted the truth, she wanted to understand.

A footstep sounded from the balcony, the shape of a woman appearing from behind the dark drape. She was tall with lank black hair and a hunch over her left shoulder giving her a pronounced stoop. The image of this figure haunted Abby, as though they had met before. She pushed the thought to the back of her mind, sure she would have remembered such a character. The woman held a tuft of dark hair in her left hand, the owner of which Abby recognised at once from her nightmare vision: it was her father. Her other hand was held aloft and holding the unmistakable glint of a dagger, poised and ready to strike.

'NO!' Abby screamed, rushing forward and ramming her shoulder into the woman's exposed midriff.

The hag let out a blood-curdling scream, throwing Abby to one side and plunging the dagger into her father's exposed chest. She released her victim, discarding the blade in his blood-soaked torso, and turned her wicked attention to Abby, clawing at her with broken nails and rotten teeth like a rabid dog in the throes of hunger.

Abby fell back, the shock at what she had just witnessed befuddling her mind. She stole a glance at her father: he lay propped against the mirror-covered wall only a foot away, his lifeblood seeping from the open wound at his chest. She barely registered the burning pain inflicted by her attacker as she scratched and gouged at her young skin, pinning her to the floor, such was the shock of this revelation.

Suddenly the weight lifted, gangly arms flailing in the air above her face now meeting nothing but her victim's shaky breath. A thick arm had wrapped around her throat, pulling her back, away from the source of her anger. Then she was gone from view, the billowing of drapes the only evidence of her exit.

Abby crawled over to her father, careful not to touch the blade protruding like an abnormal limb from his chest, and gave him a hug.

'Daddy,' she coughed between sobs, the tears flowing freely across her cheeks mixing with the spreading pool of blood on the polished marble below. 'Don't leave me,' she pleaded, 'Not now I know the truth.'

Even as she spoke she could feel the energy ebbing away from his mortal form, the glow of life receding forever, until his body slumped in her arms, his last breath a sigh of forgiveness.

Abby pulled her eyes from the limp corpse of her father, tears blurring her vision of the figure that had risen, unseen, from her chair in the corner. A bitter cackle filled her ears, bringing with it memories of a night so many years ago: the night her mother died.

She watched from a cot at the bottom of a large bed. A beautiful woman slept in that bed, her face an angelic picture of happiness in the duskiness of the evening light. The silken drapes hanging from the lavishly carved four-poster bed fluttered in a cool breeze as a door opened, a hooded figure entering and quietly stepping across the deep pile carpet.

The figure reached the bed, bending over the sleeping body, mumbling incoherent words in a tongue Abby could not comprehend. The darkly clad figure raised its right arm, the sleeve of its robes falling to the elbow. Abby followed the slender arm, taking in the pearly white skin, a small shape tattooed at the wrist forming the rough shape of a bird, the long, slender fingers gripping something that glittered like gold.

To her horror she recognised the object: it was a ceremonial dagger, the jagged blade heavily polished and inscribed with the ancient words of power, the hilt beautifully carved in rosewood beholding the royal seal. She tried to scream, to warn her mother of the danger this visitor represented, but to no avail as her screams were lost in the stillness of the air; and then the blade dropped.

Abby's senses snapped back to the present, her aunt's delirious cackling racking her body with an urgent need for revenge. She knew only one thing: this wretched figure was responsible for the loss of her mother and the years of pain and loneliness she had endured since.

She jumped to her feet, raising Salankia in one fluid motion, her training taking control of her actions, one sole purpose feeding every muscle of her athletic body. Stepping forward she raised her sword, her arm becoming one with the blade, the bond of flesh and steel focused on the task at hand. One final step and she was within striking distance, bringing the long blade in an arc downwards towards the exposed head of her tormentor.

Inches from its target the blade stopped, halted in its path by an immoveable object. Her eyes followed the line of her blade, searching for the source of its disruption and finding it in the form of an elegant rapier, which she traced to its owner. She gasped in horror when the identity of her aunt's protector became evident as the hood of the crimson robe fell from his face.

It was Tom.

Abby recoiled, stumbling backwards across the room, slipping on the expanding pool of her father's blood and falling unceremoniously onto her back, Salankia slipping from her hand. She squirmed across the cold expanse of marble, trying to regain some of her poise before Tom reached her. He stepped to her side, looking down at her struggling body, a look of serenity on his face. Then, to her surprise, he offered her a hand.

She reluctantly accepted his help and let him guide her to a nearby chair.

'Where did you come from?' she asked shakily, unsure what to feel. 'And why did you stop me from dispatching her?' She gestured towards her aunt.

Tom looked her in the eyes, his iridescent irises flaring momentarily.

'I have been with you since our meeting on the ridge above Ravensburn. I have kept my presence a secret, but I could not let her destroy you, my dear,' He said, his gaze dropping to the floor. 'To lose you would be more than I could bear.'

Abby's heart jumped, the anger within her rekindled in an instant.

'I had her. I could have finished this war here and now!' she screamed, her blood now boiling.

Tom's form visibly shrank. 'I-I could not take the chance. You mean too much to me,' he muttered, his voice no more than a murmur. 'I love you.'

Abby's anger exploded. 'I don't love you, Tom. I feel nothing,' She said harshly, her face as hard as stone.

The iciness had returned to her eyes; a look Tom had seen many times before as she had slaughtered her enemies as she was slaughtering him now. Her demeanour was as cold as the surrounding landscape, her actions hard and calculated.

He groped at a wafer-thin tendril of hope: it was all that was left. She had to love him; what future was there for this world otherwise? His life, once vibrant and meaningful, was over: the only woman he had ever loved was denying him his very life's blood. His head throbbed, not just with the pressure in his sinuses as a result of the hours of misery and heartache but from the undeniable reality that she no longer wanted him. She, the love of his life, his only reason for being, was sitting there in all her beauty and splendour, denying him his heart's only desire. His world was shattered. He wanted to lash out, destroy all that they had created, put an end to this world and the misery it held. But in his heart he yearned for her, wanting her with every particle of is being, desperate to feel the warmth of her embrace, the soft words of understanding that had once been so plentiful.

'I love you!' he spluttered, his body racked by a wave of fear and emotion. 'Surely that means something?'

Abby said nothing.

He burst into a fit of tears, his heart splitting with the pain of rejection. The agony he felt at the loss of something so precious was unbearable; the certainty of their future lost in that instant. He looked at her through the haze of his tears, the moisture giving an angelic shine to her features, her beauty unfaltering in his eyes. *This is the woman who has torn open your chest, exposing the shrivelled, diseased muscle of your heart and squeezed the last drops of life from it like the juice of an orange with her cold, loveless words*, his mind was screaming; and yet he still loved her with all his might.

'It's over,' she said with absolute finality, casually casting him off like last season's shoes.

His hope, eternally linked to his continued existence, began to fade along with his physical form: for without love he was nothing. Without love he did not exist.

43
Belladora

Spurred on by Tom's apparent defeat, although a little puzzled by his disappearance, Abby pushed herself up and strode over to the wizened form of her aunt, collecting Salankia on the way and feeling the blade once again bond with her very DNA.

She barely registered the pounding on the door or the muffled shouts from her friends outside the room; this was her battle, and she was going to end it now.

She raised the blade and drove it straight through her enemy's heart, the cold steel sliding through her decrepit torso with ease as if she were made of butter. Withdrawing the steel Abby stared, puzzled by the absence of reaction or blood. The ancient figure remained, glaring at her with fresh hatred in those old eyes, and then she began to snigger, the cold, hard crow of evil.

'Do you think you can hurt me with your mortal toys, young Abigail?' she sniggered, her face contorting into a grimace of amusement. 'You and your feeble friends are no match for me. My blood dried up long ago and the heart you so keenly skewered is just a shrivelled lump of coal in this frail carcass. I have transcended the restrictions of this mortal plane and as such have become more than just the sum of my people: I AM A GOD.'

Abby suddenly felt pressure on her chest, a tightness around her heart, like it was trapped in the vice-like grip of a seizure. Her mind began to spin, nausea filling her throat as the realisation formed that she could not draw breath. Panic began to take control, a warm buzz rippling from the nape of her neck across her scalp, the release of adrenaline triggered by her fear of death. She stumbled backwards several steps, clutching at her collar to release the life-giving oxygen her lungs so urgently needed. Her sword discarded in her desperation for life.

Belladora was visibly shaking by this point, her frail frame on the point of collapse, the ecstasy of the moment she had dreamt of so long almost in her grasp. A clap of thunder boomed in the air outside, winds whipping into a violent frenzy as the serene glow of the night sky filled with angry, blackened clouds. A streak of pure white lightning forked across the sky, incinerating the majestic form of an ancient oak. Shards of icy hale hammered into the veil of soft snow encompassing the royal gardens, smashing stone and plant life without discretion. The ferocity of the storm matched the euphoric high of the witch's fever, her sense of domination in this world enveloping the very atmosphere.

Then she suddenly froze. Her eyes enlarged to the point of bursting, her pupils becoming so small they were mere pin pricks in a vast expanse of emerald green - for she shared her sister's eyes. A hissing sound emerged from somewhere inside her dilapidated form. She took an involuntary step backward and was prevented by the solid oak of the dressing table.

Abby, abruptly released from the grip of death, gasped a lungful of air, feeling the life-giving energy flowing back to her muscles, clearing her mind and soul. Confused by this sudden change, she looked around her, convinced that she could not have possibly caused this transformation. It was then that she spotted the culprit.

It was Pook, her Nibblet friend.

He sat on the floor just behind her, his jet-black fur bristling slightly, pearly white fangs shining through the small aperture of his mouth; but this was no fearsome sight.

'H-hello, Pook,' Abby spluttered, her surprise barely hidden, the tension in the room dipping for a moment. 'How did you get in here?'

She bent to stroke his silky back but stopped short, feeling an energy flowing in the very air around him. Pook stood and stepped forward, ignoring the tall girl by his side, his attention fixed purely on Belladora.

The witch screeched, a noise like that of a trapped animal filling the room. She shuffled around the furniture, tipping over a large mirror in her haste, the shattering glass spilling across the stone floor. She backed slowly towards the open doors and the balcony beyond.

Pook casually padded after her, a low growl releasing from his feline form. As he passed Abby his fur brushed the hide of her boot, sending a tingle through her leg and into her spine. It slowly travelled upwards, spreading a sensation throughout as if she were standing on a vibrating platform. The feeling finally reached her head with the explosive force of a sneeze. Her eyes watered, her sinuses filling momentarily; and then it was gone, leaving as though through the top of her skull.

Heat swelled in her chest, intensifying into a plume of fire inside her. She grasped at her tunic, frantically pulling at the toggles to dispel the fiery source, releasing the family of

Poggles like miniature flaming arrows launched by an invisible bow. They joined the figures on the balcony, buzzing around Belladora's head like a swarm of angry wasps.

Pook took advantage, pouncing onto his victim's chest, his razor-sharp claws embedded into her tattered clothing, fangs now drawn in a deadly grimace.

Belladora staggered back against the ornately twisted railings, fending off the snapping jaws and buzzing wings of her attackers with thrashing arms, a scream of agony escaping from her ancient throat.

Abby, mesmerised by this sudden flurry, joined them in the cool air, carefully avoiding entanglement in the ensuing attack. Her breath caught as her lungs filled, not with the freezing air she had expected but with the smouldering fumes of burning flesh. She stared out into the gardens, her eyes focusing immediately on a causeway of glowing embers, the snow consuming the surrounding landscape rapidly melting in a steamy reduction. With this thaw she could see lines of warriors streaming towards the palace, dispatching Squakor in their wake; her army locked in a triumphant surge through the gardens.

Her attention snapped back to focus as a fresh screeching filled her ears. This, however, was not the increasingly desperate screams of her aunt but the shriek of metal on metal, wood on wood, as the fabric of the balcony distorted, twisting like the branches of a sapling on a windy day. The railing behind Belladora parted and, with strangely comical slow motion, she fell backwards into the burning air. The Poggles hovered where she had once been, their glow diminishing to a cool hue, but Pook remained consumed in his ferocious attack and plummeted with the witch. Their forms fell towards the soft earth below, lost at the last moment in a cloud of thick crimson smoke.

The door behind them crashed open, replaced by the hulking bulk of Arnold, his mass making short work of the timber frame. He stepped into the room, followed closely by Apollo and Emily; their faces red and wet with sweat.

'Abby!' Emily squealed as she ran across the room, flinging her arms around her friend, tears pouring from her puffy eyes.

Apollo and Arnold joined them, apparently ignoring the body of her father slumped against the wall.

'What happened, and where is the witch?' Apollo asked, his blade at the ready.

Abby looked over the balustrade to the ground below. 'She's down there,' she replied, her voice weary. But to her surprise there were no bodies or even a sign of impact, just wisps of crimson smoke floating in the stilling air.

44
The end?

Abby fell to her knees next to the still form of her father's body. She had asked for a moment of privacy in the aftermath of recent events. Her companions were reluctant but understanding in her time of loss. She could hear their voices quietly debating her future in the hallway outside the now repaired door.

She looked down at her father's face; his features were calm, the look of anguish gone, replaced by the familiar look of contentment she loved so much.

'Daddy,' she sobbed, her tears flowing again, 'I love you so much.'

She threw her arms around him to hug him one last time but the hilt of the blade still protruding from his chest caught her.

'Ouch!' she complained as she withdrew.

A spike of anger flared in the pit of her stomach. This dagger symbolised the end of not only her father's life but also her mother's. She recognised the carved rosewood handle, the royal seal so carefully embossed. Her anger swelling, she grasped this symbol of death and, with all the strength she could muster, tugged it from her father's body. An echo resonated throughout the room as the discarded blade clanged to the polished marble of the blood soaked-floor, embedding itself into the stone as if into mud.

Abby took the lifeless body into her arms, sobbing with all her heart: this was her father, the only person she had ever truly known and trusted. Even though her life had changed so much, her love for him had never faltered.

'I wish this wasn't so,' she blubbered into his motionless chest. 'I wish I could bring you back; change things so we could explore this existence together.'

At that moment she was disturbed by a buzzing sound, like the irritating vibration of the mobile phone she had discarded seemingly so long ago. Her eyes settled on her backpack in a corner of the room. She stood and, on unsteady legs, ambled over to the pack. *What can be making that noise?* she thought, her curiosity temporarily overwhelming her grief. She rummaged around inside her bag, passing over her wand, juju berries and all sorts of paraphernalia she had collected on her journey until she reached the source of the commotion.

She pulled out a little wooden box, its vibrations sending pleasant tingles down her arm. Holding it up to the light, she read the inscription that had appeared.

'Welcome, Princess, to the casket of the rose
The truth, in all its pain and glory, is all we propose
You seek to ask; a question you must now pose
But be warned, for answers can forebode
Much pain or laughter, offers the rose.'

She examined the box. The timber was highly polished with an almost liquid appearance to its surface, the gold lettering fading again as she watched. With her heart in her mouth she opened the lid, cautiously peering inside, unsure what to expect. Her eyes fell on a simple piece of folded parchment. She removed it and, with shaking hands, unfolded the tiny scrap. On it were six short words that read:

Believe and it will be true

Abby did not understand. She hated not understanding. She threw the box and its cryptic message across the room, not caring as the gift clattered against the far wall.

She returned to her father, crouching over him, fresh tears welling in her swollen eyes. A single drop passed from her cheek, landing on her father's blood-stained shirt. It rolled unhindered across the surface of the fibrous material, meandering from side to side like a miniature stream finding its way across a grassy mountainside, towards the site of the fatal wound. Abby, oblivious, continued sobbing in the haze of grief until suddenly she jumped back, resting on her haunches.

'I'm sure he moved!' she mumbled to herself, feeling the embarrassment rise to her cheeks.

She looked down at her father, who remained motionless, lying propped against the wall, as he had fallen; his eyes closed, a look of peace on his face.

'You're just being silly,' she told herself, trying to force a modicum of self-control.

She was about to call the others to return when a low groan interrupted her, stopping the sound in the folds of her dry throat.

'Abigail?' asked a low, rasping voice; so weak it sounded only inches from death.

She leant forward, unwilling to believe what her ears were telling her.

'Is that you, my dear?' asked the voice with a quiet cough.

Abby's heart swelled, emotions rolling over her like breakers on a sandy beach, each one replacing the last with fresh vitality: confusion, hope, fear, love - a constant bombardment of feelings that made her dizzy. Through all of these came happiness; happiness she had not experienced for many a day now, the happiness that only existed when in the presence of one being.

'DADDY!' she squealed and flung her arms around his neck, hugging tighter than ever before.

The door crashed open behind them, once again splintering to the floor under the might of Arnold.

'Princess. Are you all right?' said Apollo's concerned voice.

'It's my father!' she answered, turning to face the expanding crowd shuffling into the room. 'He's alive.'

45
A new day

Abby wasn't sure what had happened next. A flurry of bodies had consumed her vision and strong arms had pulled her to her feet, guiding her from the room and into the bedchamber in which she now sat. She thought she had heard her father's voice barking orders from the far side of the thick wall, but she could not be sure. She was so tired: it had been a long day that had turned into a very long night and she longed for sleep. But she would not allow herself such a luxury until she knew her father was truly alive.

A beam of light found its way through a gap in the heavy drapes hanging at one of the tall openings on the far wall. Abby wandered over, narrowly avoiding a low table in the haze of sleep deprivation. She tugged at the dusty material, heaving the old curtains aside to reveal a pair of solid timber shutters. Before she had chance to test the functionality of their hinges the shutters sprang open, bathing her in the most glorious sunlight.

Morning had arrived.

She stepped out onto the balcony. The sun had risen only a hand's breadth above the horizon, but its strength had already dispatched most of the snow; patches hid in secluded corners of shadow, fearful of the shinning orb's hot touch. She took a deep breath, the air fresh and soothing to her raw lungs, its coolness invigorating her exhausted limbs and clearing the cobwebs of slumber from her clouded mind.

She listened to the world, her world: the Roden warriors' befuddled minds after an evening of excess celebration; Arnold sleeping in the corridor beyond her room, his dreams of glory and battle; Apollo meditating in a private garden on the other side of the palace; the moments of joy as the various subjects, casts and creeds expressed their happiness in their own special way. One voice, however, broke through the ramblings of so many - it was a voice she knew so well, a voice she would always be glad to hear: that of her father.

She turned to face him in the knowledge that he was near, dropping into his waiting arms like a babe once again. It was like the last jigsaw piece slotting into place: her life felt complete again, her feelings of sorrow and loss evaporating like the morning mist in the heat of her father's love. She knew there was much to be done - cities to rebuild, people to rehome - but for a few minutes she was content to be lost in the heaven of this moment.

Gilbert released his daughter, guiding her to sit on the lavish bed.

Abby looked into his handsome face. His eyes were bright with a lust for life once again; the smile had returned to his lips.

'I thought you were dead,' she spluttered, fresh tears forming in her eyes.

Her father smiled. 'I was, my dear. I was.'

Abby was too tired to understand. 'Then how?' she managed.

Gilbert took her into his arms. 'Love is the strongest of all the magic in this world, my dear. It was your love for me that brought my spirit back from the next world.'

'I do love you, Daddy,' Abby mumbled into his jacket, happy to be back in his arms. 'So much.'

They sat for hours, discussing their future in this world, what it meant to be royalty and, naturally, which was to be her room. Eventually Abby asked the one burning question in her mind: what had happened to Belladora?

Gilbert was about to answer when a waft of jasmine floated past her nose, the fragrance stirring new emotions as her mother's shimmering form joined them, joining in their family bond.

'I can answer that, my dear,' Cassandra said, giving her husband a coy smile. 'Your friend, the Nibblet …'

'Pook.' Interjected Abby.

'Yes, Pook,' her mother continued. 'He is a native of this world. Their kind has lived in this land for millennia, far longer than our ancestors. As such, his link with the nature of this world provides magic much stronger than any, even our darkest sorcerers. It was that which Belladora recognised and feared so, and it was that which destroyed her.'

Abby gave her mother a bewildered look. 'But if Pook is so powerful, why is he not king?'

Gilbert laughed. 'The Nibblet have no interest in ruling or politics. They are simple creatures, living in harmony with their environment.'

Cassandra continued. 'As royalty, we simply guide the creatures under our protection in the true way of life: the co-existence with all living things.'

Gilbert stood, straightening his robes. 'Enough of this talk,' he said, his authority impressive. 'We have a visitor.' He walked out onto the balcony.

Abby looked at her mother for an explanation.

'We had better see who it is!' she said, and followed her husband.

Abby shrugged and got to her feet, following her parents into the sunshine. As she stepped onto the balcony her father was asking a question.

'So who is this then?'

Abby recognised one of their visitors immediately; it was the Nibblet.

'Pook!' she squealed and ran over to him.

Crouching, she gave him a hug, his long black fur tickling her nose. Releasing him, she turned her attention to his companion. 'So who is this then?' she asked.

'Poooook!' replied the Nibblet with a cheeky wink, looking over at the petite feline form sat next to him. Her short black fur was silky and emerald green eyes squinted in the brightness of the day.

'Why, I think he's in love!' Cassandra laughed, taking in the two felines as they basked in the morning sun.

Later that evening, after a sumptuous meal and two helpings of apple pie with lashings of custard, Abby retired to bed, her parents fussing about her, checking blankets and pillows, then kissing her goodnight.

She smiled to herself; she could sleep now. Life was good …

The Nousidian Chronicles

The saga continues in the second book of The Nousidian Chronicles

The Enlightenment of Abigail Brown

Concluding with the final book in this trilogy, but by no means the end of the story

The Existence of Abigail Brown

Acknowledgements

The author would like to thank all who have had input into the production of this novel: to all my friends and family who have shown undying faith in my endeavours, to Hope in the wilderness of that distant country; to Phil whose stubborn views and obscure suggestions contribute eternally to the wonder of my life; to Jane for providng the amazing images that cover this book; to Judy whose dogged determination drives me insane; to Charlie for his comma's, comments and knowledge; and to my mother who, without whose unconditional love (and constant nagging) I would not be here.

You know who you are and you all have my deepest thanks.

PS: To all those who have doubted me, and there have been a few, I would like to offer a heartfelt raspberry ...